A PROPER EDUCATION FOR GIRLS

Elaine di Rollo was born in Ormskirk, Lancashire, and now lives in Scotland, where she is a lecturer at Napier University, Edinburgh. She has a PhD in the social history of medicine from Edinburgh University. *A Proper Education for Girls* (first published as *The Peachgrowers' Almanac*) is her first novel.

ELAINE DI ROLLO

A Proper Education for Girls

VINTAGE BOOKS
London

Published by Vintage 2009

2 4 6 8 10 9 7 5 3 1

First published in Great Britain in 2008 by Chatto & Windus

Vintage
Random House, 20 Vauxhall Bridge Road,
London SW1V 2SA

www.vintage-books.co.uk

Addresses for companies within The Random House Group Limited can be found at: www.randomhouse.co.uk/offices.htm

The Random House Group Limited Reg. No. 954009

A CIP catalogue record for this book is available from the British Library

ISBN 9780099513469

The Random House Group Limited supports The Forest Stewardship Council (FSC), the leading international forest certification organisation. All our titles that are printed on Greenpeace approved FSC certified paper carry the FSC logo. Our paper procurement policy can be found at: www.rbooks.co.uk/environment

Pri[illegible]

Contents

For my mother, Jean Thomson.

ALICE

1

Travellers unfamiliar with the countryside around the Great House would come upon its boundary walls with some surprise. At first, one might wonder whether these walls, twelve feet high and clad with a rustling coat of ivy, marked the perimeter to some isolated institution – a hospital, perhaps, or an asylum. The prongs of black-painted iron that spiked the top pointed both inwards and outwards, as though their maker had been undecided whether he was trying to keep people in, or keep people out.

The gates appeared similarly well fortified, wrought from tall corkscrews of iron and tipped with bristling spears. But they were also festooned with a genial tangle of iron pomegranates and pineapples, in the midst of which a letter 'T' was vaguely discernible, as though struggling to free itself from the clustering fruits. Closer inspection revealed that the gates were rusted closed, with comfortable mounds of moss growing over their sagging lower hinges like slippers.

Mrs Talbot had designed the gates, drawing up their specifications during her first confinement. Mr Talbot had had them hammered out in one of his iron foundries in the city. He put up the gates to mark the arrival of their first child. But the boy succumbed to a fever within days of the gates' erection and, in an uncharacteristic display of manly emotion, Mr Talbot vowed that they would not be reopened until the birth of his next son. As a result, both family and visitors were, from then on, obliged to gain access through the stables.

The death of this infant son marked the handing over of Mr Talbot's iron works in the city to foremen and accountants, and his partial retirement to the country. It also signalled the birth of the Collection: the beginning of Mr Talbot's relentless accumulation of ancient and modern artefacts from all corners of the known world. It was, he declared at the outset, to be a Collection that embodied and quantified progress; one that demonstrated the triumph of human ingenuity over nature and history. A Collection that served to enlighten those who looked upon it, and in its richness and diversity to rival all others (apart from that held by the British Museum, of course, but then one had to know one's limitations).

It was not long before every room in the house had become home to a variety of items lovingly selected as representing the very best of human achievement. Wherever one looked – whichever door one opened, whichever shadow one peered into – Mr Talbot's artefacts and antiquities could be found. Suits of armour rubbed shoulders with fossilised sea creatures and display cases of Greek pottery. Medieval fireplaces, torn from their hearthstones in the castles of Europe and rebuilt against the walls of the Great House, reared beside stuffed animals and bronze statues. Cases filled with regiments of gassed and pinned butterflies lined the walls above ingenious mechanical inventions, military accessories and the most modern of scientific instruments. The stables were packed with the latest innovations in farming machinery, the conservatory replete with botanical specimens.

On occasion, Mrs Talbot expressed reservations about the growing number of seemingly indiscriminate items that came to crowd the halls, drawing rooms and numerous chambers of her home. But then she died giving birth to Lilian, Alice and Emily – triplets, unique to medical science in the whole of southern England and, as such, the most prized curiosities in their father's entire museum.

Without his wife to restrain him, Mr Talbot's Collection expanded further. And when little Emily followed her mother and brother into the grave, he sought solace in the possession of still more things. Members of the household, both family and servants, came to accept that they might return to their rooms to find that they had been graced, in their absence, with a German grandfather clock, a stuffed grizzly bear, a case of Napoleonic swords or some other unexpected item.

'This is your heritage,' Mr Talbot would say to his remaining two daughters, who seemed now to exist only to irk his sense of perfection. 'Your past, present and future. This family made its fortune in industry and engineering. Clearly, it is to human ingenuity and to its legitimate offspring – progress – that we owe our wealth, our success and our current situation in life. And yet . . .' and here he would pause to brush a philosophical hand across his glossy whiskers. 'Progress can only be understood with reference to the past. We are giants, but in turn we stand on the shoulders of giants. I am paraphrasing Newton, of course, one of England's greatest thinkers. Now, both of you, if you are to serve any purpose in this house you must understand the Collection as fully as I do myself. To this end I require you to write a short essay on the origins and purpose of *this* piece.' He would dab his handkerchief at an eye moist with emotion and run his fingers over the flank of a stuffed and mounted platypus, the cogs and wheels of a machine for peeling sixty apples simultaneously, or the bulging hips of a porcelain vase.

It was only when his daughter Lilian was obliged to leave the Great House that Mr Talbot's enthusiasm for collecting showed any sign of wavering. In the weeks that followed Lilian's disgrace and preceded her departure, and for some time after that, Mr Talbot neither added to, nor adjusted, his

Collection in any way. The clocks stopped ticking; the models and engines stood silent. The conservatory was locked and the furnace for the hot house grew cold. A silent mantle of dust gently gathered over everything – including, it seemed, over the memory of his daughter's disgrace.

Eventually, Mr Talbot received an invitation from the Society for the Propagation of Useful and Interesting Knowledge that proved too intriguing for him to pass over. A Mr Bellows was to speak on the subject of aeronautical machines.

'You should go, Father,' Alice said soothingly. 'What greater symbol is there of man's dominion over the heavens, as well as the earth, than a flying machine?'

Mr Talbot found himself unable to disagree. Within a week the entire Collection was gleaming once more, and Mr Bellows had been installed in the attic with his plans, his books and his models.

'I have shone the light of enquiry into every corner of civilisation,' Mr Talbot declared one evening at dinner. 'I have explored every niche of human endeavour, every chink of history and science. I have, if you like, anatomised progress. And now, to record the most prized artefacts in my Collection I intend to employ an expert in the very latest techniques of image creation. A photographer.' He concluded the sentence with a tremendous exhalation of breath, as though simply uttering the word were a relief, like the lancing of a boil.

No one spoke. Across the cluttered expanse of the dining table, Alice and her father's Aunt Lambert exchanged glances.

'There are certain enquiring and inspired members of the Society for the Propagation of Useful and Interesting Knowledge', continued Mr Talbot, 'who are interested in particular items in my possession. Were I to have a photographic record of such pieces, I might be able to satisfy the curiosity of these fellows simply by offering them a picture to look at. Besides, I believe Fenton is doing this sort of thing for the British Museum and what's good enough for them is good enough for me.'

'I believe these cameras can capture images the human eye is unable to detect,' quavered a voice out of the gloom. 'Ghosts and fairies. Angels. An incubus even. I should very much like to see some of these ethereal beings. Perhaps this photographer fellow will oblige?'

'Ghosts and fairies?' thundered Mr Talbot. 'Really, Mother! This is science, not fancy. Chemistry and optics, not the absurd dreamings of a romantic mind.'

'I understand that many of these insubstantial images are created when the human subject moves away during the exposure time,' said Alice. 'They are no more fairies and spirits than you or I. But we can ask the photographer himself. I'm sure he'll be able to give you a more satisfactory explanation – perhaps he will even provide a demonstration.'

'You seem to know a lot about it,' Mr Talbot grunted in his daughter's direction. He fumbled in a waistcoat pocket for his gold toothpick.

'I did some reading on the subject.'

'Well, you might like to read some more. I'd like you to furnish me with a full explanation of how the photographic process works, before this photographer fellow gets here. I don't want to appear foolish, after all. Perhaps you would condescend to give me a few lessons, too.'

'Of course, Father,' murmured Alice, knowing that her father would lose interest in the project almost as soon as it had begun. (Though not before the photographer had arrived and made himself comfortable, of course.) They would then be saddled with the man indefinitely, she thought irritably. Why, it had taken her an age to get rid of the two cuneiform translators, who had spent most of their time arguing about the inscriptions on Mr Talbot's Sumerian tablets. And was not Mr Bellows still at work up in the attic? So many experts had visited over the years that it was impossible to recall who they were and what they had come for. Some had stayed for weeks, some for months. Others, she fancied, were still living alone and forgotten in the upper reaches of the house, wandering the Collection-crammed corridors in search of their former selves. As for what had happened to Lilian – had her father learned nothing from the experience?

'Do we really need a photographer?' she said. 'Surely there are enough people here as it is?' Alice surveyed her four great-aunts and her grandmother, whose faces were ranged in baleful desiccation round the dinner table.

Aunt Lambert nodded her agreement. 'Indeed. This is another of your schemes, Edwin. A waste of time and money, just like all the others.'

'And why get Alice involved?' asked Aunt Statham. 'She has enough to do.'

'Ladies, please,' whispered Old Mrs Talbot.

'Come, Edwin, my dear,' said Aunt Pendleton gently. 'You know Alice has very little recreational time, once she has recorded and researched and filed and goodness only knows what else she gets up to on your behalf –'

'I don't mind, Aunt. Really,' said Alice hastily, fearing Aunt Pendleton was about to extol the virtues of womanly pastimes, such as needlepoint or visiting the poor. 'I've already experimented a little with Father's camera. The results are not unpleasant.'

'Oh yes,' said Aunt Rushton-Bell. 'You have made some beautiful pictures, my dear. You are quite the photographer yourself. Edwin, Alice is right. Perhaps we don't need this photographer fellow at all. Alice herself could photograph the Collection, if that is what you want?'

It had been many years since Mr Talbot had listened to an opinion voiced by his female relations and his aunts' words fluttered past him like moths into the darkness. Instead, he heard only that Alice had acquired some practical familiarity with one of his items.

'My dear, your loyalty to the Collection and the knowledge that underpins it is commendable. You know, I regard you as my curator? Ah, such a calling. I tell you, Alice, your youth may be over, but oh, the glories of the mind that accompany a lifetime devoted to tending the finest examples of man's skill and ingenuity. Surplus women are seldom granted such opportunities.'

Alice felt her face turn red.

Mr Talbot dabbed at his eye with a napkin. 'Just make sure the fellow doesn't break anything. My good friend Cattermole recommends him, but one can never be too careful.' He glared at the pale faces of his aunts, blinking, unnerved for a moment by this sepulchral jury, and turned again to Alice. 'I'm sure I can rely on you to do your duty?' He did not appear to expect an answer, but turned to gaze greedily at his most recent acquisition, a life-sized electroplated statue depicting *Truth Overcoming Prejudice*. Truth was naked, apart from a strategically draped sheet that seemed to have all but slipped from her hips as she raised her hands in alarm. She had the appearance of having just emerged from a hot bath, her face registering surprise and disgust that she had trodden on the slippery coils of the serpent of Prejudice that someone had carelessly left on the floor.

'And what, may I ask, do we know of this photographer?' persisted Aunt Lambert.

'The fellow has a university degree in . . . something or other. Medicine, I think. Worked at St Thomas's with Cattermole for a while, taking photographs of diseased body parts and tumours and suchlike.'

'And his name, pray?'

'Blake.' Mr Talbot prised himself out of his chair to run an admiring hand over Truth's electroplated thigh. He stole a glance at his fingertips, as though checking for dust, but appeared to be satisfied with their cleanliness.

'And when is he coming, this Mr Blake?' said Alice.

'That's of no consequence to you,' snapped Mr Talbot. 'Your business is with the Collection, not with the specialists I employ.' He gave his daughter a close stare, as if to ascertain whether she had changed at all since his glance had last rested upon her. He observed her large ears, her heavy eyebrows and low hairline. What did young men look for in a woman these days, he pondered, his hand resting for a moment on Truth's burnished rump. Was it a slender neck? Soulful eyes? Graceful hands? In his own youth it had been shoulders – soft, white, sloping shoulders. He glanced at the corresponding parts of his daughter's figure. Her shoulders were square. Her neck unremarkable. Her eyes too curious (her gaze almost hostile, he noticed with some disquiet). As for her hands – they were large square hands; hands not unlike his own, other than the fact that his had wiry black hairs sprouting from their backs and hers appeared to be curiously stained with brown blotches. No, he concluded with some relief, Alice was as ugly as ever. It was Lilian who had been beautiful. 'Not that *you'll* catch his eye,' he muttered to himself, though it was loud enough for the entire table to hear. 'I'll have no worries on that score.'

The aunts glanced at each other in silent consternation.

'But I need to know when he is coming,' insisted Alice, meeting her father's critical stare. 'His accommodation must be arranged –'

'My dear Alice,' interrupted Aunt Lambert. 'Do we not have a maid who can look after Mr Blake's accommodation?'

'I'm not certain. Father has been economising . . .'

'What, *again*? Edwin, surely you have not dismissed *all* the maids?' Aunt Lambert raised her hands to her throat. The aunts muttered uneasily among themselves. Who would turn down their beds and lay out their nightclothes? Who would bring their tea in the afternoon and stoke the fire in the drawing room? Would they have to take turns in blacking the grate? It really was too much . . .

'A week on Monday,' bellowed Mr Talbot, stalking towards the door. 'He comes a week on Monday.'

2

It was customary for the women of the Talbot household to retreat to the conservatory after dinner. This they did every evening of the year, seeing no need to restrict their use of the place to the spring and summer months. Now, in the darkness of a March evening, lamps within the greenery created small spheres of light like gleaming bubbles of air in a dark fish tank. But it was a tropical fish tank as, beneath wrought-iron grids in the floor, hot-water pipes burbled and throbbed like the intestines of some huge organism. It was a place free from the overbearing presence of Mr Talbot, as the conservatory – in particular the tropical conservatory – was the one room in the Great House where he was least likely to be found. Secretly, Alice suspected that her father felt uncomfortable with the soft, vulnerable greenness of botany, preferring instead the hard, virile facts elicited when man harnessed nature for his own ends. She also suspected that the heat in the hot house made him sweat uncomfortably and the humid atmosphere caused his beard to curl, which he hated. It was for this reason that she kept the heating turned up as high as the plants could tolerate. She also knew that the real reason her father had lost all interest in his botanical Collection was because of Lilian. Lilian had adored the conservatory.

Unlike Mr Talbot, his elderly aunts and his aged mother found the heavy warmth of the hot house comforting. Over time, they had colonised this man-made jungle with the trappings of a civilised parlour, so that among the foliage there lurked numerous armchairs, sofas and footstools. There were also a surprising number of tables – side tables, card tables, writing desks, a rosewood dining table, even a sideboard. It was like finding a drawing room in the middle of a rain forest.

'What are you doing?' Alice addressed Aunt Statham. Beneath the drooping tendrils of a passiflora stood a huge dining table. Its surface was littered with jars of water and turpentine, some sprouting brushes, some silted with a spectrum of pigments.

'Something I should have done a long time ago,' replied Aunt Statham. She lowered herself on to a sofa scarred with bursting welts of horsehair and liberally smeared with red paint. It teetered with canvases, stretched flat on to wooden frames or rolled up into tubes. 'I have decided to retire from painting. The light in here is impossible. The plants have grown so huge that I can hardly see what I'm doing. And my eyesight is going, of course.'

'I can prune everything back,' said Alice.

'It's my fingers too. They're so stiff, you know. And they shake a little too much these days. I can hardly hold the brush steady.'

'You never could, dear,' murmured Lambert.

'Besides,' continued Aunt Statham, ignoring the interruption. 'My paintings are everywhere. DaVinci has made his bed out of a canvas – he couldn't get to his basket any more.' She pointed to the large orange tomcat coiled on a sagging painting situated above a hot-water pipe. 'Would you move him, my dear, and stack that picture with the others? I'm going to get Sluce to take the whole lot up to the attic.'

The cat opened acid-yellow eyes and glared at Alice's approaching hands. She raised it gingerly, as though it were a hot cake, and placed it, still curled in a ball, on a stool.

To her surprise, the cat had been sleeping on her sister's face. 'I'd forgotten you'd painted Lilian,' she said, dusting the portrait free of hairs. 'You must have done this just before she left.'

'Yes,' said Aunt Statham. 'I never finished it. She's supposed to be holding an orchid – you know how she loved them – but I couldn't get the hands right. Or the orchid. It was Lilian who could paint flowers. You know that. Of course, she didn't paint anything else, so it's not surprising she was good at it. She did some beautiful pieces. What a pity your father put them all on the fire.'

'I have one or two hidden away,' said Alice.

'Quite right. Just don't let your father know, or he'll have them off you in a trice. It's a pity you don't paint yourself, my dear, or I could have bequeathed my materials, and my paintings, to you. But then not everyone is gifted with the artistic genius. You have the right idea. Accept your limitations and take up photography. There's no skill required to do that, is there?'

'A little.'

'But there's no drawing involved,' insisted Aunt Statham. 'It's all simply chemical reactions and so forth. You've said so yourself many times.'

'I suppose I have,' said Alice. She was not really listening. She held up the painting of Lilian, turning it this way and that in the feeble lamplight. Aunt Lambert was right. It was not very good, though Aunt Statham had managed to capture Lilian's half-amused smile. Aunt Statham had given Lilian a knowing look, though this might have been the result of the canvas stretching beneath the weight of the cat. Alice found it unsettling. 'Photography's not quite that straightforward, Aunt,' she said absently. 'There's the light. And the exposure time. It's very easy to get it wrong, you know.'

'But the camera simply copies what is directly before you,' insisted Aunt Statham. 'It's not art, is it? Art involves skill and time, patience and insight. Passion, even. *You* simply point your camera box at the subject and your chemicals do the work. Where's the skill in that? A camera may capture the image in all its detail, but it can't capture the spirit of the subject.'

'The camera will render painting obsolete, Mrs Statham,'

declared Aunt Lambert briskly as she dealt the cards for whist. 'Particularly portraits. But then we're all obsolete in the end. Are you in, dear? You can pair up with Mrs Pendleton. Or Mrs Rushton-Bell.'

'Obsolete? Surely not,' cried Aunt Statham. 'Why, a photograph simply shows us as we are – tired, gap-toothed, old and dull. There is no flamboyance in photographs. No mystery. No fervour or feeling. Oh no, we will always need portraits and painting. How else will we hide the drab reality of our appearance from posterity?' Aunt Statham unrolled a canvas that had already been removed from its frame and gazed fondly at its subject – a ferocious-looking old man with the high neckerchief and extravagant sideburns of the previous century. 'Ah, Mr Reynolds.' She sighed. 'Such *passion*.' She began a dreamy recitation of all the artists she had once known – including him whose portrait she was now holding. There were many of them, it seemed, and all had marvelled at her beauty and vitality, this last being a quality they felt unable to capture with anything other than the most vivid of media. Oils it had been, every time. 'Certainly a photograph would have been useless,' she added, eyeing Aunt Lambert. 'And will the photographers of today be as charming as the artists they supplant?'

'We'll soon find out,' said Alice. 'Mr Blake will be with us by next week.'

But Aunt Statham had not been looking for an answer to her question. She was lost in a whirling past that no one but she remembered. Ah, how the young men had danced and leaped around her. What toasts had been made in her honour. What glances had been exchanged as would-be lovers lunged after fallen handkerchiefs and knelt to kiss gloved fingers . . . Alice found herself wondering how Mr Blake could possibly hope to match the enthusiasm of these bohemian admirers.

'Ah well.' Aunt Statham sighed. 'They were all penniless, of course. And then I met my husband. He was not artistically inclined in any way. A clergyman. Like Lilian's husband, but not so meanly proportioned. Still, he was a dull fellow compared to the other young men of my acquaintance, dull though reliable. But that was all a long time ago now. Perhaps this photographer fellow will make a nice husband for you, my dear?'

'Alice doesn't need a husband,' snapped Aunt Lambert. 'And Lilian didn't need one either. That was her father's idea. He should have left her alone. And sending her off to India too, as if being the wife of that dreadful fellow were not punishment enough.'

'But she managed to leave this place,' said Alice, 'which is what she wanted.'

'He'll never forgive her, you know,' said Old Mrs Talbot. 'Edwin can be so stubborn.' She sighed. 'But then obedience in a daughter is more than a virtue, it's a necessity. Edwin was harsh, but, well, can one blame him?'

'Of course one can,' retorted Aunt Lambert. 'It was his own fault.'

'You're lucky he hasn't taken it out on you, Alice,' said Aunt Pendleton. 'He might have locked you up.'

'Ah, but you see I'm not likely to have Lilian's opportunity,' said Alice. 'He told me so himself. Mainly because no man would want me – I'm too ugly.'

'Oh, no!' gasped the aunts.

'Oh, yes,' said Alice. She smiled at their horrified faces.

'Oh, Alice.' The aunts sighed again. But they did not look her in the eye for they knew it was true. Where Lilian's skin was flawless and pale, Alice's was rough in texture and as dismal as whey. Lilian's hair was fine and soft but, although the same pale brown in colour, Alice's was dull and wiry. And whereas Lilian's figure was slim and well proportioned, Alice's seemed angular – a breastless, waistless and hipless body that no amount of corsetry and couture could mould or conceal.

'Of course,' said Aunt Lambert, moving the subject on to

spare Alice's feelings. 'If your mother had been around things might have been very different. She certainly wouldn't have sent her daughter off with a missionary man. Poor Lilian. She didn't know any better.'

Alice said nothing. Lilian, she knew, had always been fully aware of what she was doing, even when things did not turn out quite the way she had planned.

'Still, I doubt she's enjoying being saddled with a husband,' added Aunt Statham. 'She would have been better off without him. They can be so demanding. And in that heat too. Well, perhaps he'll slake his beastly appetites in the bazaar and leave Lilian in peace.'

'Lydia, please,' murmured Old Mrs Talbot. There was a silence, the only noise being the drip of water from somewhere deep within the foliage. The aunts exchanged glances. Alice felt the hot, moist air of the conservatory pressing against her face and neck like warm, sticky hands. Beside her, Aunt Rushton-Bell shuffled the playing cards uneasily.

'I gave her my late husband's topi and his rifle before she left, you know,' said Aunt Lambert after a moment. 'For all his faults Mr Lambert was actually quite keen on women being able to look after themselves. Not that he had much choice in the matter. I've never been one to allow a man to speak for me and I certainly never needed one to take care of me when we were in India. I'm sure Lilian will be the same.'

Alice blinked, suddenly feeling tears pricking at her eyes. The passing of time had made the separation from her sister no easier to bear. The days were measured by those activities they had always undertaken together: watering the peach tree, tending to the orchids, supervising the cleaning of the Collection. Now, Alice performed these tasks alone and unaided, and she found that she did not have the stomach for any of them. The aunts might be sisters to one another, she reflected, but not one of them could know what it was like to have a sister who had shared *everything* – every moment of life, every pleasure, every disappointment, every unhappiness. It had seemed as though even their thoughts were alike, their feelings in sympathy at all times, often with hardly a word passing between them. But now Lilian had gone. She had made her decisions and would have to live with the consequences, just as she, Alice, had to do.

'Now then, my dear, where shall we put this Mr Blake when he comes?' said Aunt Lambert brightly, patting Alice on the hand.

'I wonder whether he'll play whist,' said Aunt Pendleton.

'What about Lilian's room?' said Alice. 'No one's been in it since she left. He could go in there.'

'But what if she comes back?' said Old Mrs Talbot.

'She's not coming back,' said Aunt Lambert irritably. 'You know that.'

From beneath the iron grids in the floor came a dull throbbing sound, like the beating of an immense heart buried deep within the building. The aunts peered at each other through the leafy lamplight, their eyes wide.

'It's just the heating,' observed Alice to no one in particular as she rolled her sister's portrait into a tube. 'I really must bleed those pipes.'

3

The coach deposited Mr Blake at the gates, which were, of course, welded closed. Having discovered this surprising fact, Mr Blake abandoned his luggage (apart from his precious camera in its wooden box) where the coachman had left it and wandered off around the walls in search of an entrance. At length he found his way through the stable at the back of the house. He walked round the building to the front and rang the bell.

He was greeted, after a considerable wait, by a manservant

so advanced in age that he seemed scarcely able to pull the door wide. For a moment it seemed as though the man had not, in fact, answered Mr Blake's knock at all, but had simply been passing by and had decided, on impulse, to take a look outside.

'Good morning,' said Mr Blake. 'I believe I'm expected?'

The man muttered something that sounded disconcertingly like an expletive and receded back into the house, pushing the door closed. Mr Blake waited and rubbed his hands together to keep them warm. He took a deep lungful of frosty air and blew out a cloud of breath.

Despite this inconvenient start to his new commission, Mr Blake was greatly relieved to be away from London, with its crowded and filthy streets, and its damp and foul air. He was even more relieved to be away from St Thomas's, though he had to admit that working for Dr Cattermole had been memorable in many ways. For a start, it had allowed him to develop his photography skills, while his medical training, what there was of it, had meant that he had always known exactly what the Doctor was talking about. Together, they had taken hundreds of photographs – amputees' stumps; organs, sliced and laid out neatly for the camera; suppurating ulcers; burst appendices and faces consumed by syphilis – all had passed under the scrutiny of Dr Cattermole's lens.

'It's about detail,' Dr Cattermole had said, standing over an eviscerated cadaver and rubbing his hands hungrily. 'What we're providing is a visual catalogue of sickness and disease. A catalogue that lets us chart the balance between good health and bad – the road back to health, the numbing horror of stasis, or the descent into mortification. All equally fascinating journeys.' Mr Blake had nodded, though he had been troubled by the Doctor's growing zeal in his quest to locate the most gruesome manifestations of disease.

Now, waiting outside the Great House, Mr Blake shuddered. The stench of carbolic and decomposition that had pervaded the mortuary seemed to cling to him still. He banged on the door. 'Hello?' he shouted. 'Is anybody there? Hello? *Hello*?' The door jerked open and he found himself staring at a tall, angular woman, wearing what looked like a printer's apron.

'There's no need to shout,' the woman said.

'I beg your pardon,' he stammered. 'I thought your man had forgotten me.'

'Who, Sluce?' She smiled suddenly. 'He probably had.' She held out her hand. 'I'm Alice Talbot. I assume you're Mr Blake, the photographer?'

He took her hand. She had long fingers which, he noticed with some surprise, were as blotched and streaked with brown stains as her apron. He was even more surprised to feel that her grip was as strong as a man's. A feeble spring sun emerged, briefly, from behind the clouds. But rather than lighting up her features, its glare illuminated a fine layer of hairs that covered her cheeks and upper lip like the down on a peach. Why, he thought, she was really quite ugly. But then the sun went in again and she was, he realised, simply plain.

'Someone will bring your luggage in,' she said.

Mr Blake gave a slight bow.

She looked at the wooden camera box. 'Is that all you have?'

'The rest is at the gates. They seem to be welded closed. Perhaps your man would . . .'

'They *are* welded closed. This house is not like most other houses,' said Alice. 'Did Dr Cattermole tell you that?'

'My dear Miss Talbot,' said Mr Blake. 'I have just spent six months in a mortuary. I can assure you that that is not like most other places, either.'

Alice shrugged and led him into the hall.

Twelve grandfather clocks stood to attention against the wall at the foot of the staircase, each one sullenly chipping away at the time. 'Twelve clocks?' Mr Blake ventured bleakly.

'My father winds them once a week,' said Alice. 'He is

vigilant as to their accuracy.' Mr Blake saw her glance at him out of the corner of her eye; saw her smile at his bemused expression. 'They chime together,' she said. 'Exactly together.'

'It must be very loud,' he observed, for want of something more insightful to say. 'And this is – what, exactly?' He pointed to a mass of cogs and wheels squatting beneath a huge glass dome.

'A section of Mr Babbage's difference engine. It was taken to bits after the Great Exhibition. Mr Babbage said it had been poorly displayed, its future significance ignored by an unimaginative multitude. My father secured a part of it for the Collection.'

'And what does it do?'

'Nothing.'

'Ah.'

'It doesn't work without the rest of its numbered cogs and wheels. Mr Babbage said that if he had been adequately supported by the government and allowed to finish the project there was no knowing what it might have led to.'

Mr Blake nodded. He had no idea what she was talking about.

'It's a calculation machine,' said Alice gently.

'I shall be sure to take its picture,' said Mr Blake. He followed Alice through the crowded hallways.

She pushed open a pair of double doors. 'This', she said over her shoulder, 'is the hot house. The temperate house, in which I have established a small studio, is further on. I'll take you through.'

The doors to the hot house closed silently, sealing the two of them within. The atmosphere was leaden with moisture and Mr Blake felt instantly as though he had been submerged, fully clothed, in a warm clear broth. He mopped his forehead and looked about anxiously. High above, desperate leaves pressed against the glass ceiling like hands. Shrubs and bushes clawed at his clothes and slapped at his camera as he followed

Alice through the greenery. Everything seemed to be swathed in moss or squeezed by creepers and climbers. Here and there some of the larger specimens had split open their pots and dribbled grainy pyramids of soil onto the floor. Those bricked into the foundations had heaved against their constraints, causing floor tiles to crack and buckle. Others had burst through completely, providing obscene glimpses of hairy wrists and knuckles of root. Through the foliage, for a moment, Mr Blake was sure he glimpsed a collection of unoccupied furniture – tables and chairs, a sideboard even – but he could not be sure.

'And does your father still add to his botanical collection?' he panted, struggling to keep a grip on his camera.

'No,' snapped Alice.

Mr Blake raised his eyebrows, but said nothing.

'My father rarely comes here,' added Alice after a moment, as though realising how ungracious she sounded. 'He had the conservatory built – the biggest in England, of course; it's twenty-six feet high, one hundred feet in length and fifty feet wide – but it was my mother who grew the plants. When she died my sister and I looked after them. But my father never comes here now. He rarely came even when my mother was alive; though he was happy to indulge her interest in botany. And my sister's.'

'And now?' persisted Mr Blake, stumbling over a shaggy root as thick as a ship's mooring rope. 'Now, who cares for this place?'

'Now, I work here alone.'

'And your father indulges *your* taste in botany, I hope?' Mr Blake smiled what he hoped was a smile of charm and sincerity, but Alice did not turn round to see it.

They passed through another set of double doors. Instantly the air became cool and dry, the foliage less dense and tangled, and the light brighter. Mr Blake breathed a sigh of relief. His eye was caught by a vast wheeled bucket standing in a clearing beside the building's glass wall. He gazed at it in amazement. The huge brass wheels supported a bucket made of thick oak planks, tarred like the sides of a ship. Here and there patches of moss and lichen adhered to its hull like beards of seaweed and patches of barnacles. The bucket contained a tree.

'Why is that tree on wheels?' he asked, before he could stop himself.

'So that it can be moved,' said Alice. Her tone suggested that the question was a foolish one.

'Why does it need to be moved?'

Alice clicked her tongue. 'It's a peach tree,' she said. 'My mother loved peaches. She used to wheel the tree between the temperate house and the hot house so as to give it the best growing conditions. Sometimes it goes outside altogether. Its fruits are quite remarkable. That's not the original tree, of course, there have been a few of them, over the years. It's a system of my mother's own devising. Unique, I believe. Now then, is there anything else?'

Mr Blake shook his head. 'No,' he said. 'Thank you.'

'As I was saying.' Alice pointed to a bench against the glass wall. 'I set up a small studio here. It's north facing, so it's always bright without being sunny, though I have to cut back the foliage every now and again. The shed – you can see it in the shrubs there – I have been using as a darkroom.'

'Are you a photographer?'

'Did you think I was wearing this apron to flatter my figure?'

'Forgive me. I didn't expect . . . I mean, your father didn't say . . .' Mr Blake coloured.

'You didn't expect to find a photographer *already* here?' suggested Alice.

'No.'

'And you are shocked to find a woman thus attired?'

'Yes. Well, a little, perhaps . . . That is to say, I mean no, no, of course not. Your attire is . . . as one would expect from anyone engaged in such a pastime.' Mr Blake passed his camera from one hand to the other.

'Your camera must seem heavy now,' said Alice, observing his discomfort. 'I often put mine into Aunt Rushton-Bell's bath chair and wheel it about, rather than carrying it. Will you not put it down?'

'No, thank you,' said Mr Blake. 'I shall keep hold of it.' He forced himself to smile. He knew his face was crimson and he shivered as a bead of moisture trickled down his temple.

'What, exactly, did my father ask you to do here?' asked Alice suddenly.

'He asked me to photograph the Collection.'

'All of it?'

'His favourite pieces.'

'Is that all?'

'As far as I'm aware that is all he requires from me.'

'As far as you are aware?'

Mr Blake nodded. The long journey from London, the humidity of the hot house, the weight of his camera and the fact that he desperately wished someone would offer him a cup of tea, had combined to make him quite weak. He felt himself wilting under her interrogation. 'He said he might find more for me to do, once I got here.'

'I see. And what sort of subjects do you prefer to photograph, Mr Blake? Surely body parts and diseased flesh are not your main interest?'

The photographer hesitated. She was looking directly into his eyes and he felt his own gaze falter. 'Oh, no,' he replied. 'The work in the mortuary was temporary. I was helping Dr Cattermole . . .' He stopped. He found he didn't want to talk about his work with Dr Cattermole. 'Still life compositions and landscapes – ruined abbeys and castles – are among my favourite subjects. But I have taken many portraits, too. People have spoken very highly of my work. Why, you yourself should sit for me.'

'I'm too pale,' said Alice.

'Ah, but even the palest flower can be photographed to show its true beauty if the light is correct,' said Mr Blake with a dazzling smile. To his relief, he saw a slight blush tinge Alice's cheeks. At last! He had been beginning to wonder whether she was a woman at all, with her assertive gaze and inquisitorial conversation. Encouraged, he put down his camera and pulled a small bundle of cards out of his pocket. 'Look at these, Miss Talbot.' He handed the cards to Alice. Each one bore the dim calotype of a tiny flower.

'I photographed these last spring, when Dr Cattermole was called away one afternoon. Despite his instructions that I should continue with my tasks, I left the mortuary and took a long walk through Hyde Park. Even now I can remember how good it felt to be out of that dank and chilly place, if only for an afternoon. Before I left the park I collected a small posy from the grass and surrounding flowerbeds.' He gave Alice a wistful smile. 'A memento of my one afternoon of freedom, I suppose. A reminder that there is beauty in nature, rather than simply the death and disease that I saw on Dr Cattermole's slab every day.

'Back in my rooms, before this tiny posy wilted, I took its likeness – together as a bunch, then separate images of each flower: buttercup, honesty, daisy, a sprig of broom, a few delicate strands of sweet-smelling lily of the valley . . . Despite their dainty size and soft colour, the camera captured every detail perfectly.' He drew an illustrative finger gently down the stem of honesty. 'You see?' he murmured. 'The trick is to get the light just right. And, of course, the exposure time.'

After developing these images, though naturally he did not mention it to Alice, Mr Blake had visited a local prostitute – a woman of indeterminate age with an air of silent resignation about her. The moth-eaten silk flowers in her straw-coloured hair had bobbed and trembled as she earned her shilling and Mr Blake had been unable to tear his gaze away from them as they danced before his eyes in a monstrous parody of nature. In the warm confines of her room, the stench of the mortuary had emanated powerfully from him, so that afterwards even the doxy herself had commented on his strange and unsettling smell. He had left her feeling as though death had been riding on his shoulders throughout, gleefully panting its foetid breath into the woman's face. It had made him uneasy, although he reminded himself that he had been careful to choose a whore whose face did not betray those signs of disease with which his work for Dr Cattermole had made him so familiar.

Afterwards, on returning to his lodgings, he had found his flowers wilted, their petals scattered about the table top like a handful of confetti. Feeling less than satisfied by his own behaviour, Mr Blake had taken solace in his depictions of nature, each immortalised in a sepia image no bigger than a playing card.

'I have kept them in my pocket ever since,' he said. 'To look at whenever I need to remind myself of the beauty and simplicity of the natural world.'

Alice was examining the images closely. 'They're very well executed,' she said. She returned the photographs. 'No doubt it was these pictures that won my father over.'

'Oh, no, Miss Talbot. These particular pictures are private,' said Mr Blake warmly. 'Dr Cattermole spoke to your father about me. I didn't actually show Mr Talbot any of my work.'

'Dr Cattermole spoke for you? Are you sure that was wise?' Alice gave a humourless smile. 'Well, you're here now,' she added. 'So whatever he said was agreeable to my father.'

Mr Blake attempted a laugh, but the sound that emerged was more like a cough. 'Indeed,' he said. He gazed at his feet. He found he could no longer look her in the face.

4

In the evening, as usual, Alice collected the aunts from the hot house. Murmuring to one another about the inclement weather, the draughts, the lack of hot water that evening, and the fact that Mr Talbot had relocated the stuffed animals to the hall outside their bedrooms on the second floor and that all those staring beady eyes were most unsettling, they followed her in to dinner.

Alice was helping Aunt Rushton-Bell into her chair as Mr Talbot strode into the room. Mr Blake followed. He was wearing a smoking jacket several sizes too large. Alice had not seen him since their conversation in the temperate house, after which Mr Blake had suddenly seemed anxious to get started. He had insisted that he alone carry his photography equipment. For the next hour or so, as she sat with her aunts in the hot house, Alice had heard him passing backwards and forwards through the rustling greenery, his breathing becoming more and more laboured, his footsteps slower and slower as he transported his boxes of plates, his bales of paper, his crates of chemicals, trays, bowls, tripods, head clamps and sundry other items through the conservatory.

Now, thought Alice, he was looking dishevelled and peevish; his dark curly hair was flattened against his head and his eyes were perplexed. He seemed uncomfortable in the smoking jacket, and brushed at the lapels with fingers stained black and brown, like her own, with nitrates of silver. She peered closely at his curious costume. The jacket was one of her father's.

'Has anyone seen Mr Blake's trunk?' bellowed Mr Talbot, by way of introduction. 'He has mislaid it.'

'Mislaid it? Oh dear,' murmured Old Mrs Talbot.

'When did you last see it, Mr Blake?' asked Aunt Rushton-Bell.

'It disappeared on its way to my room,' said Mr Blake.

'Sluce was supposed to have brought it over from the gates. I have no idea where it went.'

'Keep an eye out for it,' said Mr Talbot. 'You especially, Alice. A large black trunk. It's got to be in the house somewhere. And if you see Sluce, ask him. We need it back. Mr Blake needs it back.' He cleared his throat. 'Well, then. That's that.'

'Do you play whist, Mr Blake?' called Aunt Pendleton from the far end of the table.

'Never mind what he does or doesn't play,' thundered Mr Talbot. 'He's a photographer. He's here to take photographs, not to play cards.' He thumped Mr Blake on the back. 'Now, sir, you must be hungry.'

Mr Blake was indeed hungry and, for a while, was unable to focus his attention on anything other than the food on his plate. Around him, he was dimly aware of conversation, though his brain was too fogged by gluttony to comprehend it. He looked up only once. Alice was pushing her food about her plate, though she touched none of it. No wonder she was so thin. He smiled at her, but she looked away. He speared another roast potato.

At last Mr Blake found himself able to attend to the discussion that was going on. It appeared to concern other visitors to the house.

'Oh, yes,' Aunt Lambert was saying, 'Mr Bellows. He's been here longer than all the others.'

'Is he still here?' Mr Talbot looked startled. 'I'd quite forgotten about him. Are there any others still hanging about?'

'Not now,' said Alice. 'At least, I don't think so. The translators have left. So has Dr Slater.'

'Dr Slater. Was that the fellow who burned his face?' asked Aunt Rushton-Bell.

'I beg your pardon?' said Mr Blake.

'Dr Slater was searching for a cure for facial pustules.' Alice addressed the photographer. 'His own complexion was sadly afflicted with the condition and he smeared some of the preparation he had formulated upon his own face to see whether it would help.'

'But it burned him,' interrupted Aunt Statham. 'Like acid. It was as though he'd rubbed his skin off with a pumice stone.'

'He ran screaming through the house clawing at his face to get the stuff off, as I recall,' added Aunt Lambert. 'He burst into my dressing room and plunged his entire head into my washbasin. Apparently he had emptied his own that morning and had forgotten to fill it again before he began his experiments. It was just in time. The poor fellow could hardly speak for weeks, even after his bandages were removed. Certainly, he never looked quite right afterwards. He didn't get rid of his skin condition either.'

'He tested everything on himself,' said Alice. 'Mostly he drank his own medicines and observed the consequences. He had a special emetic to take if he felt that he had inadvertently poisoned himself.'

Mr Blake felt the eyes of the entire table resting on him. Was he required to comment on Dr Slater's bizarre behaviour? Was he supposed to ask for more details about Mr Bellows? He hastily swallowed his mouthful of potato. But it lodged uncomfortably in his oesophagus, like a mouse in an organ pipe, and a muffled 'I see' was all he could manage.

'He was convinced that the cures for all man's ailments could be found in plants, if only we looked hard enough,' said Alice.

'Well, they have to be good for something,' muttered Mr Talbot. 'All that useless greenery.'

Mr Blake saw Alice's brow darken. 'The natural world provides inspiration for the direction of our own progress,' she said. 'Even without their medicinal properties plants have much to offer us. Some of man's finest creations mimic their processes and structures.'

'Such as what, my dear? Such as what?'

'Well, the Crystal Palace. The building that housed the Great Exhibition. A building very similar in design to our own conservatory.'

'An excellent example, Alice,' cried Aunt Lambert, clapping her hands. 'The Crystal Palace is a marvel of size and complexity. But where did Paxton get his inspiration? Why, from nature! From plants.'

'Precisely,' said Alice. 'Paxton's structure was based on Amazonian lily-pads – huge circular leaves strong enough to bear the weight of a child due to their supporting network of veins.'

'That's as may be, but civilisation is man's triumph over nature.' Mr Talbot reached beneath the table and produced a twelve-inch rectangular box. He placed it gently on the table top beside his plate. 'Look here. I was saving this for later but now seems as good a time as any.' He ran an admiring finger over the varnished wooden surface of the box. 'The perpetual mousetrap. A small but ingenious addition to the Collection. A device capable of resetting itself and trapping mice continuously.'

Alice glanced at Mr Blake, who waved a fork cheerily. 'Oh, don't mind me,' he said, nodding and smiling. 'Cattermole used to talk about diseased cadavers at the dinner table. It'll take more than a mere mousetrap to put me off, I can tell you.'

There was a polite pause. 'Quite so,' said Mr Talbot. He cleared his throat. 'As I was saying, most traps can catch and kill only one mouse at a time, but this one, why, due to its spring-loaded turnstile mouse door it flips the mouse through to a chamber at the rear and is instantly primed to receive another. It can catch up to twenty-eight live mice in a single trap. More, if the holding chamber is made larger. Indeed, there could be no limit to its capacity if the holding chamber were made bigger. Ingenious, don't you think? A humble example of progress, of man's resourcefulness triumphing over the natural proclivity of the mouse for procreation and pestiferousness. I shall try it in the stables tonight.'

Alice shook her head. 'And what would anyone want with twenty-eight live mice? Really, Father, take the thing off the table. It should be in the kitchen, along with the cat.'

'With this there will be no need for cats.'

'But Alice is right,' said Aunt Lambert. 'This progress of yours is simply the exchange of one set of conditions and restrictions for another.'

'Exactly,' said Alice. 'A cat would *eat* the mice it catches. By its natural urges it rids us of vermin and sustains itself. Your mousetrap still leaves the problem of what to do with twenty-eight mice.'

'And, by implication, what to do with the nation's cats.' Aunt Lambert and Alice exchanged smiles.

Mr Talbot's face grew red. 'My dear Aunt, would you have us abandon all efforts for improvement? And you, Alice. Do you say that the conditions in which you live are no better than those of your forefathers? No, you do not. Man's dedication to invention and manufacture has transformed the lot of even the humble working man. Take slum dwellers. Progress in theories of disease causation and new methods of sanitation have transformed their quality of life. Not to mention the impact a mousetrap such as this might have upon their infested homes.'

'But before the slum dwellers appeared in their droves in our cities, were they not happier, and healthier, living in the countryside?' asked Alice. 'I admit, improved sanitation allows them to avoid the cholera and this means that they live longer. But longer lives spent in miserable conditions. Who benefits from this, Father? The slum dwellers? I doubt whether they would regard an extra five years of life caught in poverty and servitude as progress, with or without this mousetrap to remind them how lucky they are!'

Mr Talbot's face darkened further. He turned to Mr Blake.

'She reads pamphlets, you know,' he muttered in an undertone. 'I have no idea where she gets them.'

But Mr Blake was no longer listening. He was thinking about his missing trunk. How careless of him. And how careless that he had stored his portfolios of photographs in it. Why had he not kept them with his photographic equipment, as he had originally intended to do? There were some portraits in those portfolios that Dr Cattermole seemed to think Mr Talbot would be particularly keen to see and now they were mislaid. What if someone else found the trunk and opened it? Rendered sleepy by the huge meal he had consumed, Mr Blake pressed his palms against his eyes to halt the images of white flesh and black hair that came crowding into his brain each time he thought of his missing portfolios. The portraits had been taken not two days before he left his lodgings in Whitechapel to start his commission with Mr Talbot. Taken, moreover (and much to Mr Blake's surprise), at the instigation of Dr Cattermole.

'Come now, my dear fellow, one good turn and all that?' the Doctor had said with a wink, throwing a conspiratorial arm round his apprentice's shoulders. And then he had demanded his favour-in-return, a parting gift from one man of the world to another. A secret, of course. After all, the Doctor had Mrs Cattermole to consider. Ah, if only his wife would allow him a fifteen-minute exposure, Dr Cattermole had joked, as they walked through the foul and raucous backstreets to escort a suitably endowed prostitute back to Mr Blake's lodgings.

Mr Blake had eyed his companion nervously. Mrs Cattermole, he knew, demanded much more than fifteen minutes. Indeed, she was beginning to demand too much and, as far as Mr Blake was concerned, his commission with Mr Talbot could not come soon enough.

The Doctor slapped Mr Blake on the shoulder and gave another exaggerated wink. 'You know what I mean,' he insisted. Mr Blake, assuming the question was rhetorical, gave only a wan smile.

The afternoon had passed in a blur of shock and surprise. Having worked with him every day for the past six months, Mr Blake assumed that he knew the Doctor well. Why, he had been to Dr Cattermole's house, had eaten his food and drunk his wine. He had also spent the past six weeks with his breeches down, reaming and rogering the Doctor's most intimate companion in every conceivable location in the Doctor's own house.

'He's not interested in me,' Mrs Cattermole had panted. 'He's not interested in any woman – unless she's dead and on his slab.'

But as he gazed in disbelief through the camera's unflinching eye, seeing the Doctor's pale and skinny frame jerking enthusiastically between the thighs of the prostitute, Mr Blake realised he had no idea at all who Thomas Cattermole was.

The naked Doctor had insisted on shouting instructions to Mr Blake throughout the proceedings. At one point he had extracted himself from the moist recesses of the lady to dart forward, his bobbing manhood glistening pinkly in the light from the window, to make sure the lens was correctly focused. Using a newfangled photographic technique involving collodion had at least meant that each exposure was mercifully rapid. More than once Mr Blake found himself wondering whether either Dr Cattermole or his obliging assistant (really, she was remarkably flexible for one so large) would have been able to maintain such a variety of positions for so long had he been taking photographs using the slower calotype method.

Afterwards, while Mr Blake attended to the developing process in the cupboard, the Doctor had taken a few more photographs, this time of the lady on her own: wearing her shift gathered up about her waist and sitting on the edge of a chair, dimpled thighs coyly sandwiched together; the same, but with only her stockings on. A third picture showed her standing completely nude and holding an immense globe-shaped breast in each hand, like a butcher offering two sides of beef for inspection. The woman herself had neither complained nor questioned, but had followed her instructions with bovine indifference. As Dr Cattermole paid her off, slapping her bottom when she turned to go, Mr Blake had had the feeling she had seen it all before – and more besides.

When he cleared up the detritus of the afternoon, Mr Blake realised that the Doctor had left his final three plates behind. But Mr Blake had not thrown them away as he had told himself he should. Instead, he had plunged them into the saline bath, staring at the mounds of naked female flesh that appeared before his eyes even as the memory itself mercifully faded.

Dr Cattermole had said nothing at all about that afternoon until Mr Blake was packing up his photographic equipment and preparing to leave for his commission with Mr Talbot.

Then, 'Those pictures,' Cattermole had said as he shook his apprentice's hand. 'Talbot might be interested.'

Now, Mr Blake realised with alarm that Mr Talbot was addressing him. Was shouting at him, in fact. 'Come, come,' he was saying. 'Speak up!'

'Indeed,' said Mr Blake. 'You are quite right, sir.' He had no idea what he was agreeing to, but his employer seemed satisfied.

Mr Blake looked at Alice, but her gaze told him nothing. He smiled, for reasons he could not identify, suddenly wanting her approval. She stared at him, then turned away, as though disgusted. Mr Blake felt his cheeks turn red.

'There you are,' thundered Mr Talbot. 'Mr Blake agrees and, as a medical man and a scientist, I'll wager his knowledge of public health matters is greater than your own. Now then.' He eyed Mr Blake as he rummaged in his pockets. 'Perhaps it's time the ladies left us.'

Mr Blake felt a deadening sense of gloom at the prospect of

drinking port alone with Mr Talbot. Would it be rude, or somehow unmanly, to claim exhaustion and go to his rooms?

Along with the half-smoked stump of his cigar, which was what he had been searching for, Mr Talbot extracted from his pocket a crumpled piece of paper. 'Humph,' he grunted. 'This came for you last week.' He tossed a letter across the table top to his daughter. 'I've a mind to throw it into the fire.'

The envelope was creased and corrugated with water damage, the address only visible through the scratches of pen on the surface of the paper. Mr Blake watched in surprise as Alice snatched the letter from her father's outstretched fingers, as though she expected him to change his mind and stuff it back out of sight into his pocket.

'At last!' cried Old Mrs Talbot, clapping her skeletal hands together so that her rings rattled. 'I knew Lilian would not forget us. Thank you, Edwin dear.'

'But you've already opened it,' said Alice, pointing to the torn envelope.

'This is my house. All correspondence that crosses this threshold is of interest to me. Especially if it's from *her*.' Mr Talbot banged his fist on the table. 'She has no right to communicate with anyone here. She made her choice. "Sharper than a serpent's tooth",' he muttered darkly to Mr Blake. 'Besides,' he added, looking slightly shamefaced, 'it's almost impossible to read. Silly woman must've written on wet paper. Either that or the monsoon caught it. She might as well be writing on butter.'

'But it is addressed to *me*,' Alice protested.

'What of it?' shouted Mr Talbot, his face turning purple. 'And don't think you might like to reply to it. I've removed the address for a start and my postbag is barred to you. And your aunts.' He swept the table with a suspicious glare. 'And Sluce keeps an eye on the servants so you won't be able to find yourself a courier from among their ranks either.' Mr Talbot heaved himself to his feet. He addressed Mr Blake. 'And I include you, sir, in this injunction. Do *not* be persuaded to carry a letter out of this house without my knowledge. I will search your pockets, sir. I will search your pockets. Let me also remind you,' he cried, 'that *no one* is permitted to leave this house without my express permission. *No one.* I am quite determined. You will *not* communicate with her. Now, take that foolish scribble away. Before I change my mind.'

'Poor Lilian,' said Aunt Pendleton tearfully. 'She was taken from us.'

'Is she dead?' asked Mr Blake.

'She's dead to me,' shouted Mr Talbot. 'And I'll not have her name mentioned at this table again.'

'She's in India,' explained Alice. 'She married a missionary. A Mr Fraser.'

LILIAN

1

Almost the first thing Lilian was told as she and her husband disembarked in Calcutta was that the heat of India did not agree with the complexions of European ladies.

'Be sure always to carry a parasol, my dear,' cautioned the cadaverous wife of a retired colonel. 'Especially as you are so very fair. And you can get Mitchum's Skin Food here too, sent out from London direct. It's invaluable. I myself have used it every day for years and you can see the advantages.'

Lilian had nodded and smiled, and regarded the old lady's yellowed face with interest. She wondered what state of sepulchral dehydration it would have been in had the colonel's wife not used cosmetic unctions but had simply let nature take its course as she, Lilian, was obliged to do, her husband being against such vanities as skin food and certainly unlikely to countenance transporting pots of the stuff across the subcontinent simply to provide his wife with the luxury of greasing her face like an old boot every night. And as for the parasol, why, surely she would need both hands to hold her skirts up, to push aside foliage or to fire her rifle at tigers or snakes?

'She'll not last long out here,' the colonel's wife had muttered to her companion, a thickset lady with the quivering dewlaps of a bloodhound. 'The thin, pale sort never do. If the heat doesn't kill her the mosquitoes or the water will. And if not, I'll wager she goes Home within the year.'

*

Lilian had travelled to India with her new husband, the Reverend Selwyn Fraser, whose intention it was to devote himself to missionary work among the heathen Hindus. Although a number of these native people had already been converted to Christianity, it appeared that there were still many millions of souls yet to be saved. On the long journey from England to Calcutta, Selwyn had told Lilian much about the godless practices of the Hindus – how they worshipped numerous false gods for instance, chief among them a smiling, cross-legged fellow with four arms.

In fact, Lilian was already familiar with the beliefs of Hindus, as well as Sikhs, Jains, Buddhists and Moslems. Had she not shared a bedroom with a display case filled with ceremonial daggers, bowls and slippers used in the practices of these various eastern religions? Did not a statue of Shiva stand opposite her bedroom door on the third floor of the Great House, beside a gilt-plated Buddha, a waste-paper basket in the shape of an elephant's foot and a howdah draped in coloured silks?

Feeling that his wife's response lacked the appropriate degree of disgust, however, Selwyn Fraser sought to stoke her sensibilities into an inferno of outrage by providing her with more evidence of the ill-judged superstition of the natives – how they made offerings to a snaking-armed idol in the form of coins left in one of the statue's outstretched hands. As if this were not enough, their family lives too were built upon perversity and their children married off even before they were old enough to understand the purpose of such a union. Why, until quite recently, widows would throw themselves on to the funeral pyres of their deceased husbands, the more reluctant of them being physically tossed on to the flames by the dead man's grieving relatives. Surely she must agree that under such conditions the true Church, the Christian Church, simply had to step in?

Secretly, Lilian suspected that, laid low with a violent seasickness almost as soon as the gangplank had been raised and plagued by itchy patches of redness in the folds of his skin, her husband was trying to convince himself that he had made the right decision.

They disembarked in Calcutta after a journey of three months, by which time Selwyn had developed a fretful cough and an irritable manner. Their plan was to stay in Calcutta for only a few days, while their luggage was unloaded. It made sense to travel overland using the dak ('That's the mail service, my dear,' explained the colonel's wife. 'By far the most economical means of transport, and the dak bungalows are every ten miles and provide very reasonable accommodation'), even though this meant that the journey to their eventual destination of Kushpur would take a number of weeks.

In the meantime, they were made the guests of a local magistrate who, like Selwyn, was from Edinburgh and had offered his services as host to numerous missionaries from Home. 'Why, it's always a pleasure to meet young people off to spread the Good Lord's Word,' he said. 'And, of course, the more you fellows convert, the more we have on our side, eh? Anyway, you'll see the very best of the Company's India while you're here in Calcutta. We have no lack of diversions. Indeed, there's a dance tomorrow evening. I hope you'll both attend?' He rubbed his hands together in anticipation and bared his teeth in a smile. 'And I shall be happy to show you both round the bazaar. There are many fine native craftsmen these days. They copy the European styles admirably. You'll not find such workmanship up-country, I can assure you.'

Lilian said she would be delighted, though she knew Selwyn was not so sure. They had already passed through the bazaar on their way to reserve the dak, and he had found the sights and smells offensive to his senses. Unable even to breathe without retching into his handkerchief, he had been shocked by the gangs of babbling children who grasped at his legs and pulled at his clothes, and held out their hands in supplication. Having shaken off the children, it was with considerable alarm that he realised his wife was attracting the attention of other undesirables. Beggars in the most repellent states of physical incompleteness – some without arms or legs, some missing ears or noses, some blind with flies teeming about their milky eyeballs, some without eyeballs at all – had emerged from doorways and risen up eagerly from mats at the roadside to shout and gesticulate. Lilian had tossed them some coins, but Selwyn's Presbyterian sense of economy was appalled: he took Lilian's purse off her and dragged her into the twisting maze of streets.

They emerged at last to walk along the river bank. 'I shall never get used to it here,' he muttered. Even as he spoke his face had turned grey at the sight of a pair of charred feet projecting from a funeral pyre. The man tending the ghat poked at the corpse with a long stick and Selwyn vomited as a leg was turned, its knee bending in the opposite direction to its natural articulation. He looked away . . . And yet, was not that the body of a man he could see, rotting in the water?

That evening after dinner, Lilian had asked the Magistrate whether this was possible and was informed that sadly, yes, it most certainly was. 'The corpses of people – men, women and children – as well as dogs, cats, goats and sundry other unfortunate animals, find their way into the river,' he said between puffs on his cigar. 'Usually the crocodiles eat them, but often they float, unmolested, in the water for days until they are finally dragged down, I assume by the weight of their own putrescence.'

Lilian saw her husband blanch. Like a magician beginning a conjuring trick, he produced from between his waistcoat buttons a voluminous red silk handkerchief, into which he buried his mouth and nose. The river was not fifty yards away from the sumptuous and civilised dining room in which they now sat. 'What kind of a place is this that it can juxtapose rotting corpses and crocodiles with chandeliers and gold-plated picture frames?' he cried, oblivious to the startled looks of the Magistrate's wife.

'My dear fellow.' The Magistrate laughed. 'You'll soon get used to it.'

But Lilian knew he wouldn't. She watched as Selwyn's face turned pale, as in his mind's eye he recalled the half-eaten face and bloated naked body bobbing among the refuse. 'Breathe deeply, Selwyn,' she whispered. He nodded. His breath gusted in and out in time with the gentle swishing of the punkah overhead.

The following evening there was, as promised, the ball. Lilian unfolded from her trunk the one dress she had brought that was suitable for such an occasion. Already, the damp heat of the journey had caused a greenish mildew to pepper the stiff silk fabric, though she did her best to remove the spores with rose-water. Selwyn changed into another of his heavy black suits – he had brought a number of them with him, each identical. They were ideal garments to wear while visiting the sick and needy in the slums of Edinburgh or London, but in Calcutta they seemed to drink in the heat, the heavy fabric cleaving to his skin and weighing him down until he looked as though he were about to sink to his knees, in resignation rather than prayer. Lilian picked out a fresh collar for him. Ignoring his complaints that he had never liked dancing anyway, that surely such activity in this heat would be absurd and certainly ruinous to the health, and, by the way, did she realise that the calamine lotion she had dabbed on his itchy back had stuck to his shirt, she forced him to accompany her to the ball.

There was such a shortage of ladies present that Lilian, despite her unfashionable dress, was sought out for almost every dance. As the evening whirled away beneath her feet she scarcely noticed how warm the room was becoming – though she could see other ladies flagging. The ballroom was illuminated by a hundred candles, which added to the oppressive heat, while the damp screens of fragrant grass that covered the windows, and the punkahs that slowly swept back and forth overhead, did little to halt the constantly rising temperature.

Around the ballroom ladies slumped on chairs, their faces shining with perspiration, their curls unravelling in the heat to hang in limp bands against their blazing cheeks. Beside them, crimson-faced young men in tight military uniforms or woollen suits, their collars and shirts dark with sweat, worked energetically at their partners' fans in a vain attempt to stir the stifling atmosphere into a breeze.

Lilian smiled to herself as she was waltzed across the floor by a young subaltern with a bristling blond moustache and yellow teeth. *How absurd we must look to the natives*, she thought. She gazed at the sweating, panting faces that spun round and round her in the candlelight as the Europeans leaped and pranced. *Anyone would think we were in Bath, rather than Bengal.*

She said as much to her shaggy-lipped partner and instantly regretted her outspokenness. 'My dear lady,' he said, looking surprised. 'Would you have us wearing pyjamas and refusing to eat roast beef?' And he smiled his yellow smile and spun her round once again.

Lilian was glad to leave the city, despite its claims to civilisation. Civilisation, she thought, had never seemed so hot and uncomfortable. Now, as she was bounced along in the dak, the curtains rolled up to enable her to observe the passing countryside (though this also allowed in a fearsome heat, a choking cloud of dust and numerous buzzing insects), she reflected on her good fortune to be away from it all. And, more important, to be away from Home – to be somewhere other than in the stultifying atmosphere of her father's house, surrounded by the clutter of his endless possessions.

Admittedly, the conservatory with its wealth of botanical specimens had provided a satisfying diversion, but in the end she had felt as imprisoned and constrained as the very plants that she grew. And as she had finally quitted the Great House, liberated, it seemed, by Selwyn Fraser's proposal of marriage, she had secretly prayed never to return. Now, only the thought of Alice, still at home in England, caused her any anxiety.

Over the following days, Lilian made some useful and, to her mind, necessary modifications to her way of life. As they travelled further inland across the Indian plains, rather than use a parasol to keep the blistering sun off her pale skin, she adopted a pith helmet. Instead of asking her husband to speak to the bearers, she struggled to learn the rudiments of their language so that she could ask them herself. On their second night on the road, at her request, one of the bearers had shown her how to use the rifle. She practised by blasting into pulp the pendulous fruit that hung from the mango trees at the roadside and was now proficient. She made sure that the rifle was well oiled and ready for use at all times.

They travelled only in the mornings. In the afternoons Selwyn slept, exhausted, in whatever dak bungalow they had reached. Lilian, however, was too restless to lie meekly at his side. With the rifle over her shoulder, her notebooks, paints and brushes in her bag, and her easel and paper strapped to her back, she would wander off to explore the surrounding countryside. To facilitate this, beneath her skirts she took to wearing a pair of her husband's trousers, which enabled her to climb over fallen trees and scramble up rocks with ease and no loss of dignity.

'Really, my dear,' her husband said after a week of watching his wife disappear into the brush. 'This is most irregular. What will the natives think to see a lady wandering about alone in the jungle?'

'Ram comes with me,' replied Lilian. 'And these are the plains, not the jungle.'

Selwyn's flushed face turned a deeper shade of crimson, as it always did when she contradicted him. 'Has your sense of propriety completely deserted you?' he cried. 'Besides, there may be thieves, or wild animals, awaiting you if you stray too far. This fellow "Ram" you seem so fond of will be sure to run off and leave you to your fate. What if you fall and break your leg. Or get bitten by a snake?'

Lilian pretended not to hear him.

It took almost three months to reach Kushpur. Three months in which Lilian seemed to grow in stature, while her husband appeared to dwindle. Rather than finding the heat enervating, Lilian thrived on it. Her complexion became rosy, her walk a confident stride.

'You walk like a man,' her husband complained peevishly, as he scratched at the weeping blebs of psoriasis that covered the backs of his hands. 'And what's that gibberish you're always muttering?' He scowled and gave a feeble cough. 'And for goodness sake make sure you take that hat off before we meet anyone we know.'

'Who do we know out here?' enquired Lilian mildly. She was cleaning the rifle with oil and a piece of soft cotton cloth.

'And stop fiddling with that gun. Anyone would think you were a sepoy.'

Lilian looked at her husband reproachfully. His thick sandy hair had lost its shine and now enfolded his skull in a lustreless woollen helmet. His eyes were sunken and dull, ringed with grey wizened flesh, as though the moisture was gradually being sucked out of him by the hot breeze. His skin was mottled with pink blotches and a slapdash effort with his ablutions that morning had left patches of unmown stubble dotted here and there across his hollow cheeks. A cut beneath his ear was beaded with dried blood.

'Whatever is the matter with you, Selwyn?' she said. She would never have spoken to him in such a way before she had made her escape from England. Why, he had told her that it was her silent acquiescence that had most appealed to him in his choice of her as his bride. As if she hadn't known that her father had made him a generous payment on her wedding day. Still, she thought, at least Selwyn had stopped reminding her how lucky she was to have found a husband at all.

'Remember your duty and speak to your husband with respect,' he snapped now, as though hearing her thoughts. 'Where's your gratitude? Where do you think you would be without me? I mean, if it were not for my noble work at the Magdalene asylum with Dr Cattermole your father might never have found a husband as suitable as me, nor as understanding of *who* and *what* you are.'

Lilian's face turned red, then white. She gripped the rifle she had been cleaning and fought to master the urge to discharge it into her husband's face. How little he knew! She breathed deeply to steady herself. Now was not the time to rise to Selwyn's taunts. Instead, she lowered her eyes and began packing away her cleaning materials.

Selwyn gave a dejected cough and rummaged in his pocket for a handkerchief to mop his sweating brow. 'Forgive me, my dear,' he said. 'I should not have spoken so. I'm sure you must dwell every day on the weaknesses of your character and the unhappy consequences of your actions. Of course, I realise that, at times, your gratitude is so profound as scarcely to be able to make itself felt.' He dabbed at his forehead and examined the resultant moist handkerchief. 'This place makes me feel unwell,' he muttered. 'Perhaps I have heatstroke.'

'But you've hardly been outside,' said Lilian, turning away so that she did not have to look at him.

'The cholera, then.'

'That's absurd.'

'Typhus.' Selwyn sank back into his chair with a groan. 'That's what it must be.'

'Nonsense,' said Lilian. 'Malaria, perhaps.'

'Malaria?' Selwyn looked startled. He had not thought of that. 'Is it fatal?'

'It can be. Are your hands shaking?'

'No.' He held out his hands. As he stared at them they began to twitch. 'Yes, yes, they are,' he screamed. 'Look!'

'Really, Selwyn, you are so suggestible.' Lilian sighed. 'Anyway, this is the end of our journey. We'll be in Kushpur later today. You can see the doctor there,' she added, relenting a little.

'I'm dying and you don't even care.' He sounded irritable. 'We should never have come. I don't know what I was thinking.' He groaned and scratched at his hands again. 'This infernal heat is killing me. I should have taken that parish in Kirkcudbright and that would have been an end to it.'

Indeed it would, thought Lilian. She remembered him declaring his intention to be a missionary. It was the day after their marriage. He had made love to her for the first time and, filled with a newfound confidence now that he had, at last, managed to deposit his seed in the desired location rather than on the bed sheets, he had made his announcement. Africa was his initial choice – more wild and untamed than any other continent, he had said excitedly, a mysterious place, filled with savages, never mind heathens, a place where a man could make his mark. Lilian had nodded. 'Of course, Selwyn,' she had said as her husband began to fumble with her nightdress once more. In the end, however, passage to India had proved to be more economical.

But now, with a cloud of flies circling his head and with his bible spotted with mould spores, Lilian knew that the fire of evangelism that once had burned in Selwyn Fraser's breast flickered and grew fainter with every day that passed. She knew he missed the soft rain and biting wind of home; the green grass and frisking lambs; the lingering sunsets and cold mornings. She knew he missed cheddar cheese and herrings in oatmeal. Lilian also knew that Selwyn found India to be a distasteful mixture of the pestilent, the heathen and the boring. She knew that the impossibility of getting anything done without first becoming familiar with an elaborate hierarchy of castes infuriated him, and that the inertia and monotony of the place filled him with disgust. Lilian knew all this because Selwyn himself made a point of telling her so almost every single day.

'We should have stayed at home,' he said mournfully.

Lilian turned away and scanned the plain before the dak bungalow. In the distance a cloud of dust hanging low in the air told her where a herd of bison wandered. The heat was already causing the air to buckle and fold on the horizon, and there was no sign that there would even be a breeze that day. She pulled her topi down to shield her face from the glare of the morning sun and slung the gun across her shoulder. 'I've already packed everything,' she said. 'When you're ready we'll go.'

2

By the time they arrived, the Missionary Society at Kushpur had been expecting Selwyn and Lilian for some time.

'Thank goodness you've arrived,' said the man who greeted them. 'We were beginning to wonder what had happened to you.'

'Look at these insect bites,' Selwyn replied. 'Or bug bites from one of those dreadful dak bungalows.' He shook the man's hand, introducing himself and Lilian.

'John Rutherford,' said the man, gazing at Selwyn's weeping scabs. He surreptitiously wiped his hand on his trousers.

'And my head is throbbing,' said Selwyn. 'This place is like an oven.'

'The heat takes some getting used to, I know. Even at this

time in the morning it can be quite oppressive.' Mr Rutherford eyed Lilian's topi, which she had failed to remove despite her husband's entreaties, and which bore the dusty and sun-bleached appearance of sustained usage. 'Ladies often find it particularly debilitating.' He cleared his throat. 'Though I see you have the right idea, Mrs Fraser.'

'I told her to take the wretched thing off,' muttered Selwyn. 'Why, she has only just changed back into her dress. She's been wearing a pair of my trousers since we left the Hooghly.'

'My husband has been quite ill,' interrupted Lilian, perceiving Mr Rutherford's expression. 'On more than one occasion we were obliged to send the dak on and wait for the next one. That's why we're so late arriving.'

'Do you need a doctor?' Mr Rutherford glanced at Selwyn, then at Lilian, as though unsure which one of them might be most in need of attention. 'The dispensary is only over there. I'm sure Dr Mossly would be delighted to help.'

He pointed to a building at whose entrance a crowd had gathered. As they watched, a bundle of rags was lifted from the ground and carried inside. Against the walls of the building lay other piles of tattered blankets, above each of which fizzed a furious cloud of flies. From the midst of these blankets here and there bony limbs could be seen projecting.

Selwyn gazed doubtfully at the dark entrance where the bundle had disappeared. 'If I go in there I may never come out again,' he said. He swiped angrily at a mosquito with the fly whisk he carried with him like a talisman. Lilian flinched. Could he not keep still, even for a moment?

'Anyhow, Rutherford,' he said, 'would you be so kind as to show us where we are to stay while we're here? We started at four this morning to avoid the heat and I'm beginning to feel rather faint.'

Mr Rutherford led them through a compound to a large, white-painted bungalow with an intricately fashioned wrought-iron veranda. The bungalow had once been surrounded by a garden, but this now appeared to be something of a jungle. A rampant mass of foliage was punctuated by crimson clots of geraniums and surrounded a wide skirt of lawn. Lilian's eyes were uncontrollably drawn to these garish flower heads, which seemed to be absorbing the glare of the sun, becoming brighter and brighter, until she found she could barely look at them. Even when she turned away she could still see their imprint blazing like red-hot coals on the backs of her eyes. The house itself rested on short stilts, as though it were standing on tiptoe to keep its skirts out of the dust.

'One of the Company clerks lived here,' said Mr Rutherford. 'But he's been taken ill and has retired to the mountains for some cool air. He won't be back for some time so you can stay in this house indefinitely. Well, at least until you move on.'

He pushed open the door and led them into the drawing room. Inside was green and shady, with cool wooden floors and scented grass screens over the windows. Overhead, the punkah began to move slowly back and forth, its rope pulled by a native servant sitting outside on the veranda. Every effort had been made to recreate the drawing rooms of Home and the place was cluttered with occasional tables, ornaments and potted palm trees. An enormous bearskin sprawled before the fireplace, its mounted head staring down in gloomy disbelief from an adjacent wall. In one corner, squatting on a short-legged table that seemed specially made for the purpose, they were surprised to see a large, pot-bellied hookah.

'Did this fellow actually smoke that thing?' asked Selwyn, pointing to the hookah.

'I believe he did, sometimes,' said Mr Rutherford.

'Whatever next! Still, I suppose you people are a long way from Home. It must be easy to forget how to behave sometimes.'

Mr Rutherford gave a tight smile. 'Indeed. As I said, Mr

Gilmour, the clerk in question, has had to repair to cooler climes. For his health, you understand.'

'Ah,' said Selwyn. He tapped the side of his head with his forefinger and nodded. 'I see.'

'Really, Selwyn,' said Lilian. 'You know nothing about poor Mr Gilmour. I'm sure Mr Rutherford meant no such thing.'

'Oh, yes he did,' snapped Selwyn. 'The heat turns some of these fellows mad, you know. It's all hushed up, of course. They get sent off. Up to Simla or some place like that. I'm right, aren't I, Rutherford?'

Mr Rutherford inspected the dusty toes of his shoes. 'I really wouldn't like to say,' he murmured.

From outside, a bell tolled. 'Nine o'clock,' cried Mr Rutherford with obvious relief. He rubbed his hands together, as though warming himself before a roaring fire. 'Is there anything else I can help you with?'

'Thank you, but I think we have everything we need,' said Lilian. Looking about the room, she noticed that the feet of all items of furniture were resting in saucers of water. Back home in her father's house Aunt Lambert insisted that the feet of all her furniture stand in saucers of water too. She maintained that this was the only way to prevent white ants from devouring the wood or from swarming up the legs of her chair and over her as she dozed before the fire. Aunt Lambert had spent over half a century living on the plains of India with her magistrate husband. Returning to England at the age of seventy-two, she had struggled to adapt to the more temperate climate and less rapacious insects. Lilian and Alice had taken it in turns to top up the saucers for her.

Selwyn had also spotted the saucers. Lilian saw him close his eyes and shudder.

'Has any correspondence arrived for us?' she asked, still thinking of Home. At that moment Lilian noticed a bowl of large saffron-coloured peaches sitting on the table beside the hookah. She gave a cry of pleasure and reached out to pick one up. It was as warm as flesh to the touch and she held it to her nose to inhale its familiar fragrant sweetness. The fuzzy skin felt soft as dust against her lips and she breathed in the scent of it again. She closed her eyes and, for a moment, forgot Selwyn and his angry, disgruntled expression; she forgot Mr Rutherford and that strange Kushpur drawing room. Instead, she was Home: back Home with Alice in the glorious summer heat of the hot house beside their mother's peach tree, its branches bowed beneath the weight of its numberless glowing fruits.

Soon, she knew, back in England it would be time to wheel the tree into the cooler air of the temperate house. Even between the two of them the peach tree had been almost impossible to move, its huge brass wheels catching on roots, its branches scraping and bending as they forced it through the hot house doors. How on earth would Alice manage now that she was alone? Lilian could not bear to think of it.

She opened her eyes, to find that Selwyn and Mr Rutherford were looking at her with expressions of perplexity on their faces. She blinked back her tears and put the peach back into the bowl. 'Well?' she said, more sharply than she intended. 'Mr Rutherford?'

'I'm afraid not,' said Mr Rutherford. 'But then it's not unusual for items to take many months to get here. And sometimes letters don't arrive at all. They fall into the river, or get caught in a flood or simply get lost or stolen.' He shrugged. 'And then sometimes months of post all arrives at once. I hope you weren't waiting for something important?'

'Oh, no,' said Lilian. 'Not really.' She was disappointed to have received nothing from Alice. She wondered how far on their journey back to England her own letters were. Perhaps they would pass Alice's as they made their way out to India . . . Then again, maybe both sisters' letters were bobbing down the Ganges, or blowing, lost, across the wide and dusty plains of Bengal.

'Was there anything else?' repeated Mr Rutherford,

backing towards the doorway. 'No? Well, then, I shall leave you to settle in. The khansamah I took the liberty of engaging for you will be in shortly to speak to you about your dining requirements and any other aspects of household management you might wish to discuss.' His voice echoed in from the veranda. 'Don't hesitate to ask if I can be of further assistance.'

It was not long before Selwyn and Lilian made the acquaintance of other Europeans in the cantonment, among them Mr Vine the Magistrate; Mr Ravelston, a clerk in the Company and a replacement for the absent Mr Gilmour; Mr Toomey, a civil engineer who specialised in bridges; Mr Birchwoode, the Company official in charge of ice manufacture; Dr Mossly, from the medical mission and various officers from the garrison. A number of these men were accompanied by their bored but garrulous wives, and Lilian did as she was required in her role as Selwyn's wife, spending hours sitting indoors with Mrs Ravelston, Mrs Toomey and Mrs Birchwoode, drinking tea and being informed which servants were good and which were bad, which fashions were in and which out, what perils the climate held for the complexion, for the digestive system and for the maintenance of silks and crinolines. But whenever she got the chance – when she awoke early in the morning before the sun had even streaked the sky, when Selwyn retired for a nap and the Europeans' bungalows lay in an exhausted silence beneath the blazing arc of the afternoon – she would pull on her husband's trousers beneath her skirt, don her topi and head out into the surrounding countryside with her easel.

It was only a matter of time before the news spread of her behaviour.

'My dear Mrs Fraser,' said Mrs Birchwoode, 'you will exhaust yourself.'

'Captain Forbes from the garrison has offered me the use of one of his horses,' said Lilian.

'It cannot possibly be safe,' said Mrs Ravelston.

'I take the rifle.'

But rather than assuage the fears of Mrs Birchwoode, Mrs Ravelston and Mrs Toomey, this intelligence served only to alarm them further. 'Whatever next!' cried Mrs Toomey.

'Are you mad?' Selwyn hissed when he heard. 'People are asking what sort of a man I am that I let my wife roam at will about the countryside. You are making a fool of me. We shall lose all our friends.'

'But we're leaving soon,' said Lilian. 'You said so yourself.'

'Just as well,' said Selwyn. 'Everyone is talking. Even Dr Mossly wonders about you. Perhaps you've taken leave of your senses like that fellow Gilmour. All that wandering about in the blazing sun. Perhaps I should speak to him.'

'Dr Mossly is a physician,' said Lilian, 'not an alienist.'

'He's a doctor, that's all that matters. Besides, he sees a lot of Europeans not quite in their right minds out here, you know. He told me so himself.'

Lilian shrugged. She reached for her topi.

'Where are you going now?' cried Selwyn. 'After everything I have just said.'

'To the bazaar.'

'Can't you send one of the bearers instead? Why do you always have to be wandering about?'

'I need some fresh air. But I shall take a bearer, if that makes you happy.'

The moment she left the shade of the bungalow Lilian felt the weight of the sun pressing down upon her. Selwyn was right: despite the lateness of the afternoon it was still far too hot to be outside. Even the bearer had looked at her in disbelief when she summoned him, as though wondering why his mistress could not simply stay indoors beneath the punkah like all the other European ladies. But rather than turn back, Lilian lengthened her stride. Each one took her further away from

Selwyn and each one raised her spirits more. She eyed the flowing sari of a woman walking towards her. How practical such a garment was. How cool and comfortable. Why, she, Lilian, with her spindly crêpe-sheathed arms and her tightly buttoned bodice, looked like a big black spider.

As usual, the bazaar was teeming. The reek of ordure, sweat, smoke and rotting vegetable matter mingled thickly with the smell of melted butter, grilling kebabs, spices and attar of roses, unfolding to meet her in a silent, invisible wave. At first, the presence of a memsahib in the bazaar had attracted a great deal of attention. Children, beggars, inquisitive faces of all shapes and sizes, had thronged around her, pulling at her clothes and touching her hair, and jabbering in her face in so many languages and voices that she could make no sense of any of them. She had firmly pushed her way through the crowds, telling everyone – in English, Hindi and Urdu – to go away. The crowds had parted in silence before her. After a few weeks Lilian was a familiar sight and no one bothered her at all.

Now, she plunged through the crowd, stopping only to remove her topi for a moment and wipe a sticky tendril of hair off her forehead. Her intention was to make her way to the dak, to see if any letters had come from England. The postal service arrived every two weeks and Lilian was there, waiting for it, every time. In the weeks they had now spent in Kushpur, however, she had received nothing. She found herself wondering whether Alice was still angry with her and was punishing her by refusing to write. But she knew this was unlikely. More probable was the interference of their father. And yet, she and Alice had always been able to get the better of him when they were together. Surely Alice's situation was not so difficult that she was unable to overcome whatever uninspired efforts he might make to frustrate their communication? Lilian twisted her fingers together anxiously.

A chicken, carried aloft in a wicker basket on someone's

shoulders, squawked in her face and released a cloud of feathers. Lilian started. Lost in thought she had missed her turning and was now deep into the bazaar. The bearer knew she had been heading to the dak, she thought irritably, why had he not called to her? She turned to tick him off about it, but he was nowhere to be seen. Where *had* the man got to? Lilian stood on tiptoe and scanned the crowd for him.

Suddenly, 'Miss Talbot? Surely it can't be you?' a voice spoke, almost in her ear.

She jumped and looked about. The voice had been English, but she could see no other European. The only person looking at her was a tall bearded Indian man. He leered at her, showing teeth and tongue stained vermilion with betel, and began to rummage earnestly in the pocket of his pyjama trousers.

Lilian frowned, hoping to deflect his gaze with her best memsahib glare. 'No, thank you,' she said firmly, assuming he was about to delve into some secret recess of his clothing and produce his wares for sale. 'Please leave me alone,' and she turned away.

'My dear Lilian . . .' said the voice.

Lilian blinked. 'I beg your pardon?'

'Miss Talbot. Lilian, if I may . . .'

Lilian stared at him. 'It's Mrs Fraser,' she corrected him. 'And no, you may not!'

'Of course.' The man eyed the ungloved fingers of her left hand.

'I'm sorry, sir, but I have no idea who you are,' said Lilian.

'You don't remember me? How could you forget?'

Lilian took a step backwards. Passers-by had stopped to stare at the badmash who had dared to detain a European memsahib and she found she was now surrounded by a ring of curious faces. 'How could I forget what?' she asked angrily. 'I have nothing to remember.'

Before the man could speak again another voice cried out

urgently from the crowd. 'Mrs Fraser? Mrs Fraser!' and, to Lilian's added surprise, Mr Vine the Magistrate emerged before her. 'Leave this lady alone, sir,' he shouted. 'Do you need any assistance?' He spoke to Lilian in anxious tones. 'Do you know this fellow?'

'No,' said Lilian.

'Yes,' said the Indian.

Lilian stared closely at the man's face. It was tanned a deep nut-brown, its lower half decorated with a long black beard in the midst of which a pair of betel-stained lips blazed fiendishly.

'I insist that I do not,' she repeated. Yet the voice was familiar . . . she looked again. Surely it couldn't be . . . she felt her stomach lurch.

'My dear Mrs Fraser,' Mr Vine whispered, dragging on Lilian's sleeve. 'What *were* you thinking of coming into this part of the bazaar?'

'Remember the orchids,' persisted the Indian. 'Salmon-pink orchids.'

Lilian felt the blood drain from her face. Her head swam and she swayed where she stood like a reed caught in a current. A voice spoke from a great distance. '*Mrs Fraser,*' it said. '*Mrs Fraser, take my arm, please.*' But Lilian did not heed it. Instead, she drew back her right hand and swung her fist as hard as she could into those smiling red teeth. The Indian staggered back, his hand to his mouth. One foot plunged, knee deep, into a large bowl of beans that stood beside a stall. A thin stream of cherry-coloured liquid issued from between his fingers, though whether this was blood, or simply betel-stained saliva, it was impossible to say.

3

Thanks to Mr Vine, the news of the scene in the bazaar was soon widespread intelligence. Immediately, a buzz of speculation surrounded the man whom Mr Vine had variously described as 'a veritable savage', 'dressed like a cut-throat', and 'with teeth as red as the devil's'. Ever tastier news followed: it turned out that Mrs Fraser had invited the savage to call on her for tiffin the next day.

'No doubt the man will be unable to balance a cup of tea on a saucer without spilling it,' Mr Vine said in an undertone to Mrs Birchwoode.

'Perhaps he won't want tea,' Mr Birchwoode remarked. 'He might simply take his refreshment by swigging from a goatskin.' He had laughed as the ladies, Mrs Birchwoode, Mrs Ravelston and Mrs Toomey, wrinkled their noses in distaste and raised their own cups delicately to their lips, as if to show one another how it was really done.

By four o'clock the following afternoon the Frasers' drawing room was crowded with visitors. Mrs Toomey, Mrs Birchwoode and Mrs Ravelston had invited themselves to the Frasers' bungalow, along with their husbands, as well as Mrs Birchwoode's youngest daughter, sixteen-year-old Frances, Mr Vine, Dr Mossly, and Captain Wheeler and Captain Forbes from the barracks. Mr Rutherford, who had come to see Selwyn on an altogether different matter, was also there, and found himself unable and unwilling (though he did not like to admit this to himself) to extricate himself from the assembled company. By the time everyone had found a seat, or a convenient place to stand without looking too expectant, there was scarcely any room for the caller.

Lilian was more amused than irritated by this sudden influx of people. She could feel the excitement of the ladies rising in tandem with the rising heat of the crowded room, as they sat and waited for the arrival of her heathen badmash visitor. Overhead, the giant wing of the punkah swept calmly back and forth, stirring the broiling atmosphere into ineffectual eddies. The conversation circled around and around the usual topics – the likely winner of that year's Bengal Cup, the transformation the railway would make if it ever reached this far up-country, whether the dwindling supply of ice would last for much longer . . . No one mentioned the real reason they had come. But as the clock on the mantel chimed the hour the conversation stopped and all eyes turned to the door. Was he coming? Would they be able to hear the sound of his goatskin boots tramping across the veranda?

After a moment Mrs Ravelston gave a nervous titter. 'It's like that play we saw last season. Remember, Libby? At the theatre in Calcutta. "And yet, is that a knock I hear, or a voice outside?" and everyone looking at the door.'

To hide her smile, Lilian motioned to a bearer to bring more refreshments. But Mrs Birchwoode had noticed Lilian's amusement and had clearly had enough. She set down her teacup with a sigh and gathered up her skirts to leave. Used to having their every move sanctioned by Mrs Birchwoode, the other ladies began to follow suit.

And then, in the kerfuffle that followed, as ayahs and bearers were located, as husbands shook each other's hands and teacups rattled on to trays, a man appeared in the doorway. No one heard the bearer announce him and no one noticed he was there until Mrs Birchwoode's daughter, Frances, pointed and let out a squeal. 'Is that him? But he doesn't look like a cut-throat at all. He looks just like one of us.'

'Fanny, please,' grunted her father.

'Allow me to introduce Mr Hunter,' said Lilian. 'Mr Hunter and I met in the bazaar yesterday afternoon. He is a plant specialist and travels widely throughout India to gather his specimens. Do come in, Mr Hunter. Please, sit down – if you can find a seat.'

'Are you all here to greet me?' asked Mr Hunter, looking around the room with a smile. 'How very kind.'

There was a moment's silence, while fourteen pairs of eyes took in the man before them. Although nobody mentioned it, they were all relieved (though also a little disappointed) that, rather than resembling a bandit from the deepest recesses of the bazaar, Mr Hunter looked as though he had just emerged from a gentlemen's club on Kensington High Street. The beard had been replaced by a pair of sleek black side-whiskers, the vermilion leer by an even, unstained smile. The betel-splattered native clothes had disappeared and instead he wore a fashionably cut, if somewhat densely woven, woollen frock coat and what appeared to be a brand-new pair of calfskin breeches. Despite the fact that Mr Rutherford's thermometer outside in the compound was touching on ninety degrees, other than a certain fidgetiness of demeanour (which could have been occasioned by the weight of so many eyes resting critically upon him) Mr Hunter seemed unperturbed by his change in apparel.

'He's as dark as a native,' whispered Mrs Birchwoode to Mrs Ravelston, 'but that'll be the sun from his travels. He actually looks quite respectable. Just as well, really. It would never do to have a one of us dressed as a badmash, not even for the purposes of travelling incognito.' She watched Mr Hunter bow low over young Fanny's hand. 'He seems quite charming. Very tall and handsome. Perhaps Mr Vine was mistaken.'

Mr Hunter bowed and smiled at the ladies appreciatively from between his glossy side-whiskers; the men nodded and shook his hand, muttering gruff welcomes. A space was found for him to sit, on a low settee between Mrs Birchwoode and Mrs Toomey.

'So, Mr Hunter,' said Selwyn, 'my wife has told me nothing at all about you, though I understand you have met before. At her father's house.' He eyed his wife craftily. 'She mentions the place so seldom, one would think she had forgotten all about it.'

'How could one forget old Talbot's place,' said Mr Hunter. His eyes, which were dark beneath black brows, twinkled. He looked at Lilian and smiled as he spoke. 'The Collection, as I recall, took up every inch of space, every shelf, corner and wall of that house. Why, even the room I inhabited during my stay was home to various pieces in Mr Talbot's museum – an ingenious invention called a "tempest prognosticator", to be precise, and twenty or more stuffed animals. Indeed, sir, I awoke every morning to stare into the glassy eyes of a nine-foot-tall grizzly bear. I used to hang my shirts on its outstretched paws. There are few men who can say they have had a grizzly bear as a valet.'

There was a titter from the ladies, but looks were exchanged. How bizarre it all sounded. 'My wife's father is very learned. A freethinker,' Selwyn explained hastily. 'His enthusiasm for the diversity of man's achievements is commendable.'

'Indeed,' Mr Hunter agreed. 'Many of the pieces in his Collection are the finest examples of artistic and scientific achievement.' He looked again at Lilian. 'His *botanical* Collection is particularly impressive.'

'Mr Hunter himself was responsible for some of its finer specimens,' said Lilian. 'Many of the plants are species from the furthest corners of the world, and are difficult to acquire and almost impossible to cultivate. But Mr Hunter is not a man to be put off by the impenetrable or unattainable. Such flimsy excuses! Indeed, the harder to win a prize, the harder he will try to get it. Isn't that so, Mr Hunter?'

'A commendable attitude,' said Mr Toomey. 'Leave no stone unturned, eh? That's the spirit.'

'Precisely.' Mr Hunter looked at Lilian over the rim of his teacup.

In fact, Lilian was thinking about the time she had first met Mr Hunter. He had been taking tea with her aunts in the conservatory and had been sitting, as he was now, on a low settee between two middle-aged ladies. The passing of time, she now observed to herself, had made little difference to his appearance. His whiskers were as sleek and glossy, his eyes still sparkled beneath black brows and his smile (now that this had been purged of the vermilion betel juice) still flashed white in his tanned face.

Mr Hunter had met Lilian's father at a meeting of the Society for the Propagation of Useful and Interesting Knowledge. He had been lecturing on his expedition to South America. Mr Talbot, who was at that time preoccupied with Incas, Aztecs and Mayans, had decided, on Lilian's own recommendation, to add examples of botany to his Collection of South American artefacts. Mr Hunter had been invited to stay at the Great House for as long as he saw fit – perhaps until he had written his book on 'Flora of the Andes', or until his plant specimens had become established in the conservatory. Certainly, at least until Mr Talbot's interest in him waned.

As Lilian and Alice expected, after only one or two visits to the sweltering atmosphere of the hot house their father had focused his collecting interests elsewhere. Mr Hunter was left to his own devices. It was a situation that suited everyone: Mr Talbot obtained some of the rarest orchids cultivated in England; the aunts were delighted to find the heating in the conservatory turned up; Lilian and Alice learned much about horticulture and botany that they had only guessed at before. And Mr Hunter had two young female assistants to help him with his work. In what seemed like no time at all the weeks turned into months. Mr Hunter, Lilian and Alice spent every day in each other's company.

'And did you know the word "orchid" is derived from the Greek word *orkhis*, meaning testicle?' Lilian remembered Mr Hunter asking them one day, as he gently separated two tubers.

Alice said yes, of course, their father expected them to know such etymological details. Lilian had lowered her gaze to the orchid tuber she held in her own hands.

'So many flowers and plants are named after human anatomy,' continued Mr Hunter after a moment. 'Amorphophallus, for instance. Clitoria. Chenopodium vulvaria and, of course, hymenaea.'

Alice had stared at him, as though surprised to find their botany instructor suddenly transformed into this lewd taxonomer.

Lilian had nodded. 'I suppose so,' she murmured.

'All the same,' continued Mr Hunter. 'I doubt whether quite so many orchids would grace the parlours and conservatories of England if their mistresses knew its name was so . . . descriptive.' And he had taken Lilian's hands in his and parted the tubers with her, the wet soil sliding over their tangled fingers.

A month later Mr Hunter had gone.

Dr Mossly buttonholed Lilian while she stood in a reverie beside the tea tray. She struggled to pay attention. It seemed the Doctor was asking about the possibility of her starting bible readings in the hospital. 'To raise morale.'

'But aren't most of your patients natives?' Lilian asked distractedly. 'Wouldn't they prefer a reading from their own scriptures?'

Dr Mossly's face turned red. 'Mrs Fraser,' he whispered, 'what are you saying?'

'Oh, I was only meaning . . . I was only meaning that I'd be delighted.'

'Splendid. I have some Eurasians in too. And some native Christians, of course. They'll be particularly keen.' Dr Mossly rubbed his hands together and began describing the importance of morale for a speedy recovery. From this he went on to explain why the native Hindu constitution was particularly susceptible to lowering fevers and depression (their general indolence and lassitude was to blame); and why so many of them suffered from cataracts (a lack of beef fat in the diet was answerable) . . . Lilian regarded him bleakly, but made no comment. Dr Mossly, however, was used to women saying nothing when he talked to them. He began to describe the mechanisms in place for maintaining ward hygiene.

Lilian found she could only smother a yawn by taking a mouthful of boiling tea. Her throat burning, she stole a glance at Mr Hunter. He was now in conversation with Mr Vine and did not appear to see her. She sighed and gazed out of the window. Dr Mossly's words circled her head, before flying like dust out into the sunlight to be lost on the great plains that surrounded the cantonment for miles. Lilian imagined herself drifting with them, out of the window and into the searing sky, turning on the oven-hot breeze to look down at Kushpur . . . down at the three-legged pariah dog, scabrous and almost devoid of hair, that sniffed at one of the bundles outside the dispensary . . . down at the bazaar in the native town teeming with a confusion of colours, sounds and smells . . . down at the crowd assembled at the burning ghat on the river, the flames circling the ankles of the deceased even as another carcass, white with ghee from a more economical but less effective cremation, floated past . . . The conversations of the English, the same wherever they went, ebbed and flowed around her like a sleeping draught. There was only one person in that company who, she knew, would be finding everything as absurd as she did. By now he was talking to her husband.

'My wife paints plants,' Selwyn was saying. 'Though what she can find that's worth painting in that jungle of a garden is beyond me. She used to wander off looking for the wretched things – flowers and such – on her own, but I soon put a stop to that. If she must go out she has to take a bearer with her.'

'Oh, indeed,' Mr Vine interrupted. He smiled at Lilian and shook his head as though in despair at the wilfulness of womankind. 'Anything could happen. Thugs, thieves, bandits. But she should really stay inside altogether. You wouldn't want to see a rose as precious as your lovely wife wilt and wither in this infernal heat.'

'If you require a flower, Mrs Fraser, you have only to ask me for it and it shall be yours.' Mr Hunter bowed and flashed her a brilliant smile.

'How kind,' said Lilian. 'But I wouldn't dream of troubling you.'

'Don't encourage her, Mr Hunter,' cried Selwyn. 'She spends enough time scribbling in her notebooks and making sketches of weeds as it is. Her bedroom is filled with paintings. And it's plants she paints, always plants. Why on earth she doesn't paint something else I'll never know. A still life, perhaps – that'd keep her indoors. Or a sunset – she could do that from the veranda.'

'You must be careful, Mrs Fraser,' said Dr Mossly. 'When the rains come the very air itself becomes sodden. Your paintings will become mildewed – if they are not devoured by white ants in the meantime.'

'I'm quite aware of that. I intend to send my completed work to England before the monsoon comes.'

'Ah, of course,' said Mr Hunter. 'To your father. Or your sister? How are they both? Well, I hope.'

Lilian didn't answer. Her hand was throbbing from the punch she had given Mr Hunter the day before (she could see the bruise on the side of his mouth where her fist had struck him) and she had a sudden urge to cuff him again. She had no idea whether Alice was well or not. In fact, the last time she had seen or heard from her, Alice had been crying. Her face, wet with tears, had been buried in a sodden handkerchief, her hand raised in farewell as Lilian was bundled into a carriage with Selwyn and Dr Cattermole. What would Alice say if she knew that Lilian was standing before Mr Hunter once again? The cup of tea in her hand trembled, though her expression remained indifferent.

Selwyn blundered on. 'And how long will you be in Kushpur, Mr Hunter?' he asked.

'A few weeks. A month, perhaps. But I may stay longer. It's not always up to me. The seasons dictate my timetable. The rains may keep me in one place, the thawing of the winter snows may send me to another, the spring equinox has me wanting to be everywhere at once.'

'And you have had some adventures up-country, I take it?' Mrs Birchwoode said. 'That would account for your . . . your native costume yesterday?'

'If sleeping beneath the stars and travelling by foot through the Himalaya is an adventure, then yes. If drinking from the melt-water of a glacier and bartering your boots for a few pieces of dried mutton is an adventure, or if standing on the roof of the world and seeing the sun rise pink and lilac over the mountains is what you live for, yes again. But if sleeping with a bullock in your tent to keep warm appals you, or if travelling for weeks without a decent cup of tea and a freshly starched collar simply to locate a new plant species seems like the most uncomfortable employment, then no.' He smiled. 'I leave you to be the judge.'

Mrs Birchwoode simpered appreciatively. 'How terribly exciting,' she breathed. 'I would like an adventure like that.'

'What?' snorted Mr Birchwoode. 'Do without tea, my dear? You wouldn't last two minutes. As for bartering your boots – I imagine the sunrise would prove a poor substitute for the loss of such fashionable accessories.'

Mrs Birchwoode ignored him. Selwyn gave a thin smile. Lilian found herself being scrutinised by the mirthful eye of Mr Birchwoode. 'Not like you, Mrs Fraser, eh? You could show Mrs Birchwoode a thing or two. That's it, my dear,' he shouted at his wife, 'why not go with Mrs Fraser the next time she's off about the countryside on Captain Forbes's horse? That'll be an adventure for you. No need to sleep beside a bullock and you'll be back in time for tiffin.'

Everyone smiled politely, but following Mr Birchwoode's remarks there was a silence that no one stepped into, until Mr Hunter asked about the availability of new tack for his horse, and Captain Forbes and Captain Wheeler appeared glad to offer their military opinion on the matter.

Mr Hunter got up to leave. He shook Lilian's hand. 'My pleasure, Mrs Fraser,' he said. 'I'm delighted to have this opportunity to renew our acquaintance.' And then he was gone.

'What a charming fellow,' said Mrs Toomey breathlessly at Lilian's elbow. 'And how pleasant for you, my dear, to see an old friend from Home.'

'Yes,' said Lilian, 'I suppose it is.' She closed the fingers of her right hand into a fist. Within it, she felt the hardness of a seed against her palm where Mr Hunter had pressed it. She knew without looking what plant it had come from.

4

Usually, in between expeditions, when he had returned from some remote corner of the country laden with specimens; when he had labelled everything precisely and packed up his plants into their glass travelling cases, his dried seeds, pods, leaves and flower heads into waterproof boxes, and shipped the whole lot back to London, Mr Hunter would while away his time in the bazaar. He would write up his notes, drinking cup after cup of strong, bitter-sweet coffee. He would play backgammon and perfect his grasp of Urdu, Marathi, Pushtu or Bengali. Occasionally he would work on his book about the flora of northern India, or seek out the hired affections of the bazaar's more disreputable nautch-girls.

Ordinarily, Mr Hunter would not have bothered with the companionship of the Europeans – their chit-chat bored him. But now, with his travel plans in abeyance until after the monsoon, he allowed himself to be drawn into their society. Despite the initial hostility of her welcome, Lilian, it appeared to him, was clearly glad to renew their acquaintance. And why should she not be? After all, he was by far the tallest and most handsome man in the cantonment, as well as the most interesting – unless one was fascinated by salt reports, land tax, or the conversion of the natives, and he found it hard to believe that Lilian might be at all concerned with any of these subjects, or their proponents. He wondered whether she would recall his original gift of a macuna seed. It was a long time ago now. Of course, he had been only too glad to explain that macuna was an aphrodisiac; that in India it was readily consumed as a stimulant to the appetites of the flesh. Now, beneath the nose of her husband he had given her another macuna seed. All that remained for him was to await Lilian's response.

Mrs Birchwoode disliked India. Perhaps the only thing she disliked more than India was Kushpur itself, and she continually bemoaned the fact that she was stuck up-country in what appeared to be the Company's most neglected and socially barren outpost. Why her husband could not request to be moved elsewhere, she sighed to anyone who would listen, she had no idea. And poor Fanny was fast approaching seventeen and would lose her looks in this terrible heat if she wasn't careful, and then no one would ever marry her.

Thus it was that on Mr Hunter's arrival Mrs Birchwoode had weighed him up as a possible suitor. Certainly the man had the necessary handsome looks and bearing. He also had charm and manners, despite what Mr Vine said. And yet, all this wandering about the place, scaling mountains and sleeping in tents, simply to obtain a handful of greenery? Mrs Birchwoode turned the searchlight of her matrimonial gaze elsewhere. Perhaps one of those dashing young captains from the barracks would do? But Fanny was shy and gauche, and needed encouragement.

Mrs Birchwoode decided to hold a soirée.

'Perhaps some cards – whist, or baccarat. Definitely some music. Myself on the piano, though Fanny is far superior and an excellent singer too. Some punch. Some dancing, certainly.'

She invited her favourites and as many young men as she could think of.

When Mr Hunter arrived the room was already full. The punkahs were moving overhead, but with so many people in so small a room, the impact they had was imperceptible. Mr Hunter looked about, scanning the faces that bobbed before him. Mrs Birchwoode favoured red furnishings and wall hangings, and the image that came into his mind was from an illustration of Dante's *Inferno* he had seen as a boy – the heat, the crimson décor, the prancing figures . . .

'Mr Hunter,' cried a voice. His spirits sank. It was his hostess. She beckoned him over. 'My dear Mr Hunter, I'm so glad you could come. I wonder whether you would be so kind as to settle a dispute between myself and Captain Lewis. The Captain tells me that the lands of Sikkim and Oudh are not yet a part of the Company's territory. I told him that this is simply not true, that you had been to both these places, and that clearly an Englishman can go anywhere in India and welcome to it.'

Mr Hunter was hardly listening. His eyes were fixed upon Lilian. As usual, she was dressed in plain black. But her hair shone, her eyes were as clear as the sea and her skin seemed luminous against her dark costume. She didn't need to dress in finery to take his breath away. Mrs Birchwoode, on the other hand, was wearing a voluminous creation of emerald-green shot silk, set off by violent spots of yellow velvet. Across her vast shoulders was draped a shawl of some yellow and green diaphanous material. How odd they looked sitting side by side – Lilian like a beautiful black insect, Mrs Birchwoode like the pupa of some monstrous caterpillar. Mr Hunter smothered a smile. He didn't think either of them would thank him for the comparison.

'Captain Lewis is correct, ma'am,' he said. 'I have indeed been to Oudh and Sikkim, though they're not places to which Englishmen habitually go. I went incognito, of course, and with a very small retinue of native bearers, in search of new plant species and, as such, I remained unobtrusive. But the casual visitor would be advised to steer well clear. How long these states will retain their independence is, sadly for them, another matter. I understand that the cessation of Oudh is likely to occur before the year is out, if, indeed, it has not occurred already. Violence is sure to follow.' He looked at Lilian. He knew the region well and could have talked about it all night, if only she had asked him. He knew she must be interested. She had always seemed curious about his travels. Until he had stopped her mouth with kisses.

'"Sadly for them"?' cried Mrs Birchwoode. 'Oh dear. Captain Lewis, what do you say to that? Should the natives in these areas be saddened that they may shortly enjoy the benefits of the Company's protection?'

'Certainly not, ma'am,' said Captain Lewis roughly. 'The sooner it happens, the better. For everyone.'

'But the appropriation of land is proceeding far too rapidly. Why, thousands of miles of Indian territory have been ceded to John Company in the last year alone. The loss of these lands, and their revenue, can hardly be pleasing to the Indian princes, the nawabs, the rajas, all the Indian aristocracy in fact. Why on earth would they be happy to lose their income to the British sircar? To make matters worse, the elimination of native rites and customs is causing great unrest. That old fool Dalhousie sitting on his settee in Bengal has no idea what he's doing.'

'Steady on,' protested Captain Lewis with manly gruffness. 'Dalhousie is a decent chap.'

Mr Hunter said nothing more. He had met Captain Lewis

before and hundreds like him – vigorous fellows, who knew how to shoot from horseback and wield a cutlass in a fray with deadly dexterity. Men who admired the bravery of their sepoys, but did not understand why Sikhs and Brahmans could not be the best of friends. Men who liked dancing and flirting with pretty girls, who knew the words of music hall songs and made sure to thrash their Hindu batman at least once a week to keep him in his place. Captain Lewis, he knew, thought about little beyond these robust activities. The possibility that the Honourable East India Company might not be appreciated by everyone was far too subtle a notion.

'You disagree, Mr Hunter?' enquired Mrs Birchwoode, blinking sleepily and hardly even bothering to smother a yawn.

'Not at all, ma'am. After all, who could deny the advantages of high taxation, land appropriation, military occupation and the opportunity to work on railway construction?'

A heavy silence prevailed. Captain Lewis cleared his throat and looked longingly at his friends on the far side of the room. Mr Hunter glanced again at Lilian. He was sure he detected the ghost of a smile about the corners of her mouth. He knew she would be fascinated; that she alone would appreciate his knowledge and his sarcasm. His eyes on Lilian's, he opened his mouth to add something witty . . . but Mrs Birchwoode had already lost interest. She had merely brought up the subject in the hope that Captain Lewis might be detained from joining his friends Captain Wheeler and Captain Forbes over by the punchbowl.

'At last,' she cried as a piano chord rang out, 'some music. Fanny, dear, you must sing for us.'

'I'd rather dance,' said Fanny sullenly.

'My dear Miss Birchwoode, would you do me the honour?' Mr Hunter smiled.

'Fanny's with Captain Lewis for this one,' said Mrs Birchwoode quickly.

'And you, ma'am?'

Mrs Birchwoode puffed out her cheeks and worked energetically at her fan. 'Good heavens, no! My feet would never stand it.'

Mr Hunter affected regret at this intelligence and turned to the only other female present on that settee. 'Mrs Fraser?' He led Lilian to the section of the room that had been set aside for dancing.

'I was your third choice?' she said.

'What dance is this?' asked Mr Hunter anxiously.

'The galop.'

'How do we start?'

'You stand here like this.' Lilian adjusted his arm. The music began and the dancers sprang into action.

'I had hoped to speak to you,' he said.

'Can you not dance and talk at the same time?'

'Not at this speed.' He whirled her round, looking down at his feet as he tried to make sure that he put them where they were supposed to go. But he could hardly remember the steps, and over and over again he saw Lilian flinch and gasp. Her dancing shoes now bore the unmistakable imprint of his boots.

'I had no idea you were such a terrible dancer,' she said.

'Sorry,' he muttered. He felt himself blush. What a clumsy oaf he was. This was not the impression he had hoped to make.

'But then there are many things about you that I don't know. And, of course, much about me that you know nothing of.'

'Indeed,' he grunted and kicked her shin. 'But I would like to know. I would like to know all about you.'

'You had that chance in my father's house.'

'I was a fool not to take it.' His boot grazed her toes again.

Lilian gave a sharp intake of breath. She stamped on his foot as hard as she could with her heel. 'For goodness sake! Step forward with your right foot, *then* your left.'

'I'm sorry.' He looked at her dejectedly. He was making a fool of himself. He kept leaping to the right when he should leap to the left, he hopped when he should glide and stood still when he might have hopped. And yet, did not women hate it when men hopped at all when they danced? He had forgotten how much he loathed balls and soirées. Over Lilian's shoulder he could see the Magistrate's laughing face staring directly at him and he wondered how many others had observed his lack of proficiency.

'Lily,' he said, gripping her tightly, 'I must speak to you. I must see you. Alone.'

'Meet me in the bazaar at midnight,' said Lilian. 'At the place I first met you.'

He blinked. How quickly she had agreed. Why, he had not even had to persuade her. 'Will you be able to find the way?'

'Would I suggest it otherwise?'

'Will you be safe?'

Lilian snorted.

Then the dance was over and suddenly Lilian was out of his arms. But Mr Hunter's head was still spinning and in his disorientation he lunged at what he thought was Lilian's departing hand. 'Wait,' he began, pulling her towards him. But the limb he was clutching turned out to belong to Mrs Toomey.

'Oh, Mr Hunter,' Mrs Toomey tittered into his face. 'Another dance already?' And she bared her neglected teeth at him in a dreadful rictus and swept him back into the crowd.

Lilian made her way through the narrow streets of the native town. It was late, but there were parts of the Kushpur bazaar, as in any bazaar, that remained awake no matter what time of the day or night it was. These places were hidden among a tangle of narrow alleyways along which Europeans rarely ventured – places that provided a refuge for pickpockets and thieves, for moneylenders and muggers and cut-throats of all shapes and sizes. Now, as she walked, Lilian found herself peering into the whispering doorways, the dimly lit booths, the shadows that gathered in corners, and she began to wonder at the wisdom of insisting that she make her own way through such murderous streets. She quickened her pace and kept her head down, relieved that she had chosen to wear the native male costume of turban, pyjama trousers and khurta, which she had bought in the bazaar at Rajmahal.

The sound of men's laughter echoed through the shifting darkness. She heard a movement, a gentle rustling, in the passageway behind her, but it was only one of the pathetic pariah dogs rummaging in a pile of refuse. It inched towards her, its lips peeled back over broken pointed teeth, its eyes blazing eagerly. Lilian shuddered and aimed a kick at its scrofulous shanks.

A few minutes later a man approached. He was not wearing the itchily tight-fitting clothes of a European, but Lilian knew at once that it was Mr Hunter. Only a European would march with such confidence through the dark passages of a midnight bazaar. Mr Hunter was dressed, as he had been when she had first met him in the bazaar, in pyjama trousers and tunic. A long, curved knife was stuck into his belt. He looked pleased when he saw her and eyed her boy's apparel with enthusiasm. 'I knew you'd come,' he said.

'Would you like to know what happened to me after you left my father's house?' said Lilian. She watched Mr Hunter's smile fade from his face.

Lilian had had plenty of time to think about what she might do should she ever meet the father of her dead child again.

She had had nine months to think about him as her body swelled beneath her dress and her father shouted and cursed, and stormed up and down through the hot house as though Mr Hunter might still be crouched in hiding somewhere among the foliage to be flushed out like a hare from a thicket.

When she had sailed for India with her new husband, Lilian had found yet more opportunity to reflect on her experiences. Time and distance had lent her dispassion. She had misjudged Mr Hunter, that much was certain. He had been content to take her and leave her. He had had no intention of saddling himself with a wife, not even one as beautiful and exhilarating as Lilian. And when the baby was gone she had felt – what? Sadness? Of course. Anger? Undoubtedly. Relief? She could not deny it. But then Lilian was no stranger to death. Not only had her brother, her mother and her sister already 'abandoned their corporeal envelopes' (as her father liked to put it), but the aunts (of whom there had once been many more) would also periodically expire, as though to remind those who remained of the innate frailty of the human condition and the fact that, for the Talbot household at least, the Celestial Gates were far more likely to be accessed than those wrought-iron ones her father had welded closed at the end of the park.

'I understand there is a native concoction called bhang,' said Lilian. 'I believe it's most stimulating. Do you know of a place where we can get some?'

Mr Hunter nodded. He led Lilian down a passageway and through a low, dimly lit doorway.

The room beyond made her gasp. It was filled with smoke and loud with the sound of laughter and shouting and music. Everywhere she looked dark-faced men reclined on low settees, hookahs at their sides and small glasses of dark liquid before them. Some sported eyepatches or torn ears or scars across their faces. Their betel-stained lips glowed like embers in their beards as they talked and laughed, and leered at the nautch-girls dancing to the sound of a screaming pipe and a sitar. More girls wandered between tables like waiters or entwined themselves around uninterested card-playing men. Those not thus occupied lounged on cushions along the walls, their expressions bored, as though waiting for a train. The atmosphere was rancid with tobacco, sweat, ghee and a sweetish musty smell Lilian could not place.

Mr Hunter steered her round the edge of the throng. 'Keep your head down,' he said. 'And don't look anyone in the eye.' He found a booth adjacent to the door and ushered her on to a charpoy piled with cushions.

'Are we safe here?' whispered Lilian.

'Not especially. Are we safe anywhere in India? I know everything seems serene when you're dancing away to the strains of Mr Rutherford's renditions of Chopin, but make no mistake, this country is not England, nor any part of England. Kushpur might appear sedate, dull even, but it's only because you're stuck with those dreadful Company people that it seems that way.' Mr Hunter warmed to his subject. He lowered his voice and leaned closer. 'We're nearer to the foothills here in Kushpur than we are to Calcutta or even Bombay, you know. Pathans, Sikhs, Baluchis, Afghan cut-throats, we have a lot of enemies. And don't forget the Russians crouching like jackals on the sidelines awaiting their chance. There will be some of these people here in Kushpur, in this bazaar. Perhaps even in this den of horse thieves.'

Lilian looked over her shoulder warily, as though expecting a Pathan, a Sikh or an Afghan cut-throat to wave his sabre at her. The Europeans in the cantonment were loathed and despised. This realisation was strangely exciting. Lilian smiled to herself and decided that she would let Mr Hunter do the talking. After all, she had yet to meet a man who did not enjoy the sound of his own voice above that of any other. For the time being she, Lilian, was content to listen and learn. 'Surely we're far enough south to avoid any disturbances in these remote territories?' she said.

He shook his head, relieved that she seemed to have forgotten the subject of Home. 'I don't know. I hope so. But this is Marathi country, after all. Besides, even further south the Company's not *really* master. Half of that hotchpotch of native states they claim to control are as wild as they ever were, despite their collectors and magistrates and garrisons all over the place. They're still ruled by princes and nabobs who'd slit your throat for sixpence.'

'I gather, then, that you meant what you said to Captain Lewis this evening?'

'Oh, yes. The annexation of Oudh is happening as we speak. They will resist, let me tell you. I just hope such dissatisfaction doesn't spread out of control.'

'But people have always said such things. And nothing ever happens.'

Mr Hunter nodded. 'Yes, but there's more truth in it than most people lolling on their chintz settees in their comfortable bungalows realise. Until it's too late, of course.'

'And you learned this from your plant-collecting expeditions, I assume?'

'I did. I've been all over this country. Some of the most rare and interesting specimens are found in places no Englishman has a right to be. One picks up bits and pieces of information on one's travels. It would be foolish not to. But here I am, babbling about politics like a nervous schoolboy.' He gave her a shy smile. 'You are such an attentive listener.'

'I am most interested.' Lilian sipped her bhang and smiled back.

Mr Hunter inched closer across the cushions. 'I was a fool to leave you,' he breathed.

'Oh, indeed,' said Lilian breezily. She patted his hand. 'But there's time for us now, don't you think?'

ALICE

1

On reaching the sanctuary of the hot house, the aunts gathered round Alice all talking at once.

'Is it really a letter from Lilian?'

'What does it say?'

'Where is she?'

'Is she well?'

'Is she coming Home?'

Alice pulled the crumpled envelope from her pocket.

'Shall I read it, Alice dear?' suggested Old Mrs Talbot extending a spindly hand. 'I have a lovely reading voice.'

'What else is in there?' asked Aunt Lambert, who had been staring hungrily at the envelope. 'I can see the corner of something. Is it another letter?'

'I don't know,' said Alice. 'I haven't had a chance to look at it properly. Perhaps it's just a crease in the paper.' She inspected the envelope. It was small, the single-sheet letter that had been inside it being folded over and over. But closer examination revealed that the front of it had been stiffened with card. A part of this had curled away from the envelope. Alice picked at it with a fingernail and the corner lifted further. 'I think it's a photograph,' she said. 'Or a card of some kind. It seems to be stuck.'

'A hidden picture,' breathed Aunt Statham. 'Is it a picture of Lilian?'

'Edwin's so preoccupied with his own affairs he must be neglecting his censoring duties,' muttered Aunt Lambert as the card came away in Alice's fingers.

Old Mrs Talbot seized the empty envelope and examined it through red-rimmed eyes. 'Why is the writing so faded and the paper so wrinkled? Oh my poor dear Lilian! Trapped in a strange and savage land with that maniac John Knox. Why, I should not be surprised if it was the poor child's tears that had caused the ink to run so.'

'Surely not,' said Aunt Pendleton, holding a handkerchief to her lips.

'Read the letter,' cried Aunt Statham and Aunt Lambert.

Alice squinted at the photograph. She had taken Lilian's likeness, standing beneath the peach tree with a basket of its fruit at her feet, on the day she left. Alice's eyes had been so raw with crying that she had hardly been able to see through the lens. Before her, in front of the camera, Lilian too had wept, her tears running down her cheeks and dropping on to the peaches' downy skins. Later on, distraught with loneliness, Alice returned to the place where they had spent those final moments alone. There, in the basket of peaches, she had found a pair of teardrops, caught in a velvet cleft, glinting like diamonds.

Alice kept that last portrait – an artificial memory fixed by ether and gun cotton – in the pocket of her dress. She did not need it to be reminded of Lilian, though she looked at it so often that the card had soon become tattered and worn.

Now, Alice stared hopefully at the sepia image Lilian had sent from India. How she longed to see her sister's face again.

But Lilian was not in the photograph. Instead, it showed a group of men gathered round the body of a tiger. The man in the middle, a tallish, thin fellow, had his boot on the tiger's ribcage, his rifle cocked over his arm. Alice scanned the faces of the figures on either side of him, but recognised no one.

'It's a tiger hunt,' she said. 'That's all. A group of men holding guns and standing beside a dead beast. I can't think why Lilian would send such a picture. And why would she bother to conceal it like that if that's all it shows? I don't understand.'

'Perhaps there's an explanation in the letter,' suggested Aunt Lambert.

'But Lilian would know that father would read it,' reasoned Alice. 'If she explained the picture in the letter there would be no point in hiding it.' She peered again at the photograph. It was small, an eighth-plate calotype and as such no bigger than a visiting card. The men in it were difficult to distinguish, their faces partly shaded by the topis some of them wore. Alice screwed up her eyes and held the photograph close to the end of her nose. The man on the far left of the group seemed familiar to her, but the upper half of his face was shaded by his hat and she could not be sure.

'Let me look, dear,' said Aunt Statham.

'Alice,' screeched Aunt Lambert, 'will you read that letter?'

Alice handed the photograph to Aunt Statham and turned to the disappointingly brief letter that accompanied it. The address had been torn off by her father, but the word 'ushpur' was just about visible.

'Where's "ushpur"?' said Old Mrs Talbot. 'I thought she was going to Calcutta?'

'It's Kushpur, I assume,' replied Aunt Lambert. 'It's up-country. Near Oudh. One of the Company's outposts, I seem to recall. There's a garrison, I believe, but the place is miles from anywhere. There will be few Europeans there, though things may have changed since my time in India. But perhaps it will all become clear when Alice reads the letter.'

'I doubt it,' said Alice grimly. 'It's hardly even two sides long.' She held the paper up to the lamplight.

Dear Alice [she read].
How is it I seem to miss every letter you send? Despite this, all I wish is to be well again after this endless journey. Truly, sister, life can offer no sort of hardship that's as great as banishment.

Still, a surprise came yesterday – the sudden and unexpected (but delightful) appearance after lunch of a certain Mr Ravelston, tiger hunter. The fellow declares that all his beasts are everlasting, as he loves tigerskin furnishings. How very amusing – if I don't acquire cushions you will surely think me remiss. Of course, my most beloved husband says he knows that almost nothing is as I perceive it. Nonetheless, I have offered Ravelston a commission. This simple plan is guaranteed to be of help in furnishing both this house, of course (for us together) and, come the summer, out at Simla. Then again, Alice, we may come up-country soon – October perhaps – if it is possible.

Tiger-skin cushions will, I think, grace any parlour. I shall be the envy of all the ladies!

With love to you and to my aunts,
Your sister,
Lilian.

Aunt Lambert and Alice exchanged baffled glances.

'Could you read that again, my dear?' said Aunt Pendleton. 'I think I must have misheard you.'

'What in heaven's name is she talking about?' said Aunt Lambert.

'Did you not hear? She has been sick after her long journey to this dreadful Indian backwater. Oh, the poor girl,' cried Old Mrs Talbot, sinking on to a sofa and fanning herself with a handkerchief.

'But tiger-skin cushions?' said Aunt Rushton-Bell. 'Lilian is not interested in such things, surely?'

'Indeed,' said Alice. 'And as for "my most beloved

husband", what can she mean?'

'I can't believe Lilian would write something so mundane,' said Aunt Lambert. 'Has she lost her mind? Why, it's hardly worth reading at all.'

'And what about this photograph?' asked Aunt Statham. She was holding it in shaking hands at the end of her nose. 'It doesn't look much like Lilian, though she's wearing a hat, of course. Perhaps you should try Mrs Pendleton's magnifying glass.'

'What?' said Alice. 'Lilian's not in this photograph.'

'Excuse me, my dear,' said Aunt Statham, 'but I think she is. In the middle. I am an artist. I have an artist's eye and I very rarely forget a face. Certainly not the face of one of my own relatives. Mrs Pendleton, your magnifier, if you please.'

Aunt Pendleton rooted in the drawer of the sideboard and produced a leather-bound box, prising it open with shaking hands. Scarcely able to contain her impatience, Alice waited as Aunt Pendleton slowly buffed its gleaming ellipse with her shawl. At last, she handed it over.

Alice peered through it at the photograph. The figure in the centre of the composition was tall and slim and wearing a large topi. The brim of the hat threw a shadow over the upper part of the face, but the part that was visible – the jaw unadorned with whiskers of any kind, the stray tendril of wispy hair escaping to tickle its owner's cheek, the half-amused smile – Aunt Statham was right. It was Lilian. Alice blushed. How could she not have recognised her own sister?

She was now looking through the magnifying glass at the face she had thought she recognised earlier; the man in profile, tall, with dark eyes and black side-whiskers. 'The man at the end,' she said to Aunt Statham cautiously, 'do you recognise him too?'

Aunt Statham took the magnifying glass. 'He looks familiar,' she said after a moment. 'It's Lilian's husband, isn't it? Mr Fraser?'

'No,' said Alice. 'Mr Fraser is not in this picture.'

'So who is that fellow?' said Aunt Statham with a frown. 'I know his face.'

'So do I,' said Aunt Lambert as she gazed through the lens. 'I would recognise him anywhere.' She looked up at Alice quickly. 'But surely it can't be him.'

'Who?' cried the aunts in unison. 'Who can't it be?'

Alice nodded. 'Yes,' she said. 'It's Mr Hunter.'

The following morning Alice read her sister's letter again. She pushed aside the plant leaves that pressed against the glass walls of the hot house and held the crumpled sheet up to the spring sunlight to see whether Lilian had scratched a secret message on the damp paper with a dry pen. But even with the help of Aunt Pendleton's magnifying glass she could distinguish nothing. Alice shook her head in despair. '*Tigerskin furnishings*'? '*My most beloved husband*'? Why, some of the sentences scarcely even made sense. And yet . . . Alice unfolded the letter once more. Perhaps Lilian had used a cipher, or some sort of code, to communicate?

Alice was disturbed from her thoughts by the sound of someone struggling through the hot house towards her. She heard a grunt as a foot caught on an exposed root, followed by a muttered curse and a furious thrashing of leaves. As she slid Lilian's letter into her pocket the photographer's red face emerged from between the fronds of an immense parlour palm.

'Good morning, Mr Blake.' Alice showed neither alarm nor distaste at his dishevelled appearance. 'We missed you at breakfast. My aunts assumed you had left. My father assumed you were already at work.'

Mr Blake stepped forward, hastily removing a twig from his hair. 'And may I ask what *you* thought?'

'Me?' Alice blinked. 'I didn't think anything at all.'

'Of course.' The photographer's cheeks became a deeper shade of crimson. He pulled out a handkerchief and busied himself with dabbing at a smear of green on his shirtsleeve. 'The fact is, Miss Talbot, I missed breakfast because I was exploring the grounds. The conservatory looks spectacular from outside, especially in the rosy light of daybreak. Then I made my way up to the roof, through a trapdoor in the attic. The view is quite remarkable.'

'Indeed,' said Alice, as though the roof were quite the usual place to go on arrival in someone else's house. 'An excellent idea. One can see right over to Bispham St Michael on a clear day. Sometimes the light is quite luminous.'

'Why yes, Miss Talbot. That is exactly what I found.' Mr Blake opened his mouth as though to add something else. Alice waited politely, but he appeared to change his mind. He gazed at her in silence. 'Miss Talbot, your father said I was to speak to you,' he said suddenly. 'He said you would be happy to act as my . . . my assistant. As long is it doesn't impinge on your other duties among the Collection, of course. He was most particular about that.'

'I'm sure,' murmured Alice. 'And what is your view of the situation?'

'I would enjoy some company. That is to say, I would enjoy *your* company.'

Alice's face remained impassive as she returned the photographer's gaze. 'Have you found your trunk?' she asked.

'What? No. No, I haven't found it. Have you seen it? Do you know where it might be?'

'I'm sure it'll turn up. I hope it didn't contain anything valuable?'

Mr Blake forced a smile. 'Valuable only to me, Miss Talbot.' He wiped a hand across his perspiring brow. 'Miss Talbot, would you mind awfully if we continued this conversation in the temperate house?'

Alice and Mr Blake made their way through the greenery towards the great doors that led into the temperate house. Mr

Blake sprang forward again and again, holding the foliage back to prevent overgrown leaves and creepers from slapping Alice's face and pulling her hair. But the vegetation was so dense that it soon became almost impossible for him to perform this civilised task without appearing to be about to embrace her. At first, he thought she was going to tell him to stop such unnecessary courteousness. After all, she had passed that way a thousand times without his, or anyone else's, assistance. But she merely nodded, giving him a curious look and a faint smile. He smiled back. In that damp and sweltering atmosphere Mr Blake found himself rather embarrassed by Alice's close proximity. He shook his head in disbelief – he, Henry Blake, feel uncomfortable at the nearness of a woman? He almost laughed out loud. He had never shown any self-consciousness in front of the fairer sex in his life. But as Alice's skirts brushed against his legs he felt his cheeks turn pink – not that Miss Talbot would notice his discomfort, he said to himself, his face was crimson with the heat anyway.

At last, they reached the doors to the temperate house. A naked female figure peered at them uncertainly through the greenery. It was *Truth Overcoming Prejudice*.

'Did you bring this through on your own?' said Alice in surprise.

'Sluce helped me, but he was too feeble to be of much use. And then he disappeared when my back was turned.' Mr Blake shrugged. 'All those roots across the pathway make it difficult to manoeuvre objects as large as this through to the studio. But, well, she's almost there.'

'But will you bring everything through to the temperate house to be photographed? The long-case clocks? The suits of armour? The marble statues? Mr Blake, the task is impossible.'

'We'll have to adapt our methods to suit individual pieces. I was happy to start with smaller objects – the Oriental vases or the Mycenaean pottery, for instance. But your father was most insistent that I photograph this lady first. The light in the dining room where she was lodged is poor, so I decided to bring her through. A decision I'm already regretting. I could move her no further without assistance.'

'I'll help you.'

'Oh, no.' Mr Blake swabbed his scarlet brow with his sodden handkerchief and glanced longingly at the doors of the temperate house. 'I don't require your assistance as a porter. It was your expertise as a photographer I was after. Miss Talbot, I insist.'

'As do I, Mr Blake. Have you seen these hands?' She held out strong, wide-palmed hands. 'Far better suited to moving large objects than fiddling about with needlepoint and piano playing. Can you bear to remain in the hot house a little longer? Might I suggest you take off your coat and roll up your sleeves? Good. Then shall we proceed?'

Between them, Mr Blake and Alice inched the statue forward across the pathway's uneven tiles. Mr Blake muttered under his breath as he struggled to raise its electroplated plinth over a bristling knuckle of root that had forced its way up through one of the heating vents in the floor. At this rate he would be in Mr Talbot's employ for ever, dragging cumbersome objets d'art through an ever-encroaching domestic jungle. He gave a despairing sigh. What had at first seemed like a perfect opportunity to escape the growing demands of Mrs Cattermole suddenly seemed a far more taxing and prolonged physical ordeal. He mopped his brow again. He was really beginning to feel quite weak. Alice, however, appeared entirely unaffected by the heat. Mr Blake watched as she seized one of *Truth*'s ample electroplated thighs, braced her shoulder beneath a bronzed breast and heaved. When the statue jerked forward, Mr Blake was catapulted backwards.

He disappeared from view, a mass of wide glossy fronds closing over him like the waves of the sea.

Had his head struck a rock? He could not be sure. It was

throbbing, that much he knew, but that could be the result of the heat, combined with his recent physical exertion, not to mention his lack of sleep and the after-effects of the ether-soaked handkerchief he had turned to once again in a bid to overcome his insomnia. He heard a distant voice call his name, but felt no urgency to reply. Alice's face appeared above him, framed by the canopy of bobbing leaves. The light from the glass panels of the conservatory roof lit up her hair in a golden halo. She smiled. Entranced by this angelic vision Mr Blake smiled back. How soft the earth felt beneath his head. How pleasing the smell of damp loam that filled his nostrils – nostrils sadly accustomed to the olfactory assaults of the dark room. He breathed deeply. The heat of the hot house seemed as warm and loving as a mother's embrace; the throbbing of the pipes beneath the floor at one with the beating of his heart . . .

A hand seized his shoulder and shook him roughly. 'Mr Blake? Mr Blake?'

Mr Blake scrambled hastily to his feet. 'My apologies, Miss Talbot. Yes, yes, I am quite well, thank you. Winded, but no damage done.' He pawed ineffectually at another green stain that had appeared on his waistcoat. 'I had little sleep last night, on top of my journey from London and the hours spent with your father in the stables waiting for mice to enter his perpetual mousetrap. And then the heat here . . . and I missed breakfast, of course.'

'Would you like to sit down? A glass of water perhaps? Why did you not sleep well? Was your room not to your satisfaction?'

'Perfectly satisfactory, thank you.' Mr Blake allowed himself to be led through to the aunts' furniture. He was relieved to find none of them there. He accepted the glass of water Alice brought to him, downing it in thirsty gulps.

'Then what was wrong?' insisted Alice. 'Why couldn't you sleep?'

'I have insomnia.'

'But you're a photographer. There's no need to . . . to go without sleep.'

Mr Blake raised his eyebrows. It seemed he had underestimated her once again.

'You do use the collodion process rather than the calotype method?' continued Alice briskly. 'You must, otherwise you will indeed be here for ever.'

'I do, Miss Talbot.'

'Well, then. You have all you need.'

Had she divined his weakness already? Perhaps she was testing him. He hastily composed his features into an expression of confusion. 'I'm not sure I follow you.'

Alice clicked her tongue. 'And as a trained doctor you'll be familiar with its medicinal uses. I'm referring to ether, Mr Blake. Surely you're acquainted with the stuff? It's central to the wet collodion process. You must have a substantial supply for your work. You couldn't possibly claim to be a modern photographer if you didn't.' She glared at him. 'One can inhale the fumes to some considerable soporific effect. Come, come, man. You know perfectly well what I mean.'

Mr Blake felt a need to unburden himself. She was open-minded and outspoken. An independent thinker. Surely she would have some sympathy for him; at the very least she would understand. 'I have used it many times,' he said with a rueful smile. 'But the dreams that come to me – they are almost worse than a state of perpetual sleeplessness. Sometimes I wake up exhausted.' He sighed and ran a hand through his hair. 'Perhaps it's all that time I spent in the mortuary. Last night, as you suggest, I took a little ether – the remains of a bottle I had in my pocket. But it had no perceivable effects – a loss of motor control for a while, certainly, but sleep eluded me. I think I lost consciousness for a few minutes – I'm almost certain I had a dream – but it was hardly sufficient and not at all relaxing.'

'What did you dream?' asked Alice after a moment's silence.

'Oh, nothing I can recall.' He blushed. He could not tell her that he had dreamed powerfully and vividly of a breathless encounter with Mrs Cattermole. He had woken moist and exasperated, and even more exhausted than when he had climbed into bed six hours earlier. 'You must think me mad, Miss Talbot,' he murmured, sipping the last of his water.

'Not at all, Mr Blake,' said Alice soothingly. 'Not at all.'

2

Over the following week Mr Blake and Alice made considerable progress photographing the Collection. Alice suggested using the temperate house only for portable objects. The rest of the Collection, as Mr Blake had discovered, was too cumbersome to be easily transported. Under Alice's instructions they had created two large white screens – made up of bed sheets stretched across wooden frames – which they carried through the house to be used as a backdrop and, in conjunction with a large mirror from Mr Blake's dressing room, as light reflectors. They both agreed that the light in the temperate house was far superior to anything found in the crammed rooms and corridors of the Great House, and it was the best they could do. At these times they would bring with them Mr Blake's portable darkroom for immediate developing, though it was often difficult to find enough space in which to erect it without blocking out the very light they were struggling to capture.

The ether and gun cotton necessary for coating the slides were mixed in the confined space of the portable darkroom. Despite the complicated heating system Mr Talbot had had installed within the house, it was necessary to warm the resulting mixture over a low flame until it was sufficiently liquid to coat one side of a glass plate swiftly and evenly. Mr

Blake would then slide the covered plate into his camera. After the photograph had been taken one or other of them would dive back into the dark tent and see to the development of the image. Once this was done the whole process would begin again. It was fiddly, cumbersome and time-consuming and, as the day wore on, the atmosphere within the tent became increasingly muggy and unwholesome. Mr Blake felt as though he had not tasted fresh air for months.

Initially, he had wondered at the wisdom of being squeezed into the dark tent with a young woman. A not particularly attractive young woman, he insisted to himself, but one he was, to his surprise, increasingly anxious to please. Yet Alice appeared completely unaware of any impropriety and, not wanting to appear prudish, Mr Blake said nothing. Now and again he found himself wondering whether Mr Talbot had realised that his daughter's assistance with the project would, by necessity, take place in such an intimate, if foetid, location.

As the days passed, however, Mr Blake found his concerns increasing. He told himself that it was simply the effect of the chemicals he was inhaling every day, but the fact of the matter was that he was finding it hard to concentrate on what he was doing whenever Alice was in the tent beside him. The tent was really only big enough for one and with the two of them inside Alice's skirts pressed against his legs, her hair tickled his cheek and even above the reek of the chemicals he could smell the scent of her. He could not help but recall that on those occasions in the past that he had been ensconced in a cramped place with a woman he had also gained access to whatever pleasures could be found beneath her skirts. Latterly, such liaisons had taken place in the broom cupboards, pantries and dressing rooms favoured by Mrs Cattermole.

Within the gloom of the tent Mr Blake watched Alice's face in profile as she worked. Daylight entered through a panel of red-tinted muslin, and its pink brightness gave her a healthy glow and rendered the down on her upper lip invisible, so that

Mr Blake wondered whether he had imagined it. Of course, he said to himself, he had a weakness for beauty and the female form in all its many manifestations could always be considered beautiful, one way or another. The aesthetic of the female face and figure – a dimpled cheek, a slender neck, a neat waist, a dainty foot – these things were his artistic inspiration. As a man (and what brutes men were) he could not help it if they had also at times inspired in him a more physical response.

And yet, he could not deny that there was something about Alice Talbot he was beginning to find irresistible. Perhaps he could persuade her to have her photograph taken. Portraits had been his speciality, before he had become sidetracked by the contents of Dr Cattermole's mortuary and the artefacts of Mr Talbot's Collection. And then he recalled the other portraits he had taken: the portraits he kept in the hidden pocket in the back of his trunk – his missing trunk. He winced at the memory and hastily withdrew the hand he had been about to lay on her arm.

Alice had been watching Mr Blake out of the corner of her eye. She wondered what he might be thinking as he leaned towards her, but the shadows made his expression impossible to read. Secretly, she suspected him of being rather in awe of her – clearly, he had never met a woman who spoke to him as an equal. Nor did he appear used to women who did not respond to his attempts at gallantry with a coy simper and a flutter of eyelashes. At first, that Alice did neither of these things seemed to surprise him. Latterly he appeared merely relieved. Now, she watched as he put out his hand towards her . . . and then withdrew it, a look of shame and alarm on his face.

'Perhaps we should stop,' said Alice. 'The fumes in here are becoming quite unbearable.'

'My sentiments exactly. A ten-minute break?'

'I was thinking of more than ten minutes.'

'But your father said . . .'

'My father changes his mind often. And I know for a fact that he's gone to London. He's meeting your old friend from the mortuary, Dr Cattermole. Dr and Mrs Cattermole are to stay. They'll be coming back with him tomorrow. You'll be pleased to see them, no doubt? Mr Blake, are you feeling unwell?'

'I need air,' he muttered. He emerged from the dark tent and went to stand beside the window. Below him, the conservatory stretched in a gleaming expanse of glass.

'Perhaps we might go up to the roof,' said Alice after a moment. 'The sun's out today and the wind is fresh. It's just the place to go to clear one's head.'

They made their way through the crowded corridors of the Great House. By now Mr Blake knew his way around almost as well as Alice, though he still relied on certain artefacts as signposts. At the head of a flight of stairs on the fourth floor stood a display case containing a lavishly embroidered red and yellow silk kimono. A gift to Mr Talbot from the owner of a firm of Japanese porcelain importers (and a fellow member of the Society for the Propagation of Useful and Interesting Knowledge), it was pinned like a gargantuan butterfly within a glass cabinet. This brilliant marker told Mr Blake that they were standing opposite the door leading to the attic.

To their surprise, they found the trapdoor that led out on to the roof already open. A square of blue sky illuminated the dust sheets that shrouded the attic's numerous occupants – items of the Collection that were broken or unfashionable – so that those in the farthest reaches of the eaves glimmered like spectres in the unexpected light.

'Who else would come up here?' asked Mr Blake in surprise. 'Your aunts?'

'I doubt it.'

'Your father?'

'I told you, he's away.'

'Yes, of course.' Mr Blake began to climb the steep ladder-like stair that led out on to the roof. 'Anyway, I suppose we'll soon find out.'

'Look at these marks on the floor,' said Alice behind him. 'Someone has dragged something heavy this way.' She squinted upwards, blinking in the bright light. 'Is there anyone up there?'

'Not that I can see.' Mr Blake emerged on to the roof. He stretched his arms and took a deep breath of sharp spring air.

'We can shelter from the wind over there,' said Alice, pointing to one of the huge brick chimney stacks that loomed fortress-like against the sky. She hesitated, before taking Mr Blake's proffered hand as she clambered out on to the roof.

'I know you can manage without my help,' he said. 'But I must extend the courtesy nonetheless. Besides, those skirts must be a dreadful hindrance. Especially when negotiating the top rungs of a steep stair in a high wind. Perhaps I should take your arm too. After all, the wind might catch your dress and whisk you away to Bispham St Michael like a seed from a dandelion clock.'

Alice hated gallantries. But, for once, she smiled – and took his arm.

At first, they sauntered over to the low iron railing which bounded the flat roof from the steep slope of slates. The wind was harsh on their faces, cold and unrelenting, so that they gasped for breath as it blew into their mouths and noses. Alice's skirts billowed and flapped around their legs.

Mr Blake held her arm close. 'Are you cold?'

'No.' Alice's hair was gathered tightly behind her head, but the wind pulled it this way and that, so that tendrils came loose to blow about her face like ribbons. 'I love it up here. I feel as though I could fly, don't you? Watch this.' She stepped away from him, spread her arms and leaned forward over the precipice of the roof edge, into the gale. Mr Blake watched as she swayed with the buffeting of the wind. If it dropped suddenly, she would fall.

'Miss Talbot, please!' he cried, horrified.

'Lilian and I used to see who could do this the longest,' she shouted. The wind snatched the words from her lips as soon as they were uttered. 'Why don't you try?'

'If you must do it, at least come away from the edge. You might fall.'

Alice laughed. 'But that's the whole point, Mr Blake,' and she leaned further forward. There was now more of her hair out of its pins than in. It streamed behind her, its wiriness smoothed by the wind and glinting with threads of gold in the spring sunshine.

At last she stepped back. Her face was illuminated by a spot of colour high on each cheekbone and her eyes were sparkling as she tucked her hair back into some sort of order. The photographer was gazing at her, his mouth open, gasping for breath. Perhaps he was overcome by so much cold air after the warm mugginess of the darkroom, thought Alice. Perhaps he was shocked to see a lady engaging in such foolhardy behaviour.

'Will you not try it yourself?' Alice gave him an encouraging smile. 'You might enjoy it.'

She watched as Mr Blake stepped nervously up to the edge of the roof where she had been standing only a moment earlier. The roof slates hurtled downwards in a brief lichen-blotched slope from the tips of his boots, but after this there was only air and space, and the sound of rushing wind.

'Don't look down,' Alice whispered in his ear. 'And wait for a strong gust.'

'I see my boots need cleaning,' Mr Blake murmured. He spread his arms as the gale shrieked and whistled about him, tugging at his coat and his trousers as though at the sails of a ship.

'Lean into it,' shouted Alice.

Mr Blake leaned forward. The wind held him in its invisible embrace.

Alice laughed and clapped her hands as Mr Blake's hair danced about his head; his body swayed in the gusts and currents of air, and he whooped and flapped his arms up and down, as though he were about to swoop out across the park that was spread below them like a newly laid table. He turned his head to speak to her . . . but at that precise moment the wind dropped. Mr Blake jerked, unbalanced on the roof edge. His feet skittered on the lead flashings, his arms windmilled furiously as he struggled to regain his balance. Alice heard a shriek of terror and realised with some surprise that it had issued from between the photographer's widely parted lips.

She seized his collar and wrenched him back from the precipice. 'Don't lean out so far,' she said. She spoke as though advising a child on some innocuous social grace, such as 'don't eat so much cake', or 'don't go to bed too late', rather than expressing alarm at the prospect of Mr Blake's untimely death. 'It clears the mind, don't you find?' she added, ignoring his ghostly pallor. She patted his arm. 'You'll be feeling better in a moment. The fear is part of the pleasure, after all.'

'Indeed,' croaked Mr Blake.

Alice took his arm and led him to a stone bench in the lea of a huge chimney stack. They gazed across the park in silence, their faces instinctively raised to the spring sunshine.

'I used to come up here with Lilian all the time,' said Alice.

'You must miss her,' said Mr Blake after a moment, as though searching for, but failing to find, something more meaningful to say.

'Yes,' said Alice. 'Very much.'

'She writes to you, I assume?'

'I have a letter, yes.'

'Only one?'

'Yes.'

Alice hesitated. She had read her sister's letter so often that it was in danger of coming apart. Despite her conviction that the letter was in code, she had been unable to fathom it, and the Lilian she remembered remained locked in a bland world of ladies' parlours and tiger-skin cushions. Perhaps she had been trying too hard.

'Mr Blake,' she said at last, 'are you any good at reading ciphers?'

'The sort lovers use to disguise telegrams? Or personal advertisements?'

Alice saw him blush. No doubt his own amorous assignations had sometimes been arranged through the pages of *The Times* personal advertisements – tender words of longing or demands for breathless couplings disguised as calls for absent friends, announcements about train times, or demands for the return of missing poultry.

'I have some knowledge of them,' he admitted. 'Is it encrypted by word, by phrase or by letter? Or perhaps it is a steganograph? This last is perhaps the most simple to work out, though can be difficult to write. Does the cipher itself make sense as a message?'

'It does.'

'Have you tried every second or third word? Or perhaps every fourth word if the cipher is a long one?'

Alice pulled out her sister's crumpled note. 'My knowledge of these things is slight,' she said. 'And I am so eager to know what she says I no longer seem able to think straight. Perhaps I have been expecting something more complex – last night I stayed up reading Mr Babbage's monograph on cryptography. It left me more baffled than before I began. Every fourth word you say? Might it be as simple as that?'

'Or every third, perhaps. Or every third word in each sentence.'

Alice gazed at Lilian's letter. Suddenly, before her eyes, the riddle was solved. Why had she not seen it before? 'Every third word of each sentence,' she cried. 'Apart from the last one, which is perhaps simply there to make the carrying message seem more credible. Mr Blake, thank you.' How simple it seemed, yet she had missed it, searching in vain for days for what Mr Blake had pointed out in seconds. Feeling slightly foolish she skimmed her sister's letter. *How I miss you*, she read. *All is well. This life no hardship. Great surprise – the unexpected appearance of Mr Hunter. Declares his everlasting love. Amusing, don't you think? My husband knows nothing. I have a plan to help us both. Come out, Alice. Come soon if possible.*

Alice read the message over again. '*A plan to help us both*'. Was Lilian referring to herself and Mr Hunter, or to herself and her sister? She frowned. It really was not very clear. And she already knew from the photograph that Mr Hunter had turned up. And how was she, Alice, supposed to get herself to Kushpur? Assuming that Lilian was still there. Besides, quite some time had passed since the letter had been written. All manner of things could have happened to Lilian since then . . . Alice suddenly became aware that Mr Blake was staring at her expectantly. She folded the letter and slipped it back into her pocket. 'Thank you,' she repeated firmly. The wind dropped. A silence grew between them.

Alice cleared her throat. 'So, are you enjoying your commission?' she asked.

Mr Blake shrugged. 'Some of it,' he said. 'The marble statues came out well. And the electroplated figures. But the farm machinery was rather tiresome, I must confess.'

'We're somewhat isolated here. You must find it so, especially after London. You'll be glad to see Dr Cattermole again, I imagine. And his wife. She is, I hear, a famous beauty.'

'So Dr Cattermole tells me.'

'You've not met her? But I assumed . . .'

'I have met her.'

'Well, then.'

Mr Blake stared glumly across the park.

'And I understand that she speaks very warmly of you.'

'She does?' he said without conviction.

'That's what my father said.'

Mr Blake examined his stained fingernails. 'We must order some more ether. Our supplies are getting low.'

'What, already?'

'It evaporates quickly once exposed to the air.'

'I know that, but even so, we can't have got through that much of it. Did you have an accident with it?'

He hesitated. 'In a manner of speaking,' he murmured.

Alice looked closely at Mr Blake. His complexion was pale, with dark patches of skin circling his eyes. His hair, which had once gleamed in the candlelight at her father's table, now seemed dull and lifeless, its dark curls pressed flat against his head. His smile remained as wide and brilliant as ever, though a vivid-looking sore had appeared at the corner of his mouth which, she noticed, seemed to be hindering his more dazzling dental displays. A handsome man. Alice smiled to herself. Before his departure for London, her father had reported that it had come to his attention that Mr Blake had left that city with a certain reputation among some of the ladies of his acquaintance. Not to mention any names and not that he, Talbot, was at all interested in tittle-tattle, but none other than Eliza Cattermole herself had been implicated. Of course, Mr Talbot had told his daughter this in the conviction that she would be at no risk from such a man. Not simply because, as his remaining daughter, she knew her place, but also because he firmly believed that she would never desert the Collection. Plus (and this last thought Mr Talbot had for once decided not to utter) she was far too plain to attract the attentions of a Lothario like Mr Blake.

Alice was curious rather than appalled by Mr Blake's rumoured dalliance with Mrs Cattermole. It was this that had made her mention the lady to him directly and she was surprised by the photographer's despairing reaction. Was this the response of a man in the throes of an adulterous love affair? Perhaps Mr Blake was not the roué that rumours suggested he was. And yet there was the trunk she had found, abandoned in the ballroom beside the display case of Chinese vases and the working model of a coal mine that her father had acquired at the close of the Great Exhibition. Without doubt it was the trunk Mr Blake had been trying to locate since his arrival. Naturally, she had opened it and taken a look inside. Should she mention *this* to him too? Mr Blake was not all that he seemed. She gazed at his profile as he stared across the park towards the distant blur of roofs that was Bispham St Michael. His expression was so lugubrious that she could not help but laugh. She covered her mouth with her hand, and tried to think of something diverting to say.

Then, 'just what I need,' cried a voice above them.

Alice and Mr Blake jumped to their feet. From between the shafts of two great chimneys a face peered down. It was a man's face, yellow and hairless, its dry and papery skin stretched tightly across the bones of the skull. The face split into a delighted smile, revealing a mouthful of shattered brown teeth. 'Two extra pairs of hands,' it said. 'Perfect.'

'Hello, Mr Bellows,' said Alice. 'This is . . .'

'My fellow scientist, the photographer, yes, I know,' said Mr Bellows. 'Delighted to meet you, sir.' A thin arm appeared between the chimneys. 'Jacob Bellows, inventor.'

'Henry Blake,' said the photographer, shaking the ragged claw that was extended towards him.

'I am the designer, the architect and the engineer of one of man's greatest inventions,' shouted Mr Bellows without further preamble. 'That is to say, I am the creator of the world's first aeronautical machine. In fact, I'm pleased to say I'm just about ready. I shall be airborne in a matter of minutes, if only I can enlist the help of two young people such as yourselves.' He blinked at them through eyes as watery as oysters. 'You look strong and competent. That's all that is required. I'm getting the thing into the air using a huge band of vulcanised rubber – remarkable stuff, you know, wonderfully elastic and never brittle. This rubber band is to be belted round these chimney stacks as a sort of catapult mechanism to fire the machine into the air. The wings, the tail and the lightweight body are all designed to ride the air currents. It glides rather than flies, I suppose, but then I'm certain that *flapping* is not the best mechanism for the flight of man, though clearly it suits our feathered friends. If you would just step this way.'

'Now?' asked Alice.

Mr Bellows rubbed his hands together with a sound like the chafing of sand on wood. 'Now,' he said.

3

Alice and Mr Blake followed Mr Bellows across the roof.

'I brought my flying machine up in separate pieces,' he said over his shoulder. 'Today the wind is perfect for a test flight – strong, persistent, westerly. I have positioned Sluce on Sodgers Hill. He is to await the arrival of the machine. If all goes well my calculations, based on the wind speed, the weight of the machine, the height of the building et cetera, indicate that we should manage to cover at least a mile in the air. That is to say, we should land directly at Sluce's feet.'

He led them between chimney stacks that rose like hands from the flat expanse of the rooftop. 'This strap is to be attached to the chimney pots over there and over there. It is then hooked beneath the flying machine. You must ensure that the strap is secure at both ends and that each end is fastened in exactly the same way so as to avoid torsion or unequal distribution of weight. You will then use this winding mechanism here to pull the flying machine back, so that it sits in its sling like a missile in a catapult. On a count of three, you will release it. I have created a ramp here between the chimneys to facilitate the machine's elevation. Thus, the machine will become immediately airborne – thereby avoiding tearing off the undercarriage on the railings at the edge of the roof. It will remain aloft far across the park, but will gradually descend.'

Alice looked at the aeronautical machine. Its body was as long as a bathtub, each wing more than twice as long again.

'I see you looking at the wingspan, my dear,' cried Mr Bellows above the shriek of the wind. 'I can assure you that it will fit between the chimneys. Unless the machine is not positioned directly at the centre of the sling. In which case' – he threw up his hands – 'one or both wings will be smashed off, and it is even possible that the undercarriage will be torn away and the whole machine tumble from the sky instantly, to be dashed to pieces in the stable yard below. In short, months – years – of work will be wasted.'

Alice nodded. 'There's a seat in it,' she said. 'I see you are planning on taking a trip in this thing.'

'Of course.' Mr Bellows grinned fiendishly. 'I have some vents on the wings, which I need to open and close as we go, to see whether they alter the machine's progress. I must be present. How else can the principles of science be tested?'

Alice eyed Mr Bellows in disbelief. Despite his stoop he was tall – taller than she or Mr Blake – with long, spindly legs, like a spider. She wondered how he would manage to fit into the flying machine as the space he had allocated himself looked no bigger than a coal scuttle. Still, presumably the man had tested the dimensions. She picked up one end of the rubber strap. 'Over there?'

'If you please.'

While Alice and Mr Blake did as they had been directed, Mr Bellows made some final adjustments to the winding mechanism that was to propel the machine into the air and across the park. These tasks completed, he jammed a copper cooking pot on to his head and secured it with a scarf tied beneath his chin. 'For protection,' he cried, perceiving Mr

Blake's expression. 'One never knows.'

'Perhaps I should capture this historic moment in a photograph?' said Mr Blake.

Before Alice could stop him or offer her assistance, Mr Blake had disappeared through the trapdoor in the roof like a rabbit into a magician's hat.

'He'll never manage all that equipment,' said Alice.

'Never mind that, my dear. Help me in, would you?' Mr Bellows began dragging a set of stepladders into position. 'Everything is as it should be. All you have to do is wind the machinery. The handle for the winding mechanism is underneath. Hold these steps steady, my dear, while I get inside. I'm not as nimble as I once was.'

Mr Bellows was poised on the top of the ladder, one reed-like leg extended above the hole in the body of the flying machine where he was to sit. What occurred next seemed to Alice to happen in slow motion. She could see events unfolding before her but was unable to halt their progression from mishap to catastrophe, no matter how quickly she moved. As Mr Bellows swung his leg, a sudden gust of wind seized the stepladder even as Alice's hands closed round it. Wrenched from her fingers, the ladder teetered to one side, knocking Mr Bellows from his precarious position half in and half out of the flying machine. For what seemed a few brief seconds Mr Bellows struggled to regain his balance, flailing in the wind like a scarecrow caught in a threshing machine. Then he tumbled sideways with a cry. But his foot appeared to have become entangled in the mysterious collection of wires and levers he had installed inside, so that he dangled, briefly, upside down against the wing before sliding across it and landing in a heap on the roof. He sprawled beside the overturned stepladder like an empty suit of clothes.

'Why did you not wait until I was in position before you mounted?' cried Alice.

'My leg!' groaned Mr Bellows. 'And my arm!'

'Are they broken?'

'I can move my foot – just about. But I fear my arm is dislocated in some way.'

'Mr Blake has some medical training –'

'Never mind that.' Mr Bellows gazed in anguish at his flying machine, his eyes beneath the rim of the cooking pot filling with tears. 'I'll never get up that ladder now.' He seized Alice's arm and stared wildly into her face. 'There's only one thing to be done,' he cried, dragging himself into a sitting position. 'You will have to go in my place.'

'Me?'

'Your father would wish it. You know how he applauds the testing of scientific theory by experience.'

Alice knew her father's views on the value of personal experience, but doubted very much whether he would be happy to see his remaining daughter clambering into an untested flying machine.

'I have worked on the design of this machine for many years. The wind conditions today are perfect. My calculations are exact. Someone must make the flight and make it now. I shall give you instructions. You must observe and report back to me everything you experience.'

Propped against the chimney, Mr Bellows proceeded to explain the laws of physics and the mechanics of flight, details he appeared to consider necessary for Alice to get from the roof of the house through the sky and over to Sodgers Hill. He spoke faster and faster, his voice rising as he talked to carry on the wind like the shriek of a seagull. Soon, Alice's head was spinning. As long as the machine became airborne, she thought, she would just sit tight and let the wind do the rest.

When Mr Blake re-emerged from the trapdoor with his camera box and his hastily rolled-up travelling dark tent, a scenario very different from the one he had left behind awaited him. Under Mr Bellows's instruction Alice had wound the mechanism that would catapult the flying machine out across the park. She was now wedged into the flying machine wearing Mr Bellows's cooking pot on her head. She waved cheerily to the photographer.

'Look after Mr Bellows. He's had a fall,' she cried. 'He may have broken an arm.' Behind her, she heard the sound of Mr Bellows slowly turning the handle of the winding mechanism one more time with his good arm. The flying machine inched backwards, the rubber strap groaning in protest.

'Miss Talbot!' shouted Mr Blake, flinging down his equipment and rushing forward, directly into the flight path. 'Come down from there. I insist. It's far too dangerous –'

'Mr Bellows, release the mechanism,' cried Alice. 'Mr Blake, stand back.'

'Miss Talbot –'

'Stand back, sir! Mr Bellows?'

Alice felt the body of the flying machine vibrate about her. Although it looked as sturdy as a cast-iron bathtub, it was actually made up of a wooden frame covered by thick canvas. It shuddered on its narrow wheels as it shot across the roof, hurtled up the ramp and, with a final thrumming sound from the vulcanised rubber band, was jettisoned into the air.

The wind buffeted her face and stopped her mouth, so that for a moment Alice thought she was unable to breathe. But then her breath came in great gasps, and she found herself shrieking with laughter in fear and excitement. She looked over the side. Already the house was behind her, Mr Blake (who had been obliged to throw himself to the ground in order to avoid being mown down by the flying machine as it careered towards him) a tiny figure running to the edge of the roof. Alice pulled out her handkerchief and waved.

Although she was a few inches shorter than Mr Bellows, Alice's seat within the flying machine was cramped and uncomfortable. Her elbows jarred against the sides and she had difficulty reaching some of the levers and pulleys Mr

Bellows had described to her. The machine held a steady course, but its wings creaked alarmingly so that at first Alice feared they would snap off altogether. When this did not happen she relaxed a little. She looked over the side at the treetops and hedgerows far below. She felt no fear, just exhilaration. No panic, only a thrilling sensation in the pit of her stomach. She laughed and kicked her feet in delight.

Soon, Sodgers Hill began to appear considerably closer. Alice gazed hopefully at the row of levers ranked before her. Which one would assist in her descent? She could not remember. She looked out once more at the hedges of hawthorn, the thickets of gorse and broom. A cow stared up balefully as she swept overhead. Did the ground seem nearer? A little, perhaps. She reached for one of the levers. Mr Bellows had asked her to observe and report back; it was no less than her father would have expected of her. She looked along the wings and noticed a flap rise halfway along as she pulled. The machine began to sink rapidly towards the trees. Alice hauled on another lever. The machine righted itself as another flap opened on the underside of the wing. A third lever gave her the sensation that she was gaining height; a further one had no perceivable effect at all.

The meadow that led up to Sodgers Hill came into sight, beyond the oaks at the end of the park. She was now quite clearly descending. Had Mr Bellows given her any specific instructions for landing? She was certain that he had, but could not recall what they were. Besides, it was too late now as the ground was coming towards her faster than she could think. She seized the one lever she had not yet tried . . . the machine lurched and shuddered. Alice was jerked violently in her narrow seat as the wheels touched the ground. Then she was racing through willowherb and groundsel, bouncing painfully against the sides of the flying machine so that her teeth rattled in her head and she felt as though her neck must surely snap in two, her arms break like twigs. Even if she had noticed the log that lay directly in her path there was nothing Alice could have done. She felt only the vicious jolt as the wheels smashed into it, then she was flung forward, against the rim of the casing and into nothingness.

Mr Blake watched the flying machine bear Alice off across the park. Behind him, Mr Bellows shrieked and cackled in delight. 'I knew it would work,' he shouted. 'My calculations were perfect. She should be with Sluce in no time at all.'

'Sluce is not there,' shouted Mr Blake. 'I saw him in the house just now. He said he thought it was tomorrow.'

'My arm,' whimpered Mr Bellows.

'Miss Talbot could break more than that, thanks to you,' snapped Mr Blake. He seized a scrap of the vulcanised rubber strap that lay beside Mr Bellows's toolbox and turned it into a sling. 'Keep your arm supported like this. I shall see to it when I come back.'

'Where are you going?'

'To find Miss Talbot, of course.'

'But what about me?'

'I shall send Sluce to help you. You must hope he doesn't think I mean tomorrow, or you'll be up here all night.'

Mr Blake set off immediately for Sodgers Hill. The wind had not changed direction and he had last glimpsed the flying machine heading precisely along the course Mr Bellows had planned for it. Should he go by road, or should he take what appeared to be the more economical route across the park itself? He decided on the latter. It soon became clear, however, that this was a mistake. The terrain in the woods was uneven, the ground covered with nettles and briars, which stung his hands and tore at his clothes, and the trees confused his sense of direction. Cursing himself and his stupidity, he retraced his steps. He climbed over a fence and sank up to his knees in thick brown mud. He slipped on a cow-pat. He turned his ankle on a molehill, and turned it again and again on every uneven sod of earth in his path. But at last, breathless and sweating, his clothes plastered with mud and grass stains, his boots filled with sludge and water, he staggered on to the meadow where Mr Bellows's flying machine had landed. He could see it on the slope that led up to Sodgers Hill. It seemed to be leaning to one side. There was no sign of Alice.

'Miss Talbot?' he gasped as he ran. 'Alice?'

He saw then that she was still inside the machine. Her head was forward and a trickle of blood had seeped from beneath the cooking pot and dried against her temple in a black sticky mass. He pressed his fingers to her throat. The pulse was strong. She stirred slightly at his touch and murmured something indistinct.

Alice's head lolled against Mr Blake's hand. 'She's dead,' she murmured. 'Oh Lily, she's dead.'

'No one is dead, Miss Talbot,' said Mr Blake, adopting what he hoped was a tone of life-affirming briskness. He suddenly remembered the bottle of ammonia salts he habitually kept in his pocket for when the fumes of the dark tent threatened to overcome him completely. Taking a quick fortifying sniff to clear his own senses, he wafted the open bottle beneath Alice's nostrils.

Alice's head jerked. 'Oh!' she cried, holding her hand to her nose. She blinked, her eyes registering shock and surprise. Then she frowned in pain. 'My head.'

'You struck it on the edge of the machine. Whatever possessed you to make such a journey?' Mr Blake gently removed the scarf and the makeshift helmet. 'Does that feel better?'

Alice turned slowly to look at him. 'I can see two of you. Two Mr Blakes.'

'Take my hand. Can you manage to climb out?'

'I think so.'

As Alice struggled to extract herself from the restricted

confines of the flying machine, Mr Blake suddenly realised that he had left the Great House in such haste that he had neglected to tell anyone but Mr Bellows where he was going. How he was to get Alice back there if she was incapable of walking he had no idea. She was halfway out, like an insect emerging from a pupa, when she suddenly slumped sideways.

'My head,' she murmured. 'You'll have to help me.' She reached towards him. But her sense of balance had deserted her. Her voluminous skirts lifted in the wind, almost turning inside out like a huge umbrella. He caught a glimpse of long white legs, a flash of sturdy cotton underthings, then they were both sprawled side by side on the grass.

'Please excuse me,' said Mr Blake.

Alice sat up and put her head in her hands. 'Did I reach the hill?' she asked at last.

'You did.'

'How long was I unconscious?'

'A few minutes, perhaps. You were coming to, even before I administered the salts.' The photographer adopted a confident tone. 'May I feel your pulse again?' and took her wrist. He stared at his watch, but found himself scarcely able to concentrate. In his mind's eye he saw the flash of her legs, felt the warmth of her body as she tumbled out of the flying machine into his arms. He had also noticed that the bodice of her dress was torn at the shoulder so that a wide triangle of white flesh was exposed. His gaze fixed upon it hungrily. Her skin was luminous against the dark fabric. It would feel silky beneath his fingers, he knew. Or beneath his lips. He tore his eyes away. 'Why did you do it?'

'One has to live,' said Alice. 'Exhilaration is not something one finds much of in my father's house. The opportunity presented itself so I took it.' She smiled. 'It was spectacular.'

Mr Blake's heart was pounding, his stomach fluttering. Could it be that he was about to faint with the combination of desire and admiration that was, at that moment, seizing hold of him like a paralysis? Would it be unmanly to take another prophylactic whiff of his own smelling salts?

'You might have been killed.'

'I might have been. But I wasn't. Besides, you came to save me.'

'Hardly that.' Was she teasing him? He found he didn't care.

4

Alice was woken from a shallow sleep by the sound of laughter in the hall below. A woman's laughter. Her father must have returned from London with the Cattermoles. She looked at the clock on the mantel; she had been asleep for two hours. Fortunately, she and Mr Blake had returned to the house in greater comfort than they had left it. Sluce had gone up to the roof soon after Mr Blake's departure and Mr Bellows had sent out the carriage. A wagon had brought back what remained of the flying machine. Mr Bellows had seemed indifferent to Alice's injuries, being merely concerned lest concussion make her forget what she had observed of the machine's behaviour. It was Mr Blake who had insisted that she take a warm bath and get some rest.

Alice put her hand to her head. It was throbbing where she had struck it, but at least she no longer felt dizzy. The gash was hidden beneath her hair and once the blood had been washed off it could hardly be seen. Her father would never notice. Not that he looked at her much anyway. She pulled on her dress and went downstairs to escort her aunts in to dinner.

In the hot house, the lamps were lit, glowing eerily through the overgrown foliage like campfires in the jungle.

'Alice, my dear, where have you been?' said Aunt Lambert. 'Mr Blake was asking for you. He's in the temperate house. He was here earlier, but he didn't stay long. One game of whist, then he was gone. I think he finds the heat rather oppressive. And the foliage, perhaps. It is getting out of control, you know. And there's a distinct draught. I suspect one of the plants has broken through to the outside, my dear. It must be stopped.'

Alice nodded. The place seemed as warm as ever to her, but the arthritic joints and stiff backs of the aunts were as efficient as barometers in the detection of changes in the hot house atmosphere.

'Mr Blake didn't really want to play whist,' said Aunt Rushton-Bell, shuffling her cards listlessly. 'He was just being polite. Such a pleasant young man.'

At that moment the photographer himself appeared. 'I thought I heard your voice, Miss Talbot. How are you feeling?'

'I'm quite well, thank you,' said Alice. 'We were about to go in to dinner. Will you join us?'

'I don't think so. I have some work to do –'

'Come, Mr Blake, a man must eat,' cried Aunt Statham, wagging a finger. 'You work far too hard. And an old lady like me must have an arm to lean on.'

Mr Blake looked at Alice, but she had already turned away. With Aunt Rushton-Bell on her arm she began to make her way through to the house. Aunt Pendleton, Aunt Lambert and Old Mrs Talbot followed in procession behind.

'I think you are fond of Alice,' said Aunt Statham in an undertone, seizing the photographer's arm and steering him after the others. 'I can tell, even if no one else can. I'm an artist, you know. I have an interest in physiognomy and I can see it in your face.' She blinked at him myopically. 'As a photographer you must know how expressive the face is – despite the fact that your chemical portraits render just about everyone cross-eyed and peevish-looking.'

Mr Blake smiled.

'No doubt you think me outspoken.'

'Not at all.'

'It's an old lady's privilege, of course.'

'Indeed.'

'Well, then,' Aunt Statham tightened her grip on his arm. 'Let me say this to you: have a care, Mr Blake. If you break Alice's heart, you shall have me to contend with. I'll not have that girl sent off to India, cast away from her family like her sister.' She produced a lacy handkerchief and dabbed at her eyes. 'Lilian and Alice are twins – well, triplets, but the third one died, as you probably know. To separate them like that, why, it's cruelty. I'll never forgive Edwin for it, never.'

'But Miss Talbot's sister got married. That was why she left.'

Aunt Statham dug her fingers into Mr Blake's arm so sharply that he almost cried out. The snowfall of face powder on her cheeks had been rendered sticky by the damp heat and it glimmered in the lamplight like quicklime on the cheeks of a corpse. 'Men like you come here all the time,' she whispered. 'Talbot brings them. And Lilian was the beautiful one, you see. But Alice is special too – though not everyone can see it. Don't give her cause to regret that she ever met you.'

'Miss Talbot, how delightful to see you again,' said Dr Cattermole, stepping forward with a smile. Alice forced herself to smile back.

Her father had met Dr Cattermole in the same way that he met so many of his friends and acquaintances, at a meeting of the Society for the Propagation of Useful and Interesting Knowledge. Dr Cattermole's interests were varied: he was fascinated by statistics of vice and immorality in the capital and proud to say he had compiled some useful ones of his own. He was intrigued by new scientific ideas that explained behaviour. He was also a keen advocate of surgery as a remedy for social and psychological ills, and collected all manner of medical instruments of diagnosis and cure, possessing an extensive array of forceps and speculums, a varied assortment of phrenology brain casts and a comprehensive library of photographs depicting diseased body parts, anatomised cadavers, portraits of maniacs and criminals, and surgical procedures in progress, as well as photographs of slivers of human viscera viewed through the microscope. It was this use of these two marvellous optical inventions – the microscope and the camera – which particularly attracted the notice of Mr Talbot, and not long had passed before Alice's father realised that he had found in Dr Cattermole a fellow eclectic, another dedicated gatherer of the artefacts of knowledge and progress. Soon, Dr Cattermole was a regular visitor to the Talbot household and the two men began to enjoy evenings of 'scientific amusement' together. These events usually involved playing with Mr Talbot's latest acquisitions, activities undertaken with exuberance, which often went on until the early hours of the morning.

Such was their developing relationship that it had been Dr Cattermole who had been called in to officiate at the birth of Lilian's baby. Rubbing his hands together as he laid out his instruments, he assured Alice, his horrified assistant, that he had delivered any number of fatherless babes, as the Magdalene asylum where so much of his charitable work took place was not two hundred yards from the mortuary where he spent a goodly part of each day.

Dr Cattermole had not, of course, remarked upon the numerous cases of puerperal mania among his patients. Nor had he mentioned the high incidence of mortality among the mothers and infants whom he attended when he was called away from the dissecting tables. He had not said anything at all about either of these occurrences because he had not noticed them. The possibility that he, Thomas Cattermole, might be the vector of such misfortune, as he almost never stopped to wash his hands, would not even have entered his mind.

*

Now, Dr Cattermole took Alice's fingers and raised them to his lips. His hands were cold and his lips unpleasantly moist. Cake crumbs dotted the lapels of his jacket like mould spores, and she could smell the sweetness of sugar and almonds on his breath.

'You look pale, my dear Miss Talbot,' said Dr Cattermole.

'I'm quite well, thank you,' said Alice, removing her fingers from the Doctor's grasp. 'And you have been enjoying cook's Bakewell Tart, I see.'

Dr Cattermole laughed a breathy, sugary laugh and dusted off the tell-tale crumbs. 'Of course, of course, Miss Talbot. How observant you are. You know my fondness for it. Your father had one baked especially. He is a most courteous host.' He bowed, and eyed her appreciatively.

Alice turned away.

At last, everyone was seated. Alice noted with interest that Mr Blake had busied himself with attending to the aunts' comfort so as to avoid anything but the briefest of communications with Mrs Cattermole. He had engineered his own place at the table so that he was between Aunt Pendleton and Old Mrs Talbot, and as far away from the Doctor's wife as possible.

As for Mrs Cattermole, she was sitting adjacent to Mr Talbot. She was opposite a lamp, and Mr Talbot's eyes were focused greedily upon her golden ringlets and rosy cheeks. Alice wondered whether she had taken that seat deliberately, knowing that her features were at their best when fully illuminated. Certainly, the light suited her. Her cheeks were dimpled, her skin downy, her eyes a clear blue. Her milky white shoulders – artfully revealed by the seamstress – sloped meltingly into her dress. She smiled a coquettish smile at Mr Talbot and ventured a similar look down the table to Mr Blake – who missed it, as he was preoccupied with retrieving Old Mrs Talbot's napkin from beneath her chair.

Without doubt, Eliza Cattermole was a beautiful woman, thought Alice. No wonder Mr Blake had found her irresistible. She glanced at Dr Cattermole, wondering how he would be reacting to her father's obvious lechery, and found to her discomfort that the Doctor was staring directly at her, a slight smile on his face. Alice returned his stare, but chose not to return his smile. She was feeling slightly sick and pushed the food about her plate, wondering why she had not stayed in her room.

'Have you been enjoying your new commission, Mr Blake?' asked Mrs Cattermole. She had to shout down the table. But her voice was languid; slow, with a cultivated ennui.

'It's very interesting,' said Mr Blake, scarcely lifting his eyes from his roast beef. 'The diversity of artefacts here is quite astounding.'

'More interesting than body parts?' Mrs Cattermole's fingers teased at a curl of golden hair. 'Surely not.'

Mr Blake swallowed.

'Of course it is,' cried Mr Talbot, before the photographer could answer. 'The Collection is fascinating, awe-inspiring and educative. It must be better than the contents of a mortuary.'

'But there are some aspects of your activities in London that you would be happy to go over again, Mr Blake?' murmured Mrs Cattermole.

Mr Blake glanced at Alice, but she seemed absorbed in replenishing Aunt Statham's water glass.

'Of course, Miss Talbot herself is a photographer. She helps you, no doubt,' said Dr Cattermole.

'We must put her to some use, sir,' cried Mr Talbot. 'She may as well assist the fellow. After all, she is very well informed, is most efficient and, of course, has nothing else to do.' He twinkled at Mrs Cattermole. 'Naturally, the darkroom is no place to hide away a face as lovely as yours, my dear.'

'Oh, indeed,' said Mrs Cattermole. 'All those terrible

smells. They make one feel faint. Don't you find it so, Mr Blake? You always used to say that being in the darkroom made you quite . . . breathless.'

Mr Blake's face turned pink.

'I dare say Miss Talbot finds it most oppressive,' continued Mrs Cattermole. 'Her complexion shows it – she is so very pale.'

'She's always pale,' said Mr Talbot.

'Miss Talbot is a very talented photographer,' interrupted Mr Blake loudly. 'One of the most accomplished I have come across. Her botanical photographs are especially impressive. She used the calotype method. It's much slower than collodion, but the image is sharper, the detail more defined.'

Alice said nothing. She didn't remember showing him her photographs.

'That mouse has the number "twenty-one" on its back,' observed Aunt Rushton-Bell.

'Where?' cried Mr Talbot, leaping to his feet. 'Number twenty-one, you say?' He rushed over to the curtains. Halfway up, a mouse was ascending a long velvet ridge. From the pocket of his coat Mr Talbot produced a small wooden box with a glass lid. He shook the curtain, dislodging the mouse and catching it in the box as it fell. 'Twenty-one it is!' he cried.

'Good heavens, Edwin,' murmured Old Mrs Talbot.

'This mouse has travelled at least two miles to be here this evening,' shouted Mr Talbot. 'I saw Seven in my dressing room earlier, but was not quick enough to catch it.'

The room was silent. All eyes were on Mr Talbot.

'Allow me to explain,' he said. 'You may or may not have heard of the "Perpetual Mousetrap". It is a device capable of catching any number of live mice. I had the thing in the cellar earlier this week and in a single night it accumulated no less than twenty-five of the creatures.'

Mrs Cattermole gasped and put her hand to her throat theatrically. Alice and Aunt Lambert exchanged glances.

'Being in possession of such a quantity of mice I decided to conduct an experiment,' continued Mr Talbot loudly, as though addressing a meeting of the Royal Society. 'I painted a number upon the back of each captive, from the number "one" to the number "twenty-five". A difficult job, let me tell you, but well worth it. I returned the mice to their box and took them two miles hence, to Whitmarsh Cross. I then released them at the side of the road. My aim? To ascertain whether any, or all, of these mice would return to this house – the house in which they were, perhaps, born, and in which they found shelter and sustenance, until such luxury was cut short by the efficacy of the Perpetual Mousetrap, of course. I commissioned Sluce on no account to leave the house while I was in London, but to remain vigilant in case of the appearance of one of these numbered rodents. He reported no sightings. But this one' – he patted his pocket fondly – 'this is the second I have seen this evening.'

'Fascinating!' cried Dr Cattermole, clapping his hands together.

'Indeed, sir. Perhaps the next logical step is to take them further still. Perhaps to Charringdon, six miles away, or Bispham St Michael. How far will a mouse travel to return home? It's a question, sir, which remains unanswered.' Mr Talbot returned to his seat.

'Edwin, you have a mouse in your pocket,' said Old Mrs Talbot. 'At the dinner table.'

'Allow me, sir,' said Mr Blake, standing up.

'I'll take it,' said Alice. 'If you'll excuse me?'

Alice gave a sigh of relief and sagged against the dining-room door as it closed behind her. She opened the box and released the creature. It leaped out and scurried off down the hallway, disappearing behind the cogs and flywheels of her father's apple-peeling machine.

She made her way through the dark and silent house. The

cut on her head was throbbing, but she did not feel tired. Her tread was light, and in the dark her senses were sharp and focused.

Alice stopped at her father's collection of Oriental and South American knives and swords. They were mounted on the wall opposite a tall window halfway down the stairs and were illuminated by a watery pool of moonlight. She selected a machete. She tested its blade on her finger and felt the weight and balance of the thing in her grasp. She had used it before, but was pleased to find that it had lost none of its sharpness and still felt well-suited to her hand. She sliced through the air with a swift downward slashing motion. It was perfect.

Showing a characteristic disregard for Mr Talbot's economising, the aunts had left their lamps burning in the conservatory. Alice took one from a table top and went over to the winding wrought-iron staircase leading upwards to the leafy heights of the hot house. By the time she reached the walkway that ran round the top of the building Alice was hot, dizzy and out of breath. She wiped her forehead. The staircase was not usually quite so overgrown, she thought guiltily. She really had been neglecting her pruning duties. And she had promised her sister that she would look after the place. Lilian would be disappointed had she known.

Alice held up the lamp. The walkway was almost impenetrable with foliage and the plants were close to bursting through the glass ceiling. Here and there a knotted green fist of leaves had actually cracked a pane, though none that she could see had yet broken through. She hacked her way rapidly through the tangle of stems and creepers, tossing severed leaves and branches down into the darkness below. But it was heavy going and it was not long before she was gasping with exertion. Salty stains appeared beneath her arms and down the front and back of her dress. Wiping a moustache of moisture from her top lip, in the lamplight she saw herself reflected in the freshly exposed glass wall of the conservatory – dark-ringed eyes staring out of a pale face shiny with sweat. She laughed. What would Mrs Cattermole say about her complexion now, she wondered.

She swung the machete again.

'I thought I'd find you here,' said a voice.

Alice jumped, the knife flying out of her hand. She heard a distant 'thunk' as it embedded itself in one of the aunts' tables far below. 'How did you know I'd be here?' she said.

'It's your favourite place.'

'I like the temperate house best, actually.'

'I don't believe you.'

Alice wiped her forehead. 'I must look a fright,' she muttered. 'What are you doing here?'

'I wanted to make sure you were not feeling unwell.'

'There's nothing the matter with me. I simply have a cut to my head.'

'All the same –'

'And *I* didn't show you my botanical photographs. Have you been looking through my things?'

'They were in the temperate house,' he said. 'You left a portfolio under the bench. Of course I looked at it. You'd look in mine if you found it, wouldn't you?' Alice said nothing. The ever-present drip . . . drip . . . drip . . . of water from somewhere in the foliage measured the seconds of silence. Mr Blake sighed. 'Sluce told me you had found my trunk.'

'That is correct, yes.'

'You didn't think to mention it?'

'I was going to.'

'I see. And you . . . you looked inside, I assume?'

'I did.'

Again he waited. A drop of sweat ran down the side of his face. Sixty feet below, the hot-water pipes throbbed rhythmically beneath their iron grids. Alice raised her lamp so that both their faces were fully illuminated. She noticed that the photographer looked pale.

'The only secrets in this house, Mr Blake, are the ones I keep,' she said after a moment. 'You're probably wondering whether I've seen the photographs you have hidden beneath the fabric in the lid of your portmanteau. You may also be wondering whether your relationship with Mrs Cattermole is unknown to me. And perhaps you believe me to be too innocent of the world to understand fully the recreational uses of ether?'

Mr Blake blinked in the lamplight, staring at her in surprise. 'Perhaps we should go to the temperate house to talk,' he said at last. 'It's so very warm up here. I would like the opportunity to explain myself to you. I couldn't bear it if you thought badly of me.'

'Allow me to explain,' said the photographer as soon as the doors of the temperate house had closed behind them. 'It's simple, really. Those photographs – I had nothing to do with them. That is . . . I mean . . . they're not mine. They belong to Dr Cattermole. He gave them to me. He seemed to think that your father . . . as a man with an open mind . . . a man always ready to encounter the unusual, to take risks, that he would . . . appreciate them. Dr Cattermole is your father's friend – and mine – he got me this commission, after all. So I brought them with me. Of course I've not showed them to your father yet. He has no idea that I have them.'

'If he did know, he would end your career forthwith,' said Alice.

'He would?'

'Oh yes. He might appear to have an open mind, but in reality this extends no further than the apparent freedoms he allows my aunts and me, and the devotion he exercises in the expansion and maintenance of the Collection. You must have guessed', said Alice, 'that Dr Cattermole got you the commission because of your intimacies with his wife.'

'But he didn't *know*,' cried Mr Blake.

'Can you be sure? Why else would he recommend you to a commission that had no foreseeable end? One where you would be obliged to spend month after month in the sexless and uninspiring company of an ugly spinster and her aged aunts?'

'But Mrs Cattermole said that her husband didn't care two hoots about her, or about what she did.'

'And you believed her?' snorted Alice.

'She seduced me,' he said weakly. 'She insisted. She was – she is – persistent. I came here to shake her off.'

'And now she is awaiting you upstairs.' Alice struggled to keep the laughter out of her voice. 'It makes your appetite for ether seem rather insignificant.'

'I told you, I began taking ether to get to sleep. Some of the work in the mortuary was so dreadful . . . The images from the slab seemed burned on to my brain. Ether took me to a different place altogether. A more pleasing place. The colours I saw, the visions –' He stopped talking and put his head in his hands. 'Will you tell your father these things about me, Miss Talbot?' Mr Blake shrugged despairing shoulders. 'Of course you will. You too must feel yourself deceived. You must despise me. What can I possibly do to stop you?'

'There is one thing you can do,' said Alice.

He looked up at her hopefully. 'What? What can I do?'

'You can marry me.'

LILIAN

1

The months passed. In the distance, clouds could be seen boiling on the horizon where the mountains began, but still no rain came. The Europeans complained about the heat, the stench, the flies, the avariciousness and dishonesty of the servants. Lilian attended prayers at the missionary society, bible readings in the hospital, hymns with converted Christians. Despite repeated petitions from her husband, Captain Forbes neglected to tell his sa'is not to saddle his horse for her and, while Selwyn napped beneath the punkah, she still went out on to the plains with her easel and paints. At night she met Mr Hunter in the bazaar.

Lilian never told him what had happened after he left her in her father's house and he never asked. Instead, she focused her attentions on learning all Mr Hunter had to tell about travelling through India in search of plants: the different languages, the varying terrain, the best way to pack a mule, the availability of foods and the variety and significance of native customs, the best way to dress for the mountains or the plains, the fastest way to light a campfire in the rain. Mr Hunter had never had such a devoted listener. In return, Lilian permitted him to hold her hand and kiss her cheek. Once, she even allowed him to squeeze her breast. She held out to him the possibility of more exciting intimacies in the future, though on the subject of when the opportunity for these intimacies might arise she was vague.

As for Mr Hunter, he was both intrigued and frustrated. He could not stop thinking about her. One evening she allowed him to kiss her beneath the neem tree in the garden of her own bungalow. 'Your moustache tastes of curry,' she said. Mr Hunter watched her longingly as she threw a long, muscular leg over the window ledge and climbed in at the window of her bedroom. Things were taking much longer second time around, he thought.

Mr Hunter returned to his room at the dak bungalow feeling dejected and confused. Did she want him or not? Were his advances too clumsy? Too hasty? Too confident? Was he not handsome enough? Not wealthy enough? His income was more than sufficient to make him an attractive candidate, either as a lover, or as a prospective husband, should she agree to leave the pathetic, insect-swatting Fraser. As for his height and bearing, why, he knew he cut a dashing figure. He rubbed a hand over his glossy black whiskers. Did his moustache really taste of curry? She had mentioned it more than once. He reached into his pocket and produced a bar of soap scented with lemon geranium. Perhaps that would do the trick.

And then one day a bearer from the dak was eaten by a tiger. The Europeans, rendered bored and sluggish by months of heat and inactivity, blazed into life with chatter on the subject. The beast was said to have dined on three small children from villages further up-country, plucking them from the dust where they played, or from the hovels where they slept. Driven away by angry villagers and demented through lack of food, it was now terrorising the countryside directly around the cantonment itself. Perhaps it had even gained access to the grounds surrounding the Europeans' bungalows?

Mrs Ravelston claimed to have heard the beast growling on

her veranda that very night. Mrs Birchwoode had seen it stalking across the Magistrate's garden. Mrs Toomey said that her dhobi had refused to work until the animal was apprehended, in case he was savaged by it on his way to the well. Lilian, however, had never seen the tiger, nor any evidence that it was still in the vicinity, and she had been out into the surrounding countryside almost every day that month on Captain Forbes's horse. But Captain Forbes nevertheless withdrew the use of this horse for fear that the tiger would attack it.

'It appears', said Mr Birchwoode one evening, 'that we must shoot the brute. We can't sit here cowering in our homes.' He rubbed his hands together. 'This'll liven things up.'

It transpired that several of the officers from the barracks agreed. Despite the sweltering heat, a shooting party was organised, made up of a team of native beaters, Mr Vine, Dr Mossly and Selwyn, Captain Lewis, Captain Wheeler and Captain Forbes from the barracks, Mr Toomey, Mr Ravelston and Mr Birchwoode from the Company, and Mr Hunter. A number of the ladies insisted on coming along and in no time at all the hunt had turned into an excursion, complete with bearers, ayahs, cooks, hampers of food and drink, and various conveyances into which Mrs Toomey, Mrs Ravelston and Mrs Birchwoode squeezed their ample behinds, along with the more modestly proportioned Lilian, and a reluctant and nervous Mr Rutherford.

The idea was that everyone would enjoy a picnic before the officers, along with those gentlemen who had some experience in shooting, stood in line with their guns while the beaters flushed the tiger out of the scrub and drove it towards them. Mr Vine (who proclaimed tiger extermination to be among his accomplishments), along with Selwyn (who was sure he would *like* to have such an accolade) and Mr Rutherford (who had no desire to see a tiger, dead or alive, and possessed no gun) would defend the ladies.

The party unpacked and settled itself beneath an acacia tree. Servants unloaded hamper after hamper of food and spread it out in the dappled shade made by the branches above. The fact that the tiger had last been seen mauling a native not half a mile away from the spot lent a degree of excitement that bordered on hysteria to the proceedings.

'I hope the blighter doesn't fancy a bit of this,' said Mr Birchwoode, waving a chicken drumstick. 'It's bound to taste better than a scrawny old Indian.'

'Why would he want a chicken leg when there are far nicer legs here that he could nibble on,' said Captain Wheeler. He winked at Mrs Ravelston, who let out a scream of laughter and spun her parasol.

'Steady on,' murmured Mr Ravelston, without raising his eyes from his plate of ham and cheese.

'My dear Libby,' Mrs Toomey cried to Mrs Birchwoode, 'do you think the tiger is watching us even now?'

'He'll not come near a party this size,' said Captain Lewis. 'Too much noise.'

'And if he does decide to pop in for a spot of tiffin,' said Captain Forbes, who was fiddling with the camera he had brought along, 'I'll get him to pose for his photograph.'

Mrs Birchwoode, considering herself to be somewhat neglected in all this banter, chose that moment to emit a piercing scream. 'There he is! Over there. Quick. Something moved in those bushes.'

Several men jumped to their feet. But it turned out to be only a vulture, which rose with a guttural squawk and made off through the branches of the acacia tree.

'How nervous everyone is,' observed Mr Hunter, who had remained seated. 'Perhaps it's time to find the tiger, rather than sitting here and waiting for him to find us.'

Alone with Mr Vine, Selwyn and Mr Rutherford, the ladies lost some of their sparkle. They fell to chattering about the approaching cold season in Calcutta. Mrs Birchwoode and Mrs Toomey were hoping to be there by December, while Mrs Ravelston would follow in the new year in the company of some of the officers' wives.

'I think you will have moved on from Kushpur by then, Mr Fraser?' said Mrs Toomey.

'We'll be in the Punjab,' said Selwyn. 'Won't we, Rutherford?'

'How dreadful for you, my dear,' said Mrs Birchwoode to Lilian in an undertone. 'Will you not stay here, while your husband goes up-country? And you have an unmarried sister back Home, do you not? Is she well? Could she not be persuaded to come out and keep you company? We have a dire shortage of ladies out here, as you know.'

'I have no idea whether my sister is well or not,' said Lilian bleakly. 'I've not heard from her since I left England. Besides, I'm not to stay in Kushpur, but will accompany my husband further north and west. Of course, there are compensations – there's a particular variety of blue poppy that grows in the foothills of that region. I'm hoping to paint these in their natural habitat. For this reason alone I'm looking forward to the Punjab. My sister is also fond of plants, and far more knowledgeable on the subject of their names and habitats than I. Back Home we used to tend my father's collection of botanical specimens –' She was about to add that, in fact, she and Alice had grown the blue poppies of the Punjab in the temperate house; that she had already painted these particular flowers in this artificial environment, and that Alice had photographed their dark, delicate blooms and slender, purse-like seed heads. Lilian had not needed Mrs Birchwoode's bland memsahib conversation to bring Alice into her thoughts, but she had not realised what a pleasure it would be simply to talk about her. 'My sister would adore India as much as I,' she said.

But Mrs Birchwood had turned to Mrs Toomey. 'Esme,

my dear, speaking of travel, you must tell me how you plan on heading to Calcutta this year. Not by dak, surely?' All at once the ladies were discussing the pestilent nature of some of the dak bungalows and the number of dresses required for the forthcoming season.

'We must discuss your relocation, Fraser,' said Mr Rutherford. 'You'll be off after the rains and they'll not be long coming now.'

'Of course,' said Selwyn. 'Mr Hunter has already provided me with some insight into the Punjab, but he told me nothing I didn't already know. Mr Vine, you might like to add your opinion. What do you say about the journey?'

And so the group split into two, the ladies talking about the discomforts of the journey east, the men discussing the likely difficulties of a trip west. Lilian, excluded from both conversations, picked up her sketch pad and moved away towards the trees. When no one was looking, she pulled on her topi and disappeared.

Half an hour later no one noticed the appearance of the tiger at the edge of the clearing. At least, not until one of the bearers let out a shriek and dropped the bottle of champagne he had unpacked on Mrs Ravelston's instructions.

In an instant, the picnic site became a bedlam. The servants, who had been discreetly attending to the replenishment of the Europeans' plates, fled, shouting and screaming, in all directions. The ladies screamed and clutched at each other, struggling to stand up and follow the natives out of the clearing. On her feet at last, Mrs Toomey flung herself into Mrs Birchwoode's arms, but Mrs Birchwoode was anxious to remove herself from the animal's line of vision. She pushed Mrs Toomey and thrust her directly towards the waiting tiger, shoving her on to the collation of cold meats that the bearers had laid out. Mrs Toomey screeched again, her arms flailing as she struggled to maintain her balance. Her shoe slipped on the remains of Mr Ravelston's ham and cheese, and she crashed down into the picnic, burling like a spinning top through the discarded plates.

Mrs Ravelston ran first to Mr Vine, then to Selwyn and back to Mr Vine – both of whom seemed rooted to the spot in fear – all the while emitting a high-pitched gibber.

Mrs Birchwoode, who was now hauling on Mrs Toomey's arm in an attempt to pull her from the wreckage of the picnic platters, seized a parasol with her free hand and began to poke it, rapier-like, in the direction of the tiger. 'Shoo!' she cried. 'Go on. Away with you. Shoo, I say.'

'Everyone stay together,' roared Mr Vine at last. 'Fraser, you're nearest, shoot the thing.'

'I can't,' cried Selwyn fiddling with his rifle, his fingers clumsy with fear. 'I don't know how it works.'

'Just point it and pull the trigger, man.'

But Selwyn had dropped the gun and was scrabbling in the grass to pick it up. The tiger lowered its forelegs and thrust its nose forward. Behind it, coming nearer and nearer, with shouts and cries and rattling sticks the native beaters were making a fearsome racket. The tiger hesitated, as though weighing up the options of going back the way it had come and facing the beaters, or going forwards and through the remains of the picnic.

'It's going to spring,' screamed Selwyn.

'Shoot it,' bawled Mr Vine.

Selwyn was half crouched among the wreckage of shattered crockery, his knees slipping in melted aspic, his hands shaking with such violence that he could scarcely get the rifle to his shoulder. 'Rutherford,' he called weakly. But Mr Rutherford had disappeared with the bearers and was nowhere to be seen.

Selwyn took aim. There was a roar as the shot echoed across the clearing. The screams of the ladies stopped abruptly and all eyes turned to the tiger. The animal looked up momentarily, as though wondering where the shot had landed and why everyone had stopped screaming. Behind it, voices were raised in alarm. Then the tiger sprang.

Selwyn dropped his rifle and fell to his knees. All at once the roar of another gunshot reverberated across the picnic site. The tiger, already in flight, hit Selwyn like a bag of wet sand. It crushed him to the ground, its paws on either side of his head, its body and hind legs completely covering him.

Winded and unable to breathe or move, Selwyn lay beneath the tiger's body, his eyes staring, his mouth open, the animal's jaws inches away from his face.

'It's too late,' screamed Mrs Ravelston. 'He's dead.'

'Get the animal off him,' cried Captain Forbes, who had appeared with the other officers in time to see Lilian emerge from the scrub behind her husband, put her rifle to her shoulder and shoot the tiger directly between the eyes. 'You're lucky you didn't shoot your husband in the back of the head,' he said to her.

'Selwyn was a good couple of inches to the left,' replied Lilian.

'Brilliant,' said Mr Hunter. He looked at her with admiration mingled with disbelief. 'I don't think I could have made such a shot myself.'

'Well done, Mrs Fraser,' said Captain Forbes, gazing with unconcealed admiration at Lilian's legs. Her dress was gathered up round her waist and tied there with a length of string. 'Are those your husband's trousers?'

'I suppose it was quick,' Lilian said. 'The animal can't have been in pain for any length of time.' She glanced at her husband as he lay on the grass beside the massive bulk of the tiger and she felt nothing. She looked up. Mr Hunter's eyes were upon her, the expression in them a mixture of admiration and disappointment. She knew exactly what he was thinking.

Dr Mossly held a flask of brandy to Selwyn's lips.

Selwyn downed a huge mouthful and gave a feeble cough.

'I think my ribs are broken,' he wheezed. 'I can hardly breathe. And . . . oh! My hand is bleeding. Look. The brute bit me as I went down. The pain is unbearable' and he began to sob gently into the grass. But no one was listening. Once it had been established that Selwyn was unhurt, everyone's attention had turned to the dead beast.

Mr Hunter paced out its length. 'It must be twelve feet long from nose to tail,' he said. 'A huge creature. I suppose it was hungry, otherwise it would never have approached a party like that. We were foolish to assume that it would be too afraid to attack a group of us in broad daylight.'

'Poor animal.' Lilian stroked the tiger's dusty orange stripes. 'He should have stayed in the jungle.'

'May I photograph you, Mrs Fraser?' asked Captain Forbes. 'Standing over the tiger, with your rifle.' He smiled. 'I shall send it to the *Illustrated London News*: *Mrs Lilian Fraser standing over the Beast of Kushpur, minutes after she saved an entire tea party from certain death*. What do you say?'

'At least make her take that hat off,' muttered Selwyn feebly. 'And those trousers.'

'You must stay as you are, Mrs Fraser,' said a grinning Captain Forbes. 'Perhaps you might even remove your skirts altogether.'

Selwyn collapsed with a groan. 'My chest,' he panted. 'Lilian, help me.'

But Lilian was being posed by Captain Forbes and did not hear him. She stood with Captain Wheeler, Mr Toomey and Mr Ravelston on one side, and Captain Lewis, Mr Birchwoode and Mr Hunter on the other. The tiger lay at their feet. 'Mrs Fraser, put your boot on the brute's ribcage,' said Captain Forbes from behind his camera. 'Now, everyone, stand absolutely still until I say you can move.'

2

For most of the journey back to Kushpur Selwyn talked about the tiger. How it had eyed him before it sprang (hungrily); how it had felt being crushed beneath its huge weight (suffocating); the smell of its breath (putrescent); the texture of its fur (smooth, but dusty); the sight of its eyes when they were only three inches from his own (terrifying). Dr Mossly had bandaged his grazed hand with a strip torn from one of the linen tablecloths, but Selwyn picked at it absently as he talked and scratched at his wrist where it was tied.

'I shall get the brute stuffed,' he said. 'The whole animal. Have it posed as though about to spring. They can do that sort of thing, can't they? It doesn't have to be just the head? Mind you, the head is big enough. And it would look imposing on a plaque above the fireplace. Captain Wheeler tells me there's a fellow in the sepoy ranks who can do these things. For a fee, of course, but cheaper than in the bazaar. And what a rug its skin would make. Or perhaps we could cover a settee with it. Mrs Birchwoode, you're a woman of fashionable taste, what do you think of the idea of a tigerskin settee?' And he began to talk about the other animals he would shoot in the future, so that it soon became clear to everyone that he was speaking as though it were he, rather than Lilian, who had shot the tiger.

The ladies exchanged glances. Selwyn's face had grown vivid and shiny with sweat. '"Tyger! Tyger! burning bright",' he cried suddenly. '"In the forests of the night,/What immortal hand or eye/Could frame thy fearful symmetry?" Fearful symmetry, ha, ha!' He looked at Mrs Birchwoode, who was sitting opposite him, and licked his lips. 'He was right on top of me, did you see? Right between my legs.'

'Indeed, Mr Fraser.' Mrs Birchwoode eyed Selwyn's blazing visage warily.

He leaned in closer. 'Would *you* like to lie beneath a *beast* like that? I'll wager you would.'

'Mr Fraser, I hardly think . . .'

'"In what distant deeps or skies/Burnt the fire of thine eyes?/On what wings dare he aspire?/What the hand dare seize the fire?/And what shoulder, and what art,/Could twist the sinews of thy heart?"' Selwyn's voice grew louder and louder. His face was crimson. '"And when thy heart began to beat,/What dread hand? And what dread feet?"'

'Dr Mossly,' muttered Mrs Birchwoode in an undertone, 'I fear Mr Fraser is no longer in his right mind.'

Dr Mossly was rooting in his bag. He produced a small bottle and put a few drops from it into a cup of water he had poured out and given to Mr Rutherford to hold. 'Laudanum to sedate him,' he murmured. 'It's probably just the shock making him rather . . . confused. That and the heat, no doubt. Mrs Fraser? If you would help him drink this? Make sure he takes all of it.'

By the time they arrived at Kushpur, Selwyn was asleep. Dr Mossly and Mr Rutherford helped to carry him into the Frasers' bungalow. They laid him on his charpoy and set about removing his breeches and shirt, which were wet with sweat and filthy with dust from the fall he had taken beneath the tiger. They took off his boots.

'He's lucky he was unharmed,' said Dr Mossly, untying the bandage on Selwyn's hand. Beneath the dressing were a slight cut and a graze on the knuckles. These were the only injuries he had sustained.

'Keep him cool, if you can, Mrs Fraser,' said Dr Mossly, rubbing iodine on Selwyn's scratched knuckles. 'And give him another dose of laudanum in a couple of hours, so that he gets a proper rest tonight. Don't worry. He'll be as right as rain tomorrow, you'll see.'

'Captain Forbes tells me that you took that shot without hesitating, Mrs Fraser,' said Mr Rutherford, as they left the bungalow. 'He said he had never seen anything quite like your marksmanship, not in all his days on the parade ground. I'm sorry I was unable to be there to witness it.'

The following morning Selwyn ate a hearty breakfast and went straight out to give instructions to the sepoy who was to turn the tiger's skin into decorative furnishings.

On the seventh day after the tiger hunt, Lilian woke to the sound of rain.

Over the past week she had been expecting the monsoon – the burning winds had ceased and thick swaths of cloud had gathered overhead. But each day these clouds, watched eagerly by the Europeans from their verandas, had dispersed after only a few hours. The river had swollen within its cracked and dried-out banks, tempting observers with proof of rainfall and fresh winds in other, more northerly, parts of the country. But then that too had subsided and not a single drop of rain had fallen. Now, the air was humid rather than dry.

Lilian leaned out of her window. Already the garden had been transformed into a pond, the earth being too hard and dry to absorb such a quantity of water in so short a time. Even as she watched, the rain grew heavier, obscuring the neem tree behind an avalanche of water that thundered onto the ground. For the rest of that morning Lilian and Selwyn sat on the veranda watching the inky black water falling from the sky. The sound of it hammering on the roof was deafening and served to render what passed for conversation between them impossible. Selwyn rejected lunch, complaining about the humidity. He retreated into his study.

Lilian stayed out on the veranda and carefully composed a letter in code to Alice. She had no idea whether it would ever reach her, but she knew that she had to try something. She was becoming increasingly distressed by Alice's lack of communication (and surprised by their father's continuing diligence in policing his remaining daughter's behaviour). Recently, however, these feelings had been overshadowed by a sense of foreboding. Perhaps something had happened? Perhaps Alice had been locked up or sent away? Perhaps she was sick or dying? Although she refused to succumb to such Gothic imaginings, Lilian could not help but feel anxious. The silence, the separation, were becoming unbearable. Alice, she knew, would feel the same.

It took her more than an hour to write her coded letter. She went over it again and again until it sounded as bland and innocent as possible, its hidden message brief but to the point. After such a length of time outside, the paper seemed to have absorbed the moisture in the atmosphere like blotting paper, so that the words looked as though they had been darned on to the page with black wool. But she had no time to write another if she was to sneak it, undetected, into Selwyn's postbag. As an afterthought she slipped into the envelope the photograph Captain Forbes had taken.

Afterwards, she brought out her sketchbook and leafed through its pages, looking over her drawings. Having heeded Mr Hunter's warnings about mildew and white ants, she had sent off all her completed paintings three weeks earlier in the hope that they would be away from India before the rains started. Rather than send them to Alice as she had originally intended, however, she had used what little money she had of her own to send them to Kew.

Towards dinner time, the rain stopped, though it was obvious from the ferocious blackness of the clouds that this was simply a hiatus. Lilian found Selwyn asleep in his study. When she woke him he was twitchy.

'What is it, woman? Can't you see I'm sleeping? And no, I don't want anything to eat. Nothing edible comes out of that cookhouse anyway.' He closed his eyes again and swallowed painfully, rubbing the back of his neck. 'My throat hurts and my head is throbbing. Just leave me in peace – unless you're going to tell me that you've a piece of toasted cheddar on warm soda bread for me. No? Well, then, go back to your scribbles and daubs, and shut the door behind you. And mind you don't slam it – even the sound of your voice sets my nerves a-jangling.'

When asked later, Lilian had been unable to say whether her husband was any more irritable than usual that evening. The fact that he had complained of a headache and a sore throat was, again, not unusual. Indeed, she would have been more surprised if he had not grumbled about some aspect of his health, as every day he seemed to be afflicted with one malady or another that demanded rest, or a few drops of laudanum, or a cold compress to the forehead, or a nap on his charpoy beneath the cooling waft of the punkah. So she had left him in his study and dined alone without thinking anything of it, listening all the while to the sound of the rain hammering on the roof and pouring into the muddied torrent that had once been her garden.

As she finished her turkey breast with pilau and curry, Lilian noticed that the rain had stopped. The air was dense with a suffocating moisture, so that she began to wonder whether such sweating dampness was an improvement, after all, on the dry, burning heat they had endured over recent months. She got up and opened the screens over the windows. A small insect flew in, coming to rest on the tablecloth beside her left hand. She looked at it closely. It appeared to be some sort of white ant with wings. As it landed, however, it shook its wings free, leaving them discarded on the table top. She watched while another landed next to a dish of pickles and a third and fourth beside, and in, the water jug. Another fizzed and crackled as it plunged directly into the flame of the lamp on the table. Lilian suddenly sensed what was to follow and called to a bearer to put the screens back over the windows. But it was too late. Even as she spoke a cloud of flying ants poured into the room. In less than an instant they were everywhere – in her ears and eyes and hair, filling her open mouth, crawling across her hands and her clothes, and shedding their thin paper wings to gather like drifts of confetti about the room. As Lilian sprang to her feet another plague of them surged in, dousing the lamp with a splutter, their charred bodies filling the air with a sickening sweetish smell. In no time at all the floor and the table top, the mantelpiece, the plate she had only recently eaten from, were littered with papery wings and seething with hastily moving bodies.

'Get the screens up,' cried Lilian again. 'Quickly.' Yet even as the swarm of ants abated they were followed by a different pestilence. A cloud of flying beetles burst after them as though in pursuit – small black buzzing things whose tiny legs tickled her skin as they scurried over the backs of her hands, around her neck and down her arms. She swept them away in disgust and they emitted a terrible smell, so that she was forced to hold her hand to her mouth as she dashed from the room leaving the bearers to struggle with the screens as best they could in the whirling half-dark.

In the hall Lilian brushed the remainder of the insects off her skin and out of her hair. She shuddered. It was the smell from the beetles rather than the quantity of them that appalled her – that and the tickling of falling wings and tiny feet . . . And then, from behind the closed door of Selwyn's study, she heard a scream.

Lilian opened the study door and peered into the gloom. Selwyn was in the middle of the room with his fly whisk in his hand, spinning round and round, and surrounded by a whirling tornado of ants and beetles. He was dressed in his shirtsleeves, as the evening had been warm and sticky, and the gleaming whiteness of his flapping garments seemed to be drawing the creatures hungrily towards him. Since they had already extinguished one lamp with the weight of their embraces, Selwyn's shirt appeared to them as another, more benign, light source; a glowing, billowing whiteness that they could not resist, and that they circled and fell upon and clung on to lovingly. Selwyn whirled among his insect tormentors like a dervish, his fly whisk flailing in his hand. Then Lilian noticed something else. Her husband's face was rigid, set in a grinning rictus of anguish. His body jerked and flapped, but she could see that there was something uncontrolled about his movements. He spun without stopping, his eyes staring, his grin ghastly between cheeks dark with crawling beetles. Then he fell down, still jerking like a marionette, on to the floor. Ants and beetles swarmed and fizzed over him like a coat of bubbling treacle.

Lilian heard herself screaming for help. She rushed to him and swept aside the sea of insects, but more came instantly to replace them, and still Selwyn twitched uncontrollably beneath her hands. With the help of two bearers she dragged him into the hall, slamming the study door behind her.

By the time the Doctor came, Lilian had managed to remove all the insects and Selwyn was stripped and lying on his charpoy beneath a clean sheet. He seemed to be quieter, but his body still convulsed painfully. More disconcertingly, his teeth remained clenched tight, the tendons in his neck stretched taut beneath the skin like rigging, his lips drawn back in a leer so grotesque that Lilian could not bring herself to look at him.

Dr Mossly put his bag on the washstand. He took one look at Selwyn and shook his head. 'Lockjaw,' he said grimly.

He examined Selwyn's hand where the tiger had grazed his knuckles.

'And what can you do for him?' Lilian forced herself to look at her husband's grinning face.

Dr Mossly shrugged. 'Sedation. Bleeding to remove the poisons and relax the system.'

'And these treatments are successful?'

'Well, it depends how extensively the poison has travelled through the body. I must say, the convulsions and other symptoms have manifested themselves after quite a long period, which leads me to fear the worst.' He rolled up his sleeves. 'I have a jar of leeches in my bag, Mrs Fraser. If you could provide me with some linen to mop up afterwards, I would be much obliged.'

For the next fourteen days, Dr Mossly spent much of his time with Lilian at Selwyn's bedside. He would arrive with his leeches – shiny strips of black slime in a jar – and leave with them as fat and round as billiard balls, each bloated with Selwyn's poisoned blood. Every few hours Lilian or Dr Mossly would try to dribble water and laudanum between Selwyn's clenched teeth, and would sponge his thrashing, twitching limbs with cool damp cloths. Every movement in the room, every sound they made, awoke in his body a convulsion of such violence that it seemed as though his sinews would snap. His charpoy was continually soaked with sweat so that Lilian had to change the sheet beneath him again and again, despite the jumping of his limbs caused by even the slightest touch from the bearers who lifted him.

In the intervals between deluges of rain, Mrs Birchwoode, Mrs Ravelston and Mrs Toomey visited Lilian and fortified her with tales of recovery – soldiers who had endured the amputation of entire limbs, who had developed blood poisoning and gangrene and lockjaw all at once, had risen up to fight another day. Lilian thanked them for their concern and they went away, convinced that 'Poor Mrs Fraser' had been encouraged by these fictitious solicitations.

Captains Wheeler and Lewis from the barracks also paid a visit. They had with them the tigerskin, which they had brought in the hope that the sight would cheer up Selwyn. But the sepoy who had cured it had been less proficient than either man liked to admit. They unrolled it, causing Dr Mossly to gag into his bandage box at the stench of rotting flesh, turpentine and mildew. The officers hastily rolled it up again, claiming that such a smell was quite normal from cured skins and that it would disappear in only a few days. They left it in a bundle outside on the veranda. As soon as they were out of sight Lilian ordered it to be taken away and burned.

Regardless of all Dr Mossly's efforts, Selwyn continued to decline. His face became grey, his breathing laboured, his body grew thinner and thinner. Lilian sat at Selwyn's bedside, his favourite ivory-handled fly whisk in her hand, swiping at the mosquitoes that buzzed speculatively back and forth above him. She looked at his grinning face and staring eyes, and found she had got used to this fearsome expression. But even when she contemplated his impending death, which she knew to be almost certain, she felt nothing for him at all.

3

Due to the heat and humidity, Selwyn was buried the day after he died.

Lilian had never been to the Kushpur Christian graveyard and she was surprised by the number of European gravestones, most of which marked the resting places of women and children. In the intervals between downpours, a grave had been dug for Selwyn between Mrs Clara Wilbury, beloved wife of Captain Charles Wilbury, and Mrs Thora Bonhope and her three tiny children. At thirty-six, Selwyn was the oldest person to be buried there.

The ground was thoroughly waterlogged and the pit into which Selwyn was eventually lowered had partially filled with water. The coffin, when it reached the bottom, was completely submerged. A disconcerting belch of air escaped as it slipped out of sight, a thin stream of bubbles continuing to break the surface even as Mr Rutherford read aloud from his prayer book and sent a handful of sodden earth plopping into the hole. All the while the rain fell, roaring, into the open grave.

*

The cold season brought with it a certain amount of relief to the Europeans. Selwyn's had been the only death that year – an unusual occurrence, said Dr Mossly to those assembled round Mrs Toomey's dining table, as there was almost always someone carried off by heatstroke, dysentery, malaria or typhus. Even worse, their old enemy cholera usually ravaged the native town and sometimes found its way into the Europeans' compounds.

'The Hindus have some idea that by saying prayers over a bullock and then driving it into the river to swim over to the other side, it will take the disease with it,' said Dr Mossly knowledgeably. 'The natives on the other side simply drive the beast back again. And so it goes on, the poor animal driven to and fro across the river again and again until it's too weak to climb out and simply floats away.' He laughed. 'Of course, the cholera continues to kill them off, no matter how many bullocks they send into the river. Absurd, isn't it?'

'Oh, yes,' cried Mr Vine. 'Why, I've told them time and again that it's miasma that causes the cholera – damp mists and foul air, an atmosphere characteristic of the bazaar, particularly during the monsoon. But do they listen? Of course they don't. A week later you see them forcing another of these poor creatures into the water.' He shook his head. 'Rational explanations fall on deaf ears. One can only pity them in their ignorance.'

Lilian looked at Dr Mossly, but he was smiling and nodding in agreement. Miasma and foul air? She frowned. But not three years ago, in his celebrated removal of the handle of the Broad Street pump in Soho, Dr Snow had proved that cholera was a water-borne disease. She remembered her father returning from the Society for the Propagation of Useful and Interesting Knowledge to report this news. Such a claim, her father said, had consequences for the entire water supply and sewage system of England. Determined to demonstrate the truth of this in his own home, Mr Talbot had then torn out every water pipe, drain and cistern in the Great House. Alice and Lilian had taken baths in the ornamental pool of the hot house, swimming together through the lily pads and water hyacinths. Afterwards, Lilian had sketched Alice as the Lady of Shalott, reclining in 'a space of flowers' on the island in the centre of the pool. Her damp hair, the colour of loam against her bare skin, had coiled about her head and shoulders like plant roots.

'"I am half sick of shadows",' Alice had said, smiling up at her. 'We both are, aren't we? Just like the Lady. Sick of being trapped in these "four grey walls and four grey towers". Still, at least we have each other. We don't need a "loyal knight and true" when we have each other.'

Oh, Alice, Lilian thought now. *I'll save you from the shadows. What use are men, when they bring us only pain and unhappiness*? She looked across the table at Mr Hunter, then at Mr Vine who was still holding forth about 'miasmic clouds'. *And they talk such nonsense too.*

Lilian hesitated. Should she challenge the Magistrate's ætiological certainty? Would Alice have remained silent at such mistakenness? But then the moment was past, and Mr Vine was observing that there was a ball at the Residency in a few months' time and were not the ladies looking forward to it, and had they ordered new silks from Calcutta for the *dharzi* to turn into dresses and sashes? The ladies' faces brightened. There were new ladies present. As members of the 'fishing fleet', those women sent over from England in search of husbands, they were familiar with the latest fashions back Home and had much to share with their up-country memsahib sisters on this subject. And, of course, remarked Captain Wheeler to Mr Birchwoode in a gruff and manly way, the pig-sticking season would shortly be upon them . . .

Dish after dish was brought in and laid on the table. Tureens of soup, warm bread and freshly churned butter, glistening roast fowls, two enormous mutton pies, two entire roast lambs, heaps of vegetables and mounds of potatoes gleaming with butter, followed by fluffy rice puddings and fruit tarts shining with syrup, bowls of lush mangoes and cream and melon syllabub and copious quantities of burgundy and claret.

'So, Miss Bell, what news from Home?' said Mrs Birchwoode, belching discreetly behind her napkin as she began her assault on a mountainous slice of mutton pie. Miss Bell was a cousin by marriage of Mrs Ravelston's sister. She had only recently arrived in Kushpur and was due to stay until the end of the cold season.

Miss Bell smiled nervously, as though unsure what was expected of her. 'Oh, very little.'

'Come, now, there must be something you can tell us. Last year Miss Stanford brought news of the cage crinoline. What a boon such an undergarment has proved to be. I for one was greatly relieved to dispense with so many heavy petticoats and the old horsehair crinoline is quite a thing of the past. So tell us, Miss Bell, are skirts wide or flat? Are waists high or low? Are shoulders in or out? Indeed, what new and shocking fashions have you seen at Home?'

'Well, since you ask' – Miss Bell leaned forward – 'some women have been seen in London wearing' – she lowered her voice – 'divided skirts.'

'Good heavens!'

'An American fashion, I believe.'

'Indeed. And is it catching on, this "divided skirt"?'

'Oh, no. It's considered to be rather shocking.'

'And have you seen one with your own eyes?'

'No. But I know a lady whose sister's maid saw one. And there was a picture in the *Englishwomen's Domestic Magazine* –'

'Ha!' shouted Mr Birchwoode, who had overheard this exchange. 'Divided skirts? Whoever heard of such a thing. You ladies'll be smoking next, and wearing trousers and demanding to be lawyers and doctors and politicians!' He grinned at Miss Bell. 'Tell me, have you seen any women with cheroots between their teeth? I'll wager you have.'

Miss Bell looked at her plate, unable to think of anything to say one way or the other.

'There already is a woman doctor,' said Mr Toomey. He winked at Miss Bell. 'What do you make of that, Dr Mossly? Are you ready to make room for a lady officiating at the bedside?'

'It will come to nothing,' said Dr Mossly. 'I hear this woman doctor – perhaps she should be termed a "doctress" or "doctrix" – is an American lady. Like their immodest fashions, such things may shock and disgust, but they don't become the way of the world.'

'But women may prefer the ministrations of their own sex,' said Lilian, glad that her new status as a widow granted her conversational licence. As a married woman she had been expected to acquiesce to her husband's opinion; as an unmarried woman, she had been expected to have no opinion worth hearing. Now, she could say almost whatever she chose. 'Modesty prevents many of them from admitting a male doctor's attentions,' she continued. 'Even when in the most acute physical distress. Especially during childbirth, or some other womanly condition.'

'Believe me, my dear,' interrupted Mrs Birchwoode, 'when one is in the throes of childbirth, one wants the reassurance of a knowledgeable doctor. And, naturally, doctors are men.' She smothered a yawn, so that Lilian wondered how she had found the energy to give birth at all. 'If you had had a child, my dear, you would understand.' The married women around the table, most of whose surviving children were back in England enjoying the rigours of a decent education, nodded sagely.

Lilian felt her face burning. 'But how can a man possibly know more about childbirth than a woman?' she cried. 'How can he know about her pain and suffering? Her feelings for her unborn child? Surely a woman doctor would have more understanding of these things than any man. His knowledge of physiology and anatomy is all very well, but the question is as much about sympathy and empathy as it is about the mechanics of the event itself.'

The men at the table shuffled their feet uneasily. Mr Hunter, who had remained silent throughout, stared at Lilian in astonishment.

For a moment no one said anything. Then Miss Bell cleared her throat. 'Quite so,' she murmured. She smiled nervously at Lilian. 'Mrs Fraser would find that she is not unusual in holding such views back Home. There is plenty of talk about it, in London at least.' She took a deep breath and added bravely, 'And I think . . . I think a lady doctor is a good idea.'

'Bravo,' cried Captain Forbes. He clapped his hands. 'Mrs Fraser, you have a new champion. Well spoken, Miss Bell. Will you storm the citadel and take a medical degree? Perhaps you might purchase a divided skirt after all. And Mrs Fraser too. A most practical garment, I imagine. I'm sure the dharzi would run you one up in an instant, if you give him your measurements.' He opened his cigarette case and offered it across the table. 'Cheroot, ladies?'

Lilian caught his eye, and she and the Captain laughed. A relieved Miss Bell joined in.

Lilian shook her head. 'Thank you, Captain Forbes. I prefer the hookah,' she said. 'But only after dinner, of course.'

'So I hear,' said Captain Forbes.

4

The lush emerald carpet of the cold season had barely covered Selwyn's grave before two unexpected suitors, Mr Vine and

Dr Mossly, made their intentions clear. This was greatly to the irritation of the "fishing fleet", who thought Lilian had had her chance at matrimony and, having carelessly lost a partner, should now get off the field and allow other, needier young ladies the opportunity to capture any unattached men.

Mr Hunter also registered his disappointment. 'Tell them you can't marry any of them,' he said. It had been months since his arrival in Kushpur and still Lilian had allowed him little more than a kiss. His employers in England were beginning to wonder what he was waiting for, so long had he been stalling them with excuses about the weather, the terrain and the difficulty of locating bearers of a suitable quality. But despite her limited encouragement, or perhaps because of it, he could not tear himself away. 'Tell them to stop sniffing around you like dogs.'

'I shall tell them no such thing,' said Lilian. 'Mr Vine is . . .'

'Old. And boring. And have you forgotten how he disapproves of you? You would hardly be allowed out of the house if you were married to him. There would be no more wanderings in the bazaar, no more trips on Captain Forbes's horse.'

'Mr Vine acts from a sense of rightness and with a view to my own safety. Besides, there is always Dr Mossly.'

'That old fool! Why, he knows nothing about anything.'

'Dr Mossly is a very kind man,' said Lilian.

'Kind? The reason half of the Europeans in this place are beneath the ground is thanks to him.'

Lilian shrugged. 'I have not made up my mind one way or the other.'

'You could marry me.'

But Lilian simply smiled and looked out of the window.

In their quest for Lilian's attention, a rift had grown between the Doctor and the Magistrate. Dr Mossly and Mr Vine no longer strolled about the maidan together in the evenings.

They no longer partnered each other at whist at Mrs Birchwoode's. They did not visit each other to smoke and chat on the verandas of their bungalows. Mr Vine regarded Dr Mossly's attention to Lilian's health as bothersome and unnecessary. Dr Mossly viewed Mr Vine's concern for Lilian's financial and legal status to be meddlesome and intrusive. They eyed each other with resentful suspicion and monitored Lilian for any signs of favouritism.

And yet, there were a number of subjects, had they but known it, upon which they were in accord, chief of these being her friendship with Mr Hunter and her increasing affection for all things Indian. Indeed, it was soon widespread intelligence that in the privacy of her own home the widow Fraser wore native clothing. Mrs Fraser's dhobi had reported as much to Mrs Birchwoode's dhobi; had shown him the saris and pyjama trousers he had been sent to wash. In the end, Mrs Birchwoode, Mrs Toomey and Mrs Ravelston had been obliged to pay Lilian an impromptu visit. They had found her, as reported, in the loose flowing fabrics of the bazaar, her feet bare, her hair undone. More shocking still was the fact that she was not even wearing black, but a vivid mixture of green and turquoise (they would never have admitted it, but the colours had suited Lilian's sun-bleached hair and tawny skin perfectly). There was a distinct whiff of tobacco about her and the hookah the absent Mr Gilmour had favoured had, quite clearly, been in recent use.

'Do you really think she smokes it?' wondered Mrs Ravelston.

'I see no reason to doubt the fact,' said Mrs Birchwoode.

'Perhaps some other person . . .' began Miss Forbes, who was Captain Forbes's sister and thus predisposed to view Lilian's case favourably.

'Like who? Mr Hunter, perhaps? It may well have been him. After all, it's no secret that she allows his attentions and we all know what sort of a fellow he is.'

'What sort of fellow is he?' asked Miss Forbes, who had seen Mr Hunter riding across the maidan and had noted his physical attributes with interest.

'Oh, he's quite a dreadful fellow,' said Mrs Toomey. 'He goes about the plains and mountains in search of weeds and seeds. He carries a knife in his belt and sleeps in a tent.'

'He chews betel,' added Mrs Ravelston.

'And wanders the bazaar dressed as a cut-throat,' said Mrs Birchwoode.

'Oh, yes. And as for his dancing,' said Mrs Toomey, 'I was quite black and blue from the knees down when he had finished with me. And it was only the polka!'

'And Mrs Fraser sees quite a lot of him?'

'Oh, yes. They were already acquainted back Home, of course, but, well, he visits her as often as he pleases. In the evening too, I hear.'

'Surely not,' said Mrs Ravelston. 'Have you seen him?'

'No, but you can be sure that he does.'

It was not long before such rumours reached the ears of Mr Vine and Dr Mossly. Clearly, they decided (independently of one another), it was of the utmost importance that Mrs Fraser find a husband and find one quickly.

'It is difficult for a single woman, even if she is a widowed lady like yourself, to remain above calumny and speculation,' said Mr Vine. He eyed Lilian's starched black dress with approval and pressed his thin fingers together, as though resisting an urge to reach out and touch her. 'And, indeed, as a relative newcomer to our modest up-country station, you may well find yourself curious about the natives, amused, even, by their beliefs, their way of dress, their customs. In the same way that one is curious and amused by the animals in the zoological gardens, say, or the antics of a dancing bear. But one does not have to *become* one to satisfy that curiosity.' He sighed and shook his head. 'You may not be aware of it, but there is much tittle-tattle in a place like Kushpur. The ladies in particular have not enough to occupy themselves and I fear they can be . . . unkind. They are already describing you as . . . how should I put it . . . a bibi.'

Dr Mossly was smiling shyly at Lilian from beneath his ginger eyebrows. 'Oh yes,' he said. 'A little kedgeree now and again, perhaps, but no hookah pipes, no saris.'

'And, in order that you find as many diversions as possible to keep you *occupied*, might I suggest that you attend the Residency Ball with me,' said Mr Vine. 'I know how you ladies love dancing –' He smiled. 'You do not have to decide right now. Please, take a little time to consider my proposal.'

Lilian nodded her thanks and looked out of the window. She had no intention of attending any ball with Mr Vine, though she had not the heart to tell him this in front of Dr Mossly, his rival in love. But Mr Vine had more to say. He was hesitating, a look of uncertainty upon his face, his mouth open slightly, as though the sentence he was about to utter had yet to make it to the end of his tongue. It was not like the Magistrate to struggle to make his thoughts known, thought Lilian. What fresh outrage was he preparing himself to reveal now? His face took on a resolute expression. Lilian steeled herself . . .

'In the meantime,' he said, his voice louder than it had been. 'I have to be present at a Burra Din, tomorrow evening. At the Kalee Ghat. It's only about a mile from Kushpur. The garrison will be there to keep the crowds in check and I am obliged to be in attendance . . . Perhaps you would care to accompany me? It should be a pleasant enough drive down there and you might find it interesting.'

Lilian blinked. Had she heard him correctly? 'Why yes,' she blurted. 'You are most kind to ask me. But this is a native festival, is it not?'

'It is.'

'I see.' She smiled. How could she refuse him? 'Thank you, Mr Vine. I shall look forward to it.'

Dr Mossly looked dejected. He wished he had made such an offer, though he could not understand why the Magistrate had suddenly thought it appropriate to take Mrs Fraser to such an event. He sighed. Dr Mossly was slightly older than Mr Vine and whereas the Magistrate's figure was tall and thin, with prominent knees and elbows and a bony sepulchral skull, the Doctor was short and tubby, his entire body covered with a thick layer of blubber and sheathed in soft pink skin that gathered in quivering folds about his chin and squeezed softly over the neck of his collar. He knew his nose was bulbous to the point of absurdity, but he was a good catch for the widow of a missionary. He put his handkerchief to his face, covering his nose as though about to sneeze. It was a nervous habit he had picked up in his youth, a desire to conceal his least attractive feature. Mind you, he thought, eyeing Lilian round the edge of his handkerchief, when Mrs Fraser had brought her deceased husband's clothes to the Missionary Society, the number of suits, jackets, boots, shoes, shirts and grooming accessories Mr Fraser had possessed had been far more plentiful, and of far better quality, than one generally expected to find in the closets of a man of his profession. *Perhaps she is not so badly off after all,* he mused, looking around the parlour with interest. *Perhaps she is not quite so in need of a husband as we think she is.* He caught sight of Mr Vine's smiling face in the mirror above the fireplace. How bristly the Magistrate's nostrils were and how brown his teeth. He had never noticed these defects in his friend before, but now they seemed as plain as day. Surely such an attractive young woman like Lilian would not allow herself to be courted by such a stained and hirsute individual as the Magistrate, even if he did offer to show her the native festivals? He blinked at her sadly from behind his handkerchief.

'There is also the subject of Mr Hunter,' he said. 'You know the fellow well?'

'He thinks he might know someone at Kew who would be interested in buying my paintings,' said Lilian.

'Ah, yes.' Mr Vine sighed, eyeing the numerous rolled-up watercolours that were stacked about the parlour in loose pyramids.

'The thing is,' interrupted Dr Mossly, 'Mr Hunter is a man of dubious sympathies. A man whose loyalty to the Company and its role here is questionable. Many of us fear that he has, in fact, *gone native*. It does you a disservice to be associated with him.'

Lilian sat down in a wing-backed chair. The chair had been Selwyn's favourite. Indeed, it was the very chair he had been sitting in when the insects had swarmed in through the open window. But now it was her chair. She did not have to listen to the petitions of either of these tedious men if she didn't want to. She didn't have to ask anyone's permission to do anything. Moreover, now that Selwyn was dead, the money her father had given him on their marriage was hers – which was just the way it should have been in the first place.

'The fellow is quite the infidel, too,' said Mr Vine. 'I for one have never seen him in church.' He looked to Dr Mossly for confirmation of this fact. Dr Mossly nodded his agreement, his cheeks wobbling like jelly against his collar.

Lilian said nothing. Surely the matter was best left up to the individual's conscience, she thought, assuming Mr Hunter had such a thing. Mr Vine's voice droned about her ears, mingling with the sound of bees buzzing back and forth above the geraniums outside her windows. She stole a glance at the clock on the mantel. The native she had hired to teach her the sitar was due to arrive in less than half an hour. Beside the clock was a note from Mr Hunter. It informed her that he would come over later in the afternoon with the Brahmin to help her with her Sanskrit, as she seemed to be making no progress with it on her own. It concluded with endearments that would have left Mr Vine speechless and sent Dr Mossly delving for his most voluminous handkerchief.

Lilian closed her eyes. Was it time to allow Mr Hunter further intimacies? She could not decide. Should she marry him? Not yet. Perhaps not ever . . . All at once Lilian noticed that the room had fallen silent. She opened her eyes. Dr Mossly and Mr Vine were staring at her so hungrily, that she was reminded of two pariah dogs, one fat and one thin, drooling over a prospective meal.

Lilian was dreading the journey to the Kalee Ghat. The prospect of being shut up in a hackery with the Magistrate, who could talk for hours about the need to improve the local irrigation systems; or about the dire shortage of ice pits for the manufacture of this most important luxury; or the benefits for export of manufacturing opium on an industrial scale; or the need for more thermantidotes to be installed at the kutcherry (to name but a few of his favourite topics of conversation) was almost enough to put her off from going. But her curiosity got the better of her and, when Mr Vine appeared in a carriage to take her there, she was waiting for him.

They passed through the European cantonment and on to the native town without incident. As they approached the temple, however, the road became increasingly busy and packed with people, so that it was soon almost impossible to proceed at anything more than a snail's pace. Lilian stared out of the window at the heaving multitude as she and the Magistrate inched forward in their sweltering carriage. The crowd was visibly excited; voices shouted and sang and laughed on all sides; the squall of music filled the air and Lilian caught a waft of ghee and onions on the breeze. Everyone was dressed in their most colourful attire – apart from Lilian who, in order not to upset Mr Vine, was wearing her black dress, and Mr Vine himself, who tended to wear black anyway. Everyone was heading to the temple.

'What festival did you say this was?' asked Lilian, gazing out at a group of mendicants, whose bodies were smeared from head to foot in ashes, their hair clotted with mud and twisted round their heads. Apart from shreds of cloth hanging from their waists, they were naked. One was holding his arms above his head. It appeared that he had kept them in that position for so many years that they were now withered and completely immovable. The nails of his clenched fists had penetrated the backs of his hands, to emerge on the other side like a pair of claws.

'We are going to the Churuk Pooja,' replied the Magistrate. 'The swinging by hooks.'

'Look at that!' cried Lilian, pointing to the fakir with the withered arms. 'How horrible!'

'Yes,' said the Magistrate.

'Is it some sort of penance?'

'I believe it's to fulfil some vow or other to Vishnu.' Mr Vine sighed. 'It's an act of great merit to endure so much pain. Dr Mossly assures me that the arms become numb quite quickly and that the pain soon ceases as a result. Some of these fellows hold up only one arm. This chap with both his arms up will be considered very holy, as he is almost completely dependent on others for food and help of any kind.'

'Goodness,' said Lilian. She felt slightly sick.

'Are you unwell, Mrs Fraser?' asked Mr Vine, leaning forward eagerly. 'Here, take my handkerchief.' He patted her hand. 'Yes, the mendicants can be quite frightful. But you'll have seen similar chaps in the bazaar. Not quite so appealing close up, are they?'

'No,' agreed Lilian, fanning her face with the Magistrate's handkerchief. 'It is certainly a very curious practice.'

Mr Vine stared out of the window in silence. 'I've been away from Home for thirty-five years now,' he said at last.

'I've been in Kushpur for ten of those years and seen the Churuk Pooja every year. One year there were quite a few deaths – one chap came loose . . . there was a stampede . . . some bhaji seller's booth was set alight . . . we were going to try to stop the event, to prevent such mishaps happening again, of course. The Brahmins agreed, and nodded and salaamed, but then the following year the thing went ahead as usual.' He shrugged. 'We didn't bother mentioning it again. Now, we just send the garrison in to make sure there isn't any trouble.' He sat forward and Lilian noticed that he was looking at her keenly. 'But this is a side of India, Mrs Fraser, that you don't usually see sitting in your drawing room with Mrs Birchwoode, isn't it?' he said. 'Perhaps it's a side you don't *want* to see. Certainly, I think you'll find that the Churuk Pooja illustrates most convincingly the difference between ourselves and the Indians.'

Lilian nodded. So that was why he had brought her there. She should have guessed..

Mr Vine scanned the crowd, which seemed now to stretch as far as they could see on both sides of the hackery. 'Perhaps this wasn't such a good idea after all,' he muttered.

But Lilian was leaning forward and pointing out of the window. Three tall posts, each crossed at the top by a long horizontal bamboo pole, could be seen projecting from the crowds. 'What are those things?' she asked.

'Those? Those are the swinging posts. They're the reason why everyone is here today. Look, there goes one now –'

Sure enough, Lilian watched as a man was released by the crowds. He was attached by a rope to the end of the horizontal bamboo pole, at the other end of which another rope was fastened to a horizontal pole that projected from the post at waist height. This lower pole was now turned round and round by a team of men. They ran faster and faster, like horses in a mill, until the hanging man was flying through the air, in a circle of about thirty feet in diameter, suspended on the end of the length of rope like a rag doll. In one hand he carried a bag, from which he threw flowers and sweetmeats to the baying mob below.

'Good heavens!' cried Lilian, her hands fluttering to her mouth. 'He will surely fly off.' She looked closely at the spectacle unfolding before her eyes. 'How on earth is he held on?' Then all at once she realised. The man's body was supported by eight iron hooks – four of which passed through the flesh of his back, and four through the flesh of his chest. It was by these hooks alone that he was entirely supported as he was whirled round and round through the air. Blood streamed from his wounds and spattered on to the upturned faces of those below, who shouted and surged about the base of the pole, barely held back by the militia who were stationed around each of the swings to keep the crowd at bay.

'How dreadful!' she cried.

'Please, allow me to be of assistance,' cried Mr Vine. He left his corner of the carriage and was suddenly by her side. 'I have some salts with me. The sight is indeed quite shocking and repulsive, especially to a lady and one so new to India as yourself.'

But Lilian was not listening. There were now three men hanging from the three swinging poles. She stared at them in disbelief, and at the people who shouted and screamed and danced in a frenzy beneath them. 'How disgusting, and yet, how fascinating,' she murmured. 'I assume the men swinging are well supplied with bhang and opium before they start? This fellow here is really quite wild.'

The Magistrate looked surprised. 'Yes, I believe they are. Dr Mossly attended one of them once, though they usually see to themselves. The fellow was delirious, though whether this was from the pain, or from the stimulants he had taken it was impossible to tell. Probably a mixture of the two.'

'And how long will they swing like this?'

'Oh, about half an hour.'

'And is this penance?'

'For their own sins, or sometimes for those of others. Richer men pay for the services of these fellows, of course, and get rid of their sins by proxy. It was ever thus.'

Lilian gave the Magistrate a smile. 'You are very well informed, Mr Vine.'

'I have seen it many times.' He stared out at the spectacle bleakly. 'One learns these things, whether one wants to know them or not. It is quite interesting at first. I seem to recall being intrigued, at least. But now? Now, I've been here long enough to know that we are the superior civilisation.' He gestured at the screaming crowds. 'What other conclusion can there possibly be?'

'Mr Vine,' said Lilian gently. 'Thank you for showing me this. But it is a most extreme and grotesque display. I think perhaps we should return now.'

'Of course,' said Mr Vine hastily. 'It is quite, quite unpleasant, I'm glad you agree. But you see, Mrs Fraser, you have seen so little of the place, despite your . . . wanderings on Captain Forbes's horse and your visits to the bazaar. I thought it might be useful for you to see some of its . . . less appealing sights. I trust you understand that my purpose in bringing you here was both educational and, well . . . to persuade you of the merits of being *European*.'

ALICE

1

Alice watched as expressions of despair, surprise, disbelief, pleasure and wariness made their way, one after the other, across the photographer's face.

'Marriage?' he said. 'I'm not much of a catch.'

'Surely Mrs Cattermole would disagree.'

'She's a devil,' muttered Mr Blake. 'She doesn't want to marry me. She just wants to satisfy her own pleasures.'

'Well, you can have two days to think about whether or not you wish to marry me. If you don't agree, of course, I shall be forced to tell my father everything.'

The photographer stood up. He took Alice's hands in his. 'Dear Miss Talbot,' he said. 'Alice. Of course I'll marry you.'

Alice had expected some sort of resistance at least. She cleared her throat and adopted a businesslike tone. 'Good. We can settle the details later. But perhaps secrecy is best for now.'

Mr Blake appeared not to be listening. He stepped closer. 'So, may I kiss my future wife?'

'I suppose so,' she said. 'But quickly now.'

Alice felt her cheeks turning crimson. She had not planned for this. She took a step back. Mr Blake took a step forward. They were the same height and his eyes were level with hers. Rather awkwardly, he put his arms round her. He smelt of smoke from her father's cigars, and as he squeezed her gently she also noticed a slightly musty, slightly sweaty, animal sort of smell, which she decided must be his own particular manly scent. Behind it came the unmistakable whiff of ether and the aroma of photographic chemicals. And then, before she could draw back, his lips touched hers. Alice flinched. She screwed her eyes shut and forced herself to relax. After all, it didn't feel unpleasant, only rather strange and unusual.

'Don't be afraid,' murmured Mr Blake against her cheek.

'I'm not,' retorted Alice.

'Of course not. You're not afraid of anything, are you?' Mr Blake kissed her again. This time, Alice felt his lips part and his tongue touch hers. She suppressed a shudder. It was all very different from the robust kisses she had seen exchanged between Lilian and Mr Hunter. Alice had entered the hot house to turn off the sprinklers. As she passed through the dripping foliage the sounds of laboured breathing had reached her ears. Rhythmic breathing, accompanied by gasps and murmurs, and the sound of rustling leaves. Alice had hastened forward. Perhaps one of the aunts had fallen down and was struggling to right herself.

But these particular pantings had not been made by an aunt in distress; they had been made by Lilian and Mr Hunter as they made love on the ferns beneath the warm sprinklers. Around them lay various items of hastily discarded clothing – Mr Hunter's shirt, his boots, his breeches, his waistcoat; Lilian's chemise, her stockings, her shoes, her dress, her numerous petticoats abandoned on the rocks beside the ornamental pond like huge beached jellyfish and, beneath the pruning knife that had clearly been used to hack through its constraining laces, her corset. Even as Alice watched Mr Hunter's naked buttocks rising and falling rhythmically between her sister's knees she had found herself wondering how on earth the two of them had managed to sustain their enthusiasm as they went through the laborious motions of removing so many layers of complicated clothing.

Still, whatever the answer to that question was, they were

too absorbed by what they were doing to notice Alice's curious face peering through the fern fronds. She watched as Lilian wound her legs about Mr Hunter's waist and her arms about his neck. Mr Hunter groaned, grasping at a soft white buttock as a drowning man might grasp at a lifebuoy. He began to move faster and more vigorously, so that Alice was briefly reminded of the piston on her father's steam-driven traction engine. All the while a fine mist of warm water fell upon them so that their bodies gleamed like wet marble in the gloomy Eden of the hot house.

Later, Lilian had come to Alice and told her what she had done, whispering to her sister how much she had enjoyed herself and how she was sure that Alice would relish such activities too. But Alice knew it was unlikely that any man would want to kiss her, let alone snip away her underclothes in his eagerness to get to her body.

Suddenly feeling foolish, she disentangled herself from the photographer's embrace. 'That's quite enough for now.'

Mr Blake took her hand chastely. 'Shall we tell your father?'

'We'll wait,' said Alice.

'You think he'll disapprove?'

'He'll lose his curator. Of course he'll disapprove.'

'Ah.' He sounded disappointed.

'Oh, there's no money in it, Mr Blake, apart from what you have and the small amount my mother left for me.'

'Oh. Are you sure? I mean, perhaps your father will be pleased. He must have made some sort of provision for your marriage.'

'There is no "provision". And I have no intention of ending up like Lilian. I want a legal arrangement.'

'But what's mine will be yours –'

'That's not true and you know it, whatever you may say to the contrary at the moment. The law says that everything I have will be yours for ever – money, property, children even – unless you agree before we are married that this will *not* be the case. But *your* money is always your own. Unless you die, of course.'

Mr Blake eyed Alice's supple waist. He had not touched a woman for months; not since he had last been alone with Mrs Cattermole. 'To be a loving husband is all I wish for,' he breathed, kissing Alice's fingers.

Alice snorted.

'Look here,' he said irritably, 'can't you accept a compliment? And you don't have to threaten me to get me to agree to anything, either. What are you so afraid of? Why can't you trust me? I'd have proposed to you myself, you know, only I didn't think you'd accept. I mean, you're quite aloof sometimes. I'd do anything for you, Miss Talbot. Alice. Go anywhere. You just have to say the word.'

'India,' said Alice. 'That's the word. That's where we'll go.'

Mr Blake located the machete and returned it to Alice. He had no wish to spend what remained of the evening toiling like a coolie in the tropical jungle of the conservatory.

He walked slowly through ill-lit corridors, turning right at the suits of armour and left at the teak filing cabinet, until he reached the door to his room.

'There you are!' cried Mrs Cattermole, jumping up from the edge of his bed. 'I was just about to go. I can't stay for long. Not that Dr Cattermole would notice, of course, but Mr Talbot has been most attentive and will be sure to ask where I've been.' She came towards him, her expression pettish. 'A few months ago you would not have hidden away from me in this way. Why, you would hardly have waited for me to finish my sentence before –' She gave him a coy look and sighed heavily, as though remembering that her bosom was at its most irresistible when heaving against its fabric constraints.

Mr Blake eyed the two mounds of soft white flesh that rose and fell above the neckline of Mrs Cattermole's bodice. Had she always worn dresses with collars of such unseemly lowness? He could not remember. Once he would have leaped across the room and plunged a hand eagerly between those warm pillows of flesh, scooping them out as though levering loaves of unbaked bread from their tins. This time, however, he closed his eyes and turned away.

'Mrs Cattermole, you really should return to your husband. He'll be wondering where you are.'

'He doesn't notice where I am.'

'I'm sure that's not true.'

Mrs Cattermole tossed her golden curls so that they shone in the candlelight. 'You're looking pale,' she observed. 'And you have dark circles around your eyes.' She gave him a look. 'I hope Miss Talbot isn't working you too hard in that darkroom of hers.'

Mr Blake felt his face turning red. It was in the darkroom that Mrs Cattermole had first offered herself to him, squeezing in beside him when her husband was out, being overcome by 'the fumes' and swooning deliberately into his arms, breathing into his ear that he must loosen her dress . . . just a little more . . . a little more so that she could breathe . . . Her bodice had parted beneath his hands like a mollusc opening to reveal the soft flesh within. Afterwards he had wondered whether she had replaced the original buttons with smaller ones, so easily had they slipped through their fastenings.

'Mrs Cattermole –'

'I was Eliza to you once.'

'You should go back to your husband.'

For a moment he thought she was going to strike him. She took a step forward and he staggered against the washstand as he backed away. She watched him as a kingfisher might watch a fish in a pond, waiting for the right moment to spear it and gobble it down in one.

'My dear Mr Blake, surely you are not afraid of me?' She moved closer, so that her skirts pressed against his legs like the push of an incoming tide.

Mr Blake felt a hand tugging at the buttons of his breeches.

'Come now,' Mrs Cattermole said briskly. 'You've no need to be shy.'

Mr Blake floundered out of the treacherous undertow of her ballooning skirts. 'Mrs Cattermole,' he cried, lurching into the arms of the stuffed grizzly bear that stood beside the washstand. 'Eliza. Please. Think of your husband.'

Mrs Cattermole began to weep. Mr Blake groaned inwardly. Not tears, anything but tears. Anger he could brace himself against, but with tears there was always a risk that he might compromise. He steeled himself and patted her shoulder in what he hoped was a comradely way. 'Come now,' he repeated, passing her his handkerchief.

'I am ruined,' she sobbed. 'You have tired of me? You've had enough of me?' She flung his handkerchief back at him.

Mr Blake said nothing. He sensed that she might be about to storm out and reasoned that a heavy silence on his part might increase the likelihood of this. He stared at the floor and counted the seconds.

'I carry your child and you tell me to return to my husband!' cried Mrs Cattermole, her voice louder than ever. 'How can you?' She seized his handkerchief again and buried her face in it.

Mr Blake felt as though he were falling into a pit.

'I came here to tell you this,' she said, 'to make you accept your responsibilities and to warn you against working too closely with Miss Talbot – ah! I see I have your attention now! So, you *are* attracted to her?' Her voice rose to a shriek. 'You can't reject *me* for a . . . a freak of nature like Alice Talbot? Why, she, she . . . well, let me tell you, Mr Blake, that woman . . . that woman should be in a *circus*. Oh yes! A circus. Or a museum of *grotesques*.'

Mr Blake's head was spinning, either from the port he had taken after dinner or the ether he had had before it. He opened his mouth to speak. He wanted to tell her that she was wrong; that Alice Talbot was outspoken, intelligent, brave and, he had to admit, possessed the best eye for composition that he'd ever come across. But he didn't. He didn't say anything. Instead, he closed his mouth and allowed Mrs Cattermole to continue her tirade.

'Did you know that she's neither man nor woman? Did you know that her father keeps her here as a *part* of his Collection, not simply to act as its housekeeper? Oh yes! My husband knows all about her from Mr Talbot himself and he has told me everything. Though I see from your face that *she* has told *you* nothing. You would be as well to go back to your medical books, Mr Blake. Look up the word "hermaphrodite" and see what it tells you.'

2

Alice descended from the sticky heights of the hot house. Marriage? What was she thinking of? What sort of escape would it be to move from being her father's curator to being Mr Blake's wife? It would still leave her hopelessly dependent on a man for every material need. In her pocket, her fingers felt the crumpled edges of Lilian's letter. *Come out, Alice. Come soon if possible.* But would Mr Blake really consent to sail halfway round the world in search of a sister he had never met?

Clearing away pruning offcuts was a tedious job, but Alice needed something to distract her from her own thoughts, so she set about gathering up the severed foliage, which lay in drifts about the hot house floor, stuffing armfuls of it into hessian sacks to be taken away and burned the following morning. The task seemed interminable, and by the time she had finished her dress was covered with leaves and brindled with green and brown stains. Her hands and face were filthy. Her hair had partly come down and was snagged with twigs and bits of green stuff. She was thirsty and exhausted, but her thoughts were still circling like the leaves she had sent whirling and tumbling down from the dizzy heights of the hot house.

Alice headed towards the aunts' jungle parlour. From beneath an upturned plant pot hidden among the foliage beside Aunt Rushton-Bell's whist table, she extracted a rectangular leather pouch. Unbuttoning it, she drew out one of her father's cigars. It was not often she had the chance to smoke tobacco. The aunts disapproved ('it reminds me of your father,' said Aunt Lambert with a barely suppressed shudder) and she was seldom without the company of one or other of them in the hot house. Now, however, she was alone and needed time to think. Snipping the end off the cigar with a pair of gardening scissors, she sank into Aunt Lambert's armchair, rummaging beneath the cushions for the brandy she knew her aunt kept secreted there. A glass or two would surely do something to calm her thoughts. After all, it was not every day that one proposed to a man one hardly knew. But as her fingers curled about the familiar bottle, a rustling of the foliage disturbed the dripping silence. Regretfully, Alice slipped the cigar out of sight, even as a voice called out, 'Alice? Alice! Are you there?'

'Yes, Aunt.' Alice stuffed the brandy bottle back into its chintz lair and rose to her feet. 'Is something wrong?'

'Oh, my dear.' Aunt Pendleton stumbled forward, a quivering lacy apparition emerging from the seething darkness of the jungle. The candle she carried shook violently in her hands. 'It's Mr Blake. Do come quickly. He's asking for you. Well, not exactly asking, but it was certainly your name he mentioned. I think he's lost his mind.'

'Where is he?'

'In the linen cupboard. The one on the second floor.'

Afterwards, Alice would remember how she had not felt the need to question this bizarre intelligence, believing there was bound to be a rational explanation. 'Is he locked in?' she enquired as they made their way back through the foliage. 'As a precaution. I mean, if he has gone mad one would assume incarceration to be the best course of action –'

'Oh, no. The others are with him. Mrs Rushton-Bell. Old Mrs Talbot. Mrs Statham. Mrs Lambert. They are looking after him. Smelling salts, lavender water, that sort of thing. There's talk of sending for a custard. Heavy and nutritious foods serving to lower and sedate the raging spirit, of course.'

'And is Mr Blake "raging"?' said Alice.

'Well, not exactly. But then I doubt there will be anyone in the kitchens able to furnish us with a custard at this time of night, so perhaps it's just as well. A slice of Dr Cattermole's Bakewell Tart might have served but he's probably eaten it all. He usually does.'

The linen cupboard on the second floor was adjacent to Mr Blake's room. In recent years the number of domestic servants had become so few that the linen was brought up from the wash-house as and when it was needed, or when someone remembered to see to the task. As a result the cupboard had fallen into semi-disuse. In former, more opulent, times it had been the main repository of sheets, pillows, pillowcases, blankets and eiderdowns for the entire west wing of the Great House. Its windowless walls were lined with row upon row of shelves, like a vault, upon which the snowy bales of newly washed laundry were neatly stacked. It abutted the main chimney and so was almost overpoweringly warm no matter what the temperature outside. Now, its door stood open. Alice could see within a gathering of aunts, their black scarecrow shadows thrown by the light of a single flickering candle.

'You know, I've seen Mr Blake disappear into this cupboard before,' whispered Aunt Statham confidingly as Alice joined the group. 'I assumed he was going to get some fresh bedding. After all, if one waited for anyone else to change one's sheets it would never get done.'

'I've seen him going in too,' said Aunt Lambert. 'Though I must say I never saw him come out.'

'Nor did I,' said Aunt Rushton-Bell. She stepped aside to allow Alice through. 'There he is, my dear,' she added, as though Mr Blake's prostrate body could easily be mistaken for anything other than what it was. 'He's naked, of course.'

'The heat, I suppose.' Aunt Rushton-Bell fanned her face with the handkerchief that she had, moments before, been wafting in Mr Blake's direction. 'It's a dry heat too. Most debilitating. Poor fellow.'

Alice surveyed the photographer's recumbent form. It seemed that Mr Blake had had the presence of mind to fold his clothes neatly and lay them on a stool beside the door before climbing on to one of the laundry room's middle shelves. There, among the enveloping mounds of sheets and blankets, he had created a nest for himself. The air, Alice could not fail to notice, was heavy with the reek of ether. An empty bottle glittered up at her, like a drugged eye, from the sleepy folds of linen.

'He's lucky he didn't cause an explosion,' she muttered under her breath. 'What on earth was he thinking, bringing a candle and a bottle of ether into so enclosed a space?' In Mr Blake's limp left hand Alice noticed a bundle of fabric. The colour and pattern seemed familiar and, as she pulled it free, she found it was made up of one of her own handkerchiefs (the badly embroidered initials on the corner were Alice's own reluctant handiwork), a wad of linen they used for buffing the photographic plates and what looked like a strip torn off the hem of a lady's petticoat. Alice gave these materials a tentative sniff. Feeling her own head begin to swim, she hastily thrust the bundle into her pocket.

Mr Blake's eyes rolled back in his head. He began to mumble to himself as though speaking an incantation, the same indistinct words over and over again. The aunts leaned forward, all the better to catch what he might be saying.

'Speak up, Mr Blake,' cried Old Mrs Talbot, a hand cupped round her ear.

The photographer's eyes flickered open. 'No, no, no,' he moaned. His vacant gaze seemed to focus, suddenly, on the ring of white faces that surrounded him, so that his features took on an expression of absolute terror. 'Away!' he screamed, rearing up from among the bedding. 'It's Cattermole you want, not me.' He thrashed into violent activity, the sheets and blankets winding themselves round his arms and legs tighter than any straitjacket. His gaze swept back and forth until it alighted, with something like relief, on Alice. 'Is that you?' he breathed, for a moment sounding lucid. 'Thank God.' But then he seemed to become confused again. A shadow passed across his face. 'Who *are* you?' he hissed, his eyes fixed upon her. 'And *what*?'

'Delirious,' said Aunt Pendleton. 'I heard shouting from inside the cupboard and opened the door to find him flailing and crying out as though Satan himself were in pursuit. The poor fellow looked terrified. He stared straight at me and shouted for a doctor. Then he shouted for you and told me that Dr Cattermole was a devil and not to be trusted under any circumstances.'

'I can find nothing to disagree with in that observation,' said Alice.

'Then he began to bawl what I can only assume was a music hall song about being deceived by the charms of a beautiful young lady.'

'Alice is here, Mr Blake,' shouted Old Mrs Talbot, as though the photographer were deaf, rather than deranged. 'You can speak to her now.'

Mr Blake had not taken his eyes off Alice. 'You,' he croaked. 'She told me all about you. Is it true?' A cunning look appeared on his face. 'Is that *your* secret?'

'What secret?' blared Aunt Lambert. 'What can you mean, Mr Blake?'

'He's unhinged,' whispered Aunt Statham. 'Do pull yourself together, Mr Blake,' she cried. 'Do you not realise where you are?' She reached for the candle, holding it aloft so that the shadows leaped and flickered like demons.

But the swaying candle and dancing shadows seemed only to agitate him further. 'She's coming for me,' he cried. 'Put out the lights! Quickly, now, and she might not see us.' He flapped a pillowcase at the candle, so that Alice only just managed to stop it from falling from Aunt Statham's shaking hand into the warm bedding. The hot wax splashed on to Mr Blake's naked thigh and he let out a scream. 'It's too late,' he shrieked, 'too late. I can feel her lips upon me.'

'He'll burn the place down,' said Aunt Lambert. 'We must get him out of here and into bed.'

'Get Edwin,' cried Old Mrs Talbot. 'He'll know what to do.'

'No,' said Alice. She leaned forward. 'Mr Blake,' she whispered. 'Mr Blake.'

The photographer peered at her anxiously, and Alice suddenly became aware of how she must appear – her face dirty with soil and sweat, her hair disordered, her dress stained. 'I look a fright,' she said briskly. 'But what of it? I've been working in the hot house.' She pulled aside the sheet and held up the candle. Mr Blake's face was pale and waxy. His eyes were now closed, his mouth open. His breathing was heavy and shallow. 'Perhaps we can move him while he is unconscious.'

'Why not use my chair?' said Aunt Rushton-Bell. 'The bath chair. If we could at least get him into that, then we could simply wheel him wherever he needed to go.'

And so, while in the drawing room Mr Talbot demonstrated to his guests the efficacy of one of his more recent acquisitions (a prosthetic limb designed to hold and shoot a firearm), while Dr Cattermole drank Mr Talbot's port and smoked his cigars, and winked as his host playfully pinched

Mrs Cattermole's generous thigh, while Mrs Cattermole simpered at Mr Talbot, and gasped at that prosthetic limb and shook her golden ringlets in the lamplight, two storeys above them Mr Talbot's daughter, his four aged aunts and his mother silently wheeled the naked, anaesthetised body of Mr Blake down the dimly lit hallway to the door of his bedchamber.

'It's years since I entered a gentleman's rooms that weren't my husband's,' whispered Aunt Statham excitedly. She gave a girlish titter. 'Uninvited too. What must Mr Blake think?'

'Fortunately, I imagine he is thinking very little at the moment,' snapped Aunt Lambert. 'He's drugged, isn't he, Alice? That bottle you found in the bedding contained something.'

'Ether. We use it in the photographic process.'

'Experimenting with his own chemicals? Edwin would be interested after all,' said Old Mrs Talbot. 'You know he always says a man can learn the most through direct experience. Experiment and experience lead us to knowledge and improvement, that's what he says.'

'We should put Mr Blake into bed and leave before he wakes,' said Alice. She rubbed her eyes, feeling suddenly dizzy. Mr Blake's room was suffused with the stench of ether, as though he had slopped it onto his bedding, his furniture, even his curtains before staggering out to the linen cupboard. Her aunts' squabbling voices receded into the distance, to be replaced by the rhythmic throbbing of blood in her ears. Alice felt the room lurch beneath her feet. Her head seemed suddenly as heavy as a cannon ball. She dashed the curtains aside and threw open a window.

The cold April night poured in like a draught of icy water. She took a few deep breaths. Outside, the sky was hard and clear, the moon a low yellow orb. It was a good job she had turned up the heating in the conservatory, as there was a glimmering icy mantle on the ground. How late the frost was this year. Perhaps it was time to move the peach tree through to the hot house.

A gunshot echoed out across the park, followed by men's laughter and a woman's voice.

'Bravo, Cattermole!' Her father's voice boomed out on the still air, reverberating from the silent walls of the house. 'An inspired piece of engineering, don't you think? A boon to the military, as well as to the unfortunate amputee who will now live to fight another day in the noble service of Queen and Country, rather than cluttering up the streets of our cities begging for alms.'

Alice felt a hand on her arm.

'Come away, my dear,' whispered Aunt Lambert, steering Alice towards the door. 'He seems to be asleep now. Whatever he wanted to say to you will have to wait until the morning.'

3

The next morning Mr Blake did not appear for breakfast.

Dr Cattermole and Mr Talbot had spent the better part of the night engaged in various manly activities – practising shooting at the statues on the terrace with the amputee's firearm; using Mr Talbot's newly acquired acid battery and electrical circuit to test the conductivity of various materials and, of course, pursuing numbered mice about the drawing room. Both men were late in rising. After the excitement of the night before, the aunts, too, were slow to make their way downstairs. Thus it was that Alice found herself at the breakfast table with only Mrs Cattermole for company.

At first, the two women sat in silence. Then, 'I hear you have been helping Mr Blake with his work here,' began Mrs Cattermole, giving Alice a frosty look.

'Yes,' said Alice.

'He is a most charming fellow, don't you think? And so

passionate about his chosen path. Has he taken your likeness?'

'No, he has not.'

'He has taken mine many times. But, then, I have sat for a number of well-known photographers. I have the face and the figure for it, you know. Not everyone does. You, perhaps, are not so well favoured with the natural luminescence which the camera so loves.'

'Perhaps,' said Alice.

'Well, we cannot all be so fortunate. My husband has told me that I am the perfect subject – he has taken me in numerous poses, including as various Greek goddesses Diana, Persephone, Leda.' She smiled. 'Your father, I think, has sculptures of some of these figures, so you understand what I am talking about.'

Alice nodded.

'Of course, the fuller figure is better suited to the more classical poses,' continued Mrs Cattermole. 'You are perhaps a little too *slim*, too . . . *masculine* – you will forgive me for saying it, I know – to appeal to the photographer's aesthetic sense.' She stared down her nose, as though waiting for Alice to blush, or at least look uncomfortable. 'Your own skills *behind* the camera, however, and in the darkroom, Mr Blake speaks very highly of. Though I can't see that such an oppressive place is somewhere a lady ought to be spending her time.'

'If one is to take a photograph, the darkroom is not to be avoided,' said Alice.

'So it would appear.' Mrs Cattermole breathed deeply. 'And no doubt Mr Blake is of the same opinion.'

Alice heard her father's favourite German long-cased wall clock ticking out the seconds. There was a dull 'thunk' as the minute hand shifted forward. She struggled for something polite, something anodyne and suitably banal, to say but she could think of nothing. Nor could she excise from her mind the image of Eliza Cattermole, posing for Dr Cattermole's camera as Diana, dressed only in a tendril of vine and a strategically placed bunch of grapes.

Mrs Cattermole leaned forward. Her breasts bulged against her neckline, like two large grapefruits in a bowl. 'You think he is attracted to you?' she hissed. 'He is not. He thinks he is, but he can't be. He is deceived – that much I know for sure. But I could not let him remain so. Oh, no. And now! Why, I have told him such things – things you should have told him yourself. He can no longer think of you as he did before.'

'What on earth are you referring to, Mrs Cattermole?' said Alice briskly.

The Doctor's wife was looking tired and irritable, and her eyes were puffy. Certainly, thought Alice, the lady's famous beauty was better suited to the dim yellow light of a candlelit drawing room than to the harsh and revealing glare of a bright spring morning. She wondered what it was that Mrs Cattermole had told the photographer. Alice opened her mouth to ask this very question, but Mrs Cattermole waved her hand impatiently. 'You belong *here*,' she said. 'You are *part* of the Collection. You know, you really should let Dr Cattermole photograph you. He is a medical man and most scientific in his approach.'

And then, all at once, to Alice's great relief, the air was filled with the whirring of mechanisms from the many clocks her father had gathered together in the breakfast room. The noise swelled and shivered about them, like the beating of the wings of a million insects. Mrs Cattermole's lips continued to move, but whatever sounds emerged from between them were mercifully obliterated by the arrival of eight o'clock. Alice allowed wave after wave of chimes to wash over her. As the eighth bong died away, she opened her eyes. Mrs Cattermole was silent now and looking startled. Alice took this hiatus as an opportunity, if one were needed, to excuse herself.

Later that day Mr Talbot found his daughter among the

swords and daggers, re-affixing the South American machete to the display on the wall.

'Dr and Mrs Cattermole have returned to London,' he informed her. 'But Dr Cattermole will be back in a few weeks. He and I have decided that it would be a good idea to hold an evening of experiment, enlightenment and amusement. A number of our friends from the Society for the Propagation of Useful and Interesting Knowledge will be invited. I need to speak to you about certain items in the Collection to which I would like their attention to be drawn. Oh, and Mrs Cattermole is with child. Cattermole is delighted.'

Alice said nothing.

'There are, of course, certain arrangements to be made if this evening of entertainments is to be a success,' continued Mr Talbot. He rubbed hairy-backed fingers through the wiry matting of his beard. 'I did wonder at first whether Mr Blake's photographs could be placed in albums and left in the Society's Reading Room, but Cattermole is right, as usual. A gentlemen's gathering would be far more stimulating. Cattermole has some monstrosities from his mortuary work to show to us, while I have new items to exhibit, and it would be most satisfying if these things were to be revealed to the Society members at the same time. I also have one or two experiments I should like to attempt.'

'Experiments?' said Alice warily. The last time her father had experimented, the cook had left and a new suit of her father's clothes had been ruined. It was shortly after a meeting of the Society for the Propagation of Useful and Interesting Knowledge at which a Dr Comely-Banks had been speaking on the wide range of temperatures endured by certain unusual creatures which made their homes in the geographical extremes of the world. Mr Talbot had returned home to experiment on a rat, enclosing it in a roly-poly tin and popping it into the oven. Intending to monitor its vital signs after a certain number of minutes, he was distracted by the arrival of new display cases from his London cabinetmaker. The cook had opened the tin some hours later to find the rodent within baked to a cinder. Mr Talbot had responded with exasperation to this experimental catastrophe and had climbed into the oven himself, allowing his own person to be baked, for twelve minutes at a moderate heat, all the while observing his own physiological well-being. 'No perceivable ill effects' was his overall conclusion.

'What experiments?' asked Alice again.

'Oh, nothing much.' Mr Talbot gazed at a terracotta model of St Nicholas' church in Hamburg. 'I have a plan for the manufacture of an artificial volcano – it is a simple variation of a common enough mixture used in pyrotechnic displays, but it should prove interesting nonetheless. I was thinking of using the front lawn for the purpose. The iron filings and sulphur necessary for the procedure will be arriving in a few weeks. We should have plenty of time to prepare. I shall require your help in making all the necessary arrangements.'

'I am already helping Mr Blake,' said Alice.

'Well, I shall need Mr Blake's help too, of course. He may have to call a halt to his photographic endeavours for a week or two. Where is the wretched fellow anyway?'

'I have no idea.'

'Have you seen him today?'

'No, Father.' This last was only partly true. Alice had glimpsed Mr Blake's receding back as she passed through the scientific instruments Collection. His movements were rapid and furtive, so that Alice was not even certain at first that it was he. She had called out, but he appeared not to hear, and had ducked behind a life-sized clay effigy of Sir Walter Raleigh. When Alice reached the spot where she had seen him, he had gone.

'Perhaps he is embarrassed,' Aunt Pendleton had whispered when Alice reported the photographer's elusiveness.

'He can't avoid us for ever,' Alice had replied.

'In fact,' Mr Talbot was saying, 'Mr Blake, with his knowledge of chemicals and so forth, would make the perfect assistant for the creation of the artificial volcano. A difficult and dangerous task for the uninitiated, but one in which an intrepid young man like Mr Blake would, I'm sure, be only too happy to be involved.' Mr Talbot rubbed his hands together vigorously, as though attempting to start a fire. 'Perhaps you would find the fellow for me. Send him to my study directly. We can discuss the matter there.'

'Shall I attend also? If I'm to help –'

'Your role will be administrative.' Mr Talbot cleared his throat and looked down at her sternly. 'I must say, Alice, it has come to my notice – indeed, I have Cattermole to thank for bringing it so clearly to my attention – that you are somewhat over-anxious to become involved. It is not *appropriate*. For a lady.'

Alice blinked. 'What lady?'

'Indeed!' Mr Talbot's eyes bulged. 'For instance, your use of that machete in the hot house – you think I know nothing of this? Why, I have seen you myself, wielding that blade like a gardener's assistant. And only last week I caught sight of you, with your shoulder to the stern of that peach tree's monstrous conveyance, inching it forward like a labourer in a shipyard.'

'The warm air from the heating pipes is beneficial to the fruits. I have no one else to help me now that . . .'

Alice fell silent. To mention Lilian's name would only irritate him. And yet, it was impossible to think about the peach tree without thinking about her. They had tended it together, guarding it against mould and aphids, lovingly trimming its branches and harvesting its blushing pink-and-gold fruits. Indeed, so proficient had she and Lilian become, that they coaxed two luscious crops out of the tree every year, simply by wheeling it into different parts of the conservatory. It had been Lilian's idea – Lilian had never liked to wait for anything – and she had jubilantly plucked and painted the first ripe peach. Afterwards, they sat together, their backs against one of the tree's enormous wheels, and fed one another with slices of the sweet, silken flesh.

Since Lilian's departure, however, Alice had cultivated only a single crop. The artificial environments of the conservatory meant that she had been able to choose which time of year she wanted the harvest and she had engineered it to fall in the spring – her last season with Lilian. As the fruits ripened, the cloying smell of peaches suffused the hot house. Alice found the memories it evoked almost too painful to bear.

She stared at her father bleakly. Why was he mentioning the hot house and the peach tree? He never brought up either of these subjects. This was mainly because he was not interested in them, but also because he was not interested in *her*. And yet, since Dr Cattermole's last visit, Alice had noticed that he seemed to have become more watchful than ever.

She realised that her father was still talking.

'I am not interested in your explanations,' he said. 'The examples are too numerous. Only the other day Sluce informed me that you had shown more interest in Bellows's flying machine than is appropriate. Then there is your excessive use of my camera. Your fingers are as stained as those of a printer's assistant and I have frequently overheard you instructing Mr Blake on matters pertaining to photography – a subject in which *he* is employed as a specialist – in imperious tones most ill suited to a lady in a gentleman's household which, my dear, is exactly what *you* are supposed to be.'

His voice had become louder and louder, as though he were trying to make himself heard over the hubbub of an increasingly crowded room. 'You steer a dangerous course, my dear, and may well find yourself shipwrecked on the very rocks of knowledge towards which I have unwittingly directed you.' He looked pleased with this vivid nautical metaphor and stood back to watch his daughter's reaction to it.

'What do you mean, Father?' said Alice.

Mr Talbot said nothing, but stared at her warily, as though unsure what he might be looking at.

Usually, her father hardly looked at her at all. Alice suddenly found that she too could think of nothing to say which, under the circumstances, was probably just as well.

'You see, you are not *feminine* in your demeanour,' said Mr Talbot at last, his voice unexpectedly hushed. 'Even now, your hands are upon your hips. They should be folded in your lap. I see nothing gentle and comforting in your physiognomy, only a frown of disagreement and a challenging light in your eyes.' But then all at once another, more appealing, thought seemed to leap into his mind.

'You will be an exhibit yourself, my dear. *Quod erat demonstrandum.*' He smiled and patted her on the arm. 'What a splendid idea. Now then, do see if you can find Mr Blake. Send him to me at once. You may also make yourself useful by writing to the members of the Society for the Propagation of Useful and Interesting Knowledge and inviting them to an Evening of Gentlemen's Experiments, Enlightenment and Amusement at this house on the 29th of next month.'

4

'There you are,' said Aunt Pendleton at Mr Blake's elbow.

He stifled a cry. How quietly these old ladies crept up on one.

Aunt Pendleton patted his hand. 'Alice has been looking for you. Are you feeling quite well again?' She peered into his face. 'You look a little pale, but then I imagine that is to be expected. You gave us all quite a shock, you know –'

'Yes, thank you, I am quite recovered,' interrupted the photographer hastily. 'I must apologise for causing such a disturbance. I hardly know how I can explain myself to you, or indeed how I might thank you and the other ladies for assisting me back to my room so discreetly. My recollection of events is limited, though I am aware that without your most fortuitous intervention there is no knowing what might have occurred –'

As he jabbered out his apologies, Mr Blake found himself being propelled rapidly along the hallway leading to the conservatory. Before he could even think of an excuse to turn back, the doors to the hot house had swung silently closed behind him and he was wading, like a deep-sea diver, though that familiar leaden atmosphere. He made a feeble attempt to disentangle himself from Aunt Pendleton's grasp, but she had wound her arm through his as a creeper winds about a branch. He abandoned himself to his fate, his head thumping like a tom-tom in time with the hot-water pipes beneath his feet. As though in a dream he heard Aunt Pendleton's voice describing how she had found her husband, generally such a placid and continent fellow, dead drunk and beached like a drowned man upon a sea of hymn sheets in the verger's office. It turned out that Mr Pendleton had been a sporting fellow (a vice his young wife had known nothing about), whose bluff had been finally called by the unexpected failure of Flying Billy to pass the finish line in the 1.20 at Newmarket. Attendant upon this was the loss of the entire accounts of the Temperance Society – an institution for which he had been a most highly respected treasurer and spokesman.

'What a terrible fellow he was,' said Aunt Pendleton, giving the photographer's arm a friendly squeeze. 'It appeared that he was leading a double life. Nothing like you, of course.' She winked and revealed a set of elderly teeth.

And then all at once the fronds of greenery parted and they emerged into the aunts' jungle parlour.

'Alice,' cried Aunt Pendleton. 'I have found Mr Blake for you.'

Alice was sitting at an escritoire that Mr Blake had not noticed before. It appeared to be situated in a thicket of bamboo. She looked up from her letter. 'Tea, Mr Blake?'

'Yes, please,' he said thickly.

A moment later he found himself sitting on a mildewed sofa. The tendrils of a small glossy creeper had colonised the front corner in the shape of a covetous, spindly-fingered hand. The photographer allowed himself to sink into the warm, slightly damp cushions, his cup of tea balanced on its saucer in his nearly shaking hands. If he sat there still and quiet for long enough, perhaps he too would be claimed by the surrounding greenery. And would anyone care if he was?

'What a relief it is to hear that Doctor Cattermole is no longer among us,' declared Aunt Statham with relish. 'That man brings out the very worst in Talbot. He becomes so competitive.' She gave Alice a kindly look. 'Don't worry, my dear. You know your father has been distracted by Cattermole's nonsense before. He will have forgotten all about it by next week.'

Alice nodded and gave a bleak, unconvinced smile.

'Oh, Mr Blake, did you hear, Edwin says that Mrs Cattermole is expecting a child,' said Old Mrs Talbot, reaching out to offer the photographer a plate of biscuits.

'Well,' said Aunt Pendleton, 'she'll have to abandon such tight lacing if that's the case. Mr Blake, how careless of you. Here, let me pass you a napkin.'

Mr Blake slid a glance in Alice's direction. She was gazing into the jungle somewhere above his head.

'Indeed,' said Aunt Statham. 'But then, of course, bearing children is what women are here for, is it not? In Dr Cattermole's world, at least.' She laughed. 'Each of us has failed in that capacity. I wonder what he would make of it? Perhaps he should exhibit us all.'

'No one will be exhibited,' cried Aunt Lambert. 'And especially not Alice.'

*

Alice stalked through the dimly lit corridors of the Great House with Mr Blake hurrying behind. He would have walked beside her, but the route she had chosen seemed to pass through the most cluttered thoroughfares, making it impossible to walk in any fashion other than single file.

'Alice,' called the photographer urgently, 'Miss Talbot, we must discuss last night. There are certain . . . details, certain possible facts that have come to my attention –'

'I take it Mrs Cattermole implied that you might be the father of her child?' said Alice over her shoulder.

'Yes,' said Mr Blake. His foot caught on a roll of Chinese silk that had fallen across the passageway, and he almost launched himself on top of her in his efforts to keep upright and within earshot.

'And that this prompted you to seek oblivion in the linen cupboard?'

'I am ashamed to say that yes, it did. Among other things –'

'Ignore her,' said Alice, striding forward. 'Then again, perhaps you wish *her* to be your wife?' She turned and glared at the photographer. They were outside her father's study now and she raised an impatient fist to batter on the door. Mr Blake seized her hand.

'Miss Talbot. Alice,' he whispered. 'Last night I agreed that *you* would be my wife.'

'And now?'

'Now, I have learned something. I have been told . . . certain things. About you. Rumours, facts, who knows?'

'What are you trying to say, Mr Blake?'

'I am trying to say that it has come to my attention that you might not be –' Mr Blake hesitated. How on earth could one ask such a question? What was the correct phrasing? Was there any way in which offence could be avoided? He wrung his hands.

'What?'

'It has come to my attention that you may not be . . . quite as you seem.'

'You said as much last night,' snapped Alice. 'I could make neither head nor tail of it then, and I can make neither head nor tail of it now. Mr Blake, please speak plainly.'

'Miss Talbot,' began the photographer again, his voice louder now, as though volume might come to the aid of clarity. 'You say you are to be an exhibit. A part of the Collection?'

'So my father wishes. I have already told you so.'

Mr Blake shuddered.

'What of it?' Alice too was almost shouting now. Would the man not just spit it out?

'Are you, God forgive me for asking a lady such a question, are you a . . . a hermaphrodite?'

At that precise moment the study door flew open and there was Mr Talbot himself, framed in the doorway. A smouldering cigar was clamped between his teeth. A dusty trail of grey upon the front of his waistcoat revealed the pathway its tumbling ash had taken across the burly topography of his torso. 'A hermaphrodite?' he cried. 'That's one description, certainly.' He eyed his daughter with interest mingled with hostility. 'Dr Cattermole at least would label her thus. It will be interesting to see what the other members of the Society have to say on the matter. But enough about that for now. Mr Blake, there is work to be done. I am, at this present moment, devising a system of mnemonics for Sluce,' he said. 'The man's memory is deteriorating. I hope to arrest its further decline by furnishing him with a coat of many pockets. Each pocket is numbered. In each of them I shall place an item that will remind him of his duties within the house and the various tasks I have set him to do. Can you help?'

Mr Blake said nothing. His eyes were fixed upon Alice. Alice's eyes were fixed upon the ground. Mr Talbot, and Mr Blake, took this silence for acquiescence.

*

Mr Blake spent the remainder of the day, and most of the evening, with Mr Talbot in his study helping select items for Sluce's mnemonic coat. Personally, the photographer could not see how such a garment would assist Sluce, as the objects and their associated significance were chosen by Mr Talbot with little or no input from the intended beneficiary. Sluce, however, donned his bulging-pocketed coat without complaint, and disappeared with a nod about his mysterious business in the dark and crowded hallways. Mr Talbot seemed to think it was a job well done. He hoped to report its success to the Society the following week. Mr Blake thought he had wasted an afternoon. Mr Talbot tried to detain him further by producing for discussion and experiment another of his recent acquisitions – a pair of enormously long and unwieldy brass and ivory binoculars. But Mr Blake could stand his employer's company no longer. Using indisposition as an excuse, he retired without taking any supper.

He threw open the curtains of his bedroom and pressed his forehead against the cold glass of the window. He gazed out into the black abyss beyond. Perhaps he should go out for a walk. The night air might clear his head and he had not been out of the house since rescuing Alice from Mr Bellows's flying machine. He pulled open the window. So much had happened since that hour spent on the roof, he could hardly believe that only a day had passed. It seemed an age. He blinked, his eyes smarting in the cold air. On the opposite wing, the window of Mr Talbot's study was still illuminated. Other than that single throbbing cell of life, the Great House seemed deserted, its edifice shrouded in an almost impenetrable darkness. Mr Blake shivered and slammed the window closed. It was far too late, far too cold and dark, to go out for a walk.

He threw himself on to the bed and lay staring up at the cobwebs that festooned the cornice above his head. He found himself thinking about Alice, gliding swiftly away from him in Mr Bellows's flying machine. Alice and her unexpected proposal of marriage. Alice and the look on her face as her father closed his study door on her that afternoon. He thought about Mrs Cattermole and her unborn child, about Sluce's mnemonic coat, about the photographs he had taken with Dr Cattermole and which were still in Alice's possession. He thought about the bottle of ether, which he knew was downstairs in his dark tent, if he chose to go looking for it. He pressed his hands over his eyes. His head was whirling, as though there was not a single thought he could hold on to long enough to make sense of. He had no idea what he was supposed to do for the best. No doubt, he concluded gloomily, he would do nothing, as usual.

A gentle knock at the door brought him out of his stupor. At least it wasn't the knuckle-bruising rap of his employer. Perhaps it was Aunt Pendleton with a cup of tea. She was assiduous in providing him with refreshment. The photographer opened the door.

'May I come in?' whispered Alice. She held her candle aloft, and looked quickly left and right, up and down the hall.

He closed the door behind her. Her hair was undone, he noticed. It looked as wiry as jute in the candlelight, but it shone with reds and golds he had not noticed before.

'What on earth are you wearing?' he exclaimed, before he could think of anything more appropriate to say.

'A cloak,' she replied. She held the collar close to her throat, as though fearing that the photographer might attempt to tear it off her.

'Have you been for a walk? I considered taking a turn around the grounds myself –'

'Mr Blake,' interrupted Alice, 'if I might be so bold as to ask you a question . . .'

'Of course,' said Mr Blake. 'Though I imagine that my answers will count for little in this most peculiar household.'

'In answering my question, you might find that your own curiosity is satisfied.'

He said nothing.

Alice clutched her cloak tighter. Her eyes were wide, he noticed, and her face pale in the candlelight. 'Mr Blake,' she said breathlessly. 'I know which books I might look at to put my mind at rest, but there would always be room for doubt, in your mind at least. The opinion of a man as experienced as yourself, however, why, this would be quite irrefutable, would it not?'

Mr Blake had no idea what she was talking about. 'Indeed,' he said.

'Besides,' continued Alice rapidly. 'You must see for yourself, not simply take my word for it.' She took a deep breath. 'I am resolved,' she murmured. She lowered her eyes. Mr Blake saw her lips move as though she were counting, *one . . . two . . . three* . . . then all at once she cast the cloak off her shoulders.

Alice stood still and silent, as naked as a statue in a fountain, the rumpled cloak in a dark pool about her ankles. 'Tell me,' she said after a moment of unbearable silence. 'Is this the body of a hermaphrodite? You have trained as a doctor. You have seen numerous unclothed women. You have lain with any number of them. You know their secret parts, their most intimate bodily secrets. You know what you should see when you look at them. Tell me now whether what you see before you is a woman, or a man, or some unnatural combination of both sexes. An abomination. A monster fit only for a museum.'

Mr Blake gazed at his feet. 'My dear Miss Talbot,' he murmured.

'Look at me,' she commanded. 'Look at me and tell me what you see.'

In fact, what Mr Blake saw when he looked up was a pale narrow body scarcely interrupted at all by the hills and valleys of breasts, waist or hips. He saw square shoulders and strong arms with large hands. He saw a flat stomach and long, narrow-thighed legs. He saw a triangle of darkness at the root of her belly. He stared at that dark thicket of maidenhair. It appeared as featureless as all the others he had seen, though he knew that whatever secrets it might contain could not be fathomed from ten paces away.

'I think,' whispered Mr Blake, 'that you are not a man, by any means.'

It was not enough. 'You need to see more.' Alice strode across the room and lay down upon his bed. She raised her knees and parted her legs, her eyes fixed upon the ceiling above. 'You must make sure. Look. Look! You must be certain. Tell me what you see. Tell me that you *know* I am a woman, not that you *think* I am not a man.'

Mr Blake stood gazing at the floor.

Alice stared at him over the tops of her widely parted knees. 'Come, Mr Blake,' she said. 'Tell me what I am. For both our sakes.'

LILIAN

1

Lilian's household was soon known as one at which all manner of native manufactured goods – silks and saris, furniture and works of art, paint pigments, foodstuffs, medicines and potions – would be purchased by the pale-haired bibi memsahib. The gates of her bungalow were always thronged with boxwallahs, up from the bazaar with their wares for her perusal. Lilian was guided in her choices partly by Mr Hunter and partly by certain members of her own household. British etiquette, combined with British indolence (and in acknowledgement of the caste system), meant that at least thirteen native servants were required to run a house in which no more than two Europeans resided. Lilian was aware that this number was regarded as modest to the point of meanness by both Indians and Europeans – Mr and Mrs Birchwoode and their daughter Fanny requiring upwards of forty to attend to their diverse diurnal needs. From the khansamah who attended to the dinner table, to the bawarchi and his assistant who worked in the cookhouse; the dhobi who washed her clothes and the istri wallah who ironed them, the ayah who helped her dress, the numerous bearers required to pull the punkahs and dust the furniture, the grass cutters and gardeners, the water carriers and gatekeepers, Lilian was hardly able to remember who was doing what and when, even in her own home.

At first, she had found it almost impossible to engage in conversation with any of this team of servants – even when she addressed them in their native Hindi. But persistence revealed that the sircar she had taken on shortly after Selwyn's death – a tall fellow with a knowledgeable smile who went about his tasks as superintendent of the household with noisy efficiency – had once worked for the mysteriously absent Mr Gilmour. The sircar's name was Harshad, and once Lilian had apologised to him for mistakenly addressing her demands to her deceased husband's bearer (a man of inferior caste, she was informed), rather than to Harshad himself (he had pointed impatiently to the white caste mark on his forehead and indicated the presence of the sacred thread about his neck with a despairing twitch of his garments), they got on very well indeed.

Harshad appeared to be unsurprised by Lilian's interest in Indian culture. He was pleased to buy the very finest tobacco for her hookah. He was happy to recommend a dharzi who might make her cholis, the tight-fitting bodice worn beneath her sari, and as many petticoats as she might desire. Without hesitation he had proposed his sister-in-law as her ayah (a lady of infinite patience when it came to explaining the intricacies of donning the completed saris), and turned out the existing ayah (who he claimed had been dishonest) before Lilian could even think of an objection. Harshad explained in detail the ins and outs of the caste system (which he feared she had misunderstood) – in particular, cautioning her against those Moslem servants who refused to perform certain tasks under the pretence of being afraid of losing caste. This was simply a ruse on their part, he informed her in disgusted tones, as Moslems did not have any notion of caste in the first place and simply pretended that they did to avoid their more onerous domestic duties. Harshad also revealed to her the mysteries of dasturi, that unfathomable payment that had to be made over and above the servants' wages for practically anything bought from the boxwallahs on Lilian's behalf.

'*Dasturi* a very bloody tax, memsahib,' said Harshad patiently. 'From two to four pice in the rupee. One anna, or one sixteenth of the rupee is correct. Unless Harshad himself purchase confounded item. But other servants – darwan, bawarchi, even khansamah – they are bloody well not to be trusted. For a memsahib, it can be hard, fearfully, fearfully hard, to find honest servants, damn them.'

Lilian smiled. 'Where did you learn your English?' she asked.

'Mr Gilmour, a very talkative sahib. He try to learn Hindi, but also teach Harshad English. Now, I alone among all servants speak Queen's damnable English. Mr Gilmour, a very bastard gentleman sahib, taught Harshad well – all his most beloved, his most bloody, English words.' Harshad laughed heartily at the memory of his previous employer. 'Mr Gilmour sahib a happy, happy man. Especially he enjoyed the gin and the hookah. And, at these times, especially he was happy to teach Harshad. Ah, yes. Often he would laugh and laugh when Harshad spoke those most confounded English words, damn and blast the bastard. But now –' he shook his head sadly – 'now Mr Gilmour is taken ill. A bloody sad time for Harshad.' A slow smile replaced the dolorous expression Harshad had assumed to accompany this sorrowful revelation. 'Still,' he said. 'Memsahib Fraser now takes his place. A damned happy event.'

'Indeed,' Lilian said, relieved that she had not engaged Harshad while her husband had been alive. 'Damned happy.'

Lilian's Hindi was already good, but she was determined to perfect it. She always spoke to Harshad, and any other servant, in their own language, insisting that they correct her when she made mistakes. Occasionally, Harshad would answer her in an English rich with expletives, a faint, wistful smile upon his lips as though at the memory of those merry, blaspheming hours spent under the tutelage of the drunken Mr Gilmour. Lilian did her best to discourage this, but met with little success.

Harshad soon became invaluable. He regularly accompanied Lilian to the bazaar, passing from booth to booth with her, showing her the best way to get a fair price (her haggling had been too meek); discussing the benefits of particular native concoctions for the cure of common ailments and taking her to the most respected hakim in the bazaar so that she might try them for herself. He would often go with her when she rode out of the cantonment with her easel and her paints, directing her to the best places for flowering plants or showing where the monsoon waters lingered longest with considerable pleasing effect on the surrounding greenery. When she asked to visit the temple by the burning ghat, he took her there and introduced her to the Brahman. And when she requested him to engage a sitar teacher, he found one straight away. As she took her lesson Harshad would stand by the door, in case she needed anything, his face a picture of misery.

'Harshad,' Lilian said one day. 'You look pained. Does my music not please you?'

'No, memsahib,' said Harshad replying in Hindi. 'It does not. You play very, very badly. You do not tune your instrument when you practise, which makes it even worse. Always the teacher has to tune it for you when he comes. And yet, even when he has done this you cannot move your fingers as you should. They are too small and the strings sound flat and dead, like a sick wasp trapped beneath a cup. And you do not sit in the correct way either. Everything is wrong. Really, memsahib, it pains me to say this, but it is quite clear that this instrument, this most beautiful Indian instrument, is not for you. You should not play. Perhaps some other instrument might serve. A drum, perhaps.'

'A drum?' Lilian laughed. 'Am I that bad? Ranjeet has been teaching me for weeks. He said I was doing well.'

'He goes home with a rupee in his pocket. As long as he tells you these lies he will continue to go home rewarded. Why should he tell you that you cannot play well? It is only I, Harshad, your most honest and loyal servant, who can tell the truth of this matter to you.'

'Yes,' said Lilian meekly.

'Bloody terrible noise.'

In the evenings, sometimes Harshad would tell Lilian about his Hindu gods and goddesses. How the dip in the land where Kushpur was situated was made by the imprint of Shiva's foot as he strode across the land. How Ganesh had been born as an ordinary boy but had been decapitated in war, his head replaced by that of a baby elephant on the orders of Shiva. Lilian already knew much of this from her time in her father's house, but it was pleasant to hear the stories spoken in Hindi, as they should be.

'What lovely fairy tales,' she said one evening without thinking. 'I don't know why everyone objects to them. What harm can there be in such fanciful legends?'

Harshad drew himself up, excused himself and strode from the room. Lilian sought him out to beg his forgiveness. Of course they were not fairy tales, she insisted. She was thoughtless and foolish to have said they were. Would he accept her apologies?

Harshad was mollified by the gift of a couple of chickens to take home to his wife.

2

Mr Vine decided that it might be a good idea for Lilian to give the new arrivals in Kushpur drawing lessons.

'Both Miss Bell and Miss Forbes have expressed an interest in sketching,' he said. 'Miss Forbes in particular has admired your paintings on several occasions.'

In fact, Miss Bell had merely commented on her own lack of skill with a pencil without intending that anything might be done about it, while Miss Forbes had wondered aloud in Mr Vine's company why Mrs Fraser kept so many paintings stacked about her parlour. Mr Vine, however, had taken it upon himself to interpret these observations according to his own particular needs and, having generously offered Miss Bell and Miss Forbes as Lilian's pupils, he was now sitting in Lilian's parlour, staring, as though hypnotised, at the painting currently clamped to her easel. The subject was a vine-like plant with large flowers wound tightly round the trunk of a yellowish-coloured tree. The bark had squeezed like butter against the ligature of creeper that encircled it, so that the image reminded Mr Vine most forcefully of one of Mrs Birchwoode's more opulent necklaces, a choker adorned with crimson silk flowers which appeared to squeeze the jaundiced neck of its owner in exactly the same fashion.

'Can you not simply cut the flowers and bring them home to paint?' he said. 'I mean, then you could send one of the bearers out. You wouldn't have to wander about out there yourself.'

'I like to paint the flora where I find them,' said Lilian. 'One needs to see their habitat, their environment, their chosen location. If the subject is growing beside a stream, I also paint the stream. If it grows among rocks, I paint the rocks too. And I always include the surrounding vegetation. What if such plants and flowers should disappear for ever? We would have no useful record of them without paintings such as these. Oh no, Mr Vine, to answer your question simply, I must paint the plant where I find it. I can assure you that sending out a bearer would be next to useless. Surely you can see that?'

Mr Vine gave a dejected grunt. Even before she had finished he regretted asking the question. The answer (so forcefully expressed, so confidently delivered) revealed to him how far Lilian had strayed into the thicket of independent thinking; a thicket so treacherous that unless he were able to hack through it to save her, she would find herself lost for ever. She would become like the wicked witch in a children's fairy tale: ostracised, alone, wretched and bitter.

His plan was a simple one, and simple plans were often the most effective. He was hoping that Lilian's obligations to Miss Bell and Miss Forbes would do something to keep her indoors (Miss Bell certainly was of too nervous a disposition to wander about the countryside in search of the perfect subject). In addition, the society of other young ladies might remind Lilian of the pleasures of gossip and fashion (and here the Magistrate congratulated himself on realising that Mrs Birchwoode, Mrs Toomey and Mrs Ravelston lacked the infectious effervescence of youth in their performance of these feminine offices). Finally, on the grounds that he was anxious to see how the ladies were enjoying their lessons, the Magistrate now had an excuse to visit Lilian's bungalow on any morning he chose.

Lilian, however, was irritated to be saddled with the two young women. Both Miss Bell and Miss Forbes had yet to lose the modern and optimistic outlook they had brought with them from Home, and Lilian did not find their company altogether disagreeable; but both were little more than girls, and, egged on by the older memsahibs, were becoming increasingly obsessed with the marriage credentials of every Company man, every officer, every unmarried European of Lilian's acquaintance. They were also lacking in either dedication or proficiency when it came to painting and drawing.

'Is it always so hot in Kushpur?' said Miss Bell peevishly. She fanned her face with her hand. 'I got up at five o'clock this morning simply in the hope that I would have at least an hour or two at a temperature that was less than intolerable. Mr Vine said the thermometer in the kutcherry yesterday stood at eighty-six degrees.'

'It will get much hotter, I can assure you,' said Miss Forbes knowledgeably.

'It's no wonder that the natives are always asleep. They can't have the energy for anything else. Neither do I, but Aunt Ravelston keeps sending me out on rides, or to see Fanny Birchwoode for tea. And I am covered in these horrible itchy spots because of the heat.' She lowered her voice. 'My corset chafes them terribly. Do you think anyone would mind if I wore a sari at home, like you, Mrs Fraser?'

'You could try it,' said Lilian.

'My brother says we ladies should all try it,' said Miss Forbes. 'But he also thinks that we should speak Hindi; or is it Urdu? I forget which. I've tried, but I'm not very good. Besides, Mrs Birchwoode says that one only really needs to know some basic commands and a few words to make sure the sircar knows what he's doing.'

Miss Bell scratched at a mosquito bite that stood out on her forehead like a caste mark. 'We have an infestation of muskrats beneath the house. Muskrats! Can you imagine anything more horrible?'

'It's a common occurrence,' said Lilian.

Miss Bell's rosebud mouth became a pout – an expression Lilian imagined would be habitual within a few years spent in a place like Kushpur. 'I've never seen a muskrat, but I assume they're quite large. My uncle, Mr Ravelston, came into my room last night saying he was looking for one of these dreadful creatures, which he had reason to suspect had actually entered the house. He said it might even be hiding in my bed, and he lifted the sheet where I lay.'

She looked at Miss Forbes, but the Captain's sister was surreptitiously admiring her own reflection in the surface of Lilian's teapot.

'How I wish I could go Home,' whispered Miss Bell, suddenly tearful. 'Don't you ever wish for such a thing, Mrs Fraser? Especially now Mr Fraser has . . . I mean, surely you can't actually *want* to remain in Kushpur without him?'

'Mrs Fraser likes it here,' said Miss Forbes.

'Do you?' Miss Bell looked at Lilian, her blue eyes round with disbelief.

'Yes,' said Lilian.

'But how *can* you?'

'My recollection of Home is of a cruel place. A place of tyranny, filled with selfish men,' said Lilian bitterly. 'I might want to leave Kushpur, but I have no wish to leave India, and no desire to go back Home.' But even as she spoke Lilian knew that this was not true. There was one memory of Home that was very different from those dark and pain-filled thoughts; one memory that burned as brightly as a comet in her mind. 'I don't miss Home at all,' she said. 'But I miss my sister terribly. She is dearer to me than any man, any husband could ever be. I would go Home only to fetch Alice.'

'Does she write?' enquired Miss Forbes. 'Letters can offer some comfort, at least.'

'No.' said Lilian. 'She is . . . prevented from writing. But I write to her. I write a letter to her every day, though I imagine she receives none of them.'

'I have no sisters,' interrupted Miss Bell, as though Lilian had held the floor for quite long enough, 'Indeed, no family apart from Mr and Mrs Ravelston. Mrs Ravelston is my mother's second cousin, by marriage. I suppose I have no one to go Home to, should I even be able to get there.'

'You need to find a husband,' said Miss Forbes briskly.

'That'd get you away from Uncle Ravelston and his sheet-lifting,' said Lilian.

Miss Bell looked confused.

'What about Mr Vine?' continued Miss Forbes in a businesslike manner. 'He's a good catch.'

'Oh.'

'Or Dr Mossly. Or what about Captain Lewis? He's a handsome enough fellow. My brother speaks very highly of him.'

'I do like a man with a soldierly bearing,' said Miss Bell. 'But I understand that Mrs Birchwoode has set her mind on

Captain Lewis for Fanny. As for Dr Mossly, I think he has eyes for someone else,' and she smiled knowingly at Lilian.

Lilian's teacup rattled on to its saucer.

'There is no place more illuminating to get to know a man's character than at the bedside of one's dying husband,' said Miss Bell, her head held high. 'And to watch your tender ministrations, Mrs Fraser, why, any man who witnessed such loving care could only fall in love with you. No, I was thinking more about your friend. About Mr Hunter,' and she blushed as red as a geranium. 'He is so very tall and well proportioned, though the older ladies say he is quite a savage at heart. What do you know of him? Is he married? The ladies say he's not, but you never know –'

'He's not married,' said Lilian.

'Perhaps he's looking for a wife,' said Miss Bell. 'They say he has been in Kushpur for months now, when he should really have left. I wonder what detains him?'

Miss Forbes stroked her chestnut ringlets. 'Well, I must say he was most attentive to me last week. I was walking with my brother and Captain Wheeler when Mr Hunter came over specifically to speak to me. Of course, he directed most of his remarks to my brother, but there was no mistaking it. He actually took my hand and welcomed me to Kushpur.' She smiled. 'A wife is a comfort and a blessing. Mr Hunter must surely be in need of one.'

'Perhaps he is too wild,' breathed Miss Bell.

'I believe you knew him back Home, Mrs Fraser,' said Miss Forbes.

'He was an acquaintance of my father's.'

'And what have you seen or heard of him that convinces you that he is less than gentlemanly?'

'Oh, this and that.'

'But what?' Miss Bell and Miss Forbes sat on the edge of the settee. Miss Bell's pale face grew paler; Miss Forbes pressed her lips together. Were they on the brink of discovering a scandal?

Of carrying back to Mrs Birchwoode a rumour that she had not already heard?

Lilian watched as curiosity, craftiness – even jealousy – chased across their features. The girls' appetites for gossip, encouraged by the other European ladies and sharpened by boredom, smiled hungrily at her from two pairs of eager lips. Lilian tried to remember how she had felt all those months ago when she discovered that Mr Hunter had left her father's house; when she realised that he had no intention of returning and had gone off plant-hunting without even saying goodbye. Rage and humiliation had been her foremost sentiments, though she found that she could muster no such emotions now. She tried to recall the distress and shock of finding that she was carrying Mr Hunter's child; the horror of Dr Cattermole's fingers against her skin and the cold jaws of the speculum inside her; the pain and awfulness of those moments when the child had been expelled from her womb. And then the desolation of seeing her dead baby wrapped so tightly in her cotton sheet, her tiny face bruised and contorted. Lilian had schooled herself never to think of these things, so that the memory of the infant seemed clouded and indistinct, as though she were viewing a photograph of her through a watery lens. She felt a sense of detachment from those sad and terrible times, and her misery had long since drained away, leaving only a faint desire for vengeance, and something she might perhaps have described as relief.

Lilian lowered her voice as she leaned forward. 'There was a rumour, I really have no idea how true it is, that Mr Hunter seduced a young lady. That he abandoned her without further thought for her well-being. Of course, this may simply be gossip. You should perhaps not repeat the story to anyone else, not least in case the name of this unfortunate young lady becomes known.'

'Where did you hear this?' whispered Miss Bell. 'And when?'

'Just before I was married. In England. It was well known in certain circles at the time.'

'He seduced her?'

'Oh, yes. Though I understand that she was not a reluctant participant.'

'And he ran off?'

'He had taken his pleasure. What more did he need from her?'

Miss Bell and Miss Forbes exchanged a glance.

'And where is the lady now? What happened to her?' said Miss Bell.

'Her baby died, and . . .'

'There was a baby?'

'I believe so.'

'The scoundrel,' breathed Miss Forbes.

'And the lady?' insisted Miss Bell. 'What about the lady?'

'Her fate is uncertain.'

'The poor soul. Perhaps she drowned herself.'

'Oh, I doubt it,' said Lilian.

3

A trip was arranged by Mr Vine to see the botanic gardens at Khinsamaghar. The Magistrate was assured by Mr Hunter that all manner of delightful April flowers would be on display and, as the heat of the day was not yet intolerable, it promised to be a pleasant excursion. It was clear to Mr Hunter (whose face had darkened with irritation that he had not suggested this outing himself) that this expedition had been arranged with Lilian's gratification foremost in the Magistrate's mind. Indeed, Mr Vine had initially intended to take Lilian only, for once agreeing with Lilian's unspoken opinion that the society of the other Europeans would be both irksome and tedious. But on this occasion Lilian agreed with the Magistrate's usual view that the company of these same Europeans was both desirable and useful: she would not have to be alone in his company.

As he made his way towards the ghat beside the barracks the Magistrate could not help but feel exasperated to see the broad backs and ample behinds of Mrs Birchwoode, Mrs Toomey and Mrs Ravelston. Mr Hunter had not been invited, but he had turned up anyway.

And then Mrs Birchwoode stepped aside and Mr Vine saw Lilian. He froze where he was, his fingers thrust in his pocket about to extract his watch, his mouth half open in the beginnings of a greeting. His face turned from its customary yellow to a deep shade of terracotta.

Lilian felt the hot breeze waft through the soft fabric of her new sari. Harshad had bought the diaphanous, green and yellow material from a boxwallah. It was edged with a golden, gauze-like material and the dharzi had made her a matching golden choli to wear beneath. She had asked for a turmeric-coloured underskirt, and a long pallav to go over her head to shade her from the sun and deter flies. Her ayah had helped her to dress, expertly folding and draping the six yards of shimmering fabric, twitching it this way and that until it was perfect. How simple and elegant a sari looked, once it was on, thought Lilian as she admired herself in her bedroom mirror. And yet, dressing herself in one was something she found almost impossible to achieve without looking as though she were entangled in the contents of a tailor's shop. Perhaps she would never learn to do it herself.

As Lilian left her bungalow, Harshad had expressed his approval, bowing deeply and murmuring something that sounded like 'bloody beautiful, memsahib,' as he helped her into the palanquin that was to take her to the river.

Mr Vine, however, did not echo those sentiments. 'Mrs Fraser,' he stuttered. 'Are you . . . I mean to say, you are not intending to . . . that is, how can you possibly think this form of dress is appropriate?'

'Exactly my own words, Mr Vine,' said Mrs Birchwoode in an undertone. 'But short of abandoning the trip (and so many preparations have been made), or sending her back home (and we cannot *force* her to go) what can be done?'

'Oh, leave her alone,' said Captain Forbes. 'She looks the part.'

'Yes,' said Mr Hunter, giving Captain Forbes an irritated glance. 'Mrs Fraser looks quite delightful. If you ask me, it's most sensible. I can't think why you ladies don't all do it. You must have terrible prickly heat.'

'Perhaps the point, sir,' said Dr Mossly, 'is that no one *did* ask you, as far as I am aware.'

'Are we going, or shall we stand here all day and stare at Mrs Fraser in her nautch-girl costume?' said Captain Forbes.

'I'm quite happy to stare at Mrs Fraser,' said Captain Wheeler. 'She looks prettier than any nautch-girl I've ever seen.'

'Shut up, Wheeler,' said Captain Forbes and he gave Lilian another admiring glance – much to the annoyance of Mr Hunter.

The journey was to be made by water – such a voyage proving to be faster, and without the inconvenience to throats, eyes and clothing occasioned by the clouds of dust that rose from beneath the wheels of vehicles or the feet of bearers. The band of cut-throats Mr Vine had hired to man the vessel looked as though they would be just as likely to rob their passengers and toss them overboard as transport them to their desired destination, though they hauled on ropes and heaved on the tiller willingly enough. The Magistrate shouted shrilly at the leader of the group – a burly, dark-skinned individual with an eyepatch whom Lilian was almost certain she had seen insensible with arrack in the bazaar not two nights earlier. The man ignored Mr Vine (which did not go unnoticed by certain of the Europeans), but bellowed a command of his own as the boat lurched away from the river bank and into the brown waters.

'How exciting!' squealed Miss Bell as a herd of elephants swam down the river, driven past the vessel and on towards Kushpur by a team of mahouts. 'Did you ever see such a thing?' The mahouts held on to the tails of their beasts with one hand, shouting and whisking their switches in the air with the other. The boat swayed and heaved in the roiling waters. Mrs Birchwoode's vast bulk shifted sideways, pinning Lilian securely against Mr Hunter as a frigate might pin a coil of rope to the dockside. Mrs Birchwoode did not seem to notice. She had turned her head away from Lilian, and away from the sight of the half-naked mahouts bobbing in the chocolaty water, and was speaking loudly to Miss Bell about how she had met Lord Canning at a ball at the Calcutta Residency. Mr Vine rubbed eau de Cologne on his temples. Lilian watched as the elephants struggled out of the water on the opposite bank. Mr Hunter slid his hand along the bench where they sat, his fingers hidden beneath the folds of her sari, and squeezed her hand.

The boat made its way slowly up the river. Mr Vine sat in silence, his brow moist with sweat. Although he knew he should try to avert his eyes from Lilian in her delicious native costume, the truth was that he found he was unable to keep from doing so. In the end he abandoned all pretence and allowed his gaze to remain fixed covetously on her. Beside him, Dr Mossly smiled and nodded almost continually, in the hope that Lilian would eventually notice these movements, and might smile and nod in return. Mrs Birchwoode was lecturing Miss Bell on how to show off her face and figure in order to catch herself a husband. Miss Bell's face turned pinker the louder and more indiscreet Mrs Birchwoode's remarks became, until Mr Birchwoode (who appeared to be selectively deaf to his wife's voice) at last stirred himself to interrupt her by pointing out a group of sepoys lounging on the river bank. The soldiers were staring directly at them.

'Can they not see who we are?' said Captain Lewis after a moment. He stood up, in case the sepoys should be in any doubt as to what such pale faces and such red uniforms might represent. The sepoys remained where they were, sitting and squatting on the ground. Captain Wheeler and Captain Forbes also stood up. The sepoys watched with burning eyes as the boat passed. Eventually, some of them struggled to their feet. Half of their number saluted; one or two of them with their left hands. Captain Lewis's face turned thunderous at such an insult, and he was all for putting ashore and taking his sword to the miscreants. Holding on to a rope end, he leaped precariously on to the side of the boat, waving his sabre and shouting bloodthirsty curses. A distressed murmuring broke out among the ladies.

'Such insolence,' said Captain Wheeler. He joined Captain Lewis at the side of the boat (though he was too indolent to leap up beside him) and spat into the water.

'There's nothing we can do,' said Captain Forbes. 'They'll be out of sight behind a bend in the river in a moment, and you'll never see them again. Besides, you'll only alarm the ladies if you carry on.'

'Don't you know what this uniform should mean to those fellows?' snapped Captain Lewis.

'Of course I do,' said Captain Forbes, looking at the civilians on either side of him. 'But you'll have to leave it.'

Captain Lewis and Captain Wheeler subsided. After all, there was champagne in the hampers and pretty girls to talk to – the same pretty girls whose faces were now flushed with excitement at the display of soldierly bravado they had just witnessed. The officers returned to their seats.

'Miss Forbes,' said Captain Wheeler gallantly, 'your brother tells me that he used to call you "Tibby" when you were a child. Can you tell us why?' And the incident was forgotten, carried away on a flurry of chaste giggling from Miss Forbes and Miss Bell, and a gale of manly laughter.

The gardens had once belonged to the rajah of Khinsamaghar. His inability to produce a direct heir, however, meant that on his death his entire personal fortune had been redirected into the coffers of the Honourable East India Company.

'How else would peace have been maintained in the region?' remarked the Magistrate as they berthed at the ghat below the palace and gardens. 'The Doctrine of Lapse is disliked by the nabobs, but that's only because they can't see the benefits.'

'And what happened to the rani?' said Lilian. 'After her husband died?'

'She receives a pension of some sort, I believe,' replied the Magistrate. 'She had an adopted son whom she tried to put forward, but the claim was not tenable under the terms of the Doctrine.'

'Come, come, old chap,' said Mr Ravelston, eyeing the rump of his disembarking niece as it swayed before his eyes. 'Just forget the politics, can't you? Everyone's happy enough.'

'How delightful,' cried Mrs Toomey. The gardens were spread out before them like a regimented Eden. An artificial stream burbled down a gleaming conduit between terraces bursting with colour. Clumps of bushes and low, clipped hedges marked out a gravel pathway leading away from the river and into the rhododendron bushes. 'I don't think we've had an outing like this since, well, since . . .' Her smile froze.

Everyone looked at Lilian for signs of feminine weakness – a moist eye perhaps, a trembling lip; a pale cheek, at least.

'Well, well,' said Dr Mossly heartily, after a moment. 'I doubt that any tigers ever find their way into this place.' He gave Lilian a concerned look. 'Mrs Fraser, would you like to sit down?'

'I've been sitting down since we left Kushpur,' retorted

Lilian. 'I don't need to sit down every time someone says the word "tiger" you know.'

The other members of the party were already making their way into the garden, the ladies sheltering under parasols or large umbrella-like canopies carried by bearers. Behind them, more bearers toiled up the slope, their backs bent beneath the weight of several hampers generously filled with food and drink.

'Does the Company maintain these gardens?' asked Lilian. Why had she never come here before? It was no more than a day's ride away. She was certain she would have remembered if Harshad had said something about them. Or Mr Hunter. Perhaps the superintendent would be interested in acquiring some of her paintings.

'Yes.' Mr Hunter spoke before Mr Vine could answer. 'Various species are collected from all over India and brought here for cultivation. Some fail, but many succeed. It provides the basis for the cultivation of new crops – indigo, hemp, mahogany, tea.'

'And you have collected species for this garden?'

'Not this one,' said Mr Hunter briskly. A misunderstanding between himself and the wife of the garden's superintendent had ensured that he had not been employed to provide specimens for the Company's gardens at Khinsamaghar, but he was not about to share this information with Lilian. 'Though I've collected many species for the Calcutta gardens. And Kew, of course, as well as for private collections like your father's.'

'And you will be off again on another trip soon, I understand?' said Dr Mossly with a smile.

'Yes. Quite soon.'

'When, exactly?' Dr Mossly's smile became fixed.

'Soon.'

'Do you need any help with your preparations for departure? My assistant in the hospital is not too busy just now. Perhaps I should send him over?'

'You had better go before the rains, had you not?' interjected Mrs Birchwoode. 'While the weather is not too hot. Before the middle of April would be advisable.'

'Good heavens, Libby,' cried Mr Birchwoode, 'anyone would think you were trying to get rid of the fellow.'

'Shall we settle ourselves beneath that tree?' said Mr Hunter, pointing towards the only visible shade in the garden. He offered his arm to Miss Bell. He was wearing his riding boots and his new calfskin breeches. So what, if he was holding the arm of another young lady? Perhaps it was time Lilian realised that she was not the only pretty girl in Kushpur.

Miss Bell threw Mrs Birchwoode a fearful look. She accepted Mr Hunter's arm as though he had offered her a dead carp to lay her hand on, though Mr Hunter was too busy looking at Lilian to notice. Lilian, however, had taken Dr Mossly's arm. She was pointing out the cathedral arches of the banyan tree, and appeared unmoved by the sight of Mr Hunter's manly thighs and well-cut breeches.

'How hot it is.' Mrs Ravelston sighed.

The party made its way towards the shade of the banyan tree. The Europeans stood by and watched as the bearers unpacked the numerous hampers and spread the contents on white linen cloths on the ground.

'What tree did you say this was?' said Miss Bell, forgetting, for a moment, that she was not supposed to be talking to the disreputable Mr Hunter. 'And what are these pole-like things? Are they holding it up?'

'It's a banyan tree. A sort of fig tree, actually, sacred to the Hindus. And to Buddhists. They say it represents immortality. Those "poles", as you call them, are special roots that grow from the branches to support the canopy. They act as props as the tree gets wider. As a result, the banyan tree seems to live for ever, because it just keeps on growing and putting down these roots like stilts as it goes. In Sanskrit the tree is called bahupada, which means "one with many feet". There are all sorts of stories about the banyan tree, you know. The natives believe it offers a home to tree spirits called yakshas, and half-human half-animal gods called kinnaras. And, of course, they will also tell you that there are celestial musicians living in its branches. As you can imagine, with all these mythical creatures and suchlike living up there, it's considered very bad luck to cut down a banyan tree.'

Miss Bell watched greedily as a bearer lifted an enormous game pie and two bottles of claret from a wicker basket.

'There's a statue of the Buddha,' said Lilian, pointing through the forest of banyan roots. 'And there's a peepul tree just behind. The Hindus say the peepul is the marriage partner of the banyan. The female to the banyan's male. They say these trees should be planted together, with a ceremony like marriage taking place to celebrate their union.'

'Whatever will they think of next?' said Dr Mossly. And everyone laughed and turned their attention to the feast before them.

Captain Wheeler proposed a game of hide and seek. 'The ladies can hide, the gentlemen can seek. What do you say?'

There were empty bottles here and there among the refuse of the picnic. The conversation had got louder, the laughter more ungoverned as the afternoon had passed. Mr Toomey was wearing Mrs Ravelston's hat. Mrs Birchwoode was purple with laughter at the sight. Mrs Toomey had picked some flowers and entwined them in Mr Birchwoode's beard.

'He looks like a character from *A Midsummer Night's Dream*,' shrieked Mrs Ravelston.

'Bottom!' cried Mr Ravelston and he reached over to tickle his niece as everyone shouted with laughter.

Dr Mossly had fallen asleep, his mouth wide open. Mr Vine, usually so restrained, had allowed his disappointment at having to share this excursion with so many others to erode his self-discipline, so that his teeth were exposed in a port-stained smile. Generally unfamiliar with moderation, the officers had soon become boisterous. Captain Lewis had challenged his fellow officers to hold geranium stems between their teeth, boasting that he could use his sword to lop the flowers off them blindfolded. Captain Forbes had ended up with a bleeding ear and Captain Wheeler had refused, so that the others had set upon him to make him eat a geranium . . . The ladies squealed as Captain Wheeler was wrestled to the ground. The bearers looked on impassively.

'So what about it?' said Captain Wheeler, spitting geranium petals. 'Us chaps will count to twenty, and you ladies run away and hide. We'll flush you out like hounds in a rabbit warren.' And he threw back his head and howled like a dog, so that everyone laughed again.

Mrs Birchwoode was dragged to her feet by Miss Bell and Mrs Toomey.

'Get along, Libby,' shouted her husband. 'We've already counted to five.'

Lilian followed Mrs Birchwoode and Mrs Toomey through the perpendicular roots of the banyan tree. The men had counted to twelve. Mrs Birchwoode slumped against the statue of Buddha. Mrs Toomey, unwilling to leave her friend, dodged behind the wide shiny trunk of the peepul tree. Lilian left them both, hastening on and emerging into the brightness of the afternoon. She took a deep breath. What a relief it was to get away, even if it was for only a few minutes. Perhaps she should just keep on running and never stop. Somewhere ahead she could hear the sound of water tumbling over rocks, somewhere behind Captain Wheeler bellowing that the gentlemen were coming, 'ready or not!' To her left the shining greenery of a vast rhododendron swept gracefully to the ground, its leaves crowned over and over again by huge crimson flowers. Lilian plunged into it, fighting her way through its heavy, low-slung branches.

As the foliage closed behind her she heard footsteps coming

up the path, accompanied by the sound of laboured breathing. Lilian watched Miss Bell hurry past, her hand to her side where her corset was tightest. Her bonnet was crooked on her head and her cheeks were red. Miss Bell stopped for a moment and looked back the way she had come. She fumbled in her pocket and produced a handkerchief, which she laid purposefully on the ground in the middle of the path. In the distance, Lilian could make out the red of an officer's coat as he made his way rapidly through the banyan tree in their direction. Looking over her shoulder, Miss Bell started at the sight. Her button-sided boots skittered on the pathway, and with a rustle of crinoline and a gasp of 'Oh!' she was gone.

A minute later Captain Wheeler raced up, following Miss Bell like a greyhound after a hare. He seized the handkerchief and examined the initials. He sniffed at it and gave a howl like a dog, an action that elicited a fit of giggling from somewhere not far ahead.

But now more footsteps were approaching. A lavish but unproductive clearing of a throat told Lilian that it was Mr Vine. She remained out of sight where she was and, sure enough, a moment later the Magistrate appeared. Lilian held her breath. Would he pass by? But no. Mr Vine had stopped. He was looking about for any likely hiding places and his eyes lingered on the rhododendron bush for so long that it seemed as though he was staring straight at her.

At that moment a twig snapped. Lilian half turned, but a man's arms were about her waist and holding her tightly before she could say or do anything. Mr Hunter pressed his lips to her ear and whispered, 'You had better not shout out, unless you want Mr Vine to take my place.' And then his mouth was upon hers, so that she couldn't have called out even if she had wanted to.

For a moment Lilian was furious. How arrogant he was. Why had she never noticed this characteristic when he was at her father's house? After all, Alice had pointed it out to her on countless occasions. But she had not listened, so convinced had she been that he was in love with her. And why would she not be convinced? Had he not told her so often enough? What liars men were.

Yet now was not the time to be angry, said a voice in her head. She must stay in control of the situation, no matter what happened. Lilian relaxed into his arms. All would be well, she reminded herself. This time she would be nobody's fool. Besides, Mr Hunter was without doubt an attractive man and a most interesting companion. She returned his kiss, and his embrace, with apparent enthusiasm.

Over Lilian's shoulder, through a chink in the rhododendron's armoured foliage, Mr Hunter saw Mr Vine cock his head, listening. He mopped his brow again and fanned his face unenthusiastically with his handkerchief. Within the rhododendron Mr Hunter kissed Lilian's neck. She gasped as he squeezed her left breast through the thin fabric of her choli and, taking advantage of the looseness of her sari, slid his fingers between her legs. Lilian bit his ear. Mr Hunter winced. Mr Vine, on the brink of moving on, hesitated. He looked closely at the rhododendron once again.

'Mrs Fraser?' he said hopefully. 'Mrs Fraser?'

Lilian and Mr Hunter stood in silence, their arms about each other. Mr Hunter kissed her again, greedily and with confidence, despite Mr Vine's proximity. He pressed her (with some difficulty due to the arrangement of the branches) against the trunk of the rhododendron.

'Mrs Fraser?' hissed Mr Vine, sounding suddenly urgent. 'Is that you?'

'Is she there, George?' said another voice. Lilian recognised the apologetic tones of Dr Mossly. 'Mrs Fraser, are you in there?' the Doctor shouted. 'Come out. The game's up.' He listened for a moment. Then, 'I think you must be mistaken.'

Within the rhododendron Mr Hunter parted Lilian's legs

with his knee. 'Marry me,' he whispered in her ear. 'Marry me and come away with me. Away from Kushpur and all these dreadful people.' He kissed her once more, so that she was not able to answer at first, and pinched her nipple with his thumb. Lilian gasped. Mr Hunter gave her buttock a friendly squeeze. Mistaking silence for acquiescence, he began to undo his breeches. His blood was roaring in his ears, his hands shaking with excitement; he could think of nothing but what was about to take place. He had waited so long, had not seen a bazaar prostitute for weeks, so intent was he on gaining his prize. And now he was about to claim it, those two old fools would not leave them alone. He was almost of a mind to shout out, to tell them to go away and let him make love to her in peace. But then all at once Lilian disentangled herself from his embrace and, like a wisp of smoke on the breeze, slipped past him (he had no idea how she managed it, as suddenly there seemed to be branches everywhere). He tried to stop her, tried to catch hold of her, but his breeches had fallen about his ankles in cloth fetters and he succeeded only in tottering in a circle like a mechanical toy before crashing backwards among the leaf debris in an ungainly sprawl.

'Lily,' he hissed. 'Where are you going?'

'Do you really want to marry me? You must ask me properly,' whispered a voice in his ear. He felt her lips against his own, her tongue darted against his and then she was gone.

'Mr Vine. Mr Mossly. So you have found me,' cried Lilian, emerging dishevelled and breathless from the dark cave of the rhododendron. 'Well done, gentlemen. Now, before we return to the others, I must confess to being most curious to see the water garden. Mr Hunter assures me it is quite the most beautiful sight. Do you think you might be able to show me where it is? I'm sure I can hear the sound of water up ahead.'

Within the bush Mr Hunter staggered to his feet. He dusted ants off his legs and fastened his breeches. How infuriating she was. He watched as she sauntered away with the Magistrate on one arm and the Doctor on the other. He wished he could simply forget about her, as he had once done, but now he knew he could not. She was everything he wanted. Still, he said to himself, he had kissed her; had touched her; had almost made love to her, in fact. He was sure that those were things Mr Vine and Dr Mossly would never do. Mr Hunter sighed dejectedly as Lilian and her companions disappeared from view. He could not help but feel sick with jealousy nonetheless.

4

Mr Hunter went to visit Lilian. His purpose was to tell her that he intended to leave Kushpur, heading north and east into Oudh and from thence to Sikkim, perhaps via Kathmandu. Everything was arranged. The path he would take through the wildest areas of the mofussil, across the plains and over the mountains, would be dangerous, the places he would explore unfamiliar to the majority of Europeans. It was a trip he would make alone, for reconnaissance purposes; after all, there would be no point in dragging a team of porters all the way to Kathmandu and beyond if the local nawabs would not even let him pass through their territories. Once he had established that such a venture could be successful, he would return with a full expedition the following spring. All he needed was a horse and a mule to carry his camp items. And Lilian.

His mouth was dry as he crossed the compound to Lilian's bungalow. This was not because he was in any way nervous about the journey he intended to make – after all, he had travelled up the country and back many times. No, his mouth was dry because he had resolved to ask Lilian whether she would accompany him on his travels as his wife. He had rehearsed his speech many times. He would get down on his knees. He would hold her hand and not let it go until she had given him an answer. He would beg her forgiveness again and again for abandoning her in England . . . but no, perhaps it would be better if he didn't mention that, a most perfidious action on his part but one which, so it seemed to him, she had already forgotten. Surely to remind her of his selfishness and treachery would be a mistake. And anyway, he said to himself, his proposal of marriage would wipe out any suggestion of dubious conduct in the past.

Whether Lilian agreed to marry him or not, however, Mr Hunter was now committed to leaving Kushpur. He had begun to grow the beard he would need to complete his transformation back into the badmash he had resembled when Lilian first met him in the bazaar. As a result, his cheeks were already covered with a dense crop of black stubble. He rubbed his fingers across this bristly excrescence as he mounted Lilian's veranda. He was now so nervous that he could hardly remember what he had intended to say.

Mr Hunter was ushered into Lilian's parlour. When he stepped past Harshad he found that he was not alone. He felt his face redden with disappointment and annoyance as he was obliged to greet Mrs Birchwoode, Mrs Toomey, Mrs Ravelston and their husbands; Miss Forbes and Miss Bell (both ladies gasped at his appearance and took each other's hands); Dr Mossly and Mr Vine; and Captains Forbes, Wheeler and Lewis from the barracks. In fact, such was the number of visitors that Mr Hunter could find nowhere to sit and was obliged to stand beside the hookah, as though he were one of the bearers. He eyed the pipe hungrily. How he wished he could have a puff. He wondered where Lilian was.

'Apparently, Mrs Fraser is getting changed,' Mrs Birchwoode informed him, as though reading his mind. 'So this Harshad chap tells me.'

'Was she wearing those breeches again?' said Captain

Wheeler. He had come along to witness what he hoped would be an entertaining diversion from his usual routine of marching sepoys up and down the parade ground in the sun, or lounging with his fellow officers in the barracks. He grinned at Captain Forbes and Captain Lewis.

Mrs Birchwoode tut-tutted. 'Quite possibly. She is quite out of control since her husband died.'

The punkah swished back and forth overhead, causing the ostrich feathers in Mrs Birchwoode's headdress to tremble like the feelers on some gigantic insect. 'You are no doubt wondering why we are here, Mr Hunter. Clearly, we are here to tell Mrs Fraser that her behaviour simply cannot, *must not*, continue. The Magistrate has procured for her a berth Home. From Calcutta. It will be for the best if she takes it. The sun, the heat, grief at loosing one's spouse, all these things can make people behave in the oddest of ways. We have seen it all before. Our own Mr Gilmour, the previous resident of this very bungalow . . .'

Mr Hunter sighed and reached for the hookah pipe. What did it matter what these people thought of him now? He motioned to the bearer to light it. 'You know, I do prefer the way they prepare the tobacco up-country. The tobacco in Calcutta is quite bland in comparison.' He put the pipe to his lips. The jar bubbled.

'The point is, Mr Hunter,' said Mrs Birchwoode, 'the point is that one cannot *become* native. I'm not sure that Mrs Fraser understands this. I'm not sure that *you* understand this. Have you not heard of the unrest at Barrackpore? Such insolence only occurs when the native thinks he can get away with it. When he thinks we are not his master. But we *are* their masters, Mr Hunter. We are most certainly *not* their friends. Surely you, with your extensive experience of India, can see that, even if Mrs Fraser, who has spent less than two years in the country and is thus little more than a griffin, cannot.'

'The unrest at Barrackpore will come to nothing,' said Mr

Vine. 'Just a couple of sepoys inflamed with bhang, no more than that. The perpetrators were dealt with, I understand. That'll be an end to it.'

'What unrest?' said Miss Bell. Having been in Kushpur for less than a year, and thus more of a griffin than anyone else, she had no idea what Mrs Birchwoode or Mr Vine were talking about. But she remembered stopping at Barrackpore on her way up-country from Calcutta. The place had seemed uneventful enough. 'What happened?'

'A sepoy attacked a British sergeant,' said Captain Lewis. 'The fellow was almost certainly intoxicated. They hanged the blighter, along with that insubordinate jemadar who refused to arrest him. The whole of the Bengal Native Infantry was sacked to punish the lot of 'em. Deserved all they got, if you ask me. They should just bite the cartridge like anyone else and have done with it.'

'"Bite the cartridge"?' Miss Bell looked in bewilderment from Captain Lewis to Captain Forbes.

'We were issued with new rifles. Dashed fine mechanism, but you have to tear the cartridge with your teeth to open it,' said Captain Lewis, 'to pour the powder in. Then you ram the ball and empty cartridge paper down on top. The paper has to be greased – beef or pig fat – to get it down the barrel.'

'There were fires in Agra and Allahabad too,' interrupted Mr Toomey. 'Seems the unrest spread a little further than the Bengal parade ground, eh?'

'Allahabad? That's not far from here, is it?' said Miss Bell.

'"Not far"?' said Captain Lewis. 'That's like saying London is not far from Liverpool. Allahabad is a long way from here.'

'It's an even greater distance from Barrackpore to Allahabad, but the trouble spread from one to the other in under a week,' said Captain Forbes. 'The army should never have introduced those cartridges. Asking a Hindu, or a Moslem, to touch his lips to beef or pig fat – they could only take it as an insult. I said as much at the time. We'd be wise to watch out.'

'They got rid of the beef fat. Changed it to beeswax, or something. Besides, they were told to use their hands, not their teeth. The sepoys have nothing to complain about,' drawled Captain Wheeler.

'Is that so?' said Mr Hunter.

'Well, we all know where *you* stand,' retorted Mr Vine.

'There's more to this trouble than greased cartridges,' said Mr Hunter. 'Anyone who listens to what's being said in the bazaar or the barrack rooms would know that.'

'Native tittle-tattle,' stated Mr Toomey.

'The sepoys are dissatisfied,' said Mr Hunter. 'Their pay is poor, they have to fight their fellow countrymen. The military command shows no respect for caste. And as for the officers, I don't know what the Company is thinking, sending such a rabble of Whitechapel guttersnipes to lord it over high-caste Hindu men; men whose buttons they are not fit to polish.'

Captains Wheeler and Lewis leaped to their feet, their faces red. But Captain Forbes was nodding gloomily. 'He's right, some of those Company officers are quite the worst kind.'

'Good God, Forbes,' said Captain Lewis. 'Who *have* you been listening to?'

'And have you heard what Rutherford is up to these days?' Captain Forbes shook his head. 'It's a mistake.'

'Exactly,' cried Mr Hunter, 'men like Rutherford insist on trying to convert everyone. No one's seen him for months. And why is that? Because he's always at the barracks and the parade ground trying to save souls. Doesn't he see it? The Hindus don't want to be saved. Neither do the Moslems. They don't want to be Christians. Why not just leave them alone?'

'Oh, no,' said Dr Mossly. 'The Lord's work is *never* done –'

'But Hunter's *right*,' cried Captain Forbes.

'What rot you're talking, Hunter!' interrupted Captain Lewis. 'And you too, Forbes, I can't think what's got into you. The native infantry is completely loyal to the Sircar. They don't know any different –'

'But your own Captain Forbes agrees,' snapped Mr Hunter. 'It's a pity there aren't a few more who think like him. It might do your regiment some credit.' Captains Wheeler and Lewis glared at the visibly pale Captain Forbes. 'Besides,' continued Mr Hunter, 'it's not just the sepoys, is it? Look at the nabobs. They're not happy either – you can't change their laws, take their land and their taxes, and expect them to be pleased about it.' He shook his head. Would no one listen to him? Could no one but he see what was happening? 'The native infantry could ignite the whole country in two minutes but Anson and his like down in Calcutta are too blind and ignorant, too arrogant, to see the trouble coming.'

'Trouble?' whispered Miss Bell. 'Is it serious?'

'No,' shouted Captain Lewis and Captain Wheeler together. Captain Forbes shifted his feet uneasily.

Mr Vine cleared his throat. 'There's nothing to worry about at all, my dear.' He blinked at the bearer standing, unmoving, beside the door; at the punkah wallah sitting outside on the veranda, silently pulling his rope; at the meekly lowered eyes of the ayah Mrs Birchwoode had brought with her to arrange her dress and operate her personal fan. Everything was in its place and as it ought to be. These incidents on the parade ground were nothing. The army command said so themselves. Surely they should know? And besides, Captain Forbes hadn't even *been* to Barrackpore . . .

'Stuff and nonsense,' said Mrs Birchwoode briskly. With an irritated tug she removed the hem of her skirt from where it had become trapped beneath Mr Toomey's boot heel. 'One mustn't pay any attention to these tiffs among the natives. They're too lazy to have a real fight about anything. Why, Mr Birchwoode has found the bearers to be more idle that ever these last few months. One of them even left some chapattis on his desk yesterday. Just lying there in the middle of his salt reports.'

'I found some on the floor of the kutcherry,' said Mr Vine. 'Covered in ants.'

'What! Why didn't you say anything?' said Mr Hunter, looking genuinely alarmed. 'The passing of cakes signifies coming unrest.'

Mr Vine exchanged glances with Mr Ravelston and Dr Mossly.

'How rude of Mrs Fraser to leave us all waiting like this,' trumpeted Mrs Birchwoode. 'I've had quite enough. Mr Vine, be sure to tell Mrs Fraser plainly: she must become a memsahib or she must go Home. Brook no argument.' Her hips heaved against the Magistrate as she negotiated her way past a bronze statue of Shiva (a new addition to the room since Mrs Birchwoode's last visit). The other ladies gathered themselves together to follow. Like a man-of-war leading a flotilla of tugboats, Mrs Birchwoode led the exodus from Lilian's parlour.

In a few moments only Mr Vine, Dr Mossly and Mr Hunter remained. Mr Hunter subsided on to the settee vacated by Mrs Ravelston and put the hookah pipe to his lips. He looked at the door. Where on earth was Lilian? He eyed Mr Vine and Dr Mossly. If only these ridiculous fellows would go away.

'I think it only fair to tell you that I intend to ask Mrs Fraser to be my wife,' said Dr Mossly suddenly. 'I have admired her for many months and her dedicated work in the hospital has led me to believe that I have some hope of success.'

'What?' exploded Mr Hunter. He sat forward. He stared in disbelief at the small, tubby man standing beside the mantelpiece. Then he laughed and sat back again. He stretched out his long legs and crossed his ankles. 'Do you really?'

'Yes,' said Dr Mossly. His face had turned scarlet. 'My work among the native poor has endeared me to her, I am sure.'

'But I intend to take her back to England,' interjected the Magistrate. 'Her berth is secured. I myself will take her to Calcutta and ensure her safe passage. I had hoped that I might take that opportunity to make her *my* wife. There is something of an understanding between us –'

'An understanding?' spluttered Mr Hunter. 'Are you out of your mind?'

'My dear Mr Hunter. I know you consider yourself to have a special friendship with Mrs Fraser, occasioned by the fact that you and she were acquainted back Home, but I can assure you that her affection for you is that of a friend and well-wisher, and no more. She has assured me of this on more than one occasion.'

'Mr Vine, you cannot return to England. You are needed here,' cried Dr Mossly. 'Mrs Fraser need not return Home, unless she wishes it, in which case she can return with me. I have no doubt that she would rather stay in India, offering succour in the hospital with me by her side.'

'But you said yourself that she should return Home, for the sake of her health,' cried the Magistrate.

'It is a possibility, yes. But only if my petition fails. And only if she wishes it.'

'I'm sure it will fail,' boomed Mr Vine. 'She understands my intentions fully.'

'I know what we can do,' said Mr Hunter. 'Something you seem not to have thought about, but which will be sure to resolve the matter. Let's ask her, shall we? Let's ask her whom she would like to marry. Will she return to England with you, Vine? Will she work with you in the hospital, Dr Mossly? Or will she come north with me on horseback as *my* wife? Let's see what her answer is.' He rose to his feet. He didn't have to look in the mirror over the fireplace to see how his swarthy good looks and tall muscular bearing outshone these two men, one fat and pale, the other lean and wolfish. 'Harshad? Harshad! Tell Mrs Fraser we are waiting for her. Tell her Mr Hunter is here. With Mr Vine and Dr Mossly. Tell her to stop hiding in her room and come through at once. We have something important to ask her.'

ALICE

1

Mr Talbot stormed down the main hallway of the Great House, the eye of a stuffed beaver glinting hungrily in the light of his candle as he passed. In his haste, he stumbled over some unseen obstruction, banging his thigh on a display case filled with nautical instruments and grazing his knuckles on a model of the harbour on the Isle of Wight made entirely out of seashells. He cursed his own domestic economy, now that the lack of lighting in the house was causing him inconvenience. Had he passed the stairs yet? Disorientated by the crowded darkness, his route illuminated only by a dim bubble of candlelight, he could not be sure. Mr Talbot cursed once more and retraced his steps.

At length he found a flight of stairs. The thick glass face of a brass diving helmet winked knowingly at him. He climbed briskly, his face livid, his cheeks puffing like bellows. Alice's room was up here somewhere, though which door was hers he had no idea. He crept forward, his bulky frame crouched bizarrely and balanced on the tips of his toes. At each door he stopped and listened. The whole of this hallway was occupied by his female family members (he had relocated his own chambers to the other side of the Great House years ago, choosing manly isolation in a distant wing over the company of his elderly relatives) and he had no wish to find himself standing in his mother's chamber or, worse, his Aunt

Lambert's. But it was no use. He had no idea behind which door his daughter might be found. His face, in the candle-light, turned crimson with irritation. How undignified to be creeping about one's own house listening at doors.

'Alice,' he bellowed suddenly. 'Where are you? I know you aren't sleeping. Alice? *Alice*!' He waited. There was a rustling sound and a door opened on his left.

From inside her bedchamber, Alice had heard her father's whistling breath and heavy tread, despite the fact that he had tried to make his advance along the aunts' hallway as noiseless as possible. Through the keyhole she had seen him stop and listen. Now, she threw a shawl over her hastily donned night-gown and opened her door.

'What is it, Father?' she whispered. 'You'll wake everyone up if you shout like that.' She looked him up and down. Even in the feeble light of his shaking candle she could see that he was furious – his hair standing up like a chimney sweep's brush, his face black with rage. She had not seen him so incensed since Lilian left. Her scalp prickled with alarm. She tried to keep her voice calm when she spoke.

'Is something the matter?' She noticed that he seemed to be carrying a heavy item in his right hand, but she could not quite see what it was.

'Yes,' he cried. 'You shame me. You and your sister. You shame me and you shame this house. You shame your mother, God rest her soul and I thank Him that she is not here to see her daughter's ignominy.' With a flourish, he thrust into Alice's face the item he had been carrying. She found herself staring at her father's newly acquired brass and ivory binoculars. Her mouth felt as dry as a glove.

'Strumpet!' he cried.

She flinched as if he had struck her, though her reflex was, in fact, due to the flecks of spittle landing on her cheeks and nose.

'Whatever do you mean, Father?' she said, resisting the urge to wipe a hand across her face.

'You were in his room. In Mr Blake's room. Do not deny it. I saw you with my own eyes.'

Alice glanced casually at the binoculars. 'You are mistaken, I assure you.'

'Mistaken? I don't think so. My study window is *directly* opposite Mr Blake's. I saw you enter his bedchamber. I saw you . . . I saw you . . . *unclothed*. Why, it was only the fact that Mr Blake is an honourable man, a man who refused your most lewd advances, that has prevented you from being as *dishonoured* as your sister.'

Her father was bawling now, his purple face inches from her own, so that she could smell the sour reek of brandy and cigars on his breath. From either side of her Alice heard the welcome sound of doors opening, though she did not take her eyes from her father's face to see which of her aunts had emerged.

'Alice?' said Aunt Lambert's imperious voice. 'What's going on? Edwin! What brings you here at this time of night?'

'I saw Alice, my own daughter, entering a gentleman's room alone,' declared Mr Talbot with a sweep of his binocular-holding hand. 'She then proceeded to stand naked before him. *Offering* herself. Like a prostitute.'

'You must be mistaken,' said Aunt Lambert.

'I am not in any way mistaken,' shouted Mr Talbot.

'How can you be sure?' asked Aunt Rushton-Bell.

'Do you really think Alice would do such a thing?' said Aunt Statham.

'Did you actually see her?' demanded Aunt Pendleton. 'With your own eyes?'

'Such a terrible charge,' murmured Old Mrs Talbot. 'Edwin, you cannot be correct, surely.'

Mr Talbot opened his mouth. He closed it again. His eyes bulged, as though his rage and impotence were suffocating him like a scarf tightly wound about his throat. A ring of disbelieving elderly faces crowded around him, their expressions accusing in the candlelight. Mr Talbot took a step back.

'Well?' said Aunt Lambert.

'Well what?' Mr Talbot bellowed.

Corralled by his aged aunts, Mr Talbot seemed suddenly to realise that this confrontation in the dead of night was a mistake. His gaze flickered from one reproachful face to another and he looked longingly over their shoulders into the darkness, as though hoping for the emergence of an unseen supporter, or at least for the chance to break through their ranks, to head back to his own reassuringly tobacco-scented rooms – should he be able to remember in which direction lay the stairs.

'Did you actually see her?'

Mr Talbot shoved his binoculars into Aunt Lambert's face. 'What do you think these are?' he shouted, as though the possession of such an instrument were utterly decisive.

'I have no idea,' said Aunt Lambert.

'Binoculars.'

'And they do what, exactly?'

'They allow me to see in through the window of Mr Blake's room.'

'But his curtains would surely be closed, especially on so cold a night,' said Aunt Pendleton gently.

'His curtains were open.'

'And was your view of this "event" entirely unobstructed?' asked Aunt Lambert.

'There was no obstruction. I saw Alice standing in Mr Blake's room. She was unclothed. Completely.'

'And she did – what?'

'Nothing.'

'She just stood there?'

'Like a statue.'

'Did she not move at all while she was, as you describe it, *exhibiting* herself?'

'She did not. What does it matter whether she moved or not?' He sounded exasperated. 'She was there and that is that. I did not see what happened next. I dropped my binoculars. They are, after all, rather unwieldy due to their length, and the quality of the materials used in their construction makes them heavy. I was also most perturbed . . . shocked . . . *enraged* by what I had just seen. They slipped from my fingers. I then made my way as quickly as I could through the house to confront her. I would have been here sooner, would have caught her out of her room, if I had not become confused in the darkness.'

'So your view was, in fact, no more than a glimpse?'

'I saw her in there.'

'But for only an instant and she was not moving.'

'I saw her, I tell you. I know my own daughter.'

'Without her clothes on? I doubt you do, Edwin.'

'She was there,' yelled Mr Talbot.

'And Mr Blake,' said Aunt Lambert. 'What did he do?'

'Mr Blake is beyond reproach. He looked away from her and shook his head, from what I could see.'

'Which appears to be very little,' said Aunt Lambert irritably. She turned to her nephew with a flourish. 'Edwin, is it not true that Mr Blake's chamber contains a number of items of the Collection?'

'Yes, but . . .'

'Any number of which must surely have obstructed your view through the window from your own rooms on the other side of the house?'

'My dear Aunt –'

'Is not the window partly obscured by a model of the Clifton Suspension Bridge?'

'A little.'

'And is not the adjacent wall furnished with an immense display case containing your most extensive collection of bird's eggs?'

'It is, but . . .'

'Could not this also have limited your view of the goings-on in Mr Blake's room? Is not a rampant grizzly resident also?'

'That is the case –'

'And, most significantly,' cried Aunt Lambert, 'does not Mr Blake share his room with, among other things, a life-sized replica of Canova's Venus made entirely out of cement?'

'Yes!' roared Mr Talbot.

'Well,' said Aunt Lambert calmly, 'I merely suggest to you that in your enthusiasm for these newfangled "binoculars" you mistook this most fine cement artefact for . . . something else.'

Mr Talbot opened his mouth, but no words came out.

'Mrs Lambert is correct, sir,' said a voice from the shadows. Mrs Talbot jumped and Alice turned to squint into the darkness. Mr Talbot held up his candle. Mr Blake himself stepped forward. 'You may indeed have been a little too hasty in drawing your conclusions. I have shifted the cement statue nearer to the window in order to get the dressing-room door open. I fear you glimpsed this Venus, rather than any other.' He lowered his eyes discreetly. 'I do hope this relocation of certain artefacts has not caused any offence. I can move them back again –'

Mr Talbot grunted. He sounded unconvinced. 'Alice, it seems that I may have been mistaken,' he said after a moment. 'But I shall be watching you.' His voice became a whisper. 'I shall be *watching*.'

2

Mr Talbot continued with his preparations for the evening of entertainments for the Society for the Propagation of Useful and Interesting Knowledge. He decided that the ballroom should be cleared and a new selection of artefacts reintroduced. A podium was to be erected for experiments and a number of chairs set out for the audience. Mr Blake was pressed into service as mover and repositioner, with Sluce as his assistant. Sluce wore his mnemonic coat, its pockets bulging with items to assist him in his recollection of tasks and responsibilities. Periodically, under the despairing gaze of Mr Blake, he would retreat to a corner and reorganise the contents of his pockets according to some design known only to himself. Occasionally he would drift off, a look of perplexity on his face, rummaging among his clothing as though in search of a memory that told him he was needed elsewhere. As a result Sluce was of little or no help and Mr Blake found himself labouring among the Collection with only Mr Talbot for company.

After much prevarication, and after Mr Talbot had repeatedly changed his mind about which objects he wished to display, the task was completed.

'Excellent,' said Mr Talbot. 'The thematic arrangement is similar to that of the Great Exhibition. Indeed, if we had more time we might have emptied the conservatory and held our meeting in there. Still, perhaps next year.' He rubbed his hands together in excitement. 'Now, all that is left to prepare is the artificial volcano – I have the necessary materials arriving any day now. And Cattermole returns at the end of the week. He will be quite delighted with what we have done so far. He is to exhibit some monstrosities from his work in the mortuary. He also intends to present a lecture on his latest work and was hoping to use Alice as his assistant.'

'And has Alice been consulted?' ventured Mr Blake. 'She may not wish to be an assistant.'

'She is my daughter. She will do as I tell her. Besides, Alice herself has always embraced knowledge and learning. She will, no doubt, be fascinated to hear of her own fate in so auspicious a setting as a specially convened meeting of the Society for the Propagation of Useful and Interesting Knowledge.'

'Her fate?' Mr Blake swallowed.

'Why yes. Her condition can be remedied. Cattermole is most definite about that.'

'What condition? What remedy? Sir, I am a medical man myself and I see in her no medical condition that requires a remedy. She is an asset to you, to your household and your Collection.'

'You are very kind and indeed Alice has proved most useful to me in my work among the Collection, but there is much *amiss* with her.' Mr Talbot lowered his voice to a more confidential tone. 'Her sister was of a similar calibre. I allowed her too much licence so that she swiftly moved beyond redemption, but Alice, why, Cattermole assures me that Alice can be saved.'

'And can you tell me what "remedy" Dr Cattermole is proposing?' Mr Blake tried to keep the anxiety out of his voice. 'Indeed, are you quite certain Alice needs to be "saved"?'

Mr Talbot twinkled from beneath the bushy black caterpillars of his brows. 'An enquiring spirit, that's what I like to see in a man.' He pounded Mr Blake on the shoulder. 'You, sir, will have to be patient. Even I do not know what Cattermole's plans are. We must wait, and see, and *learn*.'

While Mr Blake was engaged among the Collection with Mr Talbot, Alice was given the task of sending out invitations to the various members of the Society. Once this minor chore had been completed, her father sent her away. At first she wandered the corridors, hoping that she might come upon Mr Blake about his duties. But Mr Talbot was, for once, as good as his word and wherever she found Mr Blake she found her father, directing the movement of artefacts in a booming voice, or informing Mr Blake of the merits of individual pieces. Even in the evenings Mr Talbot kept the photographer close at hand and fell to taking his meals in his study with only Mr Blake for company. Days passed and Alice found not one single opportunity to speak to the photographer alone. She began to wonder whether she might risk paying him a visit in his rooms, but she noticed Sluce skulking in the shadows. No doubt her father had instructed him to keep watch.

In the end it was Mr Blake who found Alice. She had retreated to the temperate house, to the darkroom in the shed, and was bent over the spirit lamp, moving a glass plate quickly from side to side to coat it with a mixture of ether and gun cotton. She did not hear the door open, but felt a draught of air and saw a beam of shadowy daylight fall on her workbench.

'You are supposed to knock,' she said without looking up. 'Imagine if I had been developing. The image could have been lost.'

'And you would simply have taken another.'

Alice dropped the glass plate in surprise. 'Mr Blake,' she whispered. 'If my father catches you here –'

'I shall be brief,' he said, closing the door softly behind him. He seized her hands, trying not to let his gaze be distracted by the bottle of ether that stood on her workbench. Already the fumes in the darkroom were making him thirst for it, while the heat of the place made his head swim. He blinked and swallowed. In the feeble light of the spirit lamp Alice looked more attractive than he remembered . . . But had he not sought her out in order to communicate some vital intelligence? A buzzing sound had filled his ears and his head seemed suddenly as heavy as lead.

'Alice,' he said, his tone urgent, 'there are no longer any secrets between you and I. You are a woman and that's quite clear. To me, at least. I mean to say, when you came to me in my rooms the other night I was in some doubt. But now, having seen your . . . your . . . sex, if I might be so bold as to call it such, now, as I say, I am not. That is to say, I am not in any doubt. In fact, I am quite certain. You are a woman.' He put out a hand to steady himself. 'There are, of course, aspects of my past behaviour that I would rather change, things I have done, acts I have committed about which I would rather you did not know. But I cannot turn the clock back.' The fumes in the darkroom seemed to be addling his brains, his well-prepared speech turning to gibberish on his tongue. Even as he hesitated he felt his next sentence evaporating from his head before it had made it to his lips. Her expression told him nothing. 'What I mean to say is that perhaps we are now equal. Would you be so kind as to return my photographs? Oh, and are we still to be married?' He lurched towards her. 'I think we should.'

Alice held the photographer at arm's length as he swayed in front of her. With her free hand she reached beneath her workbench, pulling out a small portfolio. She handed it to him. 'Your trunk is in my room,' she said. 'I shall have Sluce take it to you immediately.'

Mr Blake swiped the portfolio out of Alice's outstretched hand as a starving man might seize a slice of bread. He wrenched it open. Two immense sepia nipples stared at him like a pair of accusing eyes. He slammed the portfolio closed, before staggering out of the darkroom into the cool, leafy calm of the temperate house.

Alice poured Mr Blake a glass of water.

'Thank you,' he said at last.

'And I thank you, for your most gallant behaviour towards me when I presented myself in your rooms. And for denying I had done so to my father.'

'He remains convinced about what he saw.'

'He has no proof.'

'He doesn't need any.' Mr Blake sat up. 'Alice, I came to tell you that Cattermole is coming. He has something planned for you, with your father's permission, but I have no idea what it is.'

'Dr Cattermole has always been interested in me. I believe

he also wishes to make me the subject of one of his photographs.'

Mr Blake flinched. 'He does?'

'So his wife tells me. She says that he is most professional and scientific in his approach.'

'You must on no account agree to be photographed by him.'

'Then perhaps I should come with you to London.'

'But I can't go to London. I am to display my photographs of the Collection in bound volumes. I cannot refuse.' He took her hand again. 'I have no money to support a wife and must earn my keep, and yours.'

But Alice did not appear to be listening. 'Of course,' she said. 'When shall we leave?'

'After I have finished my commission here. As soon as your father pays me.'

The following morning a package arrived from Kushpur. Alice could hardly take her eyes off it as she sipped her tea, but she said nothing when her father entered the breakfast room. He had been diligent in checking for correspondence from India, whether it bore Lilian's handwriting or not. More than once he had flourished a torn-open letter beneath her nose, before tossing it on to the fire. Was there a chance that he might overlook a package? She waited in silence, her eyes now fixed intently on the untouched plate before her.

That same morning, however, a team of labourers had arrived from the village to dig a pit in the park at the front of the house. It was this pit which was to act as the crucible for Mr Talbot's artificial volcano and the men were already gathered in the stable yard at the back of the house awaiting instruction. The previous afternoon one and a half tons of sublimed sulphur and a similar quantity of iron filings had arrived, and were now stored in the wash-house near the kitchens. Such was Mr Talbot's excitement at the advancement of his plans that he did not even notice the package addressed to Alice that lay among his post on the breakfast-room sideboard. In fact, part of the reason Mr Talbot overlooked it was because it was not a package, as such, but a tube, which had rolled to the back of the sideboard and was not in his immediate line of vision – especially as he was in a hurry and did not even sit down for breakfast. Alice hardly dared to breathe as her father stalked into the breakfast room, seized his mail and immediately headed back out again to supervise the destruction of the park outside.

'Cattermole is due to arrive this morning,' he bellowed over his shoulder. 'Alice, make sure his rooms are ready. And you might come and see me in my study later this afternoon. I have something I must explain to you.' Without waiting for a reply he was gone.

Alice seized the package as soon as she heard the door to her father's study slam closed. With her aunts gathered around her in a whispering escort, she carried it off to the sanctum of the hot house.

The aunts crowded round as Alice unwrapped the tube-shaped package. It was made of thick card, rolled up and wrapped in some sort of canvas and then sealed at either end with wax. This well-sheathed package had then been covered in brown paper and tightly tied with string. Clearly, whatever was inside, Lilian had been determined to keep safe and dry.

Not wanting to damage the contents, Alice scrabbled ineffectually with her fingernails at the waxy seals. The aunts inched forward. Alice could hear the creak of Aunt Pendleton's stays as she leaned closer.

'Stand back,' cried Alice, reaching for her short-bladed pruning knife.

The knife sliced through wax, canvas, string and paper in an instant. Alice tore away the wrapping and peered into the tube. At first it seemed to be empty. Then she realised that what lay within was rolled up tightly and pressed against the inside. She inserted a finger and thumb and slowly pulled a large, thick sheet of paper into the light. She recognised what it was even before it had been unfurled.

'It's a painting,' said Aunt Statham quickly. 'A watercolour probably. Watercolours were always Lilian's favourite.'

Alice unrolled the paper with shaking hands. Aunt Statham was right. It was a painting. In fact, it was four separate paintings, as the paper had been divided into quarters, each of which contained one of Lilian's characteristically detailed plant illustrations. One showed small pink and white flowers on long thin stalks; another a winding tendril of tiny leaves with small, pale, star-shaped blooms. The third showed bright yellow flowers on individual stick-like stems. The final segment of the paper contained a hairy, angular plant, its leaves small and pointed, its flowers tiny purple knots. They stared at the paper in silence.

'Are they Indian plant species?' asked Aunt Lambert at last. 'I don't recognise any of them if they are.'

'No,' said Alice. 'They are not.'

'Then what are they?' said Old Mrs Talbot. 'The poor child. Why has she sent us this?'

'They don't look very interesting,' agreed Aunt Statham. 'Why didn't she send us something beautiful, something glorious and majestic?' She poked the painting with a scrawny finger. 'That one looks like a weed. Or something cows eat.'

'Is there anything else in the package?' enquired Aunt Rushton-Bell.

Alice shook her head.

'Perhaps she has gone mad,' said Old Mrs Talbot shakily. 'Like Ophelia. Oh, Alice! Your poor deranged sister. Who would have thought it?' Tears appeared in her rheumy eyes.

'She would not be painting like this if she were mad,' stated Aunt Lambert. 'Nor would she have had the presence of mind to package it up so securely and post it to England. For goodness sake, Connie, you always look on the black side of things.'

'Besides, Connie, dear,' said Aunt Pendleton gently, 'that would be rosemary and rue, wouldn't it. "For remembrance"? We could all do with a little of that these days, I'm sure. But these flowers of Lilian's are quite different from Ophelia's.'

Alice stared at the painting. 'Like Ophelia, in one sense,' she said. 'But she's not mad.' She laughed. 'Oh no, Lilian is most definitely not mad.'

3

The day of Mr Talbot's evening of experiment, enlightenment and education was upon them. The sulphur and iron filings had been mixed with water and buried in a huge pit beneath the ground; the ballroom had been transformed into a museum and lecture room; the invitations had been sent out and replies received. Dr Cattermole had arrived and had brought with him a number of photographs and also a range of glass jars containing formaldehyde, within which viscous yellow liquid bobbed all manner of medical monstrosities.

'I have exhibited a number of these at the Medical Society over the years,' he confided to Mr Talbot. 'I have a two-headed baby, you know.'

Alice had not been present at dinner.

'A headache,' Aunt Lambert explained.

'Perhaps I should see her,' Dr Cattermole offered, rubbing his hands together.

'You needn't trouble yourself,' Aunt Lambert said hastily. 'I'm sure it's nothing. A good night's rest is all she needs.'

But Alice did not appear at breakfast either. There was nothing Aunt Lambert could say to stop Mr Talbot and Dr Cattermole going to see for themselves what ailed her.

Alice was not in her room. She was not in the hot house. Mr Talbot muttered angrily at the inconvenience of having a disobedient daughter. With Dr Cattermole in his wake, he stalked up and down the numerous corridors and staircases of the Great House in search of her.

At one point they rounded a corner and almost knocked down Mr Bellows (whose presence in his house Mr Talbot had once again forgotten). It seemed that Mr Bellows had seen no one but Sluce for a number of weeks and his appearance had deteriorated to the extent that Mr Talbot was at first quite alarmed to find what looked like a vagabond on the top floor of his house. Mr Bellows's voluble explanation of his progress with the flying machine served only to irritate Mr Talbot further, as he could make little sense of what Mr Bellows was talking about.

'Yes, yes,' he snapped. 'Very good. Perhaps you would offer us a demonstration of some sort next time the wind is favourable.' And he invited Mr Bellows to attend the meeting of the Society for the Propagation of Useful and Interesting Knowledge that was to take place later that day. 'If I can find my daughter.'

Mr Talbot and Dr Cattermole found Alice seated at her desk in the bamboo thicket beside the jungle parlour. Aunt Pendleton dozed noisily in a chair positioned above one of the cast-iron heating vents in the floor. The peach tree dangled its fruits over her head.

Alice had been up on the walkway that ran around the top of the conservatory when her father and his friend had first come looking for her. Knowing how much he hated the broiling heat of the hot house, she had not expected them to return.

'There you are,' grunted Mr Talbot irritably. 'Come with us.'

'Never mind that, Talbot,' said Dr Cattermole stepping forward. 'We've wasted enough time already and I have still to put my specimens in some sort of order. Miss Talbot. Alice, if

I may. Let us get to the point. There are some facts concerning your health, both mental and physical, which can no longer be ignored.'

Alice looked from her father's flushed and angry face to Dr Cattermole's, and back again, but said nothing.

'As you are aware,' continued Dr Cattermole, 'it has long been your father's wish that you should be educated; that you should be fully cognisant with the contents of his Collection and what they signify. And yet, as time has passed it has come to the attention of both your father and myself that this form of education – the amassing of knowledge of a distinctly *unladylike* nature – has led you down a most unfortunate mental and physical pathway. The education of a woman is all very well. We would not, after all, want the mothers of future generations to be ignorant of the principles of morality and goodness, which form the very best gift that womankind has to offer society. Yet this education must be of the right sort. I refer, of course, to the importance of the various womanly arts – cookery, needlework, attention to religious devotion.'

'Cookery and needlework?' said Alice, mystified and a little bored by Dr Cattermole's detailed lecture.

'Indeed.' Dr Cattermole nodded. He looked at Alice closely. 'My dear Miss Talbot – and I have told your father the very same thing – it is *mis-educated* women who are responsible for much of the downward tendencies of our middle-class society.'

'I had no idea, Cattermole,' muttered Mr Talbot guiltily. 'There didn't seem any harm in it.'

'Not at first, perhaps,' said Dr Cattermole. 'But the behaviour of your daughter Lilian should have alerted you to the errors of so liberal an education. Latterly, her sexual appetite was quite ungoverned; her desire to question and challenge your authority knew no bounds. Was this the behaviour of a woman who excelled in moral sense and goodness?'

'I suppose not, since you put it like that,' said Mr Talbot.

'What has a liberal education got to do with sexual appetite?' said Alice, curious now, despite herself.

Dr Cattermole pursed his lips. 'I would not expect you to understand. I'm sure I need say no more.'

'You need say a lot more, I should think,' said Alice. 'I have no idea what you mean.'

'Dr Cattermole is quite plain in his meaning,' barked Mr Talbot. He cleared his throat and swabbed anxiously at the collar of his shirt with his handkerchief. 'But Alice can be saved, Cattermole, can she not?'

'Perhaps.' Dr Cattermole gazed at Alice until she could no longer meet the cold blue eyes that glittered behind his winking spectacles.

She shuddered, turning her attention to the palm tree that reared behind him. The palm tree had been planted by her mother only a week after the hot house had been completed. That was almost thirty-five years ago now. With no tropical storms to blow it down and no one wanting its wood for houses or boats, the palm had thrived. It was now brushing the upper panes of the hot house roof with the wide fronds of its outstretched arms. Alice wondered how long it would be before she had to cut it down. Then again, perhaps she should simply allow it to burst through the glass to the outside air. After all, what did it have to lose?

Dr Cattermole, she realised, was talking again. 'But of course, Miss Talbot,' he was saying, 'when your father erroneously decided to foster within you a spirit of enquiry and a thirst for knowledge, he had no idea that he was also sending you down a road which would eventually, inevitably, lead to the degeneration of your mind and body.' He looked Alice up and down, adjusting his spectacles as he did so. His gaze lingered on her large hands, the vague undulations of her dress where her bosom was located. 'I feel obliged to point out to you that flat-chestedness and a general absence of the female physical form, a mannish gait, irritability of temper, attacks of ill health – indeed, only last night you were unable to attend dinner due to some indefinable malady – all these stem from the wrong sort of education causing a weakening of the whole female economy. I can only concur with Dr Clarke of Harvard, when he states that any form of education that is not aimed at preparing the female for womanhood, for marriage and the family, serves to *masculinise* that female, resulting in a *hermaphroditic* condition: a woman divested of her sex, lacking in any female attractions and also, I suspect, her chief feminine functions.'

Alice opened her mouth to speak but her father put his hand on her arm. 'You would be better advised to remain silent,' he said. 'After all, you may learn something about your own condition.'

'What condition?' hissed Alice. 'There is nothing the matter with me.'

'If I might be so bold as to explain, Talbot,' continued Dr Cattermole, ignoring this whispered exchange. 'It is known to be the case that intellectual work reduces the supply of nerve-energy to the female reproductive system. The result of this lack of nerve-energy? The mind rebels, collapses even. Mania can, and will, ensue. Nymphomania too is not unknown.' He lowered his voice and leaned in closer. 'Your father also informs me that not ten days ago he saw you offer yourself to Mr Blake. Is this not degeneracy? Is it not a misapplication of the female reproductive urge?'

Dr Cattermole's face was inches from her own, so that Alice could feel his warm sugary breath on her cheek. 'My father was mistaken,' she said, turning her head away from him in unconcealed disgust. 'Ask Mr Blake if you don't believe me.'

'I do not think your father was mistaken,' hissed Dr Cattermole. 'And perhaps Mr Blake will be prevailed upon to tell us the truth – if the price is high enough.'

'And this breakdown in the mind is inevitable?' interrupted

Mr Talbot. 'My dear Cattermole, this is not what you told me when you first explained the situation.'

'I have made some enquiries,' said Dr Cattermole. 'I consulted a number of colleagues. Those who specialise in the nervous diseases of women are in no doubt.'

Alice swallowed. Was there anything she might do or say to save herself? Perhaps she should swoon, or weep, or fall to her knees and beg for forgiveness. Should she lower her eyes and say nothing? Should she call upon her father to step in and defend the education with which he had, until recently, so unstintingly provided her? But she did none of these things. She knew that her fate, whatever it was, had already been decided upon. She would be better off, surely, trying to find out what it was. 'And what are the symptoms?' she demanded. 'What evidence do you have?'

Dr Cattermole whipped a book out of his pocket and proceeded to leaf through its pages. Over his shoulder, Alice could see the margins heavily annotated with the Doctor's own scribbles.

'Here,' he cried. 'Dr Baker Brown is most erudite. The case of "Miss T.S." for instance. Her symptoms included "being impolite to visitors, being forward and open to gentlemen and staring them quite out of countenance, and spending much time in serious reading." Brown states too that she was also reported to be "most disobedient to her father's wishes". Why, Miss Talbot, can you deny that these epithets describe your own character and behaviour? Your own state of being?' He turned to Mr Talbot and added in an undertone, 'I might also add that "Miss T.S." had received not one single offer of marriage in all her thirty-four years.'

Alice looked at the ground and closed her eyes in despair.

'But the remedy is known, is it not?' interjected Mr Talbot. 'You assured me that it was.' He fidgeted sweatily, plucking at the sleeves of his coat that had slicked to his arms in the heat.

'There are a number of remedies.' Dr Cattermole smiled at

Alice. 'Fear not, child, there are ways of returning you to that most welcome state of ladylike graciousness that so becomes the fair sex. Why, Brown records that "Miss T.S." herself was quite transformed after his surgical interventions.'

'And what relevance is this to me?' said Alice. She sounded angry, but the words 'surgical intervention' were ringing in her ears so that she could hardly stop her voice from shaking.

Dr Cattermole ignored her. Instead, he turned to her father. 'But first, I think the Society would be most interested in seeing her in her present condition, Talbot.' He gazed at Alice greedily. 'Perhaps a photograph or two would suffice; with your father's permission, of course. The open hostility of your countenance is symptomatic of your condition. Charcot, in France, has photographed numerous insane patients to great acclaim.'

'I will not be photographed,' said Alice. 'And I am most certainly not insane.'

'What is the cure?' said Mr Talbot. His face was scarlet with the heat; his beard, moist with droplets of water, dangled from his chin like a hank of Spanish moss. He gazed at Alice, his expression a mixture of fear and alarm, as though he expected her to begin gnashing her teeth and rending her clothes there and then.

'The state of mind of the female is linked to her sexual function,' said Dr Cattermole briskly. 'Remedies to suppress the spirit and thus calm the overtaxed mind include injections of iced water into the rectum, and the application of leeches to the labia and cervix.'

Alice felt her skin turn cold and her head began to swim.

'In order to halt the advancement of a disease that would otherwise progress to hysteria and from thence to idiocy, mania, even death, it is often found necessary to remove the clitoris,' said Dr Cattermole.

'Surgery!' Mr Talbot looked aghast, then intrigued. 'Is it a big job?'

'No greater than removing the tip of a finger, say.'

'Well, then.' Mr Talbot patted Alice's arm. 'You have nothing to worry about. Why, Sluce has sliced the tip off three of his fingers and he is none the worse for it. Cattermole, my dear fellow, can I be assured that you have performed such a procedure before?'

'I have not, but I am eager to do so. It would be a new venture for me, though I know how devoted you are, Talbot, to extending the boundaries of our knowledge and experience.'

'Oh, indeed. Especially if the results can be guaranteed. You are certain it will be effective?'

'I have never heard of a recurrence of the disease following such a procedure.' Dr Cattermole stroked the cover of his book with the tips of his long pale fingers. 'She would not visit Mr Blake's chambers, nor the chambers of any other man, ever again.'

4

Alice wrapped her coat tightly about herself and walked to the edge of the roof. Beyond the tips of her boots the slates fell away in a steep slope, below which the lawn at the front of the house unfurled. A man strode across it with a smaller, more ragged and stooped figure in shambling pursuit. It was her father, closely followed by Sluce, inspecting the site of his artificial volcano. He had been insistent that the sods of earth be replaced once the mixture of sulphur and iron filings had been buried, and now only a certain irregularity of the warp and weft of the greensward spoke of any disturbance below ground. That, and the presence of muddy footprints leading to and from a huge heap of earth that had appeared in the ha-ha a hundred feet away.

Alice watched the two figures as they walked the

circumference of the dormant volcano. Her father searched the ground anxiously. Sluce ambled in his wake, his hands thrust deep within his mnemonic pockets. Every few steps, at intervals dictated by his master, he would produce a long, pointed stick from some inner compartment of his coat and jab at the ground, as though skewering a large, slowly baking subterranean fruit cake.

There remained only an hour or so before the Society convened in the ballroom. Alice knew that somewhere beneath her feet Dr Cattermole would be stalking her father's crowded corridors. She returned to her seat in the lea of a chimney. He would never dream of looking for her on the roof.

Huddled in her coat out of the wind, Alice did not hear the footsteps that came towards her across the rooftop.

'Tea?' Mr Blake set the tray down against the chimney and poured out two cups of tea. At first neither of them spoke. Then, 'Aunt Pendleton told me that your father had been speaking to you. With Dr Cattermole.'

Alice closed her eyes. 'It seems I am to be Dr Cattermole's first clitoridectomy.'

Mr Blake could not stop his tea from slopping into his saucer.

'With my father's permission, of course.'

The photographer stared out across the park. 'Cattermole is a determined man,' he said, 'when he wants something.'

'And I am a determined woman,' said Alice.

'I have no doubt. But you cannot hide up here for ever. Perhaps if we told your father that we are to be married?'

'It is too late for marriage to save me,' said Alice. 'Dr Cattermole said so himself. No doubt he would regard the need for surgery to be even more pressing if he understood that I had been so wilful as to have courted a man behind my father's back.'

'Those photographs,' Mr Blake said after a moment. 'The

ones you found in my trunk. Were you aware that Cattermole was . . . involved in their production?'

'Dr Cattermole has been a guest in this house many times. There is less privacy here than you might expect. It is easy to forget an item – a portfolio, a diary, a pocketbook, an album of *cartes-de-visite* – when there are so many of my father's artefacts cluttering every surface in every room.' She shrugged. 'I have known for a long time. And I knew you were his dupe. His wife poses for him too.'

'Really?'

'Mrs Cattermole admitted as much to me. You did not know?'

Mr Blake shook his head. 'Your father must disapprove, surely?'

'I have no idea. He has recently become so intimate with Dr Cattermole that there is no knowing what the two of them are up to. Cattermole officiated at my sister's confinement, you know. If you can call such butchery "confinement". I was obliged to be his assistant.' Alice closed her eyes at the thought of the Doctor's thin white fingers positioning her sister's feet in the dreadful stirrups of the operating table. She would rather leap from the roof of her father's house there and then than submit to Dr Cattermole's touch on her bare flesh. And yet, it was since he had assisted in concealing Lilian's disgrace that his influence with her father had grown. She pulled out Aunt Lambert's brandy bottle and set it down on the stone seat. 'I have this to keep me warm. I have some books with me. A lantern. I have my writing box. What more do I need?'

'You would be as well to hide downstairs. You might find it easier to avoid Dr Cattermole if you know where he is and what he is up to. There will be no escape if he finds you up here. You might hide in the ballroom. He would never dream of looking for you there.'

Alice shook her head. At that moment she did not think she

could even bear to hear Dr Cattermole's voice. She pulled her coat round her shivering shoulders and turned away.

Soon, the sun began slipping behind the oaks at the end of the park. Long fingers of shadow stole across the ground. Mr Blake remained at Alice's side. She urged him to return to the house, if not to attend the meeting then at least to gather some intelligence. But he refused to go unless she accompanied him to 'weather the storm', as he put it.

'Since you're in so nautical a frame of mind,' said Alice in response, 'you might keep an eye on the gates through this.' She produced from within her coat the long brass telescope.

Mr Blake held it unsteadily to his eyes. The weight of the thing and the stiff breeze blowing across the rooftop made his hands shake; those and the fact that the telescope was warm to the touch from its recent spell pressed against Alice's body. He gave her a sidelong glance. Would she object, he wondered, if he slipped an arm about her shoulders? Perhaps a kiss could be stolen, a reward for his uncharacteristic display of manly restraint when she had presented herself, naked, in his rooms . . . He shifted himself closer, but her apparent indifference to his nearness, combined with the coldness of the stone beneath his already freezing buttocks, dimmed his uncertain ardour.

'There's one,' said Mr Blake. A carriage could be seen at the far end of the park. It had halted in obvious bafflement at the sealed gates.

'Perhaps they'll think it's all a mistake and drive away again,' said Alice hopefully. But no. The carriage in question was joined, after a moment or two, by another, and after some consultation held between the occupants (as reported by the telescopically aided Mr Blake) they moved off, one after the other, and were eventually heard entering the stable yard at the rear of the house. Mr Talbot's welcoming voice boomed up from below, echoing from walls and chimney pots before being carried away on the rising wind. Some minutes later the shambling form of Sluce could be seen heading towards the gates, a lantern in his hand against the gathering dusk, dispatched to act as a human fingerpost directing visitors in their circumnavigation of the grounds.

Mr Blake folded the telescope.

'You can't stay up here all night,' he insisted.

'I can. I shall write to Lilian to pass the time. It is a great comfort to me to do so, even though I know she will never read my letter. In fact' – Alice's face brightened – 'I was hoping that you might smuggle something out for me. I would have asked you sooner only I was not sure –'

'You doubted me?'

'Yes.'

'But now?' Mr Blake reached for her hand.

'So you will act as my courier?'

'Oh, no,' said Mr Blake. 'It is quite impossible now. It appears that since your visit to my room . . . I am at no greater liberty than yourself. Your father has assured me that my pockets will be searched for any correspondence from you should I attempt to leave the house.'

'Would you submit to such an indignity?'

'Would I have a choice? He seems most determined.'

Alice sank back into silence.

'Has Lilian written to you again?' asked Mr Blake gently.

'She sent a painting.'

'Another coded communication?'

'Yes. She sent four paintings, each depicting different flowers or leaves. They speak their own language.'

'Which is?'

'Sweet scabious, bugloss, coltsfoot and birdsfoot trefoil.'

'And this means, what, exactly?' said Mr Blake with some impatience.

Alice looked at him closely. He had no love for her father, that much was clear. And had she not just said that she trusted him? Besides, what did it matter whom she told? 'Widowhood, false love, justice and revenge.'

'Widowhood? Revenge? For what? Upon whom?'

Alice shrugged. 'I assume Mr Fraser is dead. As for the rest, we shall have to wait and see.'

'Well,' Mr Blake shivered and pulled his coat closer round his shoulders. 'That's all very interesting, but she is in India and you are here, on your father's roof, with Dr Cattermole, his camera, his surgical instruments and a room full of onlookers awaiting you downstairs. I would suggest that writing to your sister is not likely to achieve a satisfactory resolution to your present situation.'

Alice had become used to Mr Blake's quiescent manner. Now that he had been without ether for a few days, however, she had noticed that he seemed far more able to apply his thoughts intelligently. His eyes had regained some of their sparkle and the sore beside his mouth had practically disappeared.

'Besides,' he added, 'you're surely not going to let him get the better of you? An old scoundrel like Cattermole?'

'He has not got the better of me.'

The photographer reached for the bottle of brandy. He poured a splash of it into each of their empty tea cups. 'For courage!'

Alice and Mr Blake crept along an ill-lit and musty corridor used only by servants. Mr Blake led her through a small, barely distinguishable door in the wall of the ballroom. For once Mr Talbot had cast aside all thought of economy and lamps blazed everywhere. The sound of male conversation filled the air.

'I'd forgotten this door was here,' whispered Alice.

'I saw Sluce disappearing into it. He had been helping me move this . . .' The photographer pointed to the vast piece of machinery that loomed before them. 'It's . . .'

'A steam-driven ploughing, drilling and threshing machine made by Hornsby and Son. Yes, I was obliged to write a piece about it for my father when I was a child. Industry and farming are magnificently united in this artefact, you know. It represents the triumphant harnessing of nature for the glory of the nation's larders.'

'I see.'

'Did you place it here deliberately?'

'I did. I shifted the display cases of coal fragments from the Collieries of the World in front of it and I erected a pyramid made up entirely of artificial eyeballs on top. It would take a very determined fellow to see you.'

'Aren't you going to hide here with me?'

Mr Blake squeezed her hand. For a moment Alice thought he was about to press it to his lips, but he seemed to think better of it and, with a grim nod, he disappeared into Sluce's passageway.

Alice peeped round the ploughing, drilling and threshing machine. She had never seen the ballroom so filled with people. The artefacts Mr Blake had so carefully positioned about the room projected from a seething throng of black-clad backs and waving arms, as though the house were overrun by a swarm of enormous insects. Alice recognised the veined nose and booming laugh of the inventor of the tempest prognosticator, and the tall, stooping figure and trembling hands of the cuneiform translator. She stepped back hastily into the shadows behind the threshing machine. An artificial eye of a particularly startling blue gazed accusingly at her from the top of the eyeball pyramid. Alice reached over and plucked it from its pinnacle. The fewer eyes that knew about her hiding place the better.

At length her father appeared behind the lectern that had been placed on the raised platform. He droned out a welcome . . . how delighted he was to be able to greet so many august members of the Society in his humble home. How he hoped they would find most stimulating those artefacts that he had gathered together for display within the ballroom and the surrounding corridors. . . . . On and on he rambled: the magnificence of human achievements in art and science, the need to educate through display and instruction, the importance of the Society and its members in this educative role . . . Alice slumped against the wall. She had heard it so many times before.

'There is, however, a medical theme to this afternoon's meeting,' thundered Mr Talbot.

Alice sprang to her feet.

'Throughout the room you will see certain instruments and devices pertaining to the improvement of the human body. Tools – knives, blades and scalpels – designed to facilitate abdominal surgery, or the rapid removal of unnatural growths; devices – inhalers and suchlike – for the administration of opiates and other medicines; new and ingenious prosthetic limbs, not least a false nose, imitation eyeballs in all manner of sizes and colours, and an artificial hand. I might also draw your attention to an artificial leech, which can painlessly suck blood from an infected patient; a most ingenious fulcrum and chair for the extraction of teeth; and a stomach pump which has several useful adaptations.'

There was a murmuring and a nodding of heads.

'Dr Thomas Cattermole will lead this meeting with a discussion about new developments in surgery as a means of controlling certain social ills. At the back of the room you will have noticed a number of jars containing Dr Cattermole's own personal anatomical museum. I hope you will avail yourselves of this opportunity to see various extremes and marvels of human disease and malformation.'

Alice caught sight of Dr Cattermole. He looked irritated, his face red in the candlelight, his mouth a thin angry line. She had also noticed that Dr Cattermole's anatomical museum was, in fact, attracting little attention, as though those members of the Society who were present were loath to be reminded of the possible failings and malfunctions of their own all-too-frail bodies.

'Dr Cattermole has brought his magic lantern, and will illustrate his talk with photographs and statistics of his own manufacture.'

There was a round of applause as Dr Cattermole rose to his feet. On his signal, the lamps and candles were extinguished. He opened a box and removed a glass plate, which he proceeded to slide behind the magnifying eye of his magic lantern. A photograph of a startled-looking middle-aged woman appeared upon the wall behind him. It was an expression Alice recognised, as the sitter struggled to remain still with eyes open for the duration of the exposure.

'Mania', Dr Cattermole began, 'is set to make its way through the delicate balance of the female mind up and down this country.'

Alice smelt Sluce before she saw him. A dank, earthy smell; a mixture of mud and stale food, of sweat and rotten teeth. She turned. He was standing right behind her, a look of triumph mingled with disbelief on his face. He parted withered lips to shout out that he had found her at last, right under their very noses too. Alice hesitated only for a second while her fingers curled round the shining blue-and-white orb of an artificial eye. Then she drove her fist into the centre of Sluce's grinning face.

LILIAN

1

Lilian rode out of the cantonment and towards the native town dressed in pyjama trousers and dhoti, with a turban wrapped about her head. On her feet she wore a pair of soft leather boots she had bought in the bazaar and over the whole costume a goatskin jerkin secured by a belt. Months of riding about the mofussil with her paints and easel had tanned her face and hands, so that she was now quite dark-skinned. With her pale hair tucked out of sight it was only Lilian's blue eyes that seemed out of place. Strapped behind the saddle of her pony she carried food in a canvas bag, a cooking pot and her paints, several rolls of paper and a folding easel, plus a carefully chosen selection of the camping equipment Selwyn had ordered from the Calcutta Army and Navy Stores in preparation for his trip to the Punjab. Over her shoulder hung Aunt Lambert's rifle, newly oiled and loaded and ready for use. She had also discovered a pistol and a box of ammunition hidden in a kedgeree pot in the bottom of her wardrobe – a relic, she assumed, from the mysteriously departed Mr Gilmour. This firearm she had cleaned and loaded, and wore thrust into her belt, alongside a short, curved knife she had bought in the bazaar.

Lilian had left her three suitors in her drawing room. She had a pretty good idea of what they had come for, but was not interested in finding out more. She had told Harshad to escort them to the parlour and then she had slipped away, as she had intended to do anyway, after giving Harshad orders to say nothing about her whereabouts, and a full two months' pay in advance for his co-operation.

Harshad exhibited signs of distress at her departure. 'Please, memsahib Lilian,' he said tearfully, expressing himself in English, as though this might prove more persuasive. 'Do not leave this place. Trouble coming, most certainly. Bastard chapattis mean most bloody and damnable trouble. Please, stay here and remain safe in bungalow. Cover windows. Lock door, damn it.' His eyes lit up at a sudden encouraging thought. 'Hide in blasted cookhouse,' he cried. 'Yes!'

'Goodness me, Harshad,' said Lilian in surprise. 'I don't need to barricade the doors and hide in the cookhouse to escape the attentions of the Doctor and the Magistrate. And I already have some chapattis in my saddlebags, for the journey.'

'Trouble coming,' repeated Harshad. 'Please to stay here in bungalow.'

But Lilian was not to be persuaded. She told Harshad to take the contents of the cookhouse and larder to his wife, and to pay off all the other servants. If there was any money left in the purse after he had done this (and Lilian had ensured that there would be) he was to keep this for himself.

'Keep to confounded Trunk Road,' said Harshad, shaking his head. 'Speak to no one. Bloody bandits and ruffian bastards everywhere. Tigers also most fierce. Be sure to ride bloody quickly and with purpose to avoid men and beasts.' He seized her hands and sank to his knees before her. 'Then it is goodbye, memsahib Lilian. Goodbye, damn your eyes.'

From her bedroom window, as she wound her turban about her head, Lilian had watched Mr Hunter riding across the maidan towards her bungalow. Would she miss him? Perhaps. How long would it be before any of the Europeans realised she had gone? Not long. Not that it mattered. There was nothing they could do to stop her.

*

Lilian breathed deeply, feeling her chest expand agreeably without the constraint of lacing and corsetry. She had laid her plans to get Alice away from their father and out to India and, at last, she was putting those plans into action. Perhaps she and Alice might adopt male clothing for good, she thought as she rode towards the native town. They would cut off their hair and ride astride. It was liberating to be free from the encumbrance of so many layers of complicated female clothing; to be freed from the expectations and restrictions of womanhood. A man might go anywhere; say anything, without so much as a raised eyebrow or a disapproving glance. Why should she, and Alice, not do the same?

The pony tossed its head anxiously.

Lilian patted its neck. 'You agree then, do you, boy?' She smiled and wondered what sort of pony she should get for Alice – it would have to be one that complemented her sister's athletic figure and assertive nature. Lilian pictured Alice astride a spirited chestnut, her long legs clad in breeches, her strong hands holding the reins . . . Together, they would go anywhere they pleased.

Lilian had to cross the bazaar to reach the open road. She passed through the crowds unmolested and unnoticed. But Lilian's presence in the bazaar was disregarded for reasons other than her native costume, and she had not gone far before she began to make out the sound of a disturbance above the usual din and chatter. The faces that passed her looked uneasy; their eyes wide, their expressions troubled. She felt the skin on the back of her neck prickle as the sound of shouting, the tramp of running feet and the crash of overturned wares echoed along the narrow streets. No doubt it was simply another brawl, she said to herself, an altercation between Pushtu cut-throats or Marathi horse thieves that had escalated into something vicious. India was full of one-eyed men and scarred faces; just as Dr Mossly's hospital was filled with knife wounds and torn ears. There was always something violent going on somewhere and the Kushpur bazaar was no exception. Lilian pressed on.

As she pushed her way through the busy thoroughfare, however, the shouts and screams became louder – closer and more insistent. The crowd heaved against her pony. The noise increased, a noise that Lilian suddenly realised was not made by haggling natives or the calls of booth wallahs, but was the sound of anger and fear, of violence and destruction, and it seemed to be coming not from any specific area of the bazaar but from all sides.

Lilian drew her pony to a halt. Perhaps Mr Hunter was right. Perhaps there really *was* a whiff of insurrection blowing through the bazaar. Perhaps the nabobs *were* dissatisfied with the Sircar. Certainly, Mr Hunter had spoken to her most passionately on the subject many times. Perhaps she should have listened to Harshad? But then Harshad's world, like that of so many native servants, revolved around his memsahib and the requirements of her household. Surely he would have no knowledge of, or interest in, the barrack room gossip of sepoys and the discontent of princes?

Her fingers curled round the unfamiliar handle of Mr Gilmour's pistol. Would she be obliged to defend herself? Was her native dress a mistake? White skin was protection against everything – apart from cholera and insects, of course; why, not even the Thugs had attacked Europeans – or so Mrs Birchwoode had told her. Lilian peered uncertainly into the sea of worried-looking faces that bobbed about her ankles. Suddenly she was not quite so certain.

All at once people began running – from left to right; in and out of alleyways; towards the noise and away from it. A teeming frenzy of bodies swirled and buffeted about the legs of her pony like flotsam carried on flood waters. Musket fire rang out above the din. The crowd surged. Lilian's pony reared up in alarm. Lilian grabbed hold of its mane to stop herself from being tossed into the maelstrom. A woman with a baby staggered in front of her, narrowly missing the flailing hooves. A man began pulling at her leg, trying to unseat her and drag her on to the ground. Before she had time even to think, she drew the knife from her belt and slashed at the man's fingers. He staggered back, clutching his bleeding hand, falling to the ground and disappearing instantly beneath the boiling throng as a man overboard might plunge into a turbulent sea. Lilian shouted, digging her heels into the pony's sides and urging it onwards, swiping at clutching hands and arms with her knife.

Then she noticed something else. There was now a distinct smell in the air, a charred reek that was different from the usual smells of cooking fires and spices and ghee and refuse. She looked into the sky and saw that it was dark with billowing clouds. Smoke was issuing from the direction of the river, to the north of the European enclave. The barracks were burning.

Lilian urged her pony up a passageway that led in a roundabout way to the dak bungalow, away from the sepoy barracks, and in the opposite direction from the European cantonment. If she could just get up to the Grand Trunk she could then travel north and west, out into the countryside and away from the mayhem. Even as she resolved to do this a group of men staggered into view at the head of the passageway. They were dressed not in the garb of bazaar ruffians, but in the red jackets and white cross-belts of the Native Infantry. One of them carried a burning torch. It was ungainly in the man's grasp and, as she reined in her pony, Lilian realised with a start of horror and disbelief that it was not a burning torch at all but a human arm, clothed in red with a white hand dangling like a wet glove from its cuff. With the flaming arm the sepoy set fire to each booth that he passed, the smoke swelling and dancing behind him, as though he was emerging from the clouds of hell itself.

So unreal was the sight that Lilian was reminded, fleetingly, of the Collection of prosthetic limbs that filled a display case in her father's house in a macabre gallery of wooden gestures. Perhaps this *was* a prosthetic limb, she said to herself, groping for a rational explanation. But she knew that it was not. *How frail we are*, she thought, her head spinning; *how insubstantial our bodies that we can be dismembered as easily as a marionette.*

Suddenly, as though from out of a rabbit hole, a British officer rushed into the passageway in front of the sepoys. He sprinted away from them towards Lilian. He was no one Lilian recognised, but then his face was set in a mask of such rage and fear that she didn't think she would have known who it was, even if it had been one of those officers whose smiles she had beheld across Mrs Birchwoode's dinner table on so many occasions. The man's cherry-red uniform was torn and dirty, his face bloody from a gash above his eyes, and his cutlass and pistol were gone. With the sepoys now screaming and waving their sabres behind him, he ran blindly in the direction of Lilian's horse.

Lilian saw the terror in the officer's eyes as he stared at her. She was blocking his pathway, her face streaked with smoke and spattered with blood, her pyjama trousers stained crimson. He tried to stop, but his boots slipped on a pool of dried peas and he continued to skid forward, his legs flailing as the peas scattered like ball-bearings from beneath his skittering feet. Lilian hauled on the reins. With some difficulty she managed to turn her horse in the narrow passage and, not waiting to see whether the officer followed, or whether he was engulfed by the baying mob, she charged back into the main thoroughfare of the bazaar.

In that short space of time the smoke had thickened into a sickening, greasy pall. Booths had been set alight and were burning angrily, adding acrid fumes to the reek of destruction already filling the air. To her left, the sound of exploding glass from a lemonade vendor mixed with the crack-crack-crack of unattended cooking fires from a bhaji seller next door. The body of a soldier, his red coat slathered with blood and his face smashed open like a watermelon sprawled in the dust. On either side a rabble of sepoys, their uniforms grey with dirt and smoke, ransacked stalls and overturned piles of baskets, boxes of vegetables, pitchers of grain and oil, anything that stood in their path.

Lilian whirled her horse round, looking for a way through the mob. Her senses could hardly take in what was happening. Only yesterday they had made a serene boat trip to the botanical gardens. Today, in the space of a few minutes, Kushpur had been transformed into an abattoir. She had no idea what to do, or where to go . . .

A shout brought her out of her daze and she turned just in time to see a European officer, his coat torn at the shoulder, his ears and nose streaming with blood, charging towards her. His mouth was open in a furious snarl and he raised his cutlass to strike her from her horse. There was no time to move, or even to shout a warning. There was only one thing she could do if she were not to be hacked to pieces and without hesitation Lilian did it. She pulled the pistol from her belt and emptied the contents into the man's face.

2

Mr Hunter stood on Lilian's veranda, with the Doctor and the Magistrate, and watched flames rising from the bazaar. The sun had disappeared behind a smudge of black smoke and the air tasted bitter as wormwood.

'Where can she be?' asked Mr Vine.

'You don't think she's gone to the native town, do you?' said Dr Mossly. His pale cheeks turned paler still.

'Quite possibly,' said Mr Hunter. He called to his *sa'is* to bring his horse. 'I'll ride through and see what's going on.'

'The native town is burning,' said Mr Vine irritably. 'That's what's going on. You don't need to ride into the bazaar to get a view. We can watch the fires burning from Mrs Birchwoode's roof. We'll go and inspect the damage in the morning.'

'Don't be a fool, man,' cried Mr Hunter. 'Lily might be dead already.'

At last Lilian found herself in a silent passageway. The hurricane of violence had already swept through it. A trickle of crimson water made its way sluggishly through the debris of shattered bodies, torn clothing and piles of refuse. Lilian cleaned her knife blade on her trousers and reloaded her pistol with shaking hands. A spattering of pink, spongy matter was slathered over barrel and chamber, and had turned the handle sticky. She gazed at her red-stained fingers. Then all at once she vomited lavishly on to the ground. She slumped against the neck of her pony, gasping for breath. If only she had left the week before. Still, it was too late now for such pointless thoughts.

Stupefied with fear and horror, Lilian made her way through the native town. The confidence she once had in her disguise had evaporated long ago. At any moment someone might notice who she was, and she felt frightened and vulnerable, alone in the blood-soaked bazaar with her silly costume and Company pony. She had thought she was familiar with Kushpur, with India and Indians. Now, this assumption appeared arrogant and naïve. Kushpur had become a dark and foreign place, filled with terror and resentment. It was a place she hardly recognised.

Lilian rode in a daze, passing scenes of such slaughter that she could hardly believe she was traversing the same streets she had walked a hundred times without fear. Her idea of heading to the Trunk Road seemed foolish and ill-judged. She knew she would never be able to reach it alone and what dangers might it hold for her once she got there? She wanted to burst into tears (indeed, tears had already trickled a pale pathway through the dried blood and smoke smuts on her cheeks). Whom could she turn to? Who would help her to escape from this hellish place? The answer was obvious: Mr Hunter, of course. Lilian felt relieved even at the thought of him. Mr Hunter would save her from this unfolding massacre. Mr Hunter would know what to do and where to find a place of safety. He had probably left the European enclave and returned to the native town to collect his belongings at the first sign of trouble. She would be sure to find him at the dak bungalow. Lilian turned her pony and headed into the terrifying thoroughfares of the bazaar.

She passed a European officer, lying among the refuse in the middle of the passageway. His face was slathered with blood and brains so that it matched the colour of his crimson uniform. Beside him sprawled a dead sepoy, his left arm quite gone. Only a mangled stump remained, projecting from the ragged shoulder of his military tunic. Lilian looked away. She focused her mind on the dak bungalow, a place she had visited many times to see whether there had been any post from Alice. Oh Alice. What would *she* have done, had she been at her side, as she always used to be? Alice would have kept a clear head, no matter what. She would have made her way to the dak via the quietest streets, her pistol at the ready. She would have found Mr Hunter and insisted that he help and she would brook no arguments from him. Alice had always had the measure of Mr Hunter. *Mr Hunter is an adventurer*, she had said. *A self-interested man who knows how to get out of trouble as quickly and easily as possible. He will do anything to save his own skin.* Lilian found the memory of her sister's words unexpectedly comforting.

But the dak bungalow was in flames. A crowd was gathered outside, cheering. A drunken sepoy brandishing a bottle of arrack stood on the chest of a dead officer to get a better view of the inferno. Lilian almost fainted at the sight. She swayed in her saddle, but somehow managed to remain upright. The roof of the dak bungalow collapsed, releasing a whirl of dancing sparks into the smoky air.

She resolved to return to the European cantonment. Possibly Mr Hunter was still there, perhaps at that very moment devising a plan that would outwit the bloodthirsty Indians and lead everyone to safety. After all, he had always understood the natives better than anyone else (he had told her so himself on many occasions). Besides, who but her fellow Europeans would offer her sanctuary from the slaughter?

The sepoy standing on the dead officer was watching her suspiciously. His hand strayed to the knife he carried thrust into the belt of his trousers. He waved his bottle of arrack in Lilian's direction and screamed at her to drink to the end of the Sircar's rule.

'*Shabash*!' shouted Lilian feebly. 'Death to the Sircar!' She brandished her cutlass and fired her pistol into the air. This display seemed to satisfy him, and he turned his attention to jumping up and down on the officer's chest like a monkey on a barrel organ.

Mr Hunter was hardly out of the European cantonment before he was set upon by a band of armed sepoys. He just had time to curse his own stupidity, before something cracked him on the back of the head and he slipped from the saddle on to the ground.

He came to lying on his back in a ditch at the roadside. His head was pounding, his vision blurred. How long had he been lying there? He had no idea. He struggled unsteadily to his feet. The sky appeared to be almost dark, though whether this was due to smoke (which he could now taste on the air and which made his eyes smart and his throat tickle), or simply the approach of nightfall, or perhaps even an optical illusion created by the blow to the skull he had sustained, he was not sure. He put a hand to his head. His hair was sticky with blood at the back, and a torrent of the stuff had poured from a cut above his eye down his face and on to his shirt. Mr Hunter pulled the filthy shirt over his head gingerly. Blood was still running from his hairline into his eyes, and he tore up the shirt and wrapped it round his head in a makeshift bandage. His new calfskin breeches were brown with dust and ripped extravagantly at the thigh. Every bone in his body ached. His head felt as though a cannon was going off inside it.

The only reason he was not dead, he decided, was because his attackers had erroneously assumed that the blow to his head had been fatal. He looked about. His horse was gone, his bearer had fled, his *sa'is* was lying, face down, a few yards further up the road. From the curious and unnatural angle of the man's body it was clear that he had not been as lucky as his master. Mr Hunter groaned as the world began to heave and spin around him. He sank back down on to the dusty road and put his head between his knees.

The sound of approaching horses riding at a gallop and the shouts of men startled him out of his stupor. He staggered to his feet and dived back into the ditch at the roadside as a gang of sepoys thundered past, their cutlasses waving in their hands, their faces triumphant. Their horses were laden, though with what, exactly, Mr Hunter could not tell, until a bundle carried precariously behind one of the riders' saddles came undone, scattering its glittering contents about the road. A silver teapot bounced into the bushes. A pair of sugar tongs and a silver milk jug landed beside the dead *sa'is*. An ornate silver picture frame skidded through the dust, landing inches from Mr Hunter's hiding place. The sepoys did not stop to pick up their fallen booty, but disappeared in the direction of the native town.

Mr Hunter lurched out of the ditch once more, coughing and choking on the dust thrown up by the drumming of hooves on the sun-baked earth. It settled thickly on to his bloody hair and face, and he scrubbed at it crossly, trying to get it out of his eyes and nose, but succeeding only in mixing it into a terracotta-coloured paste. He spat a mouthful of blood and mud on to the ground. How was he going to find Lilian without a horse? His progress would be impossibly slow and he would be at risk from footpads, roaming bands of looters, or whole regiments of furious sepoys . . . The sound of approaching hooves sent him diving for cover once again.

Mr Hunter scrambled back into the ditch and peeped out. Round the corner, heading to the cantonment, came a single rider. The young man's clothes were bloodstained, his turban filthy about his head, his pyjama trousers blotched with ominous rust-coloured stains. He rode low over his horse's neck, clinging on to the mane with inexpert hands as he drove the animal forward. Mr Hunter swallowed. Even from his place in the ditch he could see the man's eyes blazing, his teeth clenched tightly about the blade of a knife. And yet it was only a single cut-throat, Mr Hunter said to himself, a small, thin cut-throat at that, and one who seemed somewhat uncomfortable astride a galloping pony. There was a chance, he decided suddenly, if he was swift and strong, that he might unhorse the fellow and steal his mount.

Later he decided that the blow he had taken to the head must have addled his brains. After all, throwing oneself into the pathway of a charging horse ridden by a furious and well-armed mutineer was an act of recklessness and stupidity. Nonetheless, having concluded that anything was possible, and with only a split second to make his move, Mr Hunter reared up from his ditch and launched himself at the passing rider.

Lilian almost dropped the knife from between her teeth as the filth-covered fakir sprang up at her from his roadside bed. She tried to swerve round him, to avoid his outstretched hands, but his fingers closed about her boot like a snare and she was almost dragged from her pony on to the ground. The animal reared and wheeled in the dust.

Mr Hunter roared victoriously, oblivious to the hooves that were plunging up and down inches from his face. He grabbed hold of Lilian's waist.

She twisted from side to side trying to dislodge him without falling herself; trying to get her pistol out and point it at his face without dropping her reins. His head was sheathed in the tattered remnants of a stained and foul turban, the face below a mask of clay. His rags flapped like bandages about his shoulders. How big and strong he seemed for a supposedly half-starving mendicant. But then these roadside fakirs were always being fed by locals, thought Lilian distractedly as she tried to slice the fellow's fingers off, so it was perhaps no surprise that some of them were in better health than they pretended.

Mr Hunter hauled at Lilian's legs, trying to pull her down from the pony and, at the same time, to drag himself up. The pony screamed, its eyes rolling in its head. Lilian gasped. She was slipping down. If she could just get a grip on her rifle . . . There! Lilian rammed the butt of Aunt Lambert's rifle into the fakir's face. He slithered on to the ground, his hands to his nose. Lilian did not wait to see if he got up, but dug her heels into her pony's sides and took off towards the cantonment.

Even before she had rounded the final corner to the Europeans' bungalows Lilian could see the flames against the darkening sky. Mr Vine's house was the first she passed. His possessions – those precious things he had brought from England – were scattered like the beached booty of a wrecked ship. A wall clock was protruding from a flowerbed; a portrait of the young Queen upside down in among the canna lilies. The thick claret-coloured curtains the Magistrate had ordered direct from London, which had once hung proudly in his dining room, were piled in a heap in the middle of his garden. The ground around these relics appeared to be scattered with a thousand multicoloured fragments, which glowed and flickered like jewels in the light of the inferno that was Mr Vine's bungalow.

Lilian dismounted. She picked up a handful of what appeared to be shards of pottery. It was pottery thickly glazed in vivid turquoises, reds and yellows, rich greens and violent cobalt blues. Here and there Lilian could distinguish the disembodied fragment of an animal, a plant or an insect: a sliver of emerald seaweed; an entire glazed bumblebee. Lilian recognised the shattered remains of Mr Vine's collection of Herbert Minton majolica. It had been smashed into tiny pieces and scattered like birdseed into the dirt.

Lilian scrambled back on to her pony. Already the roof of Mr Vine's bungalow was falling in, sending an explosion of orange sparks bursting into the charred and whirling darkness. Mr Vine himself was nowhere to be seen, though whether this was a good or a bad sign Lilian had no idea. She rubbed the smoke from her eyes and rode on.

She made her way stealthily past the Europeans' bungalows. Each one appeared deserted – windows stood open with the lights inside blazing uselessly; doors were wrenched off entirely and tossed aside, the interior an ominous flickering darkness as fires within danced and smouldered. Mr Ravelston's house, like the Magistrate's, was completely ablaze. The hospital, on the far side of the maidan, was also burning. Lilian had expected to find some activity, at least some evidence that the Europeans were defending themselves: the construction of makeshift barricades, perhaps (good use could surely have been made of all those ponderous sideboards); the sound of defensive musket fire; the occasional boom of a cannon, even. Instead, there was nothing. No one appeared to have made any attempt to defend anything – until it was too late, of course. But here was a house whose lights were on and whose door was closed. Perhaps everyone had taken refuge there? Lilian halted outside Mrs Birchwoode's bungalow and dismounted. Whether the Europeans of Kushpur were inside or not was impossible to tell. She peered anxiously into the spark-filled evening for signs of movement. Seeing nothing and no one, she climbed onto the veranda and opened the door.

The place was silent, but Lilian gripped her pistol nonetheless as she crossed the threshold. She turned the corner towards the drawing room, her trembling finger tightening on the trigger. All at once she caught sight of a movement out of the corner of her eye. She swung round with a cry to behold a man, crouched as though about to spring. Lilian had time only to take in his staring eyes, his filthy face below a dirty turban and the rifle he was pointing at her . . . She blasted Mr Gilmour's pistol into his face with a scream, shattering Mrs Birchwoode's hall mirror into a thousand spears of silver. The fragments cascaded, with a sound like an overturned knife box, on to the floor.

Lilian's hands began to shake uncontrollably. She stepped forward and poked her head into Mrs Birchwoode's drawing room.

The sight that greeted her sent her staggering back into the hall as though she had been struck in the face. She screwed her eyes shut, but the picture seemed to have been burned on to her retinas as though on to one of her sister's photographic plates. That brief glimpse had been enough to show Lilian that everyone present was dead. She knew this because each person there – Mrs Birchwoode, Mrs Toomey, Miss Forbes and Miss Bell – was seated about the room in her customary pose. Their teacups were before them on the tray, and their heads had been cut from their shoulders and placed in their laps.

Lilian stumbled back down the hallway. Had no one been spared? What had happened to Mr Birchwoode, Mr Ravelston and Mr Toomey? Where were Captains Wheeler, Forbes and Lewis? Surely they had been on hand to help? It was true that the sound of musket fire could still be heard echoing across the cantonment. Perhaps they were fighting in the native town with the rest of the European officers. What about Mr Vine and Dr Mossly? She found she could hardly breathe with fear. Where was Mr Hunter when she needed him? Lilian burst out on to Mrs Birchwoode's veranda, gasping for air.

And there was that fakir again! There was no mistaking his tattered headdress and torn clothing as he struggled to mount her pony.

Lilian levelled her pistol as he tried in vain to get his foot into a stirrup as the pony reared and danced.

'Get away from my horse or I'll kill you,' she screamed.

Without waiting for a response she pulled the trigger. A whiff of powder and a deafening roar filled the air. When she opened her eyes the fakir had gone.

3

Mr Hunter crawled on to Mrs Birchwoode's veranda.

'Lily,' he croaked.

Lilian jumped at the sound of his voice. 'Mr *Hunter*?' She peered at him. 'Is that you?' She fumbled for ammunition and fed it with shaking fingers into the empty chambers of Mr Gilmour's pistol. 'God, oh God, it *is* you.' She felt hysterical tears and rage rising inside her. 'I could have killed you. Only I was so frightened I couldn't hold my arm still.'

The shadows around them seemed to jump and flicker. Mr Hunter said urgently: 'We must get away from here. Come *on*. Take my hand.'

But Lilian's eyes had taken on the fixed and glassy look of someone who has seen horrors aplenty and is no longer certain what reality might look like. She gave no sign of having heard and understood his words, and she ignored his outstretched hand. 'I didn't expect this,' she whispered. 'You said there would be trouble, but I didn't expect this.'

A figure detached itself from the neem trees at the edge of the compound. Slowly, with a stealthy creeping movement, it began making its way towards them. Mr Hunter whispered: 'Give me your pistol.'

'Mrs Fraser,' said a voice from the shadows. 'Mrs Fraser, is that you? Keep your voice down. They'll hear you. They'll come back.'

'Mr Vine?' Lilian peered into the darkness. The shadow took on the thin, round-shouldered form of the Magistrate, a sabre held out before him with shaking uncertainty.

'What happened here?' demanded Mr Hunter.

'Surely you can see what happened,' said the Magistrate hoarsely. He looked Mr Hunter up and down with unconcealed dislike. He opened his mouth, as though about to say something disparaging, but then appeared to change his mind. He shrugged, his sabre drooping in his hand until its defeated point rested in the dust. 'The natives went berserk,' he said finally. 'They cut Captain Wheeler down and set upon him like dervishes. There is nothing but a stain on the ground to show where he fell.' Mr Vine pointed across the maidan with a shaking finger. 'They stamped him into the ground. They had already overrun the officers' barracks. The place was a slaughterhouse, according to Captain Lewis. The poor chap was so shocked he could hardly speak. When they caught him they cut his tongue out and threw him down the well. As for Captain Forbes, well, I have no idea what happened to him. The last I saw of him he was galloping towards the native town. I dare say he's met the same fate.'

'And what fate is that?' whispered Lilian.

'Butchered. Even young Fanny.' Mr Vine's chin trembled. 'I'm most dreadfully sorry, Mrs Fraser,' he said. 'Fanny was so very fond of you.'

'Indeed,' said Lilian. 'And I of her.' Lilian tried to recall what Fanny had looked like, but the girl had seemed so insignificant beside the vast galleon of her mother that it was all but impossible to remember anything about her. Still, what did it matter now?

'Mr Rutherford, dear man, always so quiet and unassuming among his friends, but quite a zealot in the pulpit. Such a *missionary*. Stabbed, again and again like Saint Sebastian by the very men he had tried to bring to God. Dr Mossly burned alive in his hospital.' Mr Vine began to sob. 'The screams were terrible, terrible. And I saw that bearer of yours making off with what looked like a basket of chickens.'

'We must leave here,' said Mr Hunter, his tone urgent.

'We must wreak vengeance,' cried Mr Vine suddenly. His voice rang out into the night sky like the cry of a furious preacher. 'We must smite this godless race so that they never again rise against us. We must show no mercy.' His voice rose to a shriek. 'Already, the garrisons at Delhi, at Cawnpore, at Lucknow and Meerut, they will be coming to our aid. They will be marching . . .' He gasped and pressed his hand to his chest as though seized suddenly with indigestion. The look of rage on his face turned to one of puzzlement. He gazed at Lilian, his mouth open, his eyes wide. 'Why on earth are you dressed like that?' he said at last. He stared at her, his eyes glazed and fixed upon her turban. Then all at once he toppled forward on to the dust. Behind him, a sepoy put his foot on to the small of Mr Vine's back and tugged out the blade of his sabre from between the Magistrate's shoulder blades.

Mr Hunter fell to his knees and groped in the dirt towards the fallen Magistrate, his fingers searching frantically for a weapon of some sort – a stone, a stick, even a handful of dust. Above his head he could see the sepoy's blade glinting in the light of the burning cantonment. At last his hand curled round the hilt of Mr Vine's fallen sabre. With a sudden, swift movement Mr Hunter thrust the blade up as hard as he could into the groin of the rearing sepoy.

Screaming, the sepoy collapsed beside the Magistrate. Mr Hunter staggered backwards, and then danced forwards, the shirt around his head flying out behind him as he stabbed at the writhing body.

'D'you think his clothes would fit me?' he panted, standing back at last and eyeing his attacker's uniform.

Lilian nodded. 'He's got a horse too,' she said.

Lilian and Mr Hunter rode out of the cantonment. They were certainly not the only travellers on the road that night and the path they had chosen – which headed in the opposite direction from the native town – was as busy as a bazaar thoroughfare. All manner of people were leaving Kushpur – gangs of men wielding sticks and cudgels; bands of drunken sepoys, their insignia ripped away, their faces shining with victory; whole families, their possessions carried on their backs or loaded into hackeries, made their way slowly and purposefully along the road. Lilian saw not a single white face among all those they passed. The air was filled with the sound of singing and crying, of shouts and bursts of victorious musket fire. Here and there camps had been erected, the flickering light of numerous cooking fires illuminating the roadside like welcoming beacons. The smell of wood smoke and roasting meat reminded Lilian how hungry and thirsty she was.

'Where are they all going?' she hissed. 'Can't you find out?'

Mr Hunter nodded. '*Shabash,*' he shouted, waving the dead sepoy's cutlass at a group of men lounging beside a campfire at the side of the road. 'How many have you killed today?' He spat a mouthful of saliva he could ill spare on to the ground, then threw back his head and laughed. The men grinned at one another. Mr Hunter wiped his mouth on his sleeve. Lilian gazed at him with reluctant admiration. Certainly, he looked the part. His teeth were perhaps a little too white to pass as those of a seasoned sepoy, but no one would notice in the darkness. Besides, a few minutes chewing a quid of betel would remedy that cosmetic defect. In the meantime his dark looks and skilful horsemanship, his fluency in Urdu and Hindi, his ability to transform himself from an English gentleman into a bazaar ruffian in an instant, why, despite the danger of their present situation, had she not been so shocked and stunned by the day's events, she might even have been thrilled.

The men looked up at him, taking in his stained uniform and bloody face. 'Yes,' said one. 'We have had some heavy work this evening. There is not a white face left in the whole of Kushpur. I have lost count of the *ferringhee* throats I've cut. Certainly, *hussoor*, there is little more to be done here. We are on our way to Delhi, where they say the Sircar is at his last gasp. A sight I would not miss for all the girls in the Delhi bazaar.'

'Bravely said,' replied Mr Hunter. 'May we meet again over a pile of *ferringhee* bodies at the Kashmere Gate!' He pulled on the reins of the horse so that the animal reared beneath him. 'Death to the Sircar!'

'*Shabash*!' cried Lilian, her voice sounding shriller than she had intended.

So Delhi had fallen. Lilian and Mr Hunter turned off the Trunk Road, heading north and east into the safety of the mountains. They rode single file, for which Lilian was glad. She was preoccupied by her own thoughts and they were thoughts she could not possibly have shared with Mr Hunter. Despite the horrors she had witnessed that day, she was finding that the further they went from Kushpur, the harder it was to recollect even the most terrible of those events. She was no longer able to recall the face of the officer whose head she had blown off; she could not remember the look on Mr Vine's face as he took his last breath. Even the headless ladies sitting round their tea tray – a sight she had been certain she would never forget – had become impossible to visualise, so that it was almost as though she were remembering through a series of grainy and indistinct photographs that had been taken by somebody else.

4

They covered many miles before the forest became so impenetrable that the moon was obscured and it was too dark to ride any further.

'We can be up and away early in the morning,' said Lilian, dismounting and leading her pony into the jungle. 'I have enough in my panniers to provide us with a comfortable camp.' She produced a tinder box and some kindling, and in minutes had their own campfire burning.

Mr Hunter dismounted slowly. He felt bruised all over – in his heroic bid to drag Lilian from her horse he had sprained his shoulder and now, having been on horseback for so long, it seared as though a red-hot iron were being thrust into his body. He sank on to the ground beside the fire. He felt exhausted and, though he was annoyed to admit it, was feverish as well. He hoped it wasn't anything serious.

Lilian was rooting in her baggage. She pulled out a cooking pot and a bag of rice.

'I've been in these hills before,' said Mr Hunter, unbuttoning the dead sepoy's uniform (the fellow's coat was beginning to feel like a vice about his chest). 'They're wild and dangerous, you know. I mean, most of the nabobs north of here are only nominally loyal to the British. There are a few hill forts here and there – isolated places, mostly. Places John Company pretends to have coerced into toeing the Company line, but the local rulers do just as they always did. Mind you, there might not be any of them friends of the British now.' He winced as he struggled out of his coat. 'If they ever were in the first place, that is.'

Lilian nodded. In the light of the fire she began sharpening her knife on a whetstone she had produced from some corner of her baggage.

'Of course,' continued Mr Hunter. 'Most of these hill forts are at least a week's journey away and over the roughest terrain you can find in India. I was planning to head north anyway, you know, even before . . . before everything happened the way it did. I need to check out the lie of the land before I mount a proper expedition – bearers and baggage and so forth.'

Lilian said nothing, but tested the blade with her finger.

'Yes, a reconnaissance trip, so to speak. I need to find some new rhododendron species – they simply can't get enough of them back home, you know. Some low-growing ones would suit admirably. This corner of India is as out-of-the-way as you can get – well, once we've travelled for a few days it will be – and no one's been to see what botanical treasures it contains. I have great expectations.'

Lilian nodded.

'It's the perfect place to hide out and the perfect place to find what I'm looking for. I stand to make a small fortune if I find varieties that travel well and that can be propagated back home.' Mr Hunter shrugged. 'Of course, it's a pity I had to leave all my things behind, but you seem well equipped. Certainly I don't see what else we could do at the moment. We can pick up further supplies from villages we pass through – most of them won't have seen white faces before, though, so we'll have to tread carefully.' He rubbed his hands together. 'The place is a veritable Eden, Lily,' he said. 'You'll fall in love with it.'

'I'm sure I will,' replied Lilian.

'That's settled, then,' said Mr Hunter.

Lilian nodded again.

Mr Hunter sighed. This was a new, economical version of Lilian he had not met before. He wondered what might be the matter with her, though it did not cross his mind to ask. Instead, assuming that the horrors she had witnessed had been too taxing, he switched to colourless observations about her camping skills. 'Where did you learn to light a fire like that?'

'When I go painting, I always take a tinder box,' said Lilian mechanically. 'I find a cup of tea most refreshing. Would you like one?'

'Don't you have anything stronger?'

'Brandy.'

Mr Hunter raised his eyebrows. 'Brandy?'

Lilian rooted in her baggage again. She tossed him a bottle. 'My husband's.'

Mr Hunter took a swig. He coughed and squinted at the label. 'Your husband had expensive tastes.'

'He could afford to, on the money my father gave him. Don't drink it all. I brought it for medicinal purposes.'

'Am I not in need of medicine?' said Mr Hunter crossly. He rubbed his shoulder and touched his fingers to his still-throbbing nose. She had not bothered to ask how his injuries were. 'You know, I feel quite feverish,' he said.

'You remind me of my husband,' said Lilian, prodding the fire. 'He was always feeling unwell. Fever was one of his favourite complaints.'

Mr Hunter took another gulp of brandy. It tasted slightly odd, now he thought about it, though perhaps that was simply the taste of the blood and dust that he had licked off his lips moments before. He watched as Lilian put a handful of sticks onto the fire. Why would she not comfort him? Could she not see that he was in pain? He was aching all over. 'Where shall I sleep?' he asked, watching with hopeful eyes as she unpacked a roll of bedding.

'Wherever you like.'

Mr Hunter grinned. 'In that case –'

'As long as it's not in with me.'

'Lily, please –' he gave her a beseeching look. She seemed so distant and unattainable.

She tossed him a blanket, then poured some warm water from the pot on the fire into a billycan and went over to him. Using a strip torn from the remains of his shirt, she bathed his face, wiping away the bloody slaverings that had congealed in black crusts about his hair, and on his cheeks and eyebrows.

Mr Hunter sat still and quiet while Lilian dabbed away. He wondered whether he should take the opportunity provided by this act of tenderness to seize her about the waist . . . but something told him that this would not be such a good idea. Besides, his head was swimming and he was not sure whether he would be able successfully to execute such a movement without toppling on to the fire in a faint. So he contented himself with looking at her dreamily, admiring the softness of her dirty cheek and the curve of her lips as she bent over his face. He gave a contented sigh, blowing a draught of brandied breath into her face. Lilian briskly wiped the last of the blood from his forehead.

He sank back on to his blanket. Lilian's face seemed to be suspended above him, like a benign moon in a dark and troubled sky. Had he asked her to be his wife? He could not remember. He had thought about it for so long that now, as his head pounded and his vision blurred, he was almost certain that he had. 'Will you be my wife, Lily?' he murmured, just to be on the safe side.

Lilian laid a cold damp hand on his blazing forehead.

Mr Hunter repeated the question. At least, he tried to repeat it, but he found that he could hardly get his lips to move and the words seemed as heavy as glue on his tongue. This time, even he didn't understand the sentence he had uttered. He began to shiver again. He stared up at her, but her face seemed to have receded into the distance. He saw her take off her turban, and loosen her hair so that it fell about her shoulders like ripples of sunlit water. How lovely she was. Would she not just lie down beside him to keep him warm? He sighed happily, finding to his surprise that he no longer desired her, but was simply contented to be in her company. The pain in his shoulder had abated, and the throbbing sensation in his nose and head seemed to have gone completely. Instead, these physical discomforts had been replaced with a feeling of well-being and inertia that seemed to lap around him like a warm, soothing bath. He closed his eyes as he felt Lilian's hand stroke his brow. He reached out to touch her, to kiss her fingers or to draw her close, but he found he could barely lift his arm. He felt the rim of the brandy bottle against his lips once more and he drank deeply. After that, he felt nothing at all.

The following day Mr Hunter was no better. If anything, he was worse. Thanks to the brandy he had drunk (which had been laced with opium) he had slept soundly all night. So soundly, in fact, that Lilian had trouble rousing him.

'You look terrible.' She handed him a tin mug filled with strong black tea.

He said nothing. He was, by turns, burning with heat and shivering with cold. He sipped the tea and ate some of the rice she had cooked the night before.

'Can you ride?' asked Lilian, after she had packed everything away.

His shoulder was so stiff that he could hardly move his arm. Lilian helped him on with the dead sepoy's jacket. 'Just in case we meet any of your comrades,' she said.

They made slow progress. The jungle path they followed was scarcely a path at all, and now and again Lilian had to dismount and hack away some of the low-lying branches. In place of a machete she used Mr Vine's sabre which, although not designed for horticultural duties, performed the job well enough. As she laboured among the foliage, she was reminded of the long hours spent pruning back the larger plants in the upper reaches of her father's conservatory. The sweltering atmosphere was almost the same. At times it seemed to her as though the only thing missing was the distant throbbing of the hot-water pipes beneath their iron grids, the gentle burble of her aunts' voices as they played whist in their overgrown parlour far below. And Alice.

When they stopped – as they were obliged to do with tedious frequency to allow Mr Hunter to totter into the bush to empty his gurgling bowels – Lilian pulled out her sketch pad and pencil. Mr Hunter, for once, said nothing all day, apart from telling her that, regardless of its appearance, the path they were on was the right one – as long as they continued in a north-easterly direction. Despite the heat of the day, he wrapped himself in a blanket. By evening, he was draped across the neck of his horse, as though the humidity had melted him like wax.

On the morning of the fourth day Mr Hunter seemed a little better. His shivers had abated and he was able to mount his horse unaided. He ate a bowl of rice and a chapatti. Thus fortified, he decided once more to ask Lilian to marry him. This time he would be sure to do so when there was no chance of being misunderstood: his brain would be unclouded by fever, his loins free from the misleading sensations of desire. He smoothed his hair and washed his face and did his best, using some spit and a rub with his torn shirt, to remove some of the dirt from the dead sepoy's uniform.

When Lilian's back was turned Mr Hunter sneaked a look at his reflection in the back of a spoon. He was horrified to see how gaunt and yellow-looking he was beneath his black whiskers and beard, and tanned badmash face. Furthermore, even given the distortion of his reflection occasioned by the belly of the spoon, he could see that his nose was still as bruised and swollen as an overripe pear, his eyes still bloodshot from the brandy and opium he had been drinking. He looked like a drunk after a night spent brawling in the gutter. His confidence dimmed slightly. Perhaps he should wait a few days before he made his declaration of love. At least until the sparkle in his eye had returned and he felt a little better – less tired and plagued by the residuum of aches and shivers. After all, once she had agreed to marry him he might be called upon to perform certain husbandly offices and he wanted to have enough energy to oblige.

Mr Hunter pushed the spoon out of sight. 'I think it's a touch of malaria,' he told her. 'I must have picked it up in Calcutta. The place is built on a swamp, you know. It's riddled with fevers. You must have noticed how yellow everyone looks.' He coughed, and wiped his brow with the back of his hand. His bowels gurgled ominously. 'Of course, the conditions in Darjeeling are perfect for cinchona cultivation. The Company could grow a whole plantation and have enough quinine to keep everyone free of malaria, including the natives. But for some reason those fools in Calcutta would rather keep shipping the stuff over from Peru at great expense and with little hope of ever having enough of it to do the job properly.' He clambered on to his horse. His head was swimming and all at once he felt shivery and sick. 'Can't you cut us a path a bit quicker?' he said. 'I can make faster progress as long as you look after me.'

'I see,' said Lilian, irritably. '*As long as I look after you.* You think only of yourself. As usual.'

'But I'm not well.'

'A touch of malaria.'

'It could kill me. And we must move on, or the rebels may kill us both.'

'Oh, of course,' said Lilian. Her voice had become shrill. 'You run away as soon as things become uncomfortable, don't you? That's what you do, isn't it? You take what you want and then run away.'

Mr Hunter looked startled. 'The world has turned upside down,' he said. 'How much more uncomfortable could it be?'

'You think of yourself first and you flee the moment things get hot. You care nothing for the consequences of your actions. You have no interest in what sort of trouble you might leave behind you. What kind of a man *are* you, Mr Hunter?'

He put a hand to his throbbing head. He did not know what she was talking about. 'It's quiet now, but that's only because we're away from Kushpur. But we're not *that* far away. Come on, Lily, you know what's going on.'

'I thought you were friends with the natives? What can you possibly have to fear from them?' She rammed the bag of rice into her saddlebag. Her face was furious.

'There are plenty of them who are not my friends, I can assure you. And right now any one of them would be glad to slit my throat.'

'The fathers of women whose honour you've ruined, perhaps?' muttered Lilian.

'What on earth are you talking about? Those nautch-girls don't have fathers. Besides,' he added gruffly, 'those days are over. I've not been there for months.'

'What are *you* talking about?' said Lilian crossly.

'Nothing. Those girls.'

'What "girls"? How many of us have there been?'

'How many of whom?' said Mr Hunter desperately. 'Why are we talking about this now? It doesn't matter, surely?'

'It doesn't *matter*?' Lilian's voice echoed through the forest. 'I should think it matters very much. Unless *I* don't matter. Don't you understand? You left me. You ran away and left me in the hands of that . . . that . . . *murderer*. And you think that doesn't *matter*?'

'Murderer? You can't mean Selwyn?'

'You!' shouted Lilian. 'You left me to that . . . so-called *doctor*, with his cold, horrible hands and his knives and his hooks . . .'

Mr Hunter blinked. How bright the sunlight seemed as it streamed through the branches of the *chir* pine overhead. It hurt his eyes and made them water. He knew the day was warm, but he felt as chilled as a corpse. He wished Lilian would stop talking and mount her pony. What use was there in going over the carnage they had witnessed? Far better to forget the whole monstrous business. 'Knives and hooks?' he said. 'Come now, Lily, you must try to put everything behind you. You're very upset. And no wonder. You've seen some frightful things.'

'Upset!' cried Lilian. 'Frightful things!'

'Anyway,' added Mr Hunter briskly, 'Dr Mossly is dead. Now we really must be getting along. We can talk about all this later. Come *on,* Lily.'

At first, Lilian had not intended to say anything to Mr Hunter about her fate at the hands of Dr Cattermole. Riding away from her bungalow (how long ago it seemed), as Mr Hunter and the other Europeans awaited her in the parlour, she had thought that simply making him fall in love with her and then disappearing from his life would be vengeance enough. After all, did he not deserve to have his heart broken? And besides, she could hardly bear to remind herself of the events that had led to her expulsion from the Great House. Having to repeat them by way of explanation would simply have made her weep in front of him and this she had resolved never to do.

But since then she had shot a man; she had almost cut off another man's hand; she had passed through a swirling sea of bloodshed, had seen brutality on such a scale that she had been unable to turn away, but had stared at it, as though into the maw of hell, fixated with horror and disbelief. Now, she found that the memory of her own butchery, and of the murder of her unborn child, had returned to her with a fearful clarity. The pain she had thought deeply buried inside her heart had risen up, so that the words she uttered seemed to bubble with fury into her mouth, hardly coherent even to herself. Her sense of outrage, her feelings of anger and humiliation at Mr Hunter's abandonment, and everything that had followed on from that, now blazed within her as forcefully as on the day he had left.

The acts of violence and violation she had endured had gone unpunished; the death of her child had been without retribution.

By the afternoon Mr Hunter was worse again. That night Lilian gave him a large draught of brandy, just to stop him from shrieking in his delirium.

In the morning he was still asleep. He murmured something indistinct, but lay without moving beneath his blanket. Lilian lit a fire to heat water. She made tea, but decided to wait until he stirred before preparing any breakfast. In the meantime she erected her easel and took out her watercolours. Now that the sun had risen she could see through the gaps in the conifers. They were in a clearing overlooking a forest-clad valley, at the bottom of which a river twisted and tumbled. She could see wisps of cloud hanging above the trees, snagged on the tallest branches or caught, here and there, in a breezeless hollow. Other than the sound of birds and insects, and the far-off roar of the river, the place was silent.

Lilian sat before a yellow flower twined round a broken trunk and began to paint. How well the limpid blue and lilac of the morning sky set off the glowing, sunny lustre of the flower's petals. The painting would be a good one, she could tell. And yet, how on earth was she going to get her watercolours back to England and away from the ravages of mildew and the appetites of white ants? Already she had a number of sketches and a painting rolled up behind her saddle. And there was still the vexed question of where to send them. Should she offer them to Kew? Should she send them to the botanical gardens at Calcutta? Should she post them to Alice miles away in England?

Poor Alice, thought Lilian with a sigh; she must be wondering what had happened. No doubt the telegraph had alerted London to the horrors of the recent uprisings and everyone at Home would be sure to know about it by now. Alice would be desperate for information. Unless the news had yet to cross her father's threshold. It was quite possible that their father was so engrossed in his Collection that he had no idea what was happening in the world beyond his own front door. Certainly, this had happened before and Lilian recalled that it was with a grunt of surprise that Mr Talbot had raised his head from his tempest prognosticator to hear the news that there had been fighting in the Crimea . . .

So absorbed in her own thoughts was Lilian that she didn't hear anything until the man was right behind her. Afterwards, she wondered how he had managed to creep up on her so quietly – until she came to realise that he walked everywhere in his golden slippers as though gliding over thick, luxuriant carpets. It was with a gasp of surprise, therefore, that Lilian greeted the voice at her shoulder.

'Delightful!' he cried. 'That colour is a special favourite of mine. It reminds me most forcefully of Oxford and the buttercups that grew beside the river in Magdalen's meadows. Only it is brighter. Much brighter, of course.'

5

'Your companion seems unwell,' he added.

Lilian nodded. She was staring into a man's chubby face. His brown eyes were set above sparsely whiskered cheeks; his top lip garnished with gleaming ebony moustaches. His head was wrapped in a turban of such brilliant whiteness that Lilian's eyes ached to look at it; his rotund body swathed in brocade of such richness that she could not help but stare. She blushed, suddenly conscious of her own filthy clothing and her unkempt hair. So dirty was her own turban that she had been unable to bring herself to put it on that morning, and she had donned her battered and sun-bleached topi instead. Lilian swallowed nervously.

The man smiled cheerily, awaiting her reply in respectful silence. Two bearers in spotless white dhotis stood behind him, their eyes lowered. One held a silk canopy over his master, the other a long-handled fan made up of peacock feathers which he wafted discreetly back and forth.

'You are silent,' continued the man, when no answer was forthcoming. 'But of course, as my old tutor, Dr Rogerson of Oxford, liked to say, "it is a wise head that keeps a still tongue." Perhaps I have surprised you?'

'Indeed, sir,' Lilian managed to say at last.

'Quite so. You did not expect to see me.'

'I didn't expect to see anyone,' said Lilian. 'I didn't hear you coming.' She frowned. 'Do you always creep up on people in that way?'

'May I not walk as I please in my own kingdom?'

'But of course. I only meant – I only meant that you startled me.'

'For that I must apologise. Come, Dr Rogerson was most particular. We must shake hands and declare ourselves. My name is Ravindra Yashodhar Bhagirath Rana. I am the Maharajah of Bhandarahpur. But please, you may call me Ravi. And you are?'

'I am Miss Talbot.' Lilian shook the plump beringed hand that was held out towards her.

'And your companion?' Ravi pointed into the trees, where Lilian assumed Mr Hunter to be still asleep.

'That is Tom Hunter.'

'He wears the coat of the sepoy. The man is an Indian fellow?'

'No,' said Lilian after a moment's hesitation. 'He is English too.'

'Your husband?'

Lilian shook her head.

Ravi's brow beneath his turban creased in perplexity. 'Explain this to me please. You travel alone with a man who is not your husband? Dr Rogerson, he was most particular on that matter also. A lady, an English lady, is never alone with a man who is not her husband, her father or her brother. It is considered most improper.'

Lilian could think of nothing to say.

Suddenly Ravi's face cleared. 'Ah, Mr Tom Hunter, perhaps he is your servant?' The bearer with the peacock feather fan twitched a fly whisk above his master's shoulder, as though to indicate that duties of a real servant did not involve sleeping in the jungle while his mistress looked after herself.

'No,' whispered Lilian. 'He is . . . my travelling companion.'

'But of course.' Ravi cleared his throat and lowered his eyes discreetly. Then, after a moment contemplating this information, he shrugged. 'And yet, Dr Rogerson was an old man. Times change and "there is more than one way to skin a cat" is there not? Excellent!' Apparently satisfied with his own reasoning he smiled and repeated brightly, 'I see he is not well.'

'No,' agreed Lilian. 'But he might be a little better when he wakes.'

'Ah yes, "sleep is the best medicine", as your esteemed English saying goes.' Ravi clapped his hands. A troop of bearers dressed in gleaming white dhotis stepped into the clearing. 'You will come to my home. As my guest,' he said to Lilian. 'It is not far off, and we have elephants and horses to convey us there. We may also have medicines to suit your companion. Will you do me the honour, Miss Talbot, of riding in my howdah? My bearers will carry your Mr Hunter. He will be quite safe. Ah, but you are worried. I am a stranger to you. And yet, is it not true, as your English wisdom tells us, that "strangers are simply the friends one has yet to meet"? And now that we have met, why, we are friends, I am sure.'

'That's most generous of you, sir,' said Lilian. 'We were heading north and east. Until Mr Hunter fell ill, of course. Do you know that road? Perhaps you could help us.'

'Most certainly. As the English say, "to know the road ahead, ask those coming back." You may ask me and I shall be honoured to furnish you with answers.' Ravi broke off, a wistful smiled playing about his lips. 'Yes, yes, dear Dr Rogerson. He was a most assiduous tutor. "When the student is ready the master will appear." You English have always the proverb for the occasion. Just so.' He sighed. 'Dear Oxford. Miss Talbot, join me, please. We may reminisce together. It would be a great pleasure. And to speak in English is, to me, also the most joyful of pastimes.' He eyed Lilian's half-finished painting almost greedily. 'I would most particularly like to speak to you on the subject of your painting. You are a lover of plants? I myself am most dedicated in this capacity. I have a vegetable garden of great beauty. Indeed, it is the English vegetables that interest me most. Dr Rogerson himself grew marrows of quite fearful bigness. Perhaps we may speak of these matters also.' He lowered his voice and eyed her costume with the distaste he clearly felt, but had been politely concealing. 'Of course, when we reach our destination you may also wish to exchange your goatherd attire for something more comfortable. My bearers will provide you with all you require.'

Despite the amount of time she had spent in India, Lilian had not travelled on an elephant before. There had been a howdah draped with coloured silks outside the door of her bedroom in her father's house – as children she and Alice had played in it, pretending to punt down the hallway on their way to exotic lands and faraway places. Now that Lilian was actually in an exotic land and faraway place, she felt a thrill of excitement as she climbed the elephant to sit among the howdah's crimson and gold cushions. Ravi mounted the beast beside her.

'This howdah I use for hunting,' he panted. 'Most comfortable. Very large and spacious.' He blinked reproachfully at her muddied boots and handed her a pair of silver slippers. 'Much more comfortable, please.'

Looking down, Lilian observed a flurry of activity taking place far below about the legs of the elephant. She saw Mr Hunter's still-unconscious body being placed in a palanquin. Her easel, her barely started painting and all her possessions, she noticed being carried off by a team of bearers. Their ponies were led out of sight. Then all at once a trumpet sounded; a voice cried out, the bearers disappeared (though where they went, Lilian could not tell); and her elephant began to move forward.

It was like sitting atop a moving house. Lilian made a grab for the side of the howdah to steady herself. How high they were. She found that she was looking out into the trees at birds and insects she had not seen before. Monkeys bounded off into the foliage and butterflies flitted among the branches, neither of which she had been able to see properly from her position on horseback. From his nest among a flurry of crimson and gold cushions Ravi watched his guest with interest. A faint smile sat upon his rosebud lips.

At length they were clear of the forest and Lilian was able to see out across the valley. The river still winked and sparkled, though it appeared now to be on their right instead of their left. No doubt this was a different river, thought Lilian, as she had no recollection of crossing the other one. She looked about, pulling her topi down over her eyes and squinting into the distance. She had no idea where they were; no idea in which direction Kushpur might lie and no idea where they were going. She looked behind, across the elephant's mighty brocade-clad rear to see whether she could spot Mr Hunter's palanquin. But the line of bearers that followed in their wake appeared to be transporting a number of palanquins through the jungle, and which one might contain Mr Hunter it was impossible to tell. The sun was now warm upon her shoulders through the silken gauze of the howdah's coloured drapery. Lilian judged that they were indeed travelling in a north-easterly direction. Not that it mattered. Now that she thought about it, she realised that she was enjoying herself too much to care.

The howdah swayed gently from side to side, undulating with the elephant's giant, sedate strides. All at once the beast trumpeted – raising its trunk as though in salutation and swinging its great head from side to side so that the coloured beads on its headdress rattled and glinted in the sunlight. Lilian laughed and clapped her hands. Ravi grinned, delighted that his mode of transport was being so well received.

'I have known this elephant for many years,' he said proudly. 'Her dung I use to spread about my vegetables.'

'Indeed,' said Lilian.

'And yet still they do not grow well. Marrows, yes. But leeks? These I cannot succeed with. Sprouts also. Turnip?' He shook his head sadly. 'No. Dr Rogerson would be most disappointed. Perhaps I have not the necessary understanding. As my old tutor would say, "zeal without knowledge is the sister of folly."' He looked at Lilian, his face despondent. 'You, like myself, are fond of the kingdom of plants?'

'Yes. And you have such an abundance of the most beautiful species here. I shall run out of materials before I run out of subjects.'

'Perhaps you might agree to paint my marrows?' said Ravi eagerly.

'I would be delighted. And, of course, the flower of the marrow is particularly beautiful.'

'Yes, yes it is. A most exquisite plant. And the turnip and Brussels sprout, these also are most excellent. Delicacies such as these I had often at Oxford, cooked by Dr Rogerson's housekeeper, Mrs Heggarty. Sprouts, these I loved especially. Mrs Heggarty would prepare them for me as often as I required.' He sighed. 'But now it is the Brussels sprout that troubles me the most. It seems that this most delectable English vegetable is not to be grown in India. I have tried everything, but with no success.' Then he clapped his hands and flashed her a sudden smile of brilliant whiteness. 'And yet, has Our Lord Shiva not sent me two English gardeners to help me in my desire to grow these most exquisite vegetables?' He settled himself on his cushions and looked at Lilian eagerly. 'Advise me, please. Is my soil too hard? Too soft? Too poor? Too black? Is there too much water? Not enough water? Too much sun or shade?'

'Really, I know little about vegetable cultivation –' began Lilian.

'But you are familiar with the vegetables of which I speak?'

'Yes, but I know little about what particular conditions they enjoy.'

Ravi frowned. 'This is not what I was wanting to hear.' After a moment spent digesting this unwelcome news, however, he appeared to have a change of heart. He smiled. 'Miss Talbot. Please understand me. You know, of course, that you are a long, long way from your friends now? You might wish to consider this fact. I'm sure it will help to refresh the memories you have of your own dear English vegetables.'

Mr Hunter remembered nothing about his journey. So drugged was he with opium and brandy that he had no idea where he was or what was happening to him. He had a distant awareness of movement, a dream of being lifted by native hands and of resting on scented cushions; an impression of time passing and a journey made, but these sensations were vague and formless, and he could not have said who had moved him from his blanket on the jungle floor, nor could he have said when or why they had done so. Later, as he shivered and sweated and cried out in his delirium, he discovered to his astonishment that he was no longer in the jungle, but was on a charpoy surrounded by soft white drapery, with cooling breezes wafting across his sweating, twitching body. Perhaps this was a mirage, he murmured to himself in a moment of lucidity, and his mind had wandered to such a degree that even his sense of sight and certainty had deserted him. But then he felt cool fingers on his brow, and he knew that Lilian was with him. He relaxed. He sipped the bitter-tasting liquid that was on his lips, and when he tried to turn his head away (for it really was a most unpleasant mixture) those same fingers turned his head back again and pressed the vessel to his lips once more. Gentle hands changed his sodden sheets, lifting him and lowering him on to a cool, crisp bed of newly washed linen. Mr Hunter sighed. He murmured her name before slipping into sleep.

His skin grew yellow and flaky, his eyes became glazed and ringed with dark shadows. He lay tangled in his sweat-soaked sheets, gasping and shaking.

At last, when he emerged, weak and exhausted, from his fever, Mr Hunter found himself in a room of the most splendid proportions. He looked about through red-rimmed eyes. So he had not been dreaming after all. The room was light and airy, its walls patterned with mosaics and glittering with mirrors. Curtains made of some diaphanous material encircled his charpoy, wafting in the breeze of the gently swishing punkah. His window, he discovered when he managed to persuade the bearers to help him totter over to it, looked down on to a vast walled garden of exotic plants and trees, some of which he was sure he had never seen before.

He asked those silent bearers who attended him to move his bed over to the window so that he could see the garden. He asked for Lilian, but they shook their heads and murmured vague apologies. Then, one day, gazing listlessly out at the leafy greenness, he spotted her, in a far corner sitting behind her easel in the middle of what looked like (but surely could not possibly be) a vegetable patch. She was dressed in an azure sari and was sheltered from the hot sun by a large umbrella-like canopy held by a bearer. She looked up and saw him. She waved her paintbrush at him and smiled. Mr Hunter raised his hand. He had not the strength to do anything more.

Over the following days he slept a lot. He ate well. He recovered his strength and his face filled out again. His whiskers regained their former glossy lustre. Every day a team of silent bearers brought him food and drink in shining silverware, bathed him, clothed him, brought him books on gardening, and went away again. The books were in English and had been well thumbed. Mr Hunter dozed on his charpoy and flicked through his reading material in a desultory fashion.

Later, when he was able to leave his bed unaided, he noticed that the bearers always locked the door behind them. Mr Hunter asked repeatedly to see Lilian. Why would she not come to him? He was told that she was working in the garden on her paintings. He asked to see their master. At first, the bearers simply shook their heads. Later, they mumbled that their master was busy and would meet his guest some other time. Soon, his questions were met with a stubborn silence. Rapunzel-like, Mr Hunter gazed out of his window in despair.

One day he saw a small, tubby figure clad in gold pyjama trousers and white khurta, with a pair of what looked like Wellington boots on his feet, digging in the vegetable patch. Mr Hunter shouted and waved. The figure shouted and waved back. Later that day Mr Hunter was taken out of his room.

He was led down a wide, gleaming marble staircase. He crossed gleaming marble hallways and passed beneath glittering chandeliers. Depictions of Indian warriors enjoying the sports of war and the pleasures that follow lined the walls in a seemingly endless gallery of military triumph and reward. At length he was brought into the presence of a small, Indian gentleman with silky black whiskers and moustache. Mr Hunter was sure that it was the same fellow he had seen labouring in the garden earlier that day. Now, however, the man was seated on a golden cushion, flicking though a copy of *Glenny's Handbook for the Fruit and Vegetable Grower*. Behind him hung a row of botanical paintings. Mr Hunter recognised them as Lilian's handiwork – not least because she had signed her name on each of them. Four of them appeared to depict marrows of differing sizes and colours.

'My name is Ravindra Yashodhar Bhagirath Rana, the Maharajah of Bhandarahpur,' said the man, tossing his book aside and leaping to his feet. 'And you are most welcome in my palace.' He seized Mr Hunter's hand and pumped it enthusiastically. 'I see you have recovered.'

Mr Hunter gave a slight bow. He had never heard of Bhandarahpur. 'Yes,' he said warily. 'For which I thank you. If there is any way in which I can repay your kindness –'

'That we will come to in a moment,' said Ravi. 'But first, I see you admiring my paintings. They were, of course, executed by your lady companion, Lilian Talbot.'

'I thought so,' said Mr Hunter. 'Excuse me, but is that a marrow?'

Ravi smiled. 'It is indeed *four* marrows. Ah, what a most excellent lady she is. While you were sick she has painted my most prized vegetables, as you can see. She also painted many of the plants I hold in my garden. We have "made hay while the sun shines" as you English like to say.' He laughed. 'Ah, such conversations we have had. Her dear sister, her beloved aunts . . . Lilian – she permits me to use the familiar name – has described them all to me so that I feel that they are quite my friends. Her own sad departure from England, the untimely decease of her husband, all these histories she has explained.' He smiled benignly. 'You yourself were also mentioned.'

'I was?' Mr Hunter was unable to keep the eagerness out of his voice. Had Lilian opened her heart to this unlikely confidant? 'What did she say?'

'That you stole her honour and abandoned her in England.'

Mr Hunter blushed. 'That was a long time ago. I was a fool. I have admitted it to her. She has forgiven me.'

'Ah yes, and "let bygones be bygones". That is the expression, is it not? And you are sure of this?'

'Why would I not be sure?'

'I merely ask.'

A note of uncertainty crept into Mr Hunter's voice. 'She said she had.'

'Did she?'

'Yes.'

'But my dear Mr Hunter. Are you not familiar with that most instructive of English proverbs, "take heed of reconciled enemies and of meat twice boiled"?'

'I must confess that I have never heard that one.'

'A pity. For I can assure you, Miss Talbot says that she did *not* forgive you for deserting her. Indeed, very, very bad things happened to her afterwards as a consequence of your most ungentlemanly behaviour and cowardly departure.'

Mr Hunter blinked. 'I beg your pardon?'

'"If you would enjoy the fruit, pluck not the flower", Mr Hunter. Surely, as a man of horticulture you must know the truth of this matter?'

'Meaning what, exactly?' asked Mr Hunter in exasperation. 'Look here, my dear fellow. Where is she? I demand to speak to her.'

'"My dear fellow",' murmured Ravi. 'Ah, Oxford.' He looked at Mr Hunter brightly and shook his head. 'I do not think that you are in a position to demand anything. I am to tell you, as you have not asked her yourself, that Miss Talbot – Lilian – was to have had your child.'

'How do you . . .'

'That a doctor, a friend of her father, took it upon himself to remove the unborn babe. To . . . destroy it, so that she would not be shamed. So that her father would not be shamed.' Ravi shuddered and lowered his eyes. 'And afterwards she was married to a foolish man, denied her dowry and sent away from her beloved sister. The rest you know.'

'Why didn't she tell me this herself if it's true?' cried Mr Hunter. But even as he spoke it dawned on him that the man before him might well be speaking the truth. Had not Lilian said something similar when they were camping in the forest? He had assumed, in his delirium, that she was talking about the unspeakable acts of bloodshed and violence she had witnessed in the streets of Kushpur. But those unspeakable acts had not been perpetrated on someone else, but had happened to Lilian herself, and to her child – his child – within her own body. 'Why didn't she tell me?' Mr Hunter's voice was no more than a whisper.

'You did not ask her,' said Ravi. 'And so, "though the wound was healed, a scar remained". This English saying is most fitting. Mr Hunter, you would be sensible to remember it.'

'I need to speak to her,' said Mr Hunter. 'Where is she?'

'Oh, she has gone,' said Ravi. He picked up his copy of *Glenny's Handbook for the Fruit and Vegetable Grower* and began flicking through its pages once more.

'Gone?' said Mr Hunter, unable to believe his ears.

'Yes. But you are to stay here. I have much work for you to do. "The Devil makes work for idle hands", does he not? And that would never do.' Ravi frowned, as though suddenly remembering something. 'Oh, yes. And please do not try to follow her. Her life will be improved very much without you. I have many guards and you can be certain that they are under the most explicit instructions. Besides, we are many, many miles from anyone you might wish to call friends and these lands are fearfully, fearfully dangerous: Thugs, crocodiles, tigers . . . and mutiny, of course.' He shrugged. 'But please, enough of this unpleasant talk. We have work to do. As you English say, "Procrastination is the thief of time." This saying also is most correct.' He smiled and clapped his hands. From behind a wall hanging appeared a bearer holding a silver platter. Upon it was a small pouch of golden fabric. Ravi seized the pouch and jiggled it in his right hand excitedly.

'The seed of the Brussels sprout,' he said. 'You will grow them for me. I have also cabbage, leek, turnip . . . "As you sow, so shall you reap." Is it not so?' He regarded Mr Hunter with a mixture of perplexity and concentration. 'Now then. We are perhaps a little too late to sow these particular seeds. What would your advice be? Should we plant this instant? Should we await cooler weather?' He shrugged. 'Then again, perhaps we should simply leave them until next year? After all, we have plenty of time.'

ALICE

1

The sound of Sluce falling to the ground was masked by the applause that broke out at the conclusion of Dr Cattermole's lecture. Alice stepped past the sprawling body of her father's manservant and peeped over the threshing machine. The guests were facing the podium, behind which Dr Cattermole was nodding and shaking hands, and generally looking rather pleased with himself. His magic lantern had not been switched off and from the wall behind him the face of a woman stared in startled disbelief at the crowd of enthusiastically applauding men. Her head was encircled by a garland of flowers – put there for dramatic effect by Cattermole himself, thought Alice angrily. After all, how persuasive would his lecture have been without recourse to the customary motifs of madness? And yet, could the so-called scientific men who made up his audience not see beyond such visual tricks? Were they not insulted by his lack of scientific rigour? Had they not daughters, wives, sisters who every day demonstrated the contrary? Alice was tempted to seize another glass eye and hurl it at Dr Cattermole's head.

Sluce let out a groan. Stretched on the floor, his nostrils caked with congealing blood, he was breathing heavily. The glass eye lay beside him, staring up at Alice as though in astonishment at the assault in which it had been forced to take part. The door to the servants' passageway stood ajar, a lantern within glowing dimly against the darkness. Alice bent down and seized Sluce about the ankles. His muddy shoes emanated a powerful stench of the abyss – a blend of wet leather, freshly turned soil and sulphur. Alice dragged him over the threshold and into the flickering darkness beyond.

The door clicked closed behind her. She hauled Sluce down the passageway, deep into the manservant's lair behind the wall of the ballroom. For someone so small and thin he seemed a remarkably cumbersome load. It was like dragging a sack of wet soil. Eventually, she reached a lantern that Sluce had left burning on the Louis Quinze table beside a pile of silken cushions and an electroplated statue of Diana. Alice held up the lantern and studied him. His breathing was heavy. His eyes had rolled back into his head so that only a narrow slit of white could be seen from beneath his drooping eyelids. As Mr Talbot's indispensable familiar, Sluce, she knew, had been entrusted with the keys to the house. He would have the keys to the back and front doors, to her father's study, perhaps even to his strong box . . . There was no time to lose.

Alice began to rummage in the pockets of Sluce's mnemonic coat. From her position crouched on the floor beside the wall she could hear the rumble of conversation from the ballroom beyond. A question-and-answer session had started. It was with a thrill of horror that she realised what Dr Cattermole was talking about.

'No, I have not performed this type of surgery myself, though I do have a patient awaiting my attention. It is a procedure I have every confidence will turn the subject from a wilful and opinionated individual with questionable moral self-governance, into a meek and obedient lady.' A flutter of applause greeted this declaration.

'Why, yes,' cried Dr Cattermole in answer to another question that Alice did not hear. 'I shall be delighted to report my findings to you at a subsequent meeting of the Society. And as the gentleman suggests, I shall take photographs of the lady's physiognomy both before and after the procedure.'

Alice fumbled urgently with the cold, greasy stuff of Sluce's coat. Her fingers slid beneath a dank flap of fabric and into a bulging pocket. At the bottom of a long, sock-like recess they closed round a hard, cold object. She pulled it out. It was a silver trinket box in the shape of a turtle. Alice was sure she had seen such an item on the dressing table in her mother's room when she was a child, but she could not be certain. She placed it on the floor.

Sluce moaned and exhaled noisily, his eyelids fluttering, as though he was about to emerge from oblivion. A faint whiff of gin drifted from his half-open mouth. Alice opened the mnemonic coat. Her searching fingers yielded a silver sugar-caster the size and shape of a liturgical ornament; a candlestick; a selection of buckles and bodkins; a postcard depicting the main atrium of the Great Exhibition of 1851; a clock weight and a pendulum; a cloth bag containing eight identical spanners; the rosette from a watering can spout . . . Two pockets contained nothing more than shattered pottery fragments (if only it were so easy to get rid of one's unwanted memories, Alice though grimly).

At length, Alice sat back. She stared at the results of her labours. What had she found? Nothing, it seemed, but half the contents of a bric-a-brac shop. And how warm it was becoming under the hot gaze of the lamp. Her hands felt sticky with the touch of Sluce's horrible pockets, her head ached as she gazed at the heap of aides-mémoires. She seized the postcard of the Crystal Palace and used it to sift through the sea of objects. She opened a small lacquered box to find a selection of surgical scalpels. Another box contained a dirty handkerchief and a piece of folded oilcloth. Alice dropped the handkerchief and pulled out the oilcloth. Something heavy was wrapped within and she almost lost her grip on the item as the cloth unravelled in her hands. She found that she was holding a small mahogany frame about three and half inches in diameter. Inside the frame was a square of glass, behind which, Alice assumed, was a picture. She peered at it but could make out nothing. She squinted closer, rubbing at its surface gently with the corner of her sleeve. Then she held it up to the light.

All at once, staring out at her from above two vast, pale breasts, which appeared to be resting on the rim of her lowered corset like a pair of suet puddings carried on a tray, was Mrs Cattermole. There was no mistaking the shining ringlets and coy expression. Mrs Cattermole was lolling on a mound of cushions, her thighs spread like tumbled bolsters. The glass was well-thumbed, the surface opaque with a grubby sheen and blobbed with the greasy marks of Sluce's eager fingerprints.

Alice shuddered. The foetid warmth of the passageway was heavy with the smell of hot lamp glass and exhaled gin. It seemed to be seeping into her clothes and hair, and coating her skin like oil. The stench of sulphur from Sluce's shoes and the musty odour of his coat caught in her nostrils, so that she felt her stomach tighten with a sudden wave of nausea. She wrapped the slide in its protective coat of oilcloth and pushed it into her own pocket. Seizing the lamp, she made her way out of the dark entrails of the building in search of Mr Blake.

She passed along the hallway quickly and quietly, hoping that the items of the Collection that crowded its flanks would provide places to hide or niches to slip into should the need arise.

All at once her father's voice boomed out: 'Alice?'

Alice leaped behind a life-sized statue of the Queen made from the same pottery used in the manufacture of drains and sewers (a gift to her father from Shanks and Company).

At that instant her father rounded the corner in front of her, Dr Cattermole in his wake. 'No, Cattermole, I have no idea where she is. I have sent Sluce to find her.'

'Might I suggest that when she is found she is taken straight to the room I have prepared for her?' replied Dr Cattermole.

'I have yet to speak to Mr Blake on the matter, though I have no doubt he will be glad to be of assistance.'

'Will I have to pay him?' grunted Mr Talbot. He was standing so close to her hiding place that Alice could see the flecks of dead skin on the shoulders of his coat. She squeezed herself behind the Queen's pottery skirts until she felt as though she were about to tip the statue over.

'The boundary between madness and sanity is a slim one,' Dr Cattermole was saying, his voice shrill. 'I would suggest that we have no time to lose.'

'Of course, of course. And yet . . .' Mr Talbot wrung his hands. 'Are you quite sure, Cattermole?'

'Oh, my dear fellow, it is quite natural that you should be concerned,' replied Dr Cattermole, his tone as soft as wax. 'But it is for the best. Her gentle nature, her sweetness of countenance and docility will be restored – a most desirable outcome, surely?'

'"Docility and sweetness of countenance"?' repeated Mr Talbot doubtfully. 'I'm not sure Alice ever possessed those particular attributes, although I must confess I have always found her to be a most lively dinner companion –'

'This is no time for hesitancy, Talbot,' hissed Dr Cattermole.

Alice saw her father's shoulders stiffen beneath his coat, so that she could almost hear the seams creaking. 'We must find her,' he croaked at last. 'I cannot be sure of anything any more.'

Alice ran towards the ballroom, quickly now, in case her father and the doctor should return. Inside, the room was thronged with men – talking, nodding, jabbing at open books with bony fingers or flourishing sheaves of paper beneath each other's noses. Those more subdued members of the Society were milling around her father's artefacts, gazing with interest at the various pieces, or staring dimly into the swimming formaldehyde of Dr Cattermole's museum of bodily offcuts.

Some of them held cups of tea in their hands, though how her father, without the help of Sluce, had managed to organise refreshments for so many people Alice had no idea. She peered through the door, searching for Mr Blake, but could not see him anywhere. A few curious gazes began to turn in her direction. Alice hurried away.

She headed towards the hot house. The jungle of foliage would provide her with concealment. As the hot house doors swung closed silently behind her, the heavy atmosphere enveloped her like a mother's embrace. The drip-drip-drip of water measured out the seconds in reassuring stillness. From deep within the leafy bowels of the conservatory she could hear the gentle sounds of her aunts' voices; the soft chink of teaspoons on saucers. As she hurried through, Alice noted absently that almost all the floor tiles were now ruptured, split and buckled and twisted like card, as though unable to withstand any longer the muscular upthrust of subterranean roots. Here and there the iron grids above the hot-water pipes were entwined with further root growth, which clung to the fretwork like the shaggy fingers of an escaping prisoner. It was as though the entire building were about to burst apart. Alice winced as a rubber plant swatted her on the back of the head with a large paddle-shaped leaf. How the aunts got through such a tangle these days was anyone's guess. Yet here they were, sitting in their jungle parlour, the lamplight filtering murkily through the greenery as the sunlight might penetrate the darker depths of a weed-filled pond.

'Alice, my dear,' said Aunt Statham, peering at her through the gloom. 'There you are.'

'Alice, your father has been looking for you,' said Aunt Rushton-Bell.

'With that odious Dr Cattermole,' said Old Mrs Talbot.

Alice said nothing.

'They have something planned for you,' said Aunt Lambert. She looked at Alice closely. 'Some idea of

Cattermole's. Mrs Statham overheard them. Do you know what it is? Alice, my dear, you must let us help you.'

'I don't think anyone can help me,' said Alice gloomily. 'Apart from Mr Blake, perhaps.'

'He was looking for you too,' said Aunt Rushton-Bell, shuffling her cards. 'Not ten minutes ago.' She cupped a hand round her ear. 'Is something wrong?'

Alice opened her mouth, then closed it again. She slid a hand into her pocket, her fingers touching the greasy cover of Sluce's plate-glass slide. She had no idea what to do.

'Mr Blake seems fond of you, Alice,' said Aunt Statham 'But you know, my dear, you must beware. Men always want something more than they pretend. You'd be better off talking to us, instead. We only want to see you happy. '

'Indeed, Aunt,' said Alice. But she had heard a noise in the foliage. She took a step back, trampling Aunt Pendleton's ear trumpet beneath her heel.

The screen of bamboo, which now concealed Alice's escritoire as effectively as a garden fence, thrashed from side to side. A dishevelled Mr Blake burst forth, like a partridge flushed from a cornfield. 'Alice,' he said breathlessly. 'Miss Talbot. Thank goodness I've found you. I've been looking for you all over the place.'

'I was found by Sluce,' said Alice, 'I heard Cattermole and my father talking, they have a room set aside for me. Dr Cattermole plans to operate as soon as possible. He has all the necessary equipment here. He says that you are to help him, as his assistant – his anaesthetist and his photographer. He wishes to take pictures of the procedure. He is looking for you.'

Mr Blake reached out and took Alice by the arms. 'Well, then,' he said, smiling, 'as we have found one another at last, perhaps we might get on with it.' He looked over her shoulder. 'Dr Cattermole? If you are ready?'

Alice gasped. She spun round to see Dr Cattermole, triumph on his face, emerging from the foliage like a weasel from a bank of undergrowth. Her father loomed behind him, his face crimson, his beard beaded with moisture. Alice gave a cry of horror. She turned left and right, but there was no escape, hemmed in as she was by tables, chairs, stools and settees. Old ladies seemed to be everywhere, their mouths open, their hands shaking, their paraphernalia of sticks and shawls, baskets of knitting, card tables, and tea trays gathered about her like snares and traps set to catch the unwary. Alice staggered against Aunt Lambert's chair, almost collapsing on to it (and its occupant, who had been struggling to rise). The hot house seemed to spin about her, its warmth now a smothering blanket, its throbbing pipes a ceaseless hammering in her brain. She heard her aunts' voices raised, their teacups rattling into their saucers as they tottered about in useless indignation. She felt firm hands pin her arms and the broiling atmosphere turn heavy with the stench of ether.

2

Aunt Lambert made her way through the silent hallways of the Great House. Behind her, in stately procession, Aunt Statham held the arm of Old Mrs Talbot; Aunt Pendleton pushed Aunt Rushton-Bell in her bath chair. There were no lamps to light their way other than the ones they carried themselves. Aunt Lambert held aloft a flickering candle. Aunt Statham and Old Mrs Talbot, generally too feeble to hold anything but their sticks in one hand and one another's arms in the other, blinked over her shoulder, peering myopically into the uncertain darkness. Aunt Rushton-Bell carried a lamp, its smoking wick turning her eye sockets into hollows of empty blackness, so that she resembled a mummified cadaver being wheeled along in an open coffin. Each of them wore black, as befitted their widowed status, and their faces glimmered like bone in the wavering candlelight. This macabre pageant passed as slowly as a funeral procession between the jumping shadows of the Collection.

'Are you sure it's her?' whispered Aunt Pendleton loudly. 'In that picture?'

'Most certainly it is,' said Aunt Statham. 'I never forget a face.'

'Is this wise?' said Old Mrs Talbot. 'Perhaps we should discuss it over a nice cup of tea. I should so hate to do the wrong thing. And we have Alice to think about.'

'What is there to discuss?' asked Aunt Lambert over her shoulder. 'We can only do the wrong thing if we do nothing. Alice dropped that glass photograph in my lap for a purpose. We can't just sit about drinking tea in her hour of need. We must act, and act now.'

'But we don't know where she is,' insisted Aunt Rushton-Bell. 'There are hundreds of rooms in this house. She could be in any one of them. Besides, the door will most certainly be locked and I for one have not the strength to break it down, much as I might wish to do so.'

Aunt Lambert nodded. 'And as we cannot search every room, we must take matters into our own hands.'

The aunts nodded to one another and murmured their agreement. Their heads held high in defiant resolve, they turned the corner. In front of them the doors to the ballroom stood open, the light from Dr Cattermole's magic lantern spilling into the hall in a splash of bloody colour.

'Here we are, ladies,' said Aunt Lambert. 'Now, remember what I said. We must stick together against Talbot and his dreadful friends. They will object, of course. After all, we are only *women*; and *women* are not permitted to enter the citadel. But we must make them listen. We must stand firm. Together, we can prevail.'

'*Vive la revolution!*' cried Aunt Statham. 'I knew Talleyrand, you know, when I was a girl.'

The aunts entered the ballroom. The men within were

seated before the podium. Behind it, Mr Talbot was holding forth. 'The mixture is quite simple,' he was saying. 'Sulphur and iron filings are mixed with water in equal quantities and buried beneath the ground. The heat of the sun, combined with the warmth to be found in the earth at a depth of a few metres, is generally sufficient to start the reaction. Once the reaction starts, it is self-perpetuating.' Behind him, projected by Dr Cattermole's magic lantern, was an artist's impression of an erupting Mount Etna.

'I myself was lowered into the crater of this very volcano a number of years ago,' cried Mr Talbot, gesticulating at the image. 'A most interesting experience and one which I have recounted in my unpublished monograph "Sights and Science in Southern Italy".' He fell silent, frowning at the procession of elderly ladies tottering towards him up the aisle between the rows of occupied seats. Heads turned to see what the distraction was.

'What is it, Mother?' said Mr Talbot impatiently. He glared at Aunt Lambert, but did not address her directly. 'Can it not wait?'

'No, it most certainly *cannot* wait,' snapped Aunt Lambert. The aunts halted beside the magic lantern. Aunt Lambert turned to Aunt Rushton-Bell. 'Eliza, my dear, do you have it?'

A buzz of animated perplexity broke out from the members of the Society.

'Really, Talbot, old fellow,' said a voice, 'this is most unacceptable. Surely you are familiar with those regulations of the Society regarding the presence of *women* at our meetings?'

'Indeed,' bellowed Mr Talbot. 'Mother, be so kind as to remove yourself and take your sisters with you.'

'Wait!' cried Aunt Lambert. 'Eliza, if you please.'

Aunt Rushton-Bell, recumbent in her bath chair like a Guy Fawkes in a wheelbarrow, rummaged beneath her skirts. At last she drew out a fold of grubby oilskin. She handed it to Aunt Lambert.

Aunt Lambert handed the package to Aunt Statham. 'Wait until I am in position,' she hissed. 'And when I give you the signal' – she raised her stick and knocked on the ground with it twice – 'you know what to do.'

'My dear aunts –' cried Mr Talbot, his face crimson.

'Oh, be quiet, Edwin,' said Aunt Lambert, stepping up beside him at the podium. She cleared her throat and looked out at the sea of faces before her. Aunt Lambert's eyes and ears were not as good as they had once been, and she was unaware of the hostile glares of her audience and almost deaf to the murmur of disquiet that now infected the air like the sound of a disturbed beehive.

'What I have to say is for the benefit of all of you,' she began, waving her stick. 'You are all acquainted with Dr Cattermole, are you not? A man considered to be a most principled and honest fellow, a doctor no less, and a man of science whose search for truth, whose quest for knowledge, has both inspired and delighted you.' The buzz of uneasiness died down to a curious murmur. Aunt Lambert pounded the podium with withered fists. 'Lies!' she cried. 'Gentlemen, you have been deceived.'

There was an audible gasp. It was clear that she now had their attention, and when Mr Talbot went to seize her arm and steer her from the podium, there was a groan of disapproval.

Aunt Lambert prodded Mr Talbot away with the end of her stick. 'Deceived, gentlemen, and most sorely imposed upon,' she shouted. 'But not any more.'

'Is it now?' called Aunt Statham from her position beside the magic lantern.

'Not yet,' said Aunt Lambert.

'Not yet,' shrilled Aunt Pendleton.

'I have proof,' cried Aunt Lambert. 'Gentlemen, the man you think of as a man of knowledge and learning; the man you understand to be one who seeks to further your knowledge of the natural world; the man who claims to be working for the good of humankind in his offices as a doctor – gentlemen, this man is *not as he seems*.'

Someone in the front row leaned forward like a starving dog, his eyes wide, his mouth open, hungry for more.

'How blind you have been,' cried Aunt Lambert. 'How duped and betrayed. But be assured, gentlemen, those times are now *over*. We, my sisters and I, we are here to *expose* this deceiver.' She banged her stick on the floor.

'Is it now?' demanded Aunt Statham.

'Not yet,' hissed Aunt Lambert.

'Not yet,' shrieked Aunt Pendleton, her bony fingers clutching at her throat, her eyes wide and fixed upon Aunt Lambert. 'Not yet.'

Aunt Lambert hooked her stick over her arm and gripped the podium. 'We are here to show you his most vile secret,' she cried, 'a secret he has kept from you. A secret which demonstrates more clearly than *anything else* that your most worthy Society has been harbouring in its midst a man of the most debauched, the most depraved and corrupt personality. A man whose morals, and those of that most licentious lady, his so-called *wife*, are no better than those of a sensualist; a pander; a *pornographer*.'

Aunt Lambert pounded her stick up and down on the ground, as though crushing an invasion of beetles.

'Now?' shouted Aunt Statham.

'Now!' cried Aunt Pendleton and Aunt Lambert together.

Aunt Statham thrust the plate-glass slide into the magic lantern. Like a naked genie emerging from a bottle, on the wall behind the speechless Mr Talbot appeared the sepia picture of Mrs Cattermole. Mr Talbot staggered backwards and collapsed into a chair. He gaped at the magnified image, his mouth opening and closing like a landed trout, his eyes fixed on that dark undergrowth that sprouted like gorse above the rolling hills of Mrs Cattermole's thighs. Aunt Statham, stationed beside the magic lantern, could not help but notice that some members of the audience looked more embarrassed than shocked, as though they had seen it, or something very similar, before.

And all at once a clamour broke out. Members of the audience rose to their feet. The magic lantern rocked to and fro on its stand like a lifebuoy as the Society for the Propagation of Useful and Interesting Knowledge surged about it. Someone extinguished its light (anything to get rid of that splayed and globular image). The room was plunged into darkness. At least, the room would have been plunged into darkness had it not been illuminated by an unexpected red glow that danced and flickered through the windows, as though someone had opened the door of a huge furnace somewhere far below.

Aunt Lambert, still standing behind the podium on the raised platform at the front of the ballroom, surveyed the scene with some surprise. 'Edwin,' she cried above the noise of shouting, and the screech and clatter of chairs being pushed hither and thither about the floor. 'Edwin!'

Mr Talbot was still slumped in his chair, his eyes gazing at the space on the wall where the image of Mrs Cattermole had been displayed.

'Come, come, man,' shouted Aunt Lambert. 'Pull yourself together.' She poked him with her stick. 'Edwin!'

Mr Talbot blinked and shifted red-rimmed eyes to stare at his aunt. 'Was that really her?' he asked. But he knew it was. Why, on his last trip to London, as he sat at the Doctor's table he had eyed Mrs Cattermole's bulging cleavage with unconcealed greed as she leaned in close to hear him speak. What a lovely young woman she was, he had thought. Always so animated. And so comely too. He'd had no idea she was so shameless, so brazen. Perhaps Cattermole had been taken in by her also. Perhaps Cattermole was innocent of any wrongdoing. After all, the man worked with fallen women, did he not? At the Magdalene asylum? A little voice in Mr

Talbot's head told him that this was not really an argument in the Doctor's favour.

But now his aunt was talking. 'Yes,' she was saying, 'of course it's her. Really, Edwin, you don't mean to tell me that you had no idea?'

Mr Talbot shook his head wordlessly. 'And did Cattermole take that photograph, do you think?' he croaked.

'Undoubtedly,' stated Aunt Lambert.

'Mind you,' said Mr Talbot, 'perhaps it was Mr Blake who took it.' He leaped to his feet. All at once, as though seeing it for the first time, his gaze fell upon the red flickering light at the windows. A plume of orange and yellow matter sputtered into view in a steaming fountain. A cloud of jaundiced smoke belched into the night and the air within the ballroom filled with the unmistakable stench of sulphur. The members of the Society began streaming from the ballroom.

Mr Talbot gave a cry of delight. He pushed Aunt Lambert aside and sprang to the podium. All thoughts of Dr Cattermole or Mrs Cattermole, of Mr Blake, of Alice or any kind of photograph, fell from his mind. 'It's started,' he cried, his face illuminated like a carnival mask by the diabolical light of the artificial volcano. 'I was beginning to wonder if it would work.' Mr Talbot pounded the podium. 'Gentlemen, please,' he shouted above the din. 'If you would like to make your way out of the building and on to the terrace at the front of the house, I can assure you the best view of the unfolding spectacle can be had from there. Gentlemen?' But no one was listening. Mr Talbot was addressing the retreating backs of an already dwindling crowd.

'What about Dr Cattermole?' cried Aunt Lambert. 'And Alice? Where are they?'

Her words were drowned by the sound of an explosion. The windows rattled as a shower of earth was flung against them. Then Mr Talbot too was gone.

3

Alice could hear noises around her, though they seemed muffled, as if heard through a wall, or from underwater. She tried to move, to raise herself up, but her head was heavy and her limbs leaden. She felt her senses sharpening, her mind gradually making sense of the sounds she could hear as though she were emerging from beneath a still, dark pond. It was the voices that she had noticed first: the sound of men talking. But then a door opened and closed somewhere. Curtains were drawn, a poker rattled on a grate and coals were tipped from a coal scuttle. She could hear grunts and the sound of something large scraping across the floor. Alice forced her eyes to open, though part of her would much rather have let them remain closed so that she might sink back into oblivion. The room was dark. The only source of light – a lantern on a dressing table – was obscured by the figures of two men, who appeared to be wrestling with a large seabird. Alice closed her eyes (perhaps she was dreaming) and opened them again.

'If you would lift it backwards,' hissed a voice, 'and get the thing's beak out of my eyes. Thank you.'

Alice groaned and struggled to sit up.

'Miss Talbot.' One of the figures dropped the seabird and hastened to her side. 'Please, you must not get up yet.'

Alice recognised the voice of the photographer. 'How dare you touch me,' she mumbled, struggling to express the anger she knew she should feel. 'Get your hands off me. I shall stand if I wish.' But her words came out blurred and sluggish, and she was not sure that he had even understood her. Tears of rage and frustration sprang into her eyes. She tried to lift her arm, to slap his face, but she seemed to lack the strength, or the conviction, to do so effectively. Mr Blake patted the hand she had hoped to swing at him. 'Rest, Miss Talbot,' he said. 'The ether will leave your body soon enough.'

'You would be advised to do as Mr Blake suggests,' said Dr

Cattermole. He dug two thin white fingers into a pocket of his waistcoat and extracted a key. 'Although I would be most surprised if you were able to reach the door in your current state, you would not get much further without the help of this little fellow.' He tucked the key back out of sight beneath his ribs. 'I suggest you lie back and rest. Mr Blake, if you would be so kind as to return to assisting me with this albatross? After all, we don't want to be operating in a cramped space, do we? I would hate to knock my elbow on something and make a larger incision than necessary.' He smiled, his brown teeth appearing almost absent in the dim light. 'And I need room for the camera too, don't forget. It must face the patient directly, its eye trained upon the area to be excised.'

'I thought you were interested in the face; the physiognomy?' queried Mr Blake.

'Oh, that too,' said Dr Cattermole, waving a hand. 'But the operation itself must be captured. We must see the source of all this trouble and we must chart its removal.'

Mr Blake looked at Alice. But Alice was hardly listening. One phrase was going round and round in her head: *the area to be excised.* A wave of nausea broke over her, turning her skin clammy and filling her mouth with a bitter, metallic-tasting liquid. She struggled to stand, but succeeded only in sliding off the bed like a rag doll on to the floor. Hands came towards her and she cried out.

Mr Blake lifted her back on to the bed. 'Rest now,' he murmured into her ear, 'or the Doctor will have to restrain you.'

'Yes, indeed,' said Dr Cattermole. 'I have all the necessary means at my disposal. And the full co-operation of your father, of course.'

'Do as he says,' whispered Mr Blake. 'It will be for the best if you do.' He stroked her hair soothingly. Alice closed her eyes and turned away from him.

When Alice returned to consciousness all was silent. Dr

Cattermole and Mr Blake had gone. Three lamps were burning, illuminating the room in a glare of sickly yellow light. From the contents of the place, which she had barely been able to register before, Alice knew instantly where she was – in a bedroom at the rear of the house on the third floor, close to the attic stairs. It had been the home of Mr Talbot's collection of stuffed birds for a number of years now – ever since their previous roost, the billiard room, had been taken over by the scientific instrument Collection. Alice saw that Mr Blake and Dr Cattermole had moved the birds to the sides of the room. There was a clearing now in the centre of the floor around which the birds were gathered, as though the room were a theatre filled with an audience of beaked and beady-eyed spectators. The object of their gaze, Alice noticed with alarm, was an operating table. She blanched. She had not seen Dr Cattermole's operating table since Lilian had lain upon it. The stirrups on either side of it were the same, the cracked and shining leather upholstery as stained and worn. Beside it, on a washstand, stood a large basin, a jug and a glittering array of surgical instruments. Among these Alice recognised the silvery beak of the speculum. Next to this a jar of leeches glittered, as black as molasses in the lamplight.

Alice tried to cry out in terror, but no sound emerged from her open mouth. Her skin turned hot, then cold, her flesh recoiling in horror from the sight of the Doctor's instruments, as though spiders were crawling all over her. Her breath came in gasps and a layer of icy sweat coated her body, suddenly cleaving her dress to her legs, arms and stomach, as though she were drowning in her own terrible panic. The last time she had seen those knives and hooks, those needles and forceps, she had witnessed a degree of pain and cruelty she had not thought possible. She had seen her sister lie, motionless and bleeding, upon that couch, her legs splayed awkwardly, white beneath the crimson stickiness that covered them.

Alice tried to rise from the bed. She had to find some way

out of the room. But she discovered she could not move. Looking down, she realised that there were wide leather straps across her legs, her abdomen, her arms and chest that pinned her to the bed as surely as the dose of ether had done. Alice thrashed, as far as it was possible to do so, beneath her leather constraints. If she could just get a hand free she might be able to loosen them somehow.

But at that moment the door opened. Mr Blake and Dr Cattermole entered. The former carried his camera box, the latter a tea tray upon which sat a large pot of tea, a cup and saucer and a plate of Bakewell Tart. Dr Cattermole put down his tray on the display case of finches and poured a cup of tea. Mr Blake opened his camera box and pulled out his camera. Alice noticed that the dark tent, in which she and Mr Blake had spent so much time over the past months, had been erected in a corner behind the avian audience. Alice peered at the photographer as he fixed his camera on to a large wooden tripod positioned at the end of the operating table. Mr Blake glanced at her, but was unable to meet her gaze. Once the camera was in place, he busied himself with choosing the correct lens and with buffing the glass plates he was to use, and he made sure that his back was to her. Alice stared at him, but said nothing. How stupid she had been. Over the past months she was sure that they had developed some kind of understanding, some kind of relationship built on sincere regard, mutual respect, fondness even. It seemed she had misjudged him. She wondered how much money her father had offered the photographer to act as assistant in what was soon to take place.

'Miss Talbot,' said the Doctor, licking crumbs off his lips, 'I see you are awake again. I must apologise for the restraints I was obliged to use, but you are quite clearly a resourceful woman and we could not possibly have left you unattended. Still, we are here now.' He sipped his tea, but made no move to release Alice from her bondage. 'Of course, last time we were here it was your sister who was in need of medical attention.' He shook his head. 'How your dear father grieves over the fate of his daughters. One a fallen woman, saved only by the timely intervention of a most forgiving man of the cloth. The other, unsexed by her pursuit of knowledge and tottering on the brink of madness as a result.'

'Release me,' cried Alice. 'You are committing a grave and punishable crime to hold me here in this way. This is assault. I am held without my consent.'

'But your consent is not needed, my dear. Your condition has rendered you quite beyond reason. Your father will testify to that. Any one of my colleagues downstairs would agree.'

'What nonsense,' shouted Alice, struggling to master her fear. 'If these so-called colleagues are so much in agreement with you, why is it that you hide me away up here? Why are they not up here with you?' Alice fought against her bindings, her face becoming flushed, her hair lying disordered on the pillow. She felt terror writhing like a cold serpent within her stomach. She forced herself to sound rational. 'Come now, Doctor. Release me at once and we shall say no more about it.'

Dr Cattermole licked his fingers. 'You do realise', he said, 'that were I not able to return you to docility with a simple operation, your fate would be one of long-term restraint: a lifetime of enforced idleness, either in an asylum, or in secluded apartments within the home. Clearly, your father is anxious to avoid this, in part due to the need he has for you as his housekeeper, in part due to the stigma of having a daughter lose her mind.'

'I have not lost my mind,' said Alice as calmly as she could. 'I have been encouraged, by my father, to read, to write, to think, to express myself clearly. I have honoured his wishes by acting as his curator, his assistant in all matters pertaining to the Collection. If I am outspoken, it is because my father allowed me to be so. If I am curious, it is because he encouraged this in me. If I am intelligent, it is because I was born that way and he took advantage of this to use me in any way he saw fit. If he would rather I kept my opinions to myself he need only tell me so. There is no need to butcher me to gain my co-operation.'

'I can assure you, Miss Talbot, to ease the sufferings of the mind, we must attend to the body.' Dr Cattermole sipped his tea and wiped his lips with the edge of a folded napkin. 'In particular the *sexual* organs.'

'But *this* is madness,' cried Alice. 'You have taken against me because I don't flatter you; I don't smile and simper, and dress to delight you.' She frowned. 'And I don't pose half-naked for you and your camera.'

Dr Cattermole appeared unmoved. He chuckled. 'Ah, but you will today, my dear. You may be certain of that.'

From the tray of medical instruments beside the operating table, Dr Cattermole's speculum winked at her in the lamplight. At that moment Alice wondered whether she was the only person in the room who was capable of sensible thought. She looked at Mr Blake hopefully. After all, he had always seemed sympathetic. But he was buffing his lens and making sure the camera was secure on its tripod.

Dr Cattermole put down his plate silently and came towards her across the room. He bent over her, his face so close that she could smell the sugar and almonds on his breath. 'Without doubt, there is a certain part of you that demands my immediate surgical attention,' he whispered. 'I intend to examine the organ in question, photograph it and remove it. This I shall do for the sake of your health, of course, and in accordance with your dear father's wishes. And I shall do it with or without your consent.' He smiled. 'Be assured, Miss Talbot, I shall have that small part of you pickling in a jar by the end of the night.'

'Take these straps off me this instant,' screamed Alice.

At that moment the door burst open. Her father stood on the threshold, breathing hard. His face was livid and his hair awry. His beard appeared to be smouldering slightly; his jacket singed and peppered with flecks of yellow. He was accompanied by an atmosphere all of his own, and as he stood in the doorway the room filled with a draught of cold air laced with the stench of sulphur and smoke. He gazed around the room, his eyes staring, his mouth open, his chest rising and falling as though he had run, without stopping, all the way from the garden to the top of the house (which was, in fact, exactly what he had done).

'Cattermole,' panted Mr Talbot. 'It's started.'

'What has?'

Alice struggled beneath her restraints. 'Father, help me,' she cried.

Mr Talbot eyed his daughter warily. 'Is she mad, Cattermole?' he whispered. 'Is that why you have restrained her so?'

'Most certainly,' said Dr Cattermole.

'For goodness sake, Father,' cried Alice. 'Do I sound mad? Do I appear mad?'

Mr Talbot stared at his daughter's flushed face, at her disordered hair and wide, black-ringed eyes. 'Why, yes, as a matter of fact,' he said, 'you most certainly do.'

'What is it, Talbot?' snapped Dr Cattermole. 'You look like the devil himself.'

'The volcano,' cried Mr Talbot, his eyes blazing with passion, his face beaming. 'A most magnificent sight. Cattermole, my dear fellow. You must come down and see for yourself.'

Dr Cattermole stood up. 'I have work to do up here,' he said.

'Come, come,' urged Mr Talbot. 'This is a sight you will never see again and it will not wait. The ground has opened up and there are plumes of burning sulphur, spouts of blazing iron, smoke belching forth – why, in all my years in the iron foundries I never saw the like. It is amazing. Quite remarkable. It is the mouth of hell itself – in my own front garden. Come on, man, there is no time to lose.'

Mr Talbot disappeared from the door, with a waft of smoke like a theatrical apparition. His feet could be heard stamping down the hallway. 'Come on, Cattermole,' he shouted. 'Everything else can wait until later.'

Dr Cattermole stared longingly at the door after his friend. He hesitated for only a moment. Then, 'Make sure everything is set up as it should be,' he snapped at Mr Blake. 'I shall be back.'

As soon as the door was closed Mr Blake leaped to Alice's side. He took her hand. 'Alice,' he whispered. 'Miss Talbot. Are you unhurt?'

'If I am it's no thanks to you,' muttered Alice. 'How much did they offer you? I hope it was a lot. Or were you easily bought?'

'I had to do what I did,' said the photographer. 'How else could I help you unless I pretended to be a part of their scheme?'

Alice blinked at him. 'You are not a part of their scheme?'

'Of course not.'

'But . . .'

'There is no time to lose if you are to escape. The Doctor is interested in the artificial volcano, but he will not remain downstairs for long if he has something more interesting to do up here. He has been watching you for a long time now. He told me so himself.'

'Are you intending to release me, or to talk to me until Dr Cattermole returns?' Alice struggled beneath her bonds once again. 'Hurry!'

Mr Blake began to fiddle with the buckles.

'Just cut them,' cried Alice. 'There are all manner of knives and blades on the washstand. Come *on*, Mr Blake. You are not thinking straight.'

Mr Blake nodded and dashed to the washstand. He returned with the largest of Dr Cattermole's surgical blades. In a few moments Alice was free.

She leaped to her feet and ran to the washstand. Her head was heavy, but she felt no after-effects from the dose of ether she had been given. She gathered up all Dr Cattermole's instruments. 'Quickly, Mr Blake,' she cried. 'Open the window.'

Mr Blake did as he was asked and Alice hurled the speculum, the blades and probes, the hooks and needles and syringes out into the night. They could not see the artificial volcano from the back of the house, but a draught of night air blew in through the open window, carrying with it the unmistakable reek of sulphur. A shower of sparks whirled above them into the darkness of the night sky. Alice threw the leather restraining straps out of the window too. The stirrups from the operating table followed them. She began to drag the operating table itself across the room, but Mr Blake stopped her. 'It's too large,' he said gently. 'It won't fit. Besides, is it not time to leave? We don't want to be here when the Doctor returns.'

Alice nodded. 'But surely we're locked in,' she said. 'How can we get out? Cattermole didn't leave you with a key, did he?'

'No.'

Alice went to the door and turned the handle. She peered through the keyhole. A draught of cold air tickled her eyeball. There was no key on the other side of the door. 'He's taken it with him,' she said. She ran to the window and leaned out.

But their prison was so far from the ground that Alice felt as though she were peering over the edge of a bottomless pit. They could not jump down, or climb down. She looked up, but the edge of the roof was far away beyond a featureless stretch of brick and a lip of curlicued stonework. She ran back to the door. She banged on it. She kicked it. She rattled the handle and shouted for help.

Mr Blake watched her impotent efforts with mounting concern. 'We're trapped,' he said gloomily, sinking on to the bed. 'I should have known.' The crowd of birds seemed to be staring at him, a silent, accusing jury, their beady eyes glinting with angry reproach in the lamplight. Mr Blake eyed the bottle of ether that sat on the washstand.

'Nonsense,' said Alice. 'There must be some way out of here. We just need to find it.' She followed Mr Blake's hungry gaze to the bottle of ether. 'I thought you had given up that stuff,' she muttered, rattling at the door handle again.

'I have,' he murmured. 'I was just . . .' he stopped. 'I was just thinking,' he said slowly. 'Cattermole has had that ether for months now. It's dated from last year. It will have oxidised somewhat – it will have become unstable.' He shrugged. 'It's a dangerous plan, but not impossible to execute.'

'What?' said Alice. 'What plan?' She smiled at him suddenly. 'An explosion?'

Mr Blake smiled back. 'Quite so.'

'Can we contain it sufficiently?'

'There are bandages in Cattermole's bag. We might soak one and stuff as much of it as we can into the keyhole. What we cannot cram into the keyhole, we can tie into a bundle beneath the door handle.'

'And how would we light it without blowing ourselves up in the process?'

'Come now,' said Mr Blake. 'Can you not think of something? Am I to do all the work?'

Alice looked about. Every room in her father's house was filled with unexpected items. There must be something they might use in this bird-filled attic. Then her gaze fell upon an object standing in the corner of the room. She assumed it had been carried up by mistake with the birds when they had left their old home in the billiard room. She pointed it out to Mr Blake. 'That should do the trick,' she said. 'A billiard cue. We can affix a feather to the end and touch it to a hot coal until it burns. We shall have the longest and most cautious taper you could imagine. What more do we need?'

ALICE AND LILIAN

Lilian looked up through the canopy of leaves. She felt her heart beating in time to the gentle pat, pat, pat of water dripping from one leaf on to another, and forced herself to relax into the moist and breathless heat. The foliage was sumptuous – huge, gleaming leaves, succulent stems and sturdy, muscular trunks – everything far stronger and more vigorous than she remembered it. The ground was barely visible through the matrix of roots that criss-crossed the floor and a shaggy carpet of emerald moss grew wherever the shadow was deepest.

On the table stood the pestle and mortar Aunt Statham had once used to grind up paint pigments. Beside it a knife, a bowl of severed peaches and a mound of shelled and hulled peach stones.

The peach tree, having been wheeled through from the temperate house in its massive bucket, was thriving – as did everything in the broiling temperatures of the hot house. Its branches bowed achingly with the weight of its velvet fruits. Lilian had gathered a dozen of them, sliding her knife into the soft fold of blushing fuzzy skin and slicing through the fragrant flesh. The juices had run like nectar over her fingers as she pulled out the hard wrinkled stones and the bitter almond poison at each centre.

It had seemed, at first, that since she, Lilian, had left the Great House, Aunt Statham had given up painting altogether.

The rolls of paper and canvas that had once been stacked here and there like log piles had gone; the easel was now being used as a blackboard by Aunt Pendleton to record whist victories; the jars of water and turpentine that used to litter the table top like a hundred opened condiment jars had all been cleared away. It was only after a length of time she could ill afford that Lilian had found what she was looking for: the mortar was filled with milk and sitting on the floor beside Aunt Statham's chair; the pestle was being used as a paperweight on her sister's bamboo-bound escritoire. She had rescued these two objects and set to work, grinding the peach kernels to a paste and mixing them with sugar, before taking them to the kitchen.

Now, as Lilian sat back in Aunt Lambert's mildewed armchair, she hoped that Dr Cattermole was as partial to Bakewell Tart as he had always been. At length, she heard the sound of muted voices and the rustle of leaves. The aunts were returning.

'Well,' Aunt Pendleton was saying, 'I'm sure I never saw anything quite so outrageous in all my life. It's a relief that the woman stayed in London. Imagine if I had sat opposite her at the dinner table!'

'You saw Edwin,' said Aunt Lambert. 'He tried to blame Mr Blake. Anything to get Cattermole off the hook.'

'Can we be sure Mr Blake is above suspicion?' wondered Aunt Rushton-Bell. 'Careful, ladies, please. The roots have formed ridges across the pathway. The wheels of my chair become trapped, forcing me along a road I have no wish to follow. Last week Old Mrs Talbot almost wheeled me into the ornamental pond.'

There was the sound of grunting and the undergrowth rustled. 'I'm not sure that we can rule out Mr Blake entirely,' panted Aunt Lambert. 'But whatever his involvement, I suspect him of being coerced and misled, rather than anything more sinister. I rather doubt he has the energy or the inclination to control proceedings. No. This whole business is down to Cattermole, you can be sure of it.'

'But what can we do?' wailed Old Mrs Talbot. 'He has Alice. We don't even know where he's taken her.'

Lilian saw the leaves at the edge of the clearing begin to twitch and thrash. The tip of a stick emerged at shoulder height and a swath of Spanish moss was lifted aside, like a shaggy curtain being raised on a theatre. The aunts stepped out of the jungle into the dimly lit arena beyond.

'Perhaps we should try every room in the building until we find her,' Aunt Statham was saying. 'We can't just sit here doing nothing.'

'Don't worry, Aunt Statham,' said Lilian from her place beneath the peach tree, 'I have everything in hand.'

Four pairs of watery eyes turned to stare at the visitor sitting in the shadows beside the peach tree's huge wheeled bucket. There was a moment's silence, before the aunts surged about her like a flock of exotic hens, their claw-like hands grasping her arms, their beaked faces and wattled necks jerking stiffly above their plumage of lace and watered silk. Various feelings of pain and pleasure, delight and alarm, were expressed in elderly voices quavering with emotion, so that Lilian was reminded of the sound of anxious poultry.

'Dr Cattermole is here,' cried Aunt Pendleton, her eyes wide.

'I know,' said Lilian. 'I saw him. I was hoping he would be.'

'You must save Alice,' croaked Aunt Statham.

'Everything is in hand,' repeated Lilian.

'But . . .'

'Ladies,' cried Aunt Lambert. She held up a hand. 'Explanations can wait. Lilian has said that everything is in hand. We must ask only what we can do to help.' She blinked at Lilian. 'We have tried already, but your father is . . . well, he is too enamoured of Dr Cattermole to see him for what he is.'

'Indeed,' said Lilian mildly.

'Why are you dressed as a man?' asked Aunt Pendleton suddenly. 'And your lovely hair!'

'I was at the Meeting of the Society for the Propagation of Useful and Interesting Knowledge,' said Lilian. 'Downstairs in the ballroom. I was interested to hear what Dr Cattermole had to say. I had to dress for the occasion. You know they don't allow women in.'

'Quite,' muttered Aunt Lambert.

'Did you see us?' cried Aunt Rushton-Bell. 'We were there too. We wore our own clothes. There was no mistaking us.'

'We were not there incognito,' said Aunt Statham.

'Did you see us?' repeated Aunt Rushton-Bell urgently. 'I carried the photographic plate beneath my skirts.'

'I did see you.'

'Weren't we *magnificent*?'

'Without question.' Lilian smiled.

'But your hair,' wailed Aunt Pendleton. 'Why have you done such a thing?'

'Oh, I found it most inconvenient having long hair. Especially in India. It was so hot and dirty all the time. It was much easier just to cut it all off. A barber in the Calcutta bazaar did it. I've kept it short ever since.'

'Oh, my dear Lilian,' cried Old Mrs Talbot. 'Your crowning glory. Gone!'

'Well, I think it's quite the best idea,' said Aunt Lambert. 'I found it the most frightful ordeal washing my hair in India. One needed about three women to help. And as for the trousers you are wearing' – she blushed slightly at the sight of her great-niece's legs – 'I always found crinolines such absurd garments. So impractical. One was quite tempted by a sari, for a time, but Mr Lambert put his foot down. I allowed him this one concession and as a result endured years of the most uncomfortable clothes you can imagine. Now, I am so used to such iron-clad corsetry I fear I would hardly be able to stand upright without the assistance of whalebone and pin tucks.

Anyway, my dear, enough about that. I assume you'll be going back?'

'To India? Most certainly. And Alice will come with me.'

'Alice!' cried Aunt Pendleton, her hands flying to her mouth. 'I had quite forgotten.'

'Do you know where she is?' said Old Mrs Talbot, wringing her hands.

'Yes. And I have dealt with Dr Cattermole. At least, I hope I have.'

'They are all outside,' said Aunt Pendleton, 'watching that infernal volcano.' The aunts looked up, through the dark hands of the foliage to the glimpses of glass beyond. Here and there the night sky could be seen flickering and glowing with sparks, as though illuminated by a giant bonfire. 'Now is our chance to rescue Alice.'

Lilian stood up. '*I* shall rescue Alice,' she said firmly. 'And both of us will leave this place for ever. My dear aunts, I may never see you again.'

'Stuff and nonsense,' said Aunt Lambert briskly, squeezing Lilian's outstretched hand. 'Mrs Rushton-Bell? Show her, please.'

From a secret chink in her armoured bodice Aunt Rushton-Bell produced what looked at first glance to be a visiting card. She passed it over. '*St Peter's Mount Hotel, Bournemouth,*' read Lilian. '*Home for retired gentlewomen*.'

'We're all going,' said Aunt Statham. 'The proprietor tells me that Lord Byron stayed there once.'

'I can't think what Lord Byron might have been doing in a hotel for retired gentlewomen,' retorted Aunt Lambert. 'Are you sure you heard him correctly, dear?'

'Perhaps it was in its former days,' said Aunt Statham huffily. 'It used to be a very fashionable place, you know. I danced there, as a girl, in the arms of Lord Aldershot. Wellington himself kissed my hand. I'm quite delighted to be returning for the final waltz.'

'We've had it planned for a long time.' Aunt Lambert addressed Lilian. 'We can't stay here much longer, or the place will kill us all. There's no hot water in the mornings and no one to bring it even if there were. Most of the maids have gone – Talbot hasn't paid any of them for months.'

'The food is always cold.'

'And Edwin is an absurd dinner companion,' said Aunt Statham. 'Chasing mice up and down the curtains.'

'I saw DaVinci eating mouse number 16,' whispered Old Mrs Talbot. 'I didn't dare say anything.'

'And there are draughts blowing through this hot house that there never used to be,' said Aunt Lambert. She pulled her shawls about her shoulders, as though one such renegade draught had sneaked up there and then and skewered her between the shoulder blades. 'Some of the plants have broken through to the outside.'

Lilian made her way through the rooms and corridors of the Great House. She carried a lamp, taken from the hot house. From somewhere outside the building she could hear urgent shouting and a roaring noise that sounded like the distant shovelling of coals. The air was hot and stuffy, and thick with the musty odour of dust and antiquity. But there was also a new smell. It was pungent and foul, like the stench of rotten eggs. It made her eyes smart and her stomach heave, even as her throat tickled with the charred scent of smoke and hot metal, so that she felt as though she were walking through the corridors of Hades, rather than along a hallway in what used to be her home.

She reached the collection of suits of armour. There were thirty-four of them altogether – one of the largest collections of amour on display anywhere in the country, her father was pleased to declare. The suits of armour usually stood in proud ranks on either side of the corridor that led from the conservatory to the foot of the stairs. Since the gathering of artefacts in the ballroom for the meeting of the Society, however, their uniform rows had been disturbed and they were now gathered about in groups of five or six, leaning against one another drunkenly, as if about to burst into song or sharing a lewd joke. One or two of them were on the floor, as if they had passed out altogether. Lilian threaded her way forward, emerging at the foot of the stairs beside the first of the twelve grandfather clocks. A dark shape lay on the ground – another suit of armour, perhaps toppled over during the mass departure from the house of the members of the Society. Lilian raised her lamp, so as to avoid tripping over it. But the lamplight revealed that it was not a suit of armour at all. A jury of twelve grandfather clocks loomed impassively over the body of Dr Cattermole.

Lilian stepped forward. She raised her lamp higher, to get a good look at him. He was sprawled like a burst sack of laundry, his legs and arms spread wide. One of his shoes had come off and Lilian noticed a thick yellow nail poking from a hole in the end of his stocking. A few tell-tale crumbs of Bakewell Tart adhered to the lapels of his coat. Was he dead? It seemed so. His eyes were open, but sightless; his face a furious shade of crimson, as though he was enraged at being caught out by something as simple as a poisoned cake. The twelve silver clock faces looking down at him betrayed no more regret than Lilian's did and their ticking echoed around his corpse like the clicking of twelve disapproving tongues.

Lilian abandoned Dr Cattermole and began to climb the stairs. She knew he had taken Alice to the top storey: she had followed him up there with her tray of Bakewell Tart and tea.

From the window on the first-floor landing Lilian was at last able to view the artificial volcano and she could not help but gasp and take a step back at the sight. The wide apron of parkland in front of the house, which two hours previously had appeared to be no more than slightly disturbed, had reared up like a gargantuan molehill. The grass upon it had withered and turned brown, and the earth itself appeared to be pouring with smoke and flickering with red, dancing flames. Even as Lilian watched, the ground buckled and heaved once more. Lumps of it were flung this way and that, as though from the furious stirrings of a dragon beneath. Down the sides of this great abscess of soil and turf huge cracks had appeared, revealing a suppurating crimson mass of boiling iron and sulphur. Orange, pus-like matter flowed in steaming rivers in all directions. The centre of the volcano spouted jets of yellow steam and sprayed the air with sparks, ash and cinders. All around it black-clad figures – those members of the Society for the Propagation of Useful and Interesting Knowledge who had not already fled – ran amok like demons. In the midst of the confusion one figure stood still, his arms outstretched before the scene as though summoning Beelzebub himself. Lilian recognised the broad back of her father, at his side the hunched and shambling figure of Sluce. Even from her vantage point she could see that her father's shoes were thickly encrusted with crystals of sulphur, while a tinge of yellow, illuminated by the blazing plumes that burst, periodically, from the weeping ochre fissures in the earth, covered his hair and beard like a veil.

All at once an explosion shook the window. Lilian leaped back in alarm. Was the thing about to blow up completely? But the scene outside remained unchanged in its madness. Then Lilian found that she was standing in the middle of a whirling snowstorm. Was she going insane? She reminded herself that anything was possible in her father's house. One thing was certain, however: it could not possibly be snowing indoors. She held out her hands in astonishment. In no time at all her arms, her shoulders, her head and fingers, were covered with gentle white flakes. Lilian spluttered a few of them out of her open mouth, blinking them out of her eyes and coughing as they stuck in her throat. Feathers. She looked up. They were falling from the top of the house in a blizzard of grey and white. It had to be Alice.

Lilian raced up the stairs, two at a time. The display cases and furniture, the statues and models and machines that she flew past were now enveloped in soft white drifts. A cloud of down stirred and danced about her ankles in swirling eddies as she rushed onward and upward. At the top of the stairs, a shattered and twisted door hung from a single hinge. Lilian stopped, trying to get her breath back. Tears sprang to her eyes as she choked on a lungful of feathers. And then, through the whirling wisps, Alice stepped forward. In her hand she held a splintered billiard cue.

Alice stared at the slim man with feathers in his hair and on his coat, and blanched. Had Dr Cattermole roped in some other assistant to help him with his dreadful purpose?

'It's me,' croaked Lilian. A mouthful of feathers prevented her from adding anything more.

Mr Blake, who had been chattering excitedly after their success with the ether, watched in silence as Alice and Lilian stood before him in an embrace. He could see that Alice had forgotten about him completely, so engrossed was she in her sister's return. He eyed Lilian jealously as she stroked her sister's hair and kissed her. Really, he thought irritably, he was supposed to be betrothed to Alice and she had never allowed him such lingering embraces, such fond kisses. The sisters held hands, whispering to one another like lovers, so that Mr Blake was obliged to clear his throat to attract their attention.

Alice turned to him. 'Oh, yes,' she said. 'This is Mr Blake. The photographer. Mr Blake, this is Lilian, my sister.' Mr Blake noticed dejectedly that she had not let go of Lilian's hand.

'We are engaged to be married, your sister and I,' said Mr Blake.

Alice laughed. 'I don't think so.'

Mr Blake cleared his throat again. 'If it's because I gave you up to Dr Cattermole, I can assure you that was simply . . .'

'It has nothing to do with that,' interrupted Alice. 'Come, Mr Blake. You want a woman you can flatter, a woman who delights in your gallantries and whose feminine charms are more visible than mine. We have been friends, good friends, but that's all.' She shrugged. 'We don't need each other any more, you and I. You know it's for the best.'

Mr Blake opened his mouth to object, but as he could think of nothing to say that might refute this, he closed it again.

'You need to leave here,' said Alice briskly. 'As soon as possible. Once you are back in London, once the memory of this place has faded, you will think you had a lucky escape.'

'No, I won't,' said Mr Blake thickly. 'I won't forget.' But he knew that he would. Everyone forgot in the end. 'You can at least allow me to take a photograph. To remember you by.'

'You don't need to remember me. I don't want to be remembered. And certainly not like this.'

'We should leave,' said Lilian.

'How would you like me to remember you, then?' insisted Mr Blake. He glared at Lilian.

'I don't know,' said Alice. She regarded her sister, admiring her short hair and neat, unencumbered legs.

'Come on,' urged Lilian, pulling her sister's hand.

Alice hesitated. She looked down at her skirts. They ballooned like the full sails of a galleon about her legs. 'I suppose there's no reason why you shouldn't take my photograph,' she said to Mr Blake. 'It's the least I can do for you.'

Alice, Lilian and Mr Blake emerged through the trapdoor on to the roof.

'Do you still come up here?' asked Lilian, squeezing her sister's hand.

Alice nodded. 'Of course.'

'I've been up here too,' said Mr Blake. 'Many times. With Alice.'

The red and yellow kimono billowed about his shoulders as

the wind plucked and tugged at the silken fabric. Fortunately the weather had turned warmer at last and he did not feel cold, despite having given all his woollen underthings, his shirt, waistcoat and breeches to Alice. How persuasive the Talbot sisters were when they worked together, he thought crossly. No doubt he was lucky that the display case containing the Japanese kimono was close at hand, otherwise he might well be standing there wearing Alice's skirts and underthings. Still, he had to admit that Alice fitted his clothes perfectly and looked very well in them too. Once the trappings of femininity had been removed – her corset, her dress and petticoats – why, once she cut off her hair no one would know the difference. The pictures he had taken had turned out well. Perhaps Mr Talbot would like one, to add to his now extensive collection of photographs.

'I don't think this is a very good idea,' he shouted, struggling to secure the sash of the kimono about his waist.

'It's a perfectly excellent idea,' cried Alice.

Mr Blake cast her a sulky look. 'As you wish,' he muttered. He pushed past her and led the way through the wind and the chimneys across the rooftop.

The flying machine had undergone some modifications since Alice had last sat inside it. It was longer and sleeker. Its canvas sides had been repaired and a second seat had been fitted.

'Get in,' she shouted in Lilian's ear.

Lilian stared at the contraption. She pointed to the hole in the body between the wings. 'In there?'

'Yes, in there,' said Alice. 'Don't be afraid.'

'I'm not,' said Lilian. She eased herself into the flying machine, like an insect squeezing back into its pupa. Behind her, Alice and Mr Blake secured the huge rubber band necessary to propel the machine into the air.

'Get in then, Miss Talbot,' cried Mr Blake into the wind, 'if that's what you want to do. They say fortune favours the brave.' He gave a grudging smile.

Alice hugged him tightly. 'Thank you, dear Mr Blake.' He felt her lips against his, the tickle of her hair against his face; then she was climbing the ladder to squeeze into the front seat. Mr Blake watched as Alice pulled Mr Bellows's saucepan on to her head and secured it with a scarf. She held up her thumb. Mr Blake nodded and began winding the machinery that would catapult the flying machine into the air.

Alice felt the machine inching backwards across the roof. It seemed to take for ever, to be hardly moving at all – really, she thought, could Mr Blake not work any faster? At last it stopped. She looked back into Lilian's laughing face and smiled. She searched for Mr Blake, to shout her thanks, but he was hidden from view by the tail of the flying machine and she could not see him.

All at once they were racing across the rooftop, the machine shaking and clattering beneath them, the wind screaming in their ears. They hurtled between the chimney pots and rocketed up the launching ramp, then with a jolt and a bounce they were heading up and out into the night.

Alice looked back. The moon was round in the sky and by the light of it she could see Mr Blake running to the edge of the roof, his mouth moving in a silent shout of goodbye. Far below, the volcano roared and spluttered. She could see their father still standing before it, the Members of the Society for the Propagation of Useful and Interesting Knowledge moving like scattered deer across the park. Alice pulled a lever. She saw Mr Blake watching the flying machine as it wheeled out across the park and over the trees; as it banked and turned on a current of air, to pass one last time over the roof of the Great House. She saw him wave his arms, his kimono flapping wide as the wind caught it and gleefully tore it open. Then even he had disappeared into the darkness and all that lay before them were the stars.

Acknowledgements

Grateful homage to Evelyn Waugh, for the fate of Tony Last.

With thanks to Sarah Bryant, Marc di Rollo and Julie Coultart for reading, comments and general encouragement. Thanks to Jane Conway-Gordon and Penny Hoare for everything. Special thanks to Helen Wilson, for reasons too numerous to mention.

Bibliographical note

During the writing of this novel I consulted a large number of books, a few of which are noted here.

The opinions of Dr Cattermole are well documented, and were taken, often verbatim, from medical text books and popular journals of the period, including *Chambers's Journal of Popular Literature, Science and Arts* (Edinburgh: W&R Chambers Ltd) and Isaac Baker Brown, *On the Curability of Certain Forms of Insanity, Epilepsy, Catalepsy, and Hysteria in Females* (London: Robert Hardwicke, 1866).

For Mr Talbot's Collection, I drew on *The Crystal Palace and Its Contents: being a Cyclopaedia of the Great Exhibition of the Industry of All Nations* (London, 1851).

On the treatment of women at the hands of the medical profession see Elaine Showalter, *The Female Malady: Women, Madness and English Culture, 1830–1980* (London: Virago, 1993), especially pp. 74–100, and Ornella Moscucci, *The Science of Women: Gynaecology and Gender in England, 1800–1929* (Cambridge: Cambridge University Press, 1993).

On women and botany see Ann B. Shteir, *Cultivating Women, Cultivating Science: Flora's Daughters and Botany in England 1760 to 1860* (Baltimore: Johns Hopkins University Press, 1996).

For background on the British in India, the Honourable East India Company and the Indian Mutiny see Lawrence James, *Raj: The Making and Unmaking of British India* (London: Abacus, 1997), William Dalrymple, *White Mughals* (London: Flamingo, 2003) and Pat Barr, *The Memsahibs: In Praise of the Women of Victorian India* (London: Century, 1976).

A number of biographies of Victorian female travellers were also consulted, most significantly Fanny Parkes, *Begums, Thugs and White Mughals: The Journals of Fanny Parkes* (London: Sickle Moon Books, 2002) and Antony Sattin (ed.), *An Englishwoman in India: The Memoirs of Harriet Tytler, 1828–1858* (Oxford: Oxford University Press, 1988). See also Marianne North, *Recollections of a Happy Life* (Charlottesville and London: University Press of Virginia, 1993), Lady Wilson, *Letters from India* (London: Century, 1984), and Emily Eden, *Up The Country: Letters from India* (London: Virago, 1983)

Elaine di Rollo
Edinburgh
February 2008